GEORGE'S SECRET KEY TO THE UNIVERSE

Lucy & Stephen
HAWKING

with Christophe Galfard

Illustrated by Garry Parsons

SIMON & SCHUSTER BOOKS FOR YOUNG READERS
NEW YORK LONDON TORONTO SYDNEY

For William and George, with love

SIMON & SCHUSTER BOOKS FOR YOUNG READERS
An imprint of Simon & Schuster Children's Publishing Division
1230 Avenue of the Americas, New York, NY 10020
Text copyright © 2007 by Lucy Hawking
Illustrations by Garry Parsons copyright © 2007 by Random House
Children's Books
Diagrams on pages 110-111, 126, and 162 by Dynamo Design
Published by arrangement with Random House Children's Books, one part of the
Random House Group Ltd.
First Simon & Schuster Books for Young Readers paperback edition May 2009
SIMON & SCHUSTER BOOKS FOR YOUNG READERS is a trademark of
Simon & Schuster, Inc.
Also available in a Simon & Schuster Books for Young Readers
hardcover edition.
Book design by James Fraser and Krista Vossen
The text for this book is set in Stempel Garamond.
The illustrations for this book are rendered in pencil that was digitally edited.
Manufactured in the United States of America
21 22 23 24 25 26 27 28 29 30
The Library of Congress has cataloged the hardcover edition as follows:
Hawking, Lucy. George's secret key to the universe / by Lucy & Stephen
Hawking and Christophe Galfard ; illustrated by Garry Parsons.
p. cm.
Summary: Follows the adventures of a young boy and his neighbor friend who
travel through a computer portal into outer space, where they explore such
mysteries as black holes and the origins of the universe, while trying to evade an
evil scientist.
ISBN: 978-1-4169-5462-0 (hc.)
[1. Universe—Fiction. 2. Outer space—Exploration—Fiction. 3. Inventions—
Fiction.] I. Hawking, S. W. (Stephen W.) II. Galfard, Christophe. III. Parsons,
Garry, ill. IV. Title.
PZ7.H3134Ge 2007 [Fic]—dc22 2007026084
ISBN: 978-1-4169-8584-6 (pbk.)
0519MTN

READ WHAT THE CRITICS HAVE TO SAY ABOUT
George's Secret Key to the Universe

....

"A briefer history of time—for a younger audience."
—*USA Today*

"This adventure story by physicist Stephen and Lucy Hawking is so entertaining you won't realize you're learning about science."—*St. Petersburg (FL) Times*

"Highly educational for moms and dads to read as well. . . . A relief for the science-deficient parent in need of a little extra help."—*New York* magazine

"Combines important scientific concepts with an interstellar adventure. . . . Science class was never this much fun!"
—*Fort Worth (TX) Star-Telegram*

"Succeeds first and foremost as a good old-fashioned adventure tale."—*Natural History* magazine

"Highly creative and imaginative . . . a seamless incorporation of adventure novel and physics."
—*Canton (OH) Repository*

"In the tradition of Harry Potter, C. S. Lewis' Pevensie siblings, and Lewis Carroll's Alice."—*Boston Metro*

"Although I've heard the notion all my life that 'we are the stuff of stars,' I never understood why that was technically true until after reading this book."—*Los Angeles Times*

"Teachers will welcome this entertaining read-aloud that integrates well-presented scientific facts and theories within a charmingly illustrated chapter book."—*Booklist*

Also by Lucy and Stephen Hawking

. . . .

George's Cosmic Treasure Hunt

Find out about Stephen Hawking's books for
adult readers at **hawking.org.uk**.

To hear Lucy and Stephen Hawking talk about
George's Secret Key to the Universe, visit
secretkeytotheuniverse.com.

Acknowledgments

I am so grateful to the many people who kindly gave their support to the "George" project. Tif Loehnis at Janklow and Nesbit has been wonderful throughout the whole process, as have all her staff at Janklow UK. Eric Simonoff at Janklow and Nesbit USA gave some truly stellar guidance. In Cambridge, Christophe Galfard made a huge contribution to the creative science story line, imagery, and detail. Judith Croasdell at DAMTP has been so patient, helpful, and kind in getting us organized and providing invaluable advice. Joan Godwin deserves very special thanks for her tireless and generous backup. Sam Blackburn for his technical support and work on the audio version. The amazing care team that surround my dad—for the dedication, affection, and good humor that they bring to their work.

At Random House, I'd like to thank Philippa Dickinson, Larry Finlay, and Annie Eaton for taking on the "George" books with such enthusiasm and verve. And Shannon Park and Sue Cook for being so brilliant to work with on the project. Garry Parsons's charming illustrations have brought the story to life, and I am totally indebted to James Fraser for designing such an eye-catching and beautiful front cover. Sophie Nelson and Julia Bruce for the very thorough copyedit and proofread, Markus Poessel for his scientific fact-checking, Clare Hall-Craggs and Nina Douglas, Barry O'Donovan, Gavin Hilzbrich, Dan Edwards, Bronwen Bennie, Catherine Tomlinson, Juliette Clark, and Maeve Banham for all their hard work, encouragement, and good will.

As ever, enormous thanks to my mum and Jonathan, for everything they've done and for their unfailing kindness and endless support. But most of all, thanks to my cosmic dad. It's been such a great adventure. Thank you so much for giving me the chance to work with you. It's changed my Universe.

Lucy Hawking

Chapter One

Pigs don't just vanish, thought George as he stood staring into the depths of the very obviously empty pigsty. He tried closing his eyes and then opening them again, to see if it was all some kind of horrible optical illusion. But when he looked again, the pig was still gone, his vast muddy pink bulk nowhere to be seen. In fact, when George examined the situation for a second time, it had gotten worse, not better. The side door of the pigsty, he noticed, was hanging open, which meant someone hadn't shut it properly. And that someone was probably him.

"Georgie!" he heard his mother call from the kitchen. "I'm going to start supper in a minute, so you've only got about an hour. Have you done your homework?"

"Yes, Mom," he called back in a fake cheery voice.

"How's your pig?"

"He's fine! Fine!" said George squeakily. He threw in a few experimental oinks, just to make it sound as though everything was business as usual, here in the small backyard that was full of many, many vegetables and one enormous — but now mysteriously absent — pig. He grunted a few more times for effect — it was very important his mother did not come out into the garden before George had time to think up a plan. How he was going to find the pig, put it back in the sty, close the door, and get back in time for supper, he had no idea. But he was working on it, and the last thing he needed was for one of his parents to appear before he had all the answers.

George knew the pig was not exactly popular with his parents. His mother and father had never wanted a pig in the backyard, and his dad in particular tended to grind his teeth quite hard when he remembered who lived beyond the vegetable patch. The pig had been a

present: One cold Christmas Eve a few years back, a cardboard box full of squeaks and snuffles had been delivered to their front door. When George opened it up, he found a very indignant pink piglet inside. George lifted him carefully out of the box and watched with delight as his new friend

skidded around the Christmas tree on his tiny hooflets. There had been a note taped to the box. *Dear all!* it read. *Merry Christmas! This little fellow needs a home—can you give him one? Love, Grandma xxx.*

George's dad hadn't been delighted by the new addition to his family. Just because he was a vegetarian, it didn't mean he liked animals. Actually, he preferred plants. They were much easier to deal with: They didn't make a mess or leave muddy hoofprints on the kitchen floor or break in and eat all the cookies left out on the table. But George was thrilled to have his very own pig. The presents he'd received from his mom and dad that year were, as usual, pretty awful. The home-knitted purple-and-orange striped sweater from his mom had sleeves that stretched right down to the floor; he had never wanted a xylophone, and he had a hard time looking enthusiastic when he unwrapped a build-your-own ant farm.

What George really wanted—above all things in the

Universe—was a computer. But he knew his parents were very unlikely to buy him one. They didn't like modern inventions and tried to do without as many standard household items as they could. Wanting to live a purer, simpler life, they washed all their clothes by hand and didn't own a car and lit the house with candles in order to avoid using any electricity.

It was all designed to give George a natural and improving upbringing, free from toxins, additives, radiation, and other such evil phenomena. The only problem was that in getting rid of everything that could

possibly harm George, his parents had managed to do away with lots of things that would also be fun for him. George's parents might enjoy going on environmental protest marches or grinding flour to make their own bread, but George didn't. He wanted to go to a theme park and ride on the roller coasters or play computer games or take an airplane somewhere far, far away. Instead, for now, all he had was his pig.

And a very fine pig he was too. George named him Freddy and spent many happy hours dangling over the edge of the pigsty his father had built in the backyard, watching Freddy root around in the straw or snuffle in the dirt. As the seasons changed and the years turned, George's piglet got bigger . . . and bigger . . . and bigger . . . until he was so large that in dim lighting he looked like a baby elephant. The bigger Freddy grew, the more he seemed to feel cooped up in his pigsty. Whenever he got the chance, he liked to escape and rampage across the vegetable patch, trampling on the carrot tops, munching the baby cabbages, and chewing up George's mom's flowers. Even though she often told George how important it was to love all living creatures, George suspected that on days when Freddy wrecked her garden, she didn't feel much love for his pig. Like George's dad, his mom was a vegetarian, but George was sure he had heard her angrily mutter "sausages" under her breath when she was cleaning up after one of Freddy's more destructive outings.

On this particular day, however, it wasn't the vegetables that Freddy had destroyed. Instead of charging madly about, the pig had done something much worse. In the fence that separated George's garden from the one next door, George suddenly noticed a suspiciously pig-sized hole. Yesterday it definitely hadn't been there, but then yesterday Freddy had been safely shut in his sty. And now he was nowhere to be seen. It meant only one thing—that Freddy, in his search for adventure, had burst out of the safety of the backyard and gone somewhere he absolutely should not have gone.

Next Door was a mysterious place. It had been empty for as long as George could remember. While all the other houses in the row had neatly kept backyards, windows that twinkled with light in the evenings, and doors that slammed as people ran in and out, this house just sat there—sad, quiet, and dark. No small children squeaked with joy early in the morning. No mother called out of the back door to bring people in for supper. On the weekends, there was no noise of hammering or smell of fresh paint because no one ever came to fix the broken window frames or clear the sagging gutters. Years of neglect meant the garden had rioted out of control until it looked like the Amazon jungle had grown up on the other side of the fence.

On George's side, the backyard was neat, orderly, and very boring. There were rows of string beans strictly tied to stakes, lines of floppy lettuces, frothy

dark green carrot tops, and well-behaved potato plants. George couldn't even kick a ball without it landing *splat* in the middle of a carefully tended blueberry bush and squashing it.

George's parents had marked out a little area for George to grow his own vegetables, hoping he would become interested in gardening and perhaps grow up to be an organic farmer. But George preferred looking up at the sky to looking down at the earth. So his little patch of the planet stayed bare and scratchy, showing nothing but stones, scrubby weeds, and bare ground, while he tried to count all the stars in the sky to find out how many there were.

Next Door, however, was completely different. George often stood on top of the pigsty roof and gazed over the fence into the glorious tangled forest beyond. The sweeping bushes made cozy little hidey-holes,

THE NIGHT SKY

During the day there is only one star that can be seen in the sky. It is the star that is the closest to us, the star that has the most effect on our daily lives and for which we have a special name: the Sun.

The Moon and the planets do not shine on their own. They appear bright at night because the Sun lights them up.

In the night sky there are a few objects that can be seen that are not stars—the Moon and the planets, like Venus, Mars, Jupiter, or Saturn.

All the other shining dots in the night sky are stars, like our Sun. Some are bigger, some are smaller, but they are all stars. With a naked eye, on a clear night, away from sources of light like cities, we can see hundreds of them.

while the trees had curved, gnarled branches, perfect for a boy to climb. Brambles grew in great clumps, their spiky arms bending into strange, wavy loops, crisscrossing each other like train tracks at a station. In summer, twisty bindweed clung on to every other plant in the garden like a green cobweb; yellow dandelions sprouted everywhere; prickly poisonous giant hogweed loomed like a species from another planet, while little blue forget-me-not flowers winked prettily in the crazy bright green jumble of Next Door's backyard.

But Next Door was also forbidden territory. George's parents had very firmly said no to the idea of George using it as an extra playground. And it hadn't been their normal sort of no, which was a wishy-washy, kindly, we're-asking-you-not-to-for-your-own-sake sort of no. This had been a real no, the kind you didn't argue with. It was the same no that George had encountered when he tried suggesting that, as everyone else at school had a television set—some kids even had one in their bedroom!—maybe his parents could think about buying one. On the subject of television, George had had to listen to a long explanation from his father about how watching mindless trash would pollute his brain. But when it came to Next Door, he didn't even get a lecture from his dad. Just a flat, conversation-ending no.

George, however, always liked to know *why*. Guessing he wasn't going to get any more answers from his dad, he asked his mother instead.

"Oh, George," she had sighed as she chopped up Brussels sprouts and turnips and threw them into the cake mix. She tended to cook with whatever came to hand rather than with ingredients that would actually combine to make something tasty. "You ask too many questions."

"I just want to know *why* I can't go next door," George persisted. "And if you tell me, I won't ask any more questions for the rest of the day. I promise."

His mom wiped her hands on her flowery apron and took a sip of nettle tea. "All right, George," she said. "I'll tell you a story if you stir the muffins." Passing over the big brown mixing bowl and the wooden spoon, she settled herself down as George started to beat the stiff yellow dough with the green and white vegetable speckles together.

"When we first moved here," his mom began, "when you were very small, an old man lived in that house. We hardly ever saw him, but I remember him well. He had the longest beard I've ever seen—it went right down to his knees. No one knew how old he really was, but the neighbors said he'd lived there forever."

"What happened to him?" asked George, who'd already forgotten that he'd promised not to ask any more questions.

"Nobody knows," said his mom mysteriously.

"What do you mean?" asked George, who had stopped stirring.

"Just that," said his mom. "One day he was there. The next day he wasn't."

"Maybe he went on vacation," said George.

"If he did, he never came back," said his mom. "Eventually they searched the house, but there was no sign of him. The house has been empty ever since and no one has ever seen him again."

"Gosh," said George.

"A little while back," his mom continued, blowing on her hot tea, "we heard noises next door—banging sounds in the middle of the night. There were flashing lights and voices as well. Some squatters had broken in and were living there. The police had to throw them out. Just last week we thought we heard the noises again. We don't know who might be in that house. That's why your dad doesn't want you going around there, Georgie."

As George looked at the big black hole in the fence, he remembered the conversation he'd had with his mom. The story she'd told him hadn't stopped him from wanting to go Next Door—it still looked mysterious and enticing. But wanting to go Next Door when he knew he couldn't was one thing; finding out he actually *had* to was quite another. Suddenly Next Door seemed dark, spooky, and very scary.

George felt torn. Part of him just wanted to go home to the flickery candlelight and funny familiar smells of his mother's cooking, to close the back door and be safe and snug inside his own house once more. But that would mean leaving Freddy alone and possibly in danger. He couldn't ask his parents for any help in case they decided that this was the final black mark against Freddy's name and packed him off to be made into bacon. Taking a deep breath, George decided he had to do it. He had to go Next Door.

Closing his eyes, he plunged through the hole in the fence.

When he came out on the other side and opened his eyes, he was right in the middle of the jungle garden. Above his head, the tree cover was so dense he could hardly see the sky. It was getting dark now, and the thick forest made it even darker. George could just see where a path had been trampled through the enormous weeds. He followed it, hoping it would lead him to Freddy.

He waded through great banks of brambles, which grabbed at his clothes and scratched his bare skin. They seemed to reach out in the semidarkness to scrape their prickly spines along his arms and legs. Muddy old leaves squished under his feet, and nettles attacked him with their sharp, stinging fingers. All the while the wind in the trees above him made a singing, sighing noise, as though the leaves were saying, *Be careful, Georgie . . . be careful, Georgie.*

The trail brought George into a sort of clearing right behind the house itself. So far he had not seen or heard any sign of his wayward pig. But there, on the broken paving stones outside the back door, he saw only too clearly a set of muddy hoofprints. From the marks, George could tell exactly which way Freddy had gone. His pig had marched straight into the abandoned house through the back door, which had been pushed open just wide enough for a fat pig to squeeze through. Worse, from the house where no one had lived for years and years, a beam of light shone.

Somebody was home.

Chapter Two

George looked back down the garden, at the path along which he'd come. He knew he should go back and get his parents. Even if he had to admit to his dad that he'd climbed through the fence into Next Door's garden, it would still be better than standing there all alone. He would just peek through the window to see if he could catch a glimpse of Freddy and then he would go and get his dad.

He edged closer to the beam of bright light coming from the empty house. It was a golden color, quite unlike the weak candlelight in his own house or the cold blue neon strips at school. Even though he was so scared his teeth had started to chatter, the light seemed to draw him forward until he was standing right by the window. He peered closer. Through the narrow space between the window frame and the blind, he could just see into the house. He could make out a kitchen, littered with mugs and old tea bags.

A sudden movement caught his eye and he squinted down at the kitchen floor, where he saw Freddy, his

pig! He had his snout in a bowl and was slurping away, drinking his fill of some mysterious bright purple liquid.

George's blood ran cold—it was a terrible trick, he just *knew* it. "Yikes!" he shouted. "It's poison." He rapped sharply on the pane of glass. *"Don't drink it, Freddy!"* he yelled.

But Freddy, who was a greedy pig, ignored his master's voice and happily kept slurping up the contents of the bowl. Without stopping to think, George flew through the door and into the kitchen, where he grabbed the bowl from under Freddy's snout and threw its contents into the sink. As the violet-colored liquid gurgled down the drain, he heard a voice behind him.

"Who," it said, in distinct but childish tones, "are *you*?"

George whirled around. Standing behind him was a girl. She was wearing the most extraordinary costume, made of so many different colors and layers of flimsy fabric that it looked as though she had rolled herself in butterfly wings.

George spluttered. She might look strange, this girl with her long tangled blond hair and her blue-and-green feathery headdress, but she definitely wasn't scary. "Who," he replied indignantly, "do you think *you* are?"

"I asked first," said the girl. "And anyway, this is *my* house. So I get to know who you are, but I don't have to say anything if I don't want to."

"I'm George." He stuck out his chin as he always did when he felt cross. "And that"—he pointed to Freddy—"is my pig. And you've kidnapped him."

"I haven't kidnapped your pig," said the girl hotly. "How stupid. What would I want a pig for? I'm a ballerina and there aren't any pigs in the ballet."

"Huh, ballet," muttered George darkly. His parents had made him take dance classes when he was younger, and he'd never forgotten the horror. "Anyway," he retorted, "you're not old enough to be a ballerina. You're just a kid."

"Actually, I'm in the corps de ballet," said the girl snootily. "Which shows how much *you* know."

"Well, if you're so grown up, why were you trying to poison my pig?" demanded George.

"That's not poison," said the girl scornfully. "That's grape soda."

George, whose parents only ever gave him cloudy, pale, fresh-squeezed fruit juices, suddenly felt very silly for not realizing what the purple stuff was.

"Well, this isn't really your house, is it?" he continued, determined to get the better of her somehow. "It belongs to an old man with a long beard who disappeared years ago."

"This *is* my house," said the girl, her blue eyes flashing. "And I live here except when I'm dancing onstage."

"Then where are your mom and dad?" demanded George.

"I don't have any parents." The girl's pink lips stuck out in a pout. "I'm an orphan. I was found backstage wrapped up in a tutu. I've been adopted by the ballet.

That's why I'm such a talented dancer." She sniffed loudly.

"Annie!" A man's voice rang through the house. The girl stood very still.

"Annie!" They heard the voice again, coming closer. "Where are you, Annie?"

"Who's that?" asked George suspiciously.

"That's . . . uh . . . that's . . ." She suddenly became very interested in her ballet shoes.

"Annie, there you are!" A tall man with messy dark hair and thick, heavy-framed glasses, set at a crooked angle on his nose, walked into the kitchen. "What have you been up to?"

"Oh!" The girl flashed him a brilliant smile. "I've just been giving the pig a drink of grape soda."

A look of annoyance crossed the man's face. "Annie," he said patiently, "we've talked about this. There are times to make up stories. And there are times . . ." He trailed off as he caught sight of George standing in the corner and, next to him, a pig with purple stains around his snout and mouth that made him look as though he were smiling.

"Ah, a pig . . . in the kitchen . . . I see . . . ," he said slowly, taking in the scene. "Sorry, Annie, I thought you were making things up again. Well, hello." The man crossed the room to shake hands with George. Then he sort of patted the pig rather gingerly between the ears. "Hello . . . hi . . ." He seemed unsure what to say next.

"I'm George," said George helpfully. "And this is my pig, Freddy."

"Your pig," the man echoed. He turned back to Annie, who shrugged and gave him an I-told-you-so look.

"I live next door," George went on by way of explanation. "But my pig escaped through a hole in the fence, so I had to come and get him."

"Of course!" The man smiled. "I was wondering how you got into the kitchen. My name is Eric—I'm Annie's dad." He pointed to the blond girl.

"Annie's dad?" said George slyly, smiling at the girl. She stuck her nose up in the air and refused to meet his eye.

"We're your new neighbors," said Eric, gesturing around the kitchen, with its peeling wallpaper, moldy old tea bags, dripping faucets, and torn linoleum. "It's a bit of a mess. We haven't been here long. That's why we haven't met before." Eric ruffled his dark hair and frowned. "Would you like something to drink? I gather Annie's already given your pig something."

"I'd love some grape soda," said George quickly.

"None left," said Annie, shaking her head. George's face fell. It seemed very bad luck that even Freddy the pig should get to have nice drinks when he didn't.

Eric opened a few cupboards in the kitchen, but they were all empty. He shrugged apologetically. "Glass of water?" he offered, pointing to the faucet.

George nodded. He wasn't in a hurry to get home

for his supper. Usually when he went to play with other kids, he went back to his own mom and dad feeling depressed by how peculiar they were. But this house seemed so odd that George felt quite cheerful. Finally he had found some people who were even odder than his own family. But just as he was thinking these happy thoughts, Eric went and spoiled it for him.

"It's pretty dark," he said, peering out of the window. "Do your parents know you're here, George?" He picked up a telephone handset from the kitchen counter. "Let's give them a call so they don't worry about you."

"Um . . . ," said George awkwardly.

"What's the number?" asked Eric, looking at him over the top of his glasses. "Or are they easier to reach on a cell phone?"

"They, um . . ." George could see no way out. "They don't have any kind of phone," he said in a rush.

"Why not?" said Annie, her blue eyes very round at the thought of not owning even a cell phone.

George squirmed a bit; both Annie and Eric were looking at him curiously, so he felt he had to explain. "They think technology is taking over the world," he said very quickly. "And that we should try and live without it. They think that people—because of science and its discoveries—are polluting the planet with modern inventions."

"Really?" Eric's eyes sparkled behind his heavy glasses. "How very interesting." At that moment the phone in his hand burst into tinkling song.

"Can I get it, can I get it? Pleasepleaseplease?" said Annie, grabbing the phone from him. "Mom!" And with a shriek of joy and a flounce of brightly colored costume, she shot out of the kitchen, phone clasped to her ear. "Guess what, Mom!" Her shrill voice rang out as she pattered along the hall corridor. "A strange boy came over . . ."

George went bright red with embarrassment.

"And he has a pig!" Annie's voice carried perfectly back to the kitchen.

Eric peered at George and gently eased the kitchen door closed with his foot.

"And he's never had grape soda!" Her fluting tones could still be heard through the shut door.

Eric turned on the faucet to get George a glass of water.

"And his parents don't even have a phone!" Annie was fainter now, but they could still make out each painful word.

Eric flicked on the radio and music started playing. "So, George," he said loudly, "where were we?"

"I don't know," whispered George, who could barely be heard in the din Eric had created in the kitchen to block out Annie's telephone conversation.

Eric threw him a sympathetic glance. "Let me show you something fun," he shouted, producing a plastic ruler from his pocket. He brandished it in front of George's nose. "Do you know what this is?" he asked at top volume.

"A ruler?" said George. The answer seemed a bit too obvious.

"That's right," cried Eric, who was now rubbing the ruler against his hair. "Watch!" He held the ruler near the thin stream of water running from the faucet. As he did so, the stream of water bent in the air and flowed at an angle rather than straight down. Eric took the ruler away from the water and it ran down normally again. He gave the ruler to George, who rubbed it in

his hair and put it close to the stream of water. The same thing happened.

"Is that magic?" yelled George with sudden excitement, completely distracted from Annie's rudeness. "Are you a wizard?"

"Nope," said Eric, putting the ruler back in his pocket as the water ran down in a long straight line once more. He turned off the faucet and switched off the radio. It was quiet now in the kitchen, and Annie could no longer be heard in the distance.

"That's science, George," said Eric, his whole face shining. "Science. The ruler steals electric charges from your hair when you rub the ruler through it. We can't see the electric charges, but the stream of water can feel them."

"Gosh, that's amazing," breathed George.

"It is," agreed Eric. "Science is a wonderful and fascinating subject that helps us understand the world around us and all its marvels."

"Are you a scientist?" asked George. He suddenly felt very confused.

"I am, yes," replied Eric.

"Then how can that"—George pointed at the faucet—"be science when science is also killing the planet and everything on it? I don't understand."

"Ah, clever boy," said Eric with a flourish. "You've gotten right to the heart of the matter. I will answer your question, but to do so, first I need to tell you a bit about

science itself. *Science* is a big word. It means explaining the world around us using our senses, our intelligence, and our powers of observation."

"Are you sure?" asked George doubtfully.

"Very sure," said Eric. "There are many different types of natural science, and they have many different uses. The one I work with is all about the How and the Why. How did it all begin—the Universe, the Solar System, our planet, life on Earth? What was there before it began? Where did it all come from? And how does it all work? And why? This is physics, George, exciting, brilliant, and fascinating physics."

"But that's really interesting!" exclaimed George. Eric was talking about all the questions he pestered his parents with—the ones they could never answer. He tried asking these big questions at school, but the answer he got most often was that he'd find out in his classes the following year. That wasn't really the answer he was after.

"Should I go on?" Eric asked him, his eyebrows raised.

George was just about to say "Oh, yes, please," when Freddy, who had been quiet and docile up till then, seemed to pick up on his excitement. He lumbered upright and, with a surprising spurt of speed, he dashed forward, ears flattened, hooves flying, toward the door.

"*No-o-o-o-o!*" cried Eric, throwing himself after the pig, who had barged through the kitchen door.

"*Sto-o-o-op!*" shouted George, rushing into the next room behind them.

"Oink oink oink oink oink oink!" squealed Freddy, who was obviously enjoying his day out enormously.

Chapter Three

If George had thought the kitchen was untidy, then this next room was in a whole different dimension of messiness. It was filled with piles and piles of books, stacked up so high that some of the wobbly towers reached almost to the ceiling. As Freddy charged right through the middle of the room, notebooks, paperbacks, leather-bound tomes, and bits of paper flew up in a tornado around him.

"Catch him!" shouted Eric, who was trying to drive the pig back toward the kitchen.

"I'm trying!" George shouted back as he was batted in the face by a shiny-jacketed book.

"Hurry!" said Eric. "We must get him out of here."

With a great leap, Annie's dad hurled himself right onto Freddy's back and grabbed his ears. Using them as a sort of steering wheel, he turned the pig—who was still moving at quite some speed—and rode him like a bucking bronco through the door and back into the kitchen.

Left alone, George looked around in wonder. He had never been in a room like this before. Not only was it beautifully, gloriously messy as all the papers flying about in the air came gently down to the ground, but it was also full of exciting objects.

On the wall, a huge blackboard covered with symbols

and squiggles in colored chalk caught his eye. It also had lots of writing on it, but George didn't stop to read it. There were too many other things to look at. In the corner, a grandfather clock ticked slowly, the noise of the swinging pendulum clicking in time with a row of silvery balls suspended on very fine wire that seemed to be in perpetual motion. On a wooden stand was a long brass tube that pointed up toward the window. It looked old and beautiful, and George couldn't resist touching the metal, which felt cool and soft at the same time.

Eric walked back into the room with his shirt untucked, his hair standing on end, his glasses at

a strange angle, and a huge smile on his face. In his hand he held a book, which he had caught while riding Freddy out of the room.

"George, this is incredible!" Eric looked thrilled. "I thought I'd lost it—it's my new book! I couldn't find it anywhere. And now your pig has found it for me! What a result!"

George just stood there, hand on the metal tube, staring at Eric openmouthed. He'd been expecting to get into trouble for the damage his pig had wreaked. But Eric didn't even seem angry. He wasn't like anyone George had ever met—he never seemed to get angry, no matter what happened in his house. It was all very baffling.

"So I must thank you for all your help today," continued the peculiar Eric, putting the lost book on top of a cardboard box.

"Help?" echoed George faintly, who couldn't quite believe what he was hearing.

"Yes, help," said Eric firmly. "As you seem so interested in science, perhaps I could tell you a bit more about it, by way of a thank-you. Where shall we start? What would you like to know?"

George's mind was so full of questions that he found it hard to pick just one. Instead, he pointed at the metal tube. "What's this?" he asked.

"Good choice, George, good choice," said Eric happily. "That's my telescope. It's a very old one—four hundred years ago, it belonged to a man called Galileo. He lived in Italy, and he loved looking up at the sky at night. At that time, people believed that all the planets in our Solar System went around the Earth—even the Sun, they thought, orbited our planet."

"But I know that's not true," said George, putting his eye to the old telescope. "I know that the Earth goes around the Sun."

"You do now," said Eric. "Science is also about gaining knowledge through experience—you know that fact because Galileo discovered it all those years ago. By looking through his telescope, he realized that the Earth and all the other planets in the Solar System orbit the Sun. Can you see anything?"

"I can see the Moon," said George, squinting up the telescope, which was angled up to look out of the living room window into the evening sky. "It looks like it's smiling."

"Those are scars from a violent past, the impacts of meteorites that crashed on the surface," said Eric. "You can't see very far with Galileo's telescope, but if you went to an observatory and looked through a really big telescope, you would be able to see stars billions and billions of miles away—stars so far away that by the time their light reaches our planet, they may actually already be dead."

"Can a star die? Really?" asked George.

"Oh yes," said Eric. "But first I want to show you

OUR MOON

- A moon is a natural satellite of a planet.

- A satellite is an object that goes around a planet—like the Earth, which goes around the Sun—and *natural* means that it is not man-made.

Average distance from the Earth: 238,854 miles (384,399 kilometers)

Diameter: 2,160 miles (3,476 km), which is 27.3% of Earth's diameter
Surface area: 0.074 x Earth's surface area **Volume:** 0.020 x Earth's volume **Mass:** 0.0123 x Earth's mass **Gravity at the equator:** 16.54% of Earth's gravity at Earth's equator

- The most obvious effect the Moon's gravity has on the Earth is the tides of the oceans. The sea on the side of the Earth facing the Moon is pulled harder towards the Moon because it is closer. This raises a bulge in the sea on that side. Similarly, the sea on the side away from the Moon is pulled towards the Moon less than the Earth because it is farther away. This creates another bulge in the sea on the other side of the Earth.

- Even though the Sun's gravitational pull is much stronger than the Moon's, it has only about half the Moon's effect on the tides because it is so much farther away. When the Moon is roughly in line with the Earth and the Sun, the Moon and the Sun tides combine to produce the large tides (called "spring tides") twice a month.

The Moon circles around the Earth in 27.3 days. The way the Moon shines in the night sky is the same every 29.5 days.

- There is no atmosphere on the Moon, so the sky there is black, even during the day. And there hasn't been an earthquake or a volcanic eruption there since around the time life began on Earth. So all living organisms that have ever been on the Earth have seen exactly the same features on the Moon.

- From Earth, we always see the same side of the Moon. The first pictures of the Moon's hidden side were taken by a spacecraft in 1959.

how a star is born, and then we'll take a look at how it dies. Hang on a minute, George, while I get everything set up. I think you're going to like this."

LIGHT & STARS

☆ Everything in our Universe takes time to travel, even light.

☆ In space, light always travels at the maximum speed that is possible: 186,000 miles per second (300,000 km per second). This speed is called the speed of light.

☆ It takes light only about 1.3 seconds to travel from Earth to the Moon.

☆ Our Sun is farther away from us than our Moon is. When light leaves the Sun, it takes about 8 minutes and 30 seconds to reach us on Earth.

★ The other stars in the sky are much, much farther away from Earth than the Sun. The closest one after the Sun is called Proxima Centauri, and it takes 4.22 years for light from it to reach Earth.

★ All other stars are even farther away. The light of almost all the stars we can see in the night sky has been traveling for hundreds, thousands, or even tens of thousands of years before reaching our eyes. Even though we see them, some of these stars may not exist anymore, but we do not know it yet because the light of their explosion when they die has yet to reach us.

★ Distances in space can be measured in terms of light-years, which is the distance light travels in one year. A light-year is almost 6,000 billion miles (around 9,500 billion km).

Proxima Centauri, the closest star to the Earth after our Sun

Eric walked toward the doorway and stuck his head out into the hallway. "Ann-ie!" he shouted up the stairs.

"Ye-e-e-es," her distant voice tinkled down to them.

"Do you want to come and see *The Birth and Death of a Star?*" called Eric.

"Seen it already," she sang back. "Lots of times." They heard her feet pattering down the stairs, and a second later she stuck her head around the door. "Can I have some potato chips?"

"If we have any," replied Eric. "And if we do, you're to bring them into my library and share them with George. Okay?"

Annie smiled sweetly and disappeared into the

kitchen. They heard the noise of cupboard doors being flung open.

"Don't mind Annie," said Eric gently, without looking at George. "She doesn't mean any harm. She's just . . ." He trailed off and went over to the far corner of the room, where he started fiddling around with a computer George hadn't noticed before. He'd been too fascinated by the other objects to look at the flat silver screen with its keyboard attached. It was strange that George hadn't spotted the computer right away—he really wished he could persuade his mom and dad to buy him one. He was saving up his allowance for a computer, but at the current rate, he calculated it was going to take him about eight years to afford even a really junky secondhand one. So instead, he had to use the clunky, slow, old machines at school, which crashed every five minutes and had sticky fingerprints all over the screen.

Eric's computer was small and glossy. It looked powerful and neat—the sort of computer you might find on a spaceship. Eric hit a couple of buttons on the keyboard, and the computer

made a sort of humming noise while bright flashes of color shot across the screen. He patted the computer happily.

"You have forgotten something," said a strange mechanical voice. George jumped out of his skin.

"Have I?" Eric looked confused for a moment.

"Yes," said the voice. "You have not introduced me."

"I'm so sorry!" exclaimed Eric. "George, this is Cosmos, my computer."

George gulped. He had no idea what to say.

"You have to say hello to Cosmos," said Eric in a side whisper to George. "Otherwise he'll get offended."

"Hello, Cosmos," said George nervously. He'd never spoken to a computer before, and he didn't quite know where to look.

"Hello, George," replied Cosmos. "Eric, you have forgotten something else."

"What now?" said Eric.

"You have not told George I am the most powerful computer in the world."

Eric rolled his eyes up to heaven. "George," he said patiently, "Cosmos is the most powerful computer in the world."

"That is correct," agreed Cosmos. "I am. In the future, there will be computers more powerful than me. But there are none in the past or present."

"Sorry about this," Eric whispered to George. "Computers can be a bit touchy sometimes."

"I am smarter than Eric, too," boasted Cosmos.

"Says who?" said Eric crossly, glaring at the screen.

"Says me," said Cosmos. "I can compute billions of numbers in a nanosecond. In less time than it takes you to say 'Cosmos is great,' I can compute the life of planets, of comets, of stars, and of galaxies. Before you can say 'Cosmos is the most impressive computer that I have ever seen, he is truly incredible,' I can—"

"All right, all right," said Eric. "Cosmos, you are the most impressive computer we have ever seen. Now, can we move on? I want to show George how a star is born."

"No," said Cosmos.

"*No?*" said Eric. "What do you mean, *no*, you ridiculous machine?"

"I don't want to," said Cosmos snootily. "And I am not ridiculous. I am the most powerful computer that has ever been—"

"Oh, but *ple-e-ease*," pleaded George, interrupting him. "Please, Cosmos, I really want to see how a star is born. *Please* won't you show me?"

Cosmos was silent.

"Oh, come on, Cosmos," said Eric. "Let's show George some of the wonders of the Universe."

"Maybe," replied Cosmos sulkily.

"George doesn't have a very high opinion of science," Eric went on. "So this is our chance, Cosmos, to show him the other side of science."

"He must take the oath," said Cosmos.

"Good point—smart Cosmos," said Eric, leaping over to the blackboard.

George turned and studied the writing on it more closely. It looked like a poem.

"George," said Eric, "do you want to learn about the greatest subject in the whole Universe?"

"Oh yes!" exclaimed George.

"Are you prepared to take a special oath to do so? To promise that you will use your knowledge only for good and not for evil?" Eric was staring at George intently from behind his big glasses. His voice had changed—he now sounded extremely serious. "This is very important, George. Science can be a force for good, but as you pointed out to me earlier, it can also do great harm."

George stood up straighter and looked Eric in the eye. "I am," he confirmed.

"Then," said Eric, "look at the words on the blackboard. It is the Oath of the Scientist. If you agree with it, then read the oath out loud."

George read what was written on the blackboard and thought about it for a moment. The words of the oath didn't frighten him. Instead they made him feel tingly with excitement, right down to his toes. He read the oath out loud, as Eric had instructed.

"I swear to use my scientific knowledge for the good of Humanity. I promise never to harm any person in my search for enlightenment . . ."

The living room door opened, and Annie sidled in, clutching a huge multipack bag of potato chips.

"Keep going," said Eric encouragingly. "You're doing very well."

George read out the next part.

"I shall be courageous and careful in my quest for greater knowledge about the mysteries that surround us.

I shall not use scientific knowledge for my own personal gain or give it to those who seek to destroy the wonderful planet on which we live.

"*If I break this oath, may the beauty and wonder of the Universe forever remain hidden from me.*"

Eric clapped. Annie burst an empty potato chip package. Cosmos flashed a rainbow of bright colors across his screen.

"Well done, George," said Eric. "You are now the second youngest member of the Order of Scientific Inquiry for the Good of Humanity."

"I salute you," said Cosmos. "From now on, I will recognize your command."

"And I'll let you have some chips!" piped up Annie.

"Annie, shush!" said Eric. "We're just getting to the good part. George, you may now use the secret key that unlocks the Universe."

"Can I?" asked George. "Where is it?"

"Go over to Cosmos," said Eric quietly, "and look at his keyboard. Can you guess which one you need to press? Can you figure out which one is the secret key that will unlock the Universe for you? Annie—say nothing!"

George did as he was told. Cosmos might be the world's most powerful computer, but his keyboard was just an ordinary, familiar one, with the letters and symbols laid out in the same order as even the school's crummiest computer. George thought hard. Which key would be the one to unlock the Universe for him? He looked again at the keyboard—and suddenly he knew.

"It's this one, isn't it?" he said to Eric, his finger hovering.

Eric nodded. "Press it, George. To begin."

George's finger came down on the key marked ENTER.

Suddenly the lights in the room started to fade . . .

"Welcome," said Cosmos, playing a little computerized fanfare, "to the Universe."

Chapter Five

The room was getting darker and darker. "Come and sit here, George," called Annie, who had already settled herself on the big comfy sofa. George sat down next to her, and after a few seconds he saw a tiny beam of very bright white light. It came directly from Cosmos's screen. The beam shot out into the middle of the room, where it wavered for a second before it began to sketch a shape in the air. It moved from left to right in a straight line before dropping down toward the floor. Leaving a shining path of light behind it, it turned another corner to make three sides of a rectangle. One more right angle and the beam of light came back to its starting point. For a second, it looked like a flat shape hanging in the air, but suddenly it turned into something real and very familiar.

"But that looks like a—," said George, who could suddenly see what it was.

"A window," said Eric proudly. "Cosmos has made us a window on the Universe. Watch closely."

The beam of light disappeared, leaving the window it had drawn in the middle of Eric's living room, hanging

in midair. Although the outline was still shining with bright light, it now looked exactly like a real window. It had a big sheet of glass in the pane and a metal frame. Beyond it, there was a view. And that view was not of Eric's house, or of any house, road, or town, or anywhere else that George had ever seen before.

Instead, through the window George could see an incredible, vast darkness, peppered with what looked like tiny bright stars. He started to try and count them.

"George," said Cosmos in his mechanical voice, "there are billions and billions of stars in the Universe. Unless you are as smart as me, you will not be able to count them all."

"Cosmos, why are there so many?" asked George in wonder.

"New stars are created all the time," answered the great computer. "They are born in giant clouds of dust and gas. I am going to show you how it happens."

"How long does it take for a star to be born?" George asked.

"Tens of millions of years," replied Cosmos. "I hope you are not in a hurry."

"Tut-tut," said Eric, sitting cross-legged on the floor beside the sofa, his long, thin limbs bent at sharp angles. He looked like a friendly giant spider. "Don't worry, George, I've speeded it up quite a lot. You'll still get home for dinner. Annie, pass the chips around. I don't know about you, George, but the Universe always makes me very hungry."

"Oh dear," said Annie, sounding embarrassed. There was a rustling noise as she rooted around inside the big bag. "I'd better get some more." She leaped off the sofa and dashed back to the kitchen.

As Annie left the room, George noticed something about the view through the window onto outer space: Not all of it was covered with little stars. In the bottom corner of the window he saw a patch of total darkness, a place where not a single star shone.

"What's happening there?" He pointed.

"Let's have a look, shall we?" said Eric. He pressed a button on a remote control, and the view through the window seemed to zoom toward the dark patch. As they got closer, George realized that an enormous cloud was hovering in that spot. The window kept moving forward until they were right inside the cloud itself, and George could see it was made of gas and dust, just as Cosmos had said.

"What is it?" he asked. "And where is it?"

"It's a huge cloud in outer space, much bigger than the ones in the sky," replied Eric, "made up of tiny, tiny particles that are all floating around inside it. There are so many of these particles that the cloud is enormous—it's so big that you could put millions and millions of Earths inside it. From this cloud, many stars will be born."

Inside the cloud, George could see the particles

PARTICLES

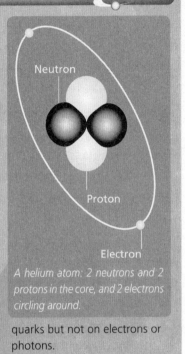

- Elementary particles are the smallest possible things that cannot be divided up into smaller particles. Examples include the electron, which carries electricity, and the photon, which carries light.

- An atom is not an elementary particle because it is made of electrons going around a nucleus in the center, like the planets go around the Sun. The nucleus is made of protons and neutrons packed tightly together.

- Protons and neutrons were previously thought to be elementary particles, but we now know they are made of smaller particles called quarks, held together by gluons, which are the particles of a strong force that acts on

A helium atom: 2 neutrons and 2 protons in the core, and 2 electrons circling around.

quarks but not on electrons or photons.

moving around, some joining together to form huge lumps of matter. These great lumps spun around and around, gathering even more particles all the time. But as the particles joined together, the spinning lumps weren't getting bigger; instead, they seemed to be getting smaller, as though something was squeezing them. It looked like someone was making gigantic dough balls in outer space. One of these giant balls was quite close to the window now, and George could see it spinning around, getting smaller and smaller all the time. As it shrank, it became hotter and hotter—so hot that George could feel the heat from where he sat on the sofa. And then it started to glow with a dim but frightening light.

"Why is it glowing?" asked George.

"The more it shrinks," said Eric, "the hotter it gets. The hotter it gets, the brighter it shines. Very soon it's going to get *too* hot." He grabbed a couple of pairs of strange sunglasses from a pile of junk on the floor.

"Wear these," he told George, putting on a pair himself. "It will soon be too bright for you to look at without glasses."

Just as George put on the very dark glasses, the ball exploded from the inside, throwing off its outer layers of burning-hot gas in all directions. After the explosion, the ball was shining like the Sun.

"Wow!" said George. "Is that the Sun?"

"It could be," Eric replied. "That's how stars are born, and the Sun is a star. When a huge

amount of gas and dust combines and shrinks to become dense and hot, as you've just seen, the particles in the middle of the ball are so pressed together they start to fuse or join up, releasing an enormous amount of energy. This is called a *nuclear fusion reaction*. It is so powerful that when it starts, it throws off the outer layers of the ball, and the rest is transformed into a star. That's what you just saw."

The star was now shining steadily in the distance. It was a beautiful sight. Without the special sunglasses, they wouldn't have been able to see much because the star was so bright.

George gazed at it, amazed by its power. Every now and then he could see huge jets of brightly shining gases

MATTER

- Matter is made of atoms of various types. The type of atom, or element, as it is called, is determined by the number of protons in the nucleus. This can be up to 118, with mostly an equal or greater number of neutrons.

- The simplest atom is hydrogen, whose nucleus contains just one proton and no neutron.

- The largest naturally occurring atom, uranium, has a nucleus that contains 92 protons and 146 neutrons.

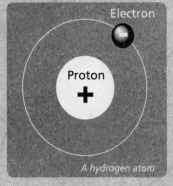

Electron

Proton

+

A hydrogen atom

- Scientists think that 90% of the total number of all atoms in the Universe are hydrogen atoms.

sent hundreds of thousands of miles from the surface at extraordinary speeds.

"And the star will keep on shining like this forever?" he asked.

"Nothing is forever, George," said Eric. "If stars shone forever, we wouldn't be here. Inside their bellies, stars transform small particles into larger ones. That is what a nuclear fusion reaction does: It fuses small particles together, and builds big atoms out of small ones. The energy released by this fusion is enormous, and that's what makes stars shine. Almost all the elements that you and I are made of were built inside stars that existed long before the Earth. So you could say that we are all the children of stars! When they exploded a long time

○ The remaining 10% are all the 117 other atoms, in various proportions. Some are extremely rare.

○ When atoms join together in chains, the resulting object is called a molecule. There are countless molecules, of various sizes, and we build new ones all the time in laboratories.

○ Before stars are born, only the simplest molecules can be found in space. The most common is the hydrogen molecule, which is inside the huge clouds of gas in outer space where stars are born. It consists of two hydrogen atoms joined together.

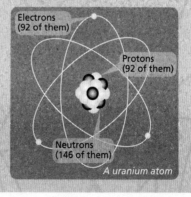

Electrons (92 of them)

Protons (92 of them)

Neutrons (146 of them)

A uranium atom

ago, these stars sent into outer space all these large atoms they created. The same will happen to the star you are looking at now, behind the window. It will explode at the end of its life, when there are no more small particles available to fuse into bigger ones. The explosion will send into outer space all the large atoms the star created in its belly."

On the other side of the window, the star was looking angry. Its bright yellow color was turning reddish as it grew and grew, until it was so big that it was almost impossible to see anything else through the window. It seemed to George that the star might explode at any moment. Eric pressed his remote control again, and the window immediately moved away from the star, which kept getting redder and bigger all the time.

"Isn't it amazing!" exclaimed Eric. "At first the ball shrinks and gives birth to a star, and then the star gets bigger and bigger! And now it is about to explode! Whatever you do, don't take off your glasses."

George watched the star in fascination. Suddenly, long after it had reached a size no one could have imagined, the most powerful explosion George had ever seen happened just in front of him. The whole star blew up, sending into outer space enormous quantities of light and red-hot gas, including all the new atoms it had created. After the explosion, George saw that all that was left of the star was a beautiful new cloud, full of extraordinary colors and new materials.

"Ooooh-ahhhh!" he said. It was like watching the most incredible fireworks display.

"You see," said Eric, "with time, the colorful cloud you now see will mix with other clouds, ones from far distant stars that have also exploded. As they cool down, all the gases from these clouds will mix together into an even bigger cloud, where stars will be born again. Near where these new stars appear, the leftover elements will gather together to become objects of various sizes—but not ones big enough to become stars themselves. Some of these objects will become balls, and with time, these balls will turn into planets. In real life, it takes a very long time for all this to happen—tens of millions of years!"

"Wow!" George was fascinated.

"But we haven't got that much time to wait, and you need to get home for your supper," said Eric, going over to Cosmos and pressing a few more keys. "So let me speed it up a bit. Here we go!"

In the blink of an eye, the tens of millions of years Eric was talking about had passed. The gas from the explosion of dozens of stars had gathered into an immense cloud. Within this cloud, new stars were appearing everywhere, until one formed just in front of the window. That star's brightness made all the other stars very difficult to spot. Some distance away from this new star, the gas left over from the cloud was becoming very cold and had started to gather into small, icy rocks. George saw that one of these rocks was heading straight for the window. He opened his mouth to warn Eric, but the rock was traveling far too quickly. Before George could say anything, it smashed into the glass with a shattering, splintering roar, seeming to shake the whole house.

George jumped in fright and fell off the sofa. "What was *that*?" he shouted to Eric.

"Oops!" said Eric, who was typing away on Cosmos. "Sorry about that. I wasn't expecting to take a direct hit."

"You should be more careful," said Cosmos crossly. "This isn't the first time we've had an accident."

"What was it?" asked George, who found he was clutching a small teddy bear that Annie must have left on the sofa. He was feeling rather dizzy.

"We were hit by a tiny comet," admitted Eric, who

was looking a little sheepish. "Sorry, everyone. I didn't mean for that to happen."

"A tiny what?" asked George, feeling the room spin around him.

Eric typed a few more commands into Cosmos. "I think that's enough for today," he said. "Are you all right, George?" He took off his glasses and peered into George's face. "You look a little green." He sounded worried. "Oh dear, I thought this was going to be fun. Annie!" he called into the kitchen. "Can you bring George a glass of water? Oh dear, oh dear."

Annie came in, walking on tiptoe. She was carefully holding a very full teacup of water, some of which was sloshing over the side. Freddy the pig was glued to her side, casting adoring glances up at her with his piggy eyes. She held the cup out to George.

"Don't worry," she said kindly. "I felt really sick too, my first time. Dad"—it was a command—"it's time to let George go home now. He's had enough of the Universe."

"Yes, yes, I think you're right," said Eric, still looking concerned.

"But it was so interesting!" protested George. "Can't I see some more?"

"No, really, I think that's enough," said Eric hurriedly, putting on a coat. "I'm going to walk you back to your house now. Cosmos, you're in charge of Annie for a couple of minutes. Come on, George, bring your pig."

"Can I come back?" said George eagerly.

Eric stopped fussing around with coats and keys and outdoor shoes and smiled. "Certainly," he said.

"But you must promise not to tell anyone about Cosmos," Annie added.

"Is it a secret?" asked George, eagerly.

"Yes," said Annie. "It's a huge great big ginormous amazing secret that is a trillion gazillion times bigger than any secret you've ever heard before."

"Now, Annie," said Eric sternly, "I've told you that gazillion is not a real number. Say good-bye to George and his pig."

Annie waved and gave George a smile.

"Good-bye, George," said Cosmos's voice. "Thank you for making use of my exceedingly powerful capacities."

"Thank you, Cosmos," said George politely.

With that, Eric ushered him and Freddy into the hallway and out of the front door and back to their real lives on planet Earth.

Chapter Six

The next day at school, George couldn't stop thinking about the wonders he had seen at Eric's house. Enormous clouds and outer space and flying rocks! Cosmos, the world's most powerful computer! And they all lived next door to him, George, the boy whose parents wouldn't even let him have an ordinary computer in the house. The excitement was almost too much to bear, especially now that George was sitting once more at his very boring desk in the classroom.

He doodled on the schoolbook in front of him with his colored pencils, trying to sketch Eric's amazing computer— the one that could make a window from thin air, and through that window show you the birth and death of a star. But even though

George could see it perfectly in his mind, his hand found it difficult to draw a picture that looked anything like what he had seen. It was very annoying. He had to keep crossing parts out and drawing them again, until the whole page looked like one giant squiggle.

"*Ow!*" he exclaimed suddenly as a missile made of a scrunched-up ball of paper hit him on the back of the head.

"Ah, George," said Dr. Reeper, his teacher. "So, you are with us this afternoon after all. How nice."

George looked up with a start. Dr. Reeper was standing right over him, staring down through his really smeared glasses. There was a large blue ink stain on his jacket, which reminded George of the shape of an exploding star.

"Do you have anything to say to the class?" said Dr. Reeper, peering down at George's notebook, which

George hastily tried to cover. "Other than 'Ow!' the only word I've heard you say today?"

"No, not really," said George in a strangled, high-pitched voice.

"You wouldn't like to say, 'Dear Doctor Reeper, here is the homework I spent all weekend slaving over'?"

"Um, well . . . ," said George, embarrassed.

"Or, 'Doctor Reeper, I've listened carefully to every word you've ever said in class, written them all down, added my own comments, and here is my project, with which you will be extremely pleased'?"

"Uh . . . ," muttered George, wondering how to get out of this one.

"Of course you wouldn't," said Dr. Reeper heavily. "After all, I'm just the teacher, and I stand here all day saying things for my own amusement and fun, with no hope that anyone will ever gain anything of value from my attempts to educate them."

"I *do* listen," protested George, who was now feeling guilty.

"Don't try and flatter me," said Dr. Reeper rather wildly. "It won't work." He whipped around sharply. "And give me that!" He shot across the classroom so fast he was almost a blur of speed and snatched a cell phone from a boy sitting at the back.

Dr. Reeper might wear tweed jackets and speak like a man from a century ago, but his pupils were so scared of him, they never tricked him the way they did teachers who were foolish enough to try and befriend them. He was a new teacher and he hadn't been at the school long, but even on his first day he had quelled a whole room full of students into silence just by staring at them. There was nothing modern or touchy-feely or cozy about Dr. Reeper, with the result that his classrooms were always orderly, his homework came in on time, and even the slouchy rebel boys sat up straight and fell quiet when he walked into the room.

The kids called him "Greeper," a nickname that came from the sign on his office door, which read DR. G. REEPER. Or "Greeper the Creeper" because of his mysterious habit of appearing without warning in far-flung corners of the school. There would be a gentle *swoosh* of thick-soled shoes and a faint smell of old tobacco, and before anyone knew it, Greeper would be bearing down on whatever secret mischief was brewing, rubbing his scarred hands with delight. No one knew how he had managed to cover both hands in red, scaly, painful-looking burn marks. And no one would ever dare ask.

"Perhaps, George," said Greeper, pocketing the cell phone he had just confiscated, "you would care to enlighten the class as to what the artwork you have been working on this morning represents?"

"It's, well, it's . . . ," whispered George, feeling his ears become hot and pink.

"Speak up, boy, speak up!" ordered Greeper. "We're

all curious to know quite what *this*"—he held up George's drawing of Cosmos so the whole class could see—"is meant to be! Aren't we, class?"

The other children snickered, delighted that Greeper was picking on someone who wasn't them.

At that moment George really hated Greeper. He hated him so much he completely forgot his fear of shame or humiliation in front of the other pupils. Unfortunately he also forgot his promise to Eric.

"It's a very special computer, actually," he said in a loud voice, "which can show you what's happening in the Universe. It belongs to my friend Eric." He fixed Greeper with a very blue stare, his eyes determined under his tufts of dark red hair. "There are amazing things in outer space, just flying around all the time, like planets and stars and gold and stuff." George was making the last part up—Eric hadn't said anything about gold in outer space.

For the first time since George had been in Greeper's class, his teacher seemed lost for words. He just stood there, holding George's book in his hands, his jaw falling open as he looked at George in wonder. "So it does work, after all," he half whispered to George. "And you've seen it. That's amazing . . ." A moment later it seemed as though Greeper were waking from a dream. He snapped George's book shut, handed it back to him, and walked to the front of the class.

"Now," said Greeper loudly, "given today's behavior, I'm going to assign one hundred lines. I want you to write neatly and clearly in your books: *I will not send text messages in Doctor Reeper's class because I am too busy listening to all the interesting things he has to say.* One hundred times, please, and anyone who hasn't finished by the time the bell rings can stay behind. Very good, get on with it."

There was an angry muttering from the classroom. George's classmates had been looking forward to seeing him being taken to pieces by the teacher, and instead, they'd all been punished for something quite different, and George had mostly been let off the hook.

"But, sir, that's not fair," whined a boy at the back.

"Neither is life," said Greeper happily. "As that is one of the most useful lessons I could possibly teach you, I feel proud that you've understood it already. Carry on, class." With that, he sat down at his desk, got out a book that was full of complicated equations, and starting flicking through the pages, nodding to himself wisely as he did so.

George felt a ruler being jabbed into his back.

"This is all your fault," hissed Ringo, the class bully, who was sitting behind him.

"*Silence!*" thundered Greeper, without even looking up from his book. "Anyone who speaks will do *two* hundred lines instead."

His hand whizzing across the page, George finished

the one hundred lines in his neat writing just as the bell rang for the end of class. Carefully he tore out the page with the picture of Cosmos on it and folded it up, tucking it into a back pants pocket before dropping his book on Greeper's desk. But George hadn't taken even two steps down the hall before Greeper caught up with him and barred his way.

"George," said Greeper very seriously, "this computer

is real, isn't it? You've seen it, haven't you?" The look in his eyes was frightening.

"I was just, um, making it up," said George quickly, trying to wriggle away. He wished he hadn't said anything at all to Greeper.

"Where is it, George?" asked his teacher, speaking slowly and quietly. "It's very important that you tell me where this amazing computer lives."

"There *is* no computer," said George, managing to duck under Greeper's arm. "It doesn't exist—I just imagined it, that's all."

Greeper drew back and looked at George thoughtfully. "Be careful, George," he said in a scarily quiet voice. "Be very careful." With that, he walked away.

Chapter Seven

The way home from school was long and hot; the unexpected heat of the early autumn sun was beating down on the asphalt, turning it soft and squishy under George's feet. He trudged along the pavement while big cars whizzed past him, leaving smelly fumes behind them as they went. In some of these enormous, shiny monsters sat the smug kids from school, watching DVDs in the backseat as their parents drove them home. Some of them made faces at George as they drove past, jeering at him for having to walk. Others waved happily, as though he would somehow be pleased to see them as they shot off into the distance in their vast gas-guzzlers. No one ever stopped and offered him a lift.

But today he didn't mind. He had plenty to think about on his walk home, and he felt glad to be alone. His mind was full of clouds in space, huge explosions, and the millions of years it took to make a star. These thoughts took him far, far across the Universe—so far, in fact, that he completely forgot an important fact about his life on planet Earth.

"Hey!" He heard a shout behind him, and it snapped him back to the here and now. He hoped it was just someone shouting in the street, a random noise that had nothing to do with him. He hurried along a little faster, clutching his school bag snugly to his chest.

"Hey!" He heard it again, this time a little closer. Resisting the urge to look back, he sped up his pace. On one side of him was the busy main road, on the other the city park, which offered nowhere to hide. The trees were too thin and straggly to stand behind, and going anywhere near the bushes was a bad idea. The last thing he wanted was to get dragged into them by the boys he feared were behind him. He kept going, getting faster every minute, his heartbeat thumping in his chest like a bongo drum.

"Georgie boy!" He heard the yell and his blood curdled. All his worst fears were confirmed. Usually when the end-of-school bell rang, George shot out of

the gates and was well on his way home while the larger, slower boys were still flicking rubber bands at each other in the coatroom. He'd heard the awful stories of what Ringo and his followers did to the kids they caught on the street. Eyebrows shaved off, hung upside down, covered in mud, left up a tree wearing only underwear, painted in indelible ink, or abandoned to take the blame for broken windows— all were whispered tales at school of Ringo's reign of terror.

But on that sunny, drowsy autumn afternoon, George had made a terrible mistake. He was walking home too slowly just when he'd given Ringo and his friends a reason to come looking for him. Angry with him for landing them with extra work in Greeper's class, they were now clearly on his tail and ready to take revenge.

George looked around. Ahead of him he saw a group of mothers pushing carriages toward an intersection, where a crossing guard stopped the traffic to let people across. Scurrying forward, he joined the moms and babies, managing to insert himself into their midst so that he was surrounded by strollers. Ambling across the road while the crossing guard held up her bright yellow sign, George tried to look as though he belonged to one of the mother-and-baby groups. But he knew he wasn't fooling anyone. As he passed the crossing guard, she winked at him and said under her breath, "Don't worry, dear, I'll hold 'em back for you for a minute. But you run along home now. Don't let those nasty boys catch you."

When George reached the other side of the road, to his surprise the crossing guard leaned her sign against a tree and stood there, glaring back at Ringo and his friends. The roar of the traffic started up again, and as George sped away he heard another menacing shout.

"Hey! We gotta get across—we need to get home and do our . . . schoolwork. . . . If you don't let us cross, I'll tell my mother and she'll come and straighten you out."

"You watch yourself, Richard Bright," grumbled the crossing guard, walking slowly out into the road with her sign.

George turned off the main road, but the sound of

heavy thudding feet behind told him they knew which way he'd gone. He was hurrying down a long tree-lined alley that ran behind the gardens of some very big houses; for once it was empty of adults who might have saved him.

George tried a few of the doors in the fences, but they were all firmly locked. He looked around in a panic and then had a flash of inspiration. Grabbing on to the lowest bough of an

overhanging apple tree, he hoisted himself up high enough to gain a foothold on the top of the fence and leaped right over it. He landed in a large prickly bush, which scratched him, ripping his school uniform. As he lay groaning silently in the shrubbery, he heard Ringo and his friends pass by on the other side of the fence, making spine-chilling comments about what they'd do to George when they got their hands on him.

George stayed still until he was sure they'd gone. Wriggling free of his school sweater, which was hopelessly tangled in the spiky bush, he struggled out of the clinging branches. His pants pockets had emptied their contents onto the ground. He scrabbled around, trying to pick up all his important things. Then he emerged from the undergrowth onto a long, flat green lawn, where a very surprised lady lay in a deck chair, sunbathing. She lifted up her dark glasses and looked at him.

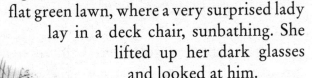

"*Bonjour!*" she said in a nice voice. She pointed toward the house. "Go zat way—ze gate is not so locked."

"Oh, *merci,*" said George, remembering his

one word of French. "And, um, sorry," he added as he rushed past her and ran along a passage by the side of her house. He went through the gate, came out onto the road, and set off for home, limping a little because he'd twisted his left foot. The streets were quiet and sleepy as he hobbled along. But the silence didn't last long.

"There he is!" A great cry went up. "*Georgie-boy!*" he heard. "*We're coming to get you!*"

George gathered the last of his strength and tried to get his legs to move fast, but he felt as though he were wading through quicksand. He wasn't far from home— he could see the end of his road—but Ringo and his gang were gaining on him. He plowed bravely forward, reaching the corner just as he thought he might collapse on the pavement.

"*We're gonna kill you!*" Ringo shouted from behind him.

Staggering, George tottered down his street. His breathing had gone all funny—the air was going in and out of his lungs in great swooshing gasps. All the scratches and bruises and bumps he'd gotten running away from Ringo were hurting, his throat was parched, and he was exhausted. He couldn't have gone much farther, but he didn't need to—he was home. He'd reached the green front door without being turned into ground meat, or something worse, by Ringo and his terrible friends, and now everything was going to be all right. All he had to do was reach into his pocket and find his key to unlock the front door.

But it wasn't there.

He turned out his pockets and found all his treasures—a marble, a Spanish coin, a length of string, a model red sports car, and a ball of fluff. But no key. He must have dropped it in the bushes when he climbed over the fence. He rang the bell, hoping his mom might have come home early. *Ting-a-ling-ling-ling!* He tried again. But there was still no answer.

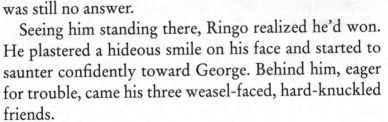

Seeing him standing there, Ringo realized he'd won. He plastered a hideous smile on his face and started to saunter confidently toward George. Behind him, eager for trouble, came his three weasel-faced, hard-knuckled friends.

George knew there was nowhere left to run. He closed his eyes and stood with his back to his front door, his stomach churning as he prepared to meet his fate. He tried to think of something to say that might make Ringo back off. But he couldn't come up with anything clever, and there wasn't much point in telling Ringo he was going to get into trouble. Ringo knew that already, and it had never stopped him before. The footsteps stopped, and George opened one eye to see what was happening. Ringo and his friends had paused halfway down the path and were having some kind of conference about what to do with George.

"No!" Ringo was saying loudly. "That's ridiculous! Let's squeeze him against the wall until he begs us to let him go!"

But just as Ringo spoke, something happened. Something so peculiar that, afterward, Ringo and his friends weren't sure if they'd dreamed it. The door of the house next to George's flew open and out of it bounded what looked like a tiny astronaut. Everyone took a step back in astonishment as the small figure in a white spacesuit with a round glass helmet and an antenna attached to the back jumped into the middle of the road, striking a fierce, karate-style pose.

"Get back," said the spacesuit in a strange metallic voice, "or I will put the curse of Alien Life on you. You will turn green, and your brains will bubble and leak out of your ears and down your nose. Your bones will turn to rubber, and you will grow hundreds of warts all over your body. You will only be able to eat spinach and broccoli, and you will never, ever be able to watch television again because it will make your eyes fall out

74

of your head. So there!" The astronaut did a few twirls and kicks that looked somehow familiar to George.

Ringo and his friends had turned a ghostly color and were stumbling backward, their mouths hanging open. They were absolutely terrified.

"Get into the house," said the spacesuit to George.

George slipped into Next Door's house. He wasn't scared of the little astronaut—he'd caught a gleam of bright blond hair through the glass of the helmet. It looked like Annie had saved him.

Chapter Eight

"Phew!" The figure in the space suit followed George into the house, slamming the front door with a backward kick of a hefty space boot. "It's hot in here," it added, pulling off the round glass helmet and flipping out a long ponytail. It was Annie, a bit pink in the face from jumping about in the heavy suit. "Did you see how scared they were?" she said to George, beaming and wiping her forehead on her sleeve. "Did you?" She strode along the hallway, making clunking noises as she walked. "Come on."

"Um, yes. Thank you," George managed to say as he trailed behind her into the same room where he'd watched *The Birth and Death of a Star* with Eric. He'd been so excited about coming back to see Cosmos again, but now he just felt miserable. He'd accidentally told horrible Dr. Reeper

about Cosmos, when he'd promised Eric he would keep it a secret. He'd had a long, frightening journey back from school being chased by the bullies, and to cap it all off, he'd been rescued by a little girl wearing a space suit. It was turning out to be a really bad day.

Annie, on the other hand, seemed to be enjoying herself immensely. "What do you think?" she said to George, smoothing down the brilliant white folds of her jumpsuit. "It's new—it just arrived in the mail." On the floor lay a cardboard box covered in stamps, marked SPACE ADVENTURES R US! Next to it was a much smaller pink suit with sequins, badges, and ribbons sewn all over it. It was dirty and worn and covered in patches. "That's my old suit," Annie explained. "I had that when I was really young," she said scornfully. "I thought it was cool to put all that stuff on it, but now I like my space suits plain."

"Why have you got a space suit?" asked George. "Are you going to a costume party?"

"As if!" Annie rolled her eyes. "Cosmos!" she called.

"Yes, Annie," said Cosmos the computer fondly.

"You good, beautiful, lovely, wonderful computer!"

"Oh, Annie!" said Cosmos, his screen glowing as if he were blushing.

"George wants to know why I have a space suit."

"Annie has a space suit," replied Cosmos, "so she can go on journeys around outer space. It is very cold out there, around minus four hundred and fifty-five

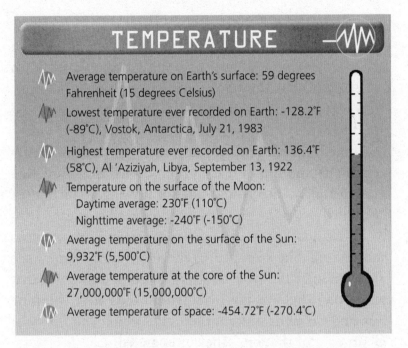

TEMPERATURE —/\/\/\

- Average temperature on Earth's surface: 59 degrees Fahrenheit (15 degrees Celsius)
- Lowest temperature ever recorded on Earth: -128.2°F (-89°C), Vostok, Antarctica, July 21, 1983
- Highest temperature ever recorded on Earth: 136.4°F (58°C), Al 'Aziziyah, Libya, September 13, 1922
- Temperature on the surface of the Moon:
    Daytime average: 230°F (110°C)
    Nighttime average: -240°F (-150°C)
- Average temperature on the surface of the Sun: 9,932°F (5,500°C)
- Average temperature at the core of the Sun: 27,000,000°F (15,000,000°C)
- Average temperature of space: -454.72°F (-270.4°C)

degrees Farenheit. She would freeze solid in a fraction of a second if she didn't wear it."

"Yeah, but —," protested George. But he didn't get far.

"I go on journeys around the Solar System with my dad," boasted Annie. "Sometimes my mom comes too, but she doesn't really like it in outer space."

George felt really fed up. He was in no mood for silly games. "No you don't," he said crossly. "You don't go into outer space. You'd have to go up in the space shuttle to do that, and they're never going to let you on board because they wouldn't know what was true and what you'd made up."

Annie's mouth had formed a perfect O.

"You just tell stupid stories about being a ballerina or an astronaut, and your dad and Cosmos pretend to believe you, but they don't really," continued George, who was hot and tired and wanted to have something good to eat.

Annie blinked rapidly. Her blue eyes were suddenly very shiny and full of tears. "I'm not making it up," she said furiously, her round cheeks turning even pinker. "I'm not, I'm not. It's all true, I don't tell stories. I *am* a ballerina, and I *do* go into outer space, and I'm going to show you." She stomped over to Cosmos. "And," she went on angrily, "you're going to come too. And that way you'll believe me." She rummaged in a shipping box and brought out another suit, which she threw at George. "Put that on," she commanded.

"Uh-oh," said Cosmos quietly.

Annie was standing in front of Cosmos, drumming her fingers on the keyboard. "Where should I take him?" she asked.

"I don't think this is a good idea," warned Cosmos. "What will your dad say?"

"He won't know," said Annie quickly. "We'll just go and come right back. It'll take two minutes. Please, Cosmos!" she pleaded, her eyes now brimming over with tears. "Everyone thinks I make everything up and I don't! It's true about the Solar System, and I want to show George so he doesn't think I tell lies."

"All right, all right," said Cosmos hastily. "Please don't drop saltwater on my keyboard; it rusts my insides. But you can just look. I don't want either of you actually to go out there."

Annie wheeled around to face George. Her face was fierce, but the tears were still flowing. "What do you want to see?" she demanded. "What's the most interesting thing in the Universe?"

George thought hard. He had no idea what was going on, but he certainly hadn't meant to upset Annie so much. He didn't like seeing her cry, and now he felt even worse about Eric. Eric had said to him only yesterday that Annie didn't mean any harm, and yet George had been pretty nasty to her. Perhaps, he thought, it would be better to play along.

"Comets," he said, remembering the end of *The Birth*

and Death of a Star and the rock that had smashed into the window. "I think comets are the most interesting things in the Universe."

Annie typed the word *comet* on Cosmos's keyboard.

"Put on your suit, George, quickly!" she ordered. "It's about to get cold." With that, she hit the button marked ENTER . . .

Chapter Nine

Once more everything went dark. The little beam of brilliant light shot out from Cosmos's screen into the middle of the room, hovered for a second, and then started to draw a shape. Only this time it wasn't making a window out of thin air. It was drawing something different. The beam drew a line up from the floor, then turned left, kept going in a straight line, and dropped back down to the floor again.

"Oh, look!" said George, who could see what it was now. "Cosmos has drawn a door!"

"I haven't just drawn it," said Cosmos huffily. "I'm much smarter than that, you know. I've *made* you a doorway. It's a portal. It leads to—"

"Shush, Cosmos!" said Annie. She had put on her helmet again and was speaking through the voice transmitter fitted inside it. It gave her the same funny voice that had so frightened Ringo and his friends. "Let George open it himself."

By now George had struggled into the big, heavy white suit and glass helmet that Annie had chucked at

him. Attached to the back of the suit was a small tank that fed air through a tube into the helmet so he could breathe easily inside it. He put on the big space boots and gloves that Annie had thrown at him, and then he stepped forward and gave the door a timid push. It flew open, revealing an enormous expanse filled with hundreds of little lights that turned out to be stars. One in particular was much bigger and brighter than the others.

"Wow!" said George, speaking through his own voice transmitter. When he'd watched *The Birth and Death of a Star*, he'd seen the events in outer space through a windowpane. But this time there didn't seem to be anything between him and outer space. It looked as though he could just step through the doorway and be there. But where? If he took that small step, where would he be?

"Where . . . ? What . . . ? How . . . ?" said George in wonder.

"See that bright star over there, the brightest star of all those you can see?" George heard Cosmos reply. "It's the Sun. Our Sun. It looks smaller from here than when you look at it in the sky. The doorway leads to a place in the Solar System that is much farther away from the Sun than planet Earth. There is a large comet coming—that is why I have selected this location for you. You will see it in a few minutes. Please stand back from the door."

George took a step backward. But Annie, who was right next to him, grabbed his suit and hauled him forward again.

"Please stand back from the door, a comet is approaching," said Cosmos as though he were announcing the arrival of a train at the station. "Please do not stand too close to the edge—the comet will be traveling at high speed."

Annie nudged George and pointed at the doorway with her foot.

"Please stand back from the door," repeated Cosmos.

"When I count to three . . . ," said Annie. "One." She held up one finger. Beyond the door, George could see a large rock coming toward them, much larger than the tiny one that hit the window the day before.

"This comet will not be stopping," continued Cosmos. "It goes straight through our Solar System."

Annie held up another finger to indicate "Two." The grayish white rock was getting closer.

"The journey time is approximately one hundred and eighty-four years," said Cosmos. "Calling at Saturn, Jupiter, Mars, Earth, and the Sun. On its way back, it will also call at Neptune and Pluto, now out of service as a planet."

"Please, my wonderful Cosmos, when we're out there on the comet, can you accelerate the journey? Otherwise it will take us months to see the planets!" Without waiting for Cosmos to reply, Annie shouted,

PLUTO

Before August 2006 there were said to be nine planets that revolved around the Sun: Mercury, Venus, Earth, Mars, Jupiter, Saturn, Uranus, Neptune, and Pluto. These nine celestial bodies still exist, of course, and are exactly the same as they were before, but in August 2006 the International Astronomical Union decided not to call Pluto a planet anymore. It is now called a dwarf planet.

This is due to a change in the definition of what a planet is. There now are three rules that need to be fulfilled by any object in space in order for it to be called a planet:

1) It has to be in orbit around the Sun.
2) It has to be big enough for gravity to make it almost round and stay that way.
3) Its gravity has to have attracted almost everything that is next to it in space as it travels around the Sun, so that its path is cleared.

According to this new definition, Pluto is not a planet anymore. Is it in orbit around the Sun? Yes. Is it almost round and will it stay so? Yes. Has it cleared its path around the Sun? No. There are lots of rocks in its orbital path. So, because it failed to fulfill the third rule, Pluto has been downgraded from a planet to a dwarf planet.

The other eight planets fulfill the three rules and so they remain planets. For planets and stars other than the Sun, an additional requirement has been agreed upon by the International Astronomical Union: The object should not be so big as to become a star itself at a later stage.

Planets around stars other than the Sun are called exoplanets. So far, over 240 exoplanets have been seen. Most of them are huge—much bigger than the Earth.

In December 2006 a satellite named *Corot* was sent into space. The quality of the detectors *Corot* is equipped with should allow for the discovery of exoplanets much smaller than before, down to about twice the size of the Earth. One such planet was detected using other means in 2007. It is called Gliese 581 c.

"Three!" grabbed George's hand, and dragged him through the doorway.

The last thing he heard was Cosmos's voice, calling as though from millions and millions of miles away, "Don't jump! It isn't safe! Come *ba-a-a-a-ack.*"

And then there was silence.

Chapter Ten

Out in the street, Ringo and his friends were still standing there, as though stuck to the pavement by some invisible force.

"What was that?" asked a small, skinny boy who went by the name of Whippet.

"Dunno," said the huge boy they called Tank, scratching his head.

"Well, *I* wasn't scared," said Ringo defiantly.

"Neither was I," chorused all the others quickly.

"I was just going to have a word with that weirdo in the space suit when it got frightened and ran away."

"Yeah, yeah, yeah," his friends all agreed quickly. "Course you were, Ringo. Course you were."

"So I think," Ringo went on, *"you"*—he pointed at the newest member of his gang—"should ring the doorbell."

"Me?" The boy gulped.

"You said you weren't scared," said Ringo.

"I'm not!" he squeaked.

"Then you can ring the bell, can't you?"

"Why can't you do it?" asked the new boy.

"Because I asked you first. Go on." Ringo glared at the boy. "Do you wanna be part of this gang?"

"Yes!" said the boy, wondering which was worse— meeting a spaceman and suffering the curse of Alien Life or making Ringo angry. He settled for the spaceman—at least he wouldn't have to see him every day at school. He edged toward Eric's front door uneasily.

"Then ring the bell, Zit," said Ringo, "or you'll be an *ex*-member of this gang."

"Okay," muttered Zit, who didn't like his special new gang name much either. The others all took a few steps backward.

The new boy's finger hovered over the bell.

"Ringo," said one of the others suddenly, "what're we gonna do if he opens the door?"

"*What're we gonna do if he opens the door?*" Ringo

© JOHN THOMAS/SCIENCE PHOTO LIBRARY

In 1996, passing within 9.4 million miles (15 million km) of the Earth, Hyakutake was one of the brightest comets of the twentieth century.

© ROYAL GREENWICH OBSERVATORY/SCIENCE PHOTO LIBRARY

Halley's Comet is visible from the Earth every seventy-six years or so. This photo was taken in 1910.

© RICHARD J. WAINSCOAT, PETER ARNOLD INC./SCIENCE PHOTO LIBRARY

Halley's Comet in 1986.

Although the Moon is usually thought of as gray, it actually has color. This image has been enhanced to reveal the subtle hues produced by the different geological features of the Moon.

This far side of the Moon can never be seen from Earth. This picture was taken by the *Apollo 16* spacecraft in 1972.

The center of the Milky Way. This cannot be seen with our eyes because there is cosmic dust in front of it. But this picture was taken in infrared light, which allows us to see hundreds of thousands of hidden stars. Within the white dot at the center is a supermassive black hole.

© NASA/SCIENCE PHOTO LIBRARY

The largest and most detailed true-color image of Saturn ever produced.

The view of Saturn when seen from the Earth through a small portable telescope.

© JOHN CHUMACK/SCIENCE PHOTO LIBRARY

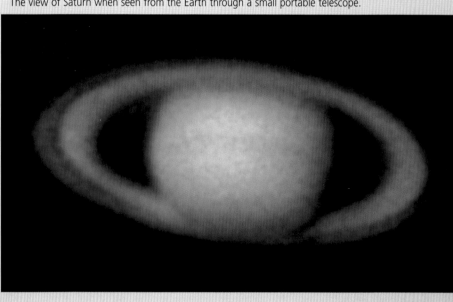

Titan is the largest moon of Saturn. It is the only known moon in the Solar System to have a thick atmosphere. This is an infrared-light picture.

Rhea is the second largest moon of Saturn. It doesn't appear to be geologically active.

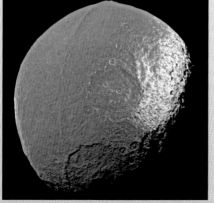

Iapetus is the third largest moon of Saturn. The heavily cratered region that dominates this image is known as Cassini Regio.

Dione is the fourth largest moon of Saturn. Its surface is mainly composed of water ice.

Tethys, the fifth largest moon of Saturn, is also probably composed of water ice.

This is an ultraviolet, green, and infrared composite image of Enceladus, the sixth largest moon of Saturn. Its surface temperature is about −328°F (−200°C), but there may be water underneath the surface.

echoed the question while he tried to think of an answer. He lookayed up at the sky as though searching for an idea. "We're gonna—" Even Ringo wasn't being his usual confident, thuggish self. But before he could come up with an answer, he let out a shout of pain. "Arrrrgggghhhh!" he yelped as a hand grabbed him by the ear and twisted it very hard.

"What," said a stern voice, "are you boys doing, hanging around in the street?" It was Dr. Reeper—Ringo and George's class teacher from school. He had

Ringo firmly by the ear and clearly didn't intend to let go. The boys were very startled to see a teacher outside the school grounds—they never imagined that teachers actually had other lives to lead or had anywhere to go but their classrooms.

"We're not doing nothing," squealed Ringo.

"I think you mean, 'We are not doing *anything*,'" corrected Dr. Reeper in a teacherly voice, "which in any case isn't true. You are obviously doing something, and if I find out that that something has to do with bullying smaller children—like, for example, George . . ." Dr. Reeper stared very hard at all the boys to see if any of them flinched at the mention of George's name.

"No sir no sir no sir no sir," said Ringo, who feared his ear might come off in the teacher's hand. "We never touched him. We were running after him because he . . ."

"Left-his-lunchbox-behind-at-school," said Whippet very quickly.

"And we wanted to give it back to him before he got home," added Zit, the new boy.

"And did you succeed?" said Dr. Reeper with a nasty smile, letting go of Ringo's ear just a little bit.

"We were just about to hand it over," improvised Ringo, "when he went into that house." He pointed at Eric's front door. "So we were ringing the bell to give it to him."

Dr. Reeper let go of Ringo's ear so suddenly that Ringo fell to the ground.

"He went in there?" Dr. Reeper questioned them sharply as Ringo staggered to his feet again.

"Yeah." They all nodded in unison.

"Why don't you boys," said Dr. Reeper slowly, "let me have George's lunchbox and I'll hand it back to him." He fished around in his pocket and brought out a crumpled ten-dollar bill, which he dangled in front of their noses.

"Who's got the lunchbox?" questioned Ringo.

"Not me," said Whippet immediately.

"Not me," mumbled Tank.

"It must be you then," said Ringo, pointing at Zit.

"Ringo, I haven't . . . I didn't . . . I wasn't . . ." Zit was panicking now.

"Very well," said Dr. Reeper, glaring at the four of them. He put the money back in his pocket. "In that case, I think you'd better scram. Do you hear me? Scram!"

Once the boys—who didn't need telling twice—were gone, Dr. Reeper stood in the street, smiling to himself. It wasn't a pleasant sight. Checking that no one else was coming or going, he went up to Eric's front window and squinted through it. The curtains were drawn, so he only had a small opening to look through. He couldn't see much, just two strangely shaped, shadowy figures, which seemed to be standing near some kind of doorway inside the house.

"Interesting," he muttered to himself. "Very, very interesting."

Suddenly, the temperature in the street dropped dramatically. For a second it felt as though air from the North Pole were blowing along the street. Strangely, the bitter wind seemed to be coming from under Eric's front door, but as Dr. Reeper bent down to investigate, it stopped. When he went back to look through the window, the two figures had gone and there was no inside doorway to be seen.

Dr. Reeper nodded to himself. "Ah, the chill of outer space—how I long to feel it," he whispered, rubbing his hands together. "At last, Eric, I've found you! I knew you'd come back one day."

Chapter Eleven

When he leaped over the threshold of the portal door, George found he was floating—not going up, not going down, just drifting in the huge, great darkness of outer space. He looked back toward the doorway, but the hole in space where it should have been had closed over as though it had never been. There was no way back now and the giant rock was getting closer all the time.

"Hold my hand!" Annie shouted to George. As he gripped her hand in its space glove even harder, he started to feel as if they were falling down toward the comet. Moving faster and faster, as if they were on a giant Tilt-a-Whirl, George and Annie spiraled toward the huge rock, getting closer and closer all the time. Beneath them, they could see that one side of the comet, the part facing the Sun, was brightly lit. But the other side, which the Sun's rays didn't reach, was in darkness. Eventually they landed in a heap on a thick layer of icy, dust-covered rubble. Luckily they'd come down on the bright side of the comet, so they could see what lay around them.

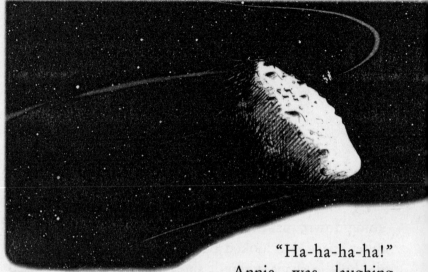

"Ha-ha-ha-ha!"

Annie was laughing as she picked herself up. She hauled George to his feet and brushed bits of dirty ice and crumbly rock off him. "So?" she said. "Do you believe me now?"

"Where are we?" said George, who was so surprised he forgot to be scared. George felt extremely light. He looked around and saw rock, ice, snow, and darkness. It was like standing on a giant dirty snowball someone had thrown into outer space. Stars blazed everywhere, their fiery glow quite different from the twinkling lights he saw from the Earth.

"We're having an adventure," replied Annie. "On a comet. And it's real—it isn't a made-up story, is it?"

"No, it isn't," admitted George. He patted her space suit awkwardly. "I'm sorry I didn't believe you, Annie."

"That's all right," said Annie generously. "No one ever

does. That's why I had to show you. Look, George!" She waved an arm around. "You're going to see the planets in the Solar System." She started to pull a length of rope out of a pocket in her space suit. On the end of the rope was a spike, like a tent peg. Using her space boot, she jammed the spike into the ice on the comet's surface.

Watching her, George gave a tiny little jump for joy. Even though he was wearing the space suit that had seemed very heavy on Earth, he couldn't believe how light he felt. So light that he thought he could leap as high as he wanted. He did another little jump across a little crack on the comet's surface. This time he went up and forward, but he didn't come down again. He seemed to be taking a giant leap, maybe hundreds of feet long! He'd never be able to find Annie again . . .

"Help! Help!" George called through the helmet as his jump carried him farther and farther away, his arms whirling in the surrounding emptiness as he tried to make himself fall down onto the comet. But it was no good. Annie was far away in the distance now— he could only just see her when he looked back. The comet's surface was passing quickly below him. He could see holes and little hills everywhere, but nothing that he could grab on to. But at last he seemed to fall.

The ground was getting closer now, and as he landed he slid on the ice near the threshold between the bright and the dark side of the comet. In the distance, he saw Annie carefully running toward him.

"If you can hear me, *don't jump again!*" she was saying in a very urgent voice. "If you can hear me, *don't jump again!* If you can—"

"*I won't!*" he called back as she reached him.

"Don't *do* that, George!" said Annie. "You could have landed on the dark side of the comet. I might never have found you! Now stand up—the boots have small spikes on their soles." She sounded very grown-up and not at all like the impish little girl he had met at Eric's house. "A comet is different from the Earth. We weigh much less here than we do there, so when we jump, it can take us a long, long way. This is a different world. Oh, look!" she added, changing the subject. "We're just in time!"

"For what?" asked George.

"For *that!*" Annie pointed to the other side of the comet.

Behind the comet was a tail of ice and dust, which was getting steadily longer. As it grew, it caught the light from the faraway Sun and glistened in the wake of the comet, making it look as though thousands of diamonds were shining in outer space.

"That's beautiful," whispered George.

For a minute he and Annie just stood there in silence.

MASS

⚙ The mass of a body measures the force needed to move it or to change the way it moves. Mass is often measured by weighing the body, but mass and weight are not the same. The weight of an object is the force attracting it to another object, such as the Earth or the Moon, and it depends on the mass of both objects and the distance between them. You weigh slightly less on top of a mountain because you are farther from the center of the Earth.

Earth | Moon

Because the mass of the Moon is much less than the mass of the Earth, an astronaut who weighs about 200 pounds (about 90 kg) on Earth would weigh only about 33 pounds (15 kg) on the Moon. So astronauts on the Moon could, with the correct training, beat any Earth-based long-jump record.

⚙ Einstein was a German physicist who was born in 1879. He discovered that energy is equivalent to mass, according to the famous equation $E=mc^2$, where "E" is energy, "m" is mass, and "c" is the speed of light. Because the speed of light is very large, Einstein and others realized that this equation suggested one could make an atom bomb, in which a small amount of mass is converted into a very large amount of energy in an explosion.

⚙ Einstein also discovered that mass and energy curve space, creating gravity.

99

As George watched the trail grow, he realized it was made up of bits of the bright side of the comet.

"The rock's melting!" said George in a panic, clutching Annie's arm. "What will happen when there's nothing left?"

"Don't worry." Annie shook her head. "We're just getting closer to the Sun. The Sun slowly warms up the bright side of the comet and the ice turns into gas. But it's okay because there's enough ice here for us to pass the Sun loads of times. Anyway, the rock under the ice won't melt. So we won't start falling through space, if that's what you're scared of."

"I'm not scared!" protested George, letting go of her arm very suddenly. "I was just asking."

"Then ask more interesting questions!" said Annie.

"Like what?" asked George.

"Like, what would happen if some of the rocks from the comet's tail fell on the Earth?"

George kicked some dust around and then said reluctantly, "All right, what would happen?"

"Now that is a good question!" said Annie, sounding pleased. "The rocks catch fire when they enter the Earth's atmosphere, and from the ground, when we look up, they become what we call shooting stars, or meteors."

They stood and gazed until the comet's tail got so long they couldn't see the end of it. But as they were watching it, the comet seemed to start changing direction: All the stars in the background were moving. "What's happening?" George asked.

"Quick!" Annie replied. "We've only got a few seconds. Sit down, George." She cleared two little spaces on the ice, speedily brushing the powder aside

with her glove. Reaching into another pocket of her
suit, she produced what looked like climbing hooks.
"Sit down!" she ordered again. She screwed the hooks
into the ground and then fastened them onto a longish
piece of cord hanging from a buckle on George's suit.
"Just in case something hits you," she added.

"Like what?" asked George.

"Well, I don't know. My dad normally does this part,"
she replied. Next, she sat down behind George and did
the same to herself. "Do you like roller coasters?" she
asked him.

"I don't know," said George, who had never been on
one.

"Well, you're about to find out!" said Annie, laughing.

The comet was definitely falling—or at least changing direction toward what seemed to be "down." From the way the stars were moving all around him, George understood that the comet was falling very fast. But he couldn't feel anything—he didn't have butterflies in his stomach, and there was no rush of air blowing past him. It wasn't at all how he had expected a ride on a roller coaster to feel. But he was starting to realize that things feel very different in outer space from the way they do on Earth.

George closed his eyes for a moment, just to see if he

COMETS

 Comets are big, dirty, and not very round snowballs that travel around the Sun. They are made up of elements created in stars that exploded a long time before our Sun was born. It is believed that there are more than 100 billion of them, very far away from the Sun, waiting to come closer to us. But we can see them only when they come close enough to the Sun to have a shiny tail. We actually have seen only about 1,000 comets so far.

 The largest known comets have a central core of more than 20 miles (32 km) from one side to the other.

 When comets come close to the Sun, the ice in them turns into gas and releases the dust that was trapped inside. This dust is probably the oldest dust there is throughout the Solar System. It contains clues about our cosmic neighborhood at the very beginning of the life of all the planets, more than 6 billion years ago.

Most of the time, comets circle around the Sun from very far away (much, much farther away than the Earth). Every now and then, one of them starts to travel toward the Sun. There are then two possibilities:

1) Some, like Halley's Comet, will get trapped by the Sun's gravity. These comets will then keep orbiting the Sun until they melt completely or until they hit a planet. Halley's Comet's core is about 9.6 miles (16 km) long. It returns near enough to the Sun to melt down a bit and have a tail that can be seen by us about every 76 years. It was near us in 1986 and will be back in 2061. Some of the comets trapped by the Sun's gravity return near the Sun much more rarely. The Hyakutake Comet, for instance, will travel for 110,000 years before coming back.

2) Because they have too much speed or because they do not travel close enough to the Sun, some other comets, like Comet Swan, never come back. They pass by us once and then start an immense journey in outer space toward another star. These comets are cosmic wanderers. Their interstellar journey can take hundreds of thousands of years, sometimes less, sometimes even more.

could feel anything at all. But no, nothing. Suddenly, with his eyes closed, he realized that something in space must be pulling them and the comet toward it for the comet to change direction like that. George instinctively knew that this something was probably much, much bigger than the comet on which he and Annie were surfing through outer space.

Chapter Twelve

When George opened his eyes again, he saw a massive pale yellow planet with a belt of rings rising in the dark sky ahead of them. They sped along on the comet, heading for a point just above the rings. From far away, the rings looked like soft ribbons. Some were pale yellow, like the planet itself; others were darker.

"This is Saturn," said Annie. "And I saw it first."

"I know what it is!" replied George. "And what do you mean, 'first'? I'm in front of you. *I* saw it first!"

"No, you weren't looking, you were too scared! You had your eyes shut!" Annie's voice rang inside his helmet. "*Ner*-ner-na-*ner-ner*."

"No I didn't!" protested George.

"Shhh!" Annie interrupted him. "Did you know that Saturn is the second biggest of the planets that move around the Sun?"

"Of course I knew," lied George.

"Oh really?" replied Annie. "Then if you knew that, you'll know which is the biggest planet of all."

"Well . . . um . . . ," said George, who had no idea. "It's the Earth, isn't it?"

"*Wrong!*" trumpeted Annie. "The Earth is teeny-weeny,

just like your silly little brain. The Earth is only number five."

"How do you know that?"

"How do I know you've got a silly little brain?" said Annie sarcastically.

"No, stupid," said George furiously. "How do you know about the planets?"

"Because I've done this trip many, many times before," said Annie, tossing her head as though throwing back her ponytail. "So let me tell you. And listen carefully," she ordered. "There are eight planets orbiting the Sun. Four are huge and four are small. The huge ones are Jupiter, Saturn, Neptune, and Uranus. But the two biggest are so much bigger than the others that they are called the Giants. Saturn is the second of the giant planets, and the biggest one of all is Jupiter. The four small planets are Mars, Earth, Venus, and Mercury," she continued, ticking them off on her fingers. "The Earth is the biggest of the small ones, but if you put these four together into a ball, you still wouldn't get anything nearly as big as Saturn. Saturn is more than forty-five times bigger than these four small planets added together."

Annie was clearly delighted to be showing off about the planets. Even though he was very annoyed by how smug she was, George was secretly impressed. All he had ever done was dig potatoes and mess around with a pig in his backyard. It wasn't much in comparison with riding around the Solar System on a comet.

As Annie talked, the comet flew nearer and nearer to Saturn. They got so close that George could see that the rings were made not of ribbons but of ice, rocks, and stones. These were all different sizes, the smallest no bigger than a speck of dust, the largest about twelve feet long. Most of them were moving much too fast for George to catch one. But then he spotted a small chunk of rock calmly floating right next to him. A quick glance behind showed that Annie wasn't looking. He reached out, snatched up the rock, and held it in his space glove! A real treasure from outer space! His heart was beating fast. The sound was so loud in his ears that he thought Annie must be able to hear it through the sound transmitter in his helmet. He suspected that taking things home from outer space was probably not allowed, so he hoped she hadn't noticed.

"George, are you all right?" asked Annie. "Why are you wriggling around like that?"

George quickly thought of something to say to divert her attention from the rock he was trying to stuff into his pocket.

THE SOLAR SYSTEM

○ The Solar System is the cosmic family of our Sun. It comprises all the objects trapped by the Sun's gravity: planets, dwarf planets, moons, comets, asteroids, and other small objects yet to be discovered. An object trapped by the Sun's gravity is said to be in orbit around the Sun.

○ Closest planet to the Sun: Mercury
  Mercury is 36 million miles (57.9 million km) away from the Sun on average

○ Farthest planet from the Sun: Neptune
  Neptune is 2.8 billion miles (4.5 billion km) away from the Sun on average

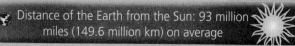
Distance of the Earth from the Sun: 93 million miles (149.6 million km) on average

○ Number of planets: 8

○ From closest to the Sun, the planets are: Mercury, Venus, Earth, Mars, Jupiter, Saturn, Uranus, and Neptune

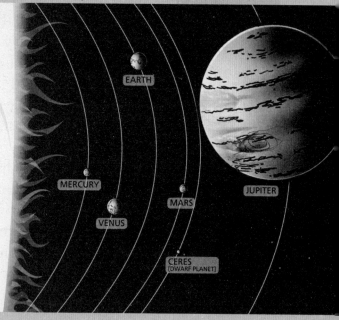

SUN

EARTH

MERCURY

VENUS

MARS

JUPITER

CERES
[DWARF PLANET]

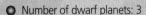
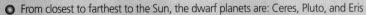

- Number of dwarf planets: 3
- From closest to farthest to the Sun, the dwarf planets are: Ceres, Pluto, and Eris
- Number of known planetary moons: 165
  Mercury: 0; Venus: 0; Earth: 1; Mars: 2; Jupiter: 63;
  Saturn: 59; Uranus: 27; Neptune: 13
- Number of known comets: 1,000 (estimated real number:1,000,000,000,000,000)

Farthest distance traveled by a man-made object: more than 9.3 billion miles (14.96 billion km). Nine billion three hundred million miles is the distance reached by *Voyager 1* on August 15, 2006, at 10:13 a.m. (Greenwich Mean Time). This corresponds to exactly 100 times the distance from the Earth to the Sun. *Voyager 1* is still traveling away.

URANUS

NEPTUNE

ERIS
[DWARF PLANET]

PLUTO
[DWARF PLANET]

SATURN

DISTANCES NOT TO SCALE

"Why did we change direction? Why did our comet move toward Saturn? Why didn't we continue in a straight line?" he babbled.

"Oh dear, you just don't know anything at all, do you?" sighed Annie. "It's lucky for you that I'm such a fount of useful scientific knowledge," she added importantly. "We moved toward Saturn because we fell toward it. Just like an apple falls on Earth, just like we fell onto the comet when we arrived, just like the particles in space clouds fall onto each other and become balls that become stars. Everything falls toward everything throughout the Universe. And do you know the name of what causes this fall?"

George didn't have a clue.

"It's called gravity."

"So it's because of gravity that we're going to fall on Saturn now? And crash?"

"No, silly! We're moving way too fast to crash. We're just flying by to say hello."

Annie waved to Saturn and shouted, *"Hello, Saturn!"* so loudly that George's hands automatically tried to cover his ears, but he couldn't because of his helmet, so instead he yelled back, *"Don't shout!"*

"Oh, I'm sorry," she said. "I didn't mean to."

As they whizzed past Saturn, George saw that Annie was right—the comet didn't fall all the way onto the giant planet but cruised straight past it. With some distance now, he could see that Saturn not only had

rings, but also a moon, like the Earth. Looking closer,
he could hardly believe his eyes! He saw another moon,
and another and yet another! In total, he saw five large
moons and even more small ones before Saturn was
too far away for him to keep counting. *Saturn has at
least five moons!* he thought. George hadn't known

SATURN

- Saturn is the sixth closest planet to the Sun.
- Average distance to the Sun: 888 million miles (1,430 million km)
- Diameter at equator: 74,898 miles (120,536 km) corresponding to 9.449 diameters at equator on Earth
- Surface area: 83.7 x Earth's surface area
- Volume: 763.59 x Earth's volume
- Mass: 95 x Earth's mass
- Gravity at the equator: 91.4% of Earth's gravity at Earth's equator

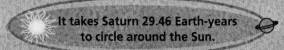

It takes Saturn 29.46 Earth-years to circle around the Sun.

- Structure: Hot, rocky core that is surrounded by a liquid metal layer that is itself surrounded by a liquid hydrogen and helium layer. There then is an atmosphere that surrounds it all.

- Winds have been recorded at speeds up to 1,116 mph (1,795 km/h) in Saturn's atmosphere. By comparison, the strongest wind ever recorded on Earth is 231 mph (371.68 km/h) at Mount Washington, New Hampshire, USA, on April 12, 1934. It is believed that wind speeds can sometimes reach over 300 mph (480 km/h) inside tornadoes. However devastating these are, these winds are still very slow compared to Saturn's winds.

So far, Saturn has 59 confirmed moons. Seven of them are round. Titan, the largest, is the only known moon within the Solar System to have an atmosphere. In volume, Titan is more than three times bigger than our Moon.

that a planet other than the Earth could have even one moon, let alone five! He looked at Saturn with respect as the giant planet with rings shrank into the distance behind them until it was just a bright dot in the starry background.

Chapter Thirteen

The comet was now traveling straight again. In front of them, the Sun was bigger and brighter than before, but still very small compared to its size when seen from the Earth. George spotted another bright dot that he hadn't noticed before, a dot that was quickly growing bigger as they approached it.

"What's over there?" he asked, pointing ahead and to the right. "Is that another planet?"

But there was no reply. When he looked around, Annie had gone. George untied himself from the comet and followed the trail of footprints she had left in the icy powder. He carefully gauged the length of his steps so that he wouldn't find himself flying off the comet again.

After climbing carefully over a small icy hill, he saw her. She was peering into a hole in

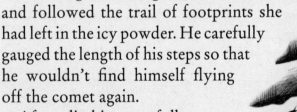

the ground. Around the hole were bits and pieces of rock that seemed to have been spat out by the comet itself. George walked over and looked down into the hole too. It was a few feet deep, with nothing much to be seen at the bottom.

"What is it?" he asked. "Have you found something?"

"Well, you see, I went for a walk—," Annie started to explain.

"Why didn't you tell me?" George interrupted her.

"You were shouting at me about not shouting!" said Annie. "So I thought I'd just go by myself. Because then there'd be no one to get *mad* at me," she added pointedly.

"I'm not *mad* at you," said George.

"Yes, you are! You're always angry with me. It doesn't make any difference if I'm nice to you or not."

"*I'm not angry!*" shouted George.

"*Yes, you are!*" shouted back Annie, balling her gloved hands into fists and shaking them at George. As she did so, something extraordinary happened. A little fountain of gas and dirt blew up from the ground just next to her.

"Now look what you've done!" complained George. But as he spoke, another little fountain erupted through the rock right next to him. It formed a cloud of dust that slowly dispersed.

"Annie, what's happening?" he asked.

"Um, it's nothing," replied Annie. "This is all fine,

don't worry." But she didn't sound very sure. "Why don't we go and sit down where we were before?" she suggested. "It's nicer over there."

But as they walked back, more and more little geysers of dust erupted around them, leaving a haze of smoke in the air. Neither of them felt very safe, but neither of them wanted to admit it. They just walked more and more quickly toward the place where they'd been sitting before. Without saying a word, they anchored themselves to the comet once more.

In the sky, the bright dot George had seen growing had become much bigger. It now looked like a planet with red and blue stripes.

"That's Jupiter," Annie said, breaking the silence. But she was whispering now. She didn't sound like the confident show-off she had been earlier. "It's the biggest of the planets, about twice the volume of Saturn. That makes it more than a thousand times the volume of Earth."

"Does Jupiter have moons too?" George asked.

"Yes, it does," replied Annie. "But I don't know how many. I didn't count them last time I was here, so I'm not sure."

"Have you really been here before?" George looked suspicious.

"Of course I have!" said Annie indignantly. George wasn't sure he believed her.

Once again, the comet and Annie and George started

to fall. As they fell, George gazed at Jupiter. Even by Saturn's standards, Jupiter was enormous.

As they flew by, Annie pointed out a big red mark on Jupiter's surface.

"That thing," she said, "is a huge storm. It's been going on for hundreds and hundreds of years. Maybe even more, I don't know. It's over twice the size of the Earth!"

As they moved away from Jupiter, George counted how many moons he could spot.

"Four big ones," he said.

"'Four big ones' what?"

"Moons. Jupiter has four big moons and lots and lots of little moons. I think it has even more moons than Saturn."

"Oh, okay," said Annie, who was sounding nervous now. "If you say so."

George was worried—it wasn't like Annie to agree with anything he said. He noticed she had shuffled a little closer to him. She slipped her hand in its space glove into his. All around them, new jets of gas and dust were springing up out of the rock, each one spitting out a small cloud. A thin haze was forming over the whole comet. "Are you all right?" he asked Annie. She had stopped showing off and being rude, and he felt sure something was very wrong.

"George, I—," Annie started to reply, when a huge rock smashed into the comet behind them, shaking the ground like an earthquake and sending up even more dust and ice into the haze.

Looking up, George and Annie saw there were hundreds and hundreds of rocks, all coming toward them at high speed. And there was nowhere to hide.

"Asteroids!" cried Annie. "We're in an asteroid storm!"

JUPITER

- Jupiter is the fifth closest planet to the Sun.
- Average distance to the Sun: 483.6 million miles (778.3 million km)
- Diameter at equator: 88,846 miles (142,984 km), corresponding to 11.209 diameters at equator on Earth
- Surface area: 120.5 x Earth's surface area
- Volume: 1,321.3 x Earth's volume
- Mass: 317.8 x Earth's mass
- Gravity at the equator: 236% of Earth's gravity at Earth's equator
- Structure: Small (compared to the overall size of the planet) rocky core surrounded by a liquid metal layer that smoothly turns into a liquid hydrogen layer as height increases. This liquid then smoothly turns into an atmosphere made of hydrogen gas, which surrounds it all. Even though it is bigger, Jupiter's overall composition is similar to Saturn's.

Great Red Spot

Earth

- The Great Red Spot on Jupiter's surface is a giant hurricane-type storm, a storm that has lasted for more than three centuries (it was first observed in 1655), but it may have been there for even longer. The Great Red Spot storm is huge: more than twice the size of the Earth. Winds on Jupiter often reach 620 mph (1,000 km/h).
- It takes Jupiter 11.86 Earth-years to circle around the Sun.
- So far, Jupiter has 63 confirmed moons. Four of them are big enough to be round and were seen by the Italian scientist Galileo in 1610. These are collectively known as the Galilean moons. They are Io, Europa, Ganymede, and Callisto, and they are about the same size as our Moon.

Chapter Fourteen

"What do we do?" yelled George.

"Nothing," shrieked Annie. "There's nothing we *can* do! Try not to get squashed! I'll call Cosmos to get us back."

The comet shot through the asteroids with incredible speed. Another large rock hit the comet just in front of them, raining down smaller rocks on their space suits and helmets. Through the voice transmitter in his helmet, George heard Annie scream. But suddenly the scream went silent—the noise just stopped like a radio being switched off.

George tried to say something to Annie through the voice transmitter, but she didn't seem to hear him. He turned to look at her. He could see she was trying to speak to him from inside the glass space helmet, but he couldn't hear anything she said. He shouted as loudly as he could: *"Annie! Get us home! Get us home!"* But it was no use. He could see now that the tiny antenna on her helmet was snapped in half. That must be why he couldn't talk to her! Did this mean she couldn't talk to Cosmos either?

Annie was nodding like crazy and holding on to George very tightly. She was trying as hard as she could to summon Cosmos to come and get them both, but the computer wasn't answering. As George feared, the device that linked her both to him and to Cosmos had been broken by the rocks raining down on them. They were stuck on the comet, flying through an asteroid storm, and it seemed there was no way out. George tried to call Cosmos himself, but he didn't know how to do it or whether he even had the right equipment. He got no reply. Annie and George hung on to each other and squeezed their eyes shut.

But just as suddenly as the storm had started, it stopped again. One minute rocks were thudding down on the comet all around them, the next the comet had flown out of the other side of the storm. Looking around, George and Annie realized how very lucky they had been to escape. The rocks were forming a huge line

that seemed to extend all the way through space. They were mainly large and scattered thinly along the line, except where the comet had flown through. The rocks here were much smaller but more densely packed.

However, they were still far, far from safe. Jets of gas from the comet were now shooting out everywhere. Soon one could erupt right underneath them. It was now so hazy from all the explosions that they could hardly see the sky. Just the Sun and a faint little blue dot that was slowly getting bigger.

George turned back to Annie and pointed at the blue dot ahead. She nodded and tried to spell out a word with the finger of her space glove in the air. George could only make out the first letter—*E*. As they got closer to it, the comet tilted slightly toward it, and George suddenly realized what Annie was trying to tell him. It was *E* for Earth! The tiny blue dot in front of him was the planet Earth. It was so small compared to the other

ASTEROID BELT

🪨 Asteroids are objects that orbit the Sun but are not big enough to be round and to be called planets or dwarf planets. There are millions of them around the Sun: 5,000 new asteroids are discovered every month. Their size varies from a few inches across to several hundred miles wide.

🪨 There is a ring full of asteroids that circle the Sun. This ring lies between Mars and Jupiter. It is called the Asteroid Belt. Even though there are a lot of asteroids in the Asteroid Belt, it is so huge and spread out that most of the asteroids there are lone space travelers. Some places, however, may be more crowded than others.

planets, and so beautiful. And it was his planet and his home. He desperately wanted to be back there now, this very second. He wrote "Cosmos" in the air with his space glove. But Annie just shook her head and wrote the word "NO" with her finger.

Around them on the comet, conditions were getting worse by the second. Hundreds and hundreds of fountains of gas and dust were erupting all over it. They huddled together, two castaways in space, with no idea how to get out of the awful trouble they had landed themselves in.

At least, George thought, in a strange, dreamlike way, I've seen the Earth from space. And he wished he could have told everyone back home how tiny and fragile the Earth was compared to the other planets. But there was no way they could get back home now. The fog of dust and gas was now so thick that they had even lost sight of the Earth's blue color. How could Cosmos have let them down like this?

George was just wondering if this was the last thought he'd ever have when suddenly a doorway filled with light appeared on the ground next to them. Through it came a man in a space suit, who unhooked them both from the comet and, one at a time, picked them up and threw them through the door. A split second later, Annie and then George landed with a bump on the floor of Eric's library. The man who had grabbed them quickly followed and the doorway slammed shut behind him. Pulling off his space helmet and glaring down at George and Annie, who were sprawled on the library floor in their space suits, Eric shouted, *"What on Earth did you think you were doing?!"*

Chapter Fifteen

"What on Earth did you think you were doing?!"

Eric was so angry that, for a moment, George wished he were still on the roller-coaster comet, heading straight for the heart of the Sun.

"Actually, we weren't on the Earth," murmured Annie, who was struggling out of her suit.

"*I heard that!*" George hadn't thought Eric could get any angrier than he already was, but now he looked so furious, George thought he might explode. He half expected to see great jets of steam burst out of his ears, just like the ones on the comet.

"Go to your room, Annie," ordered Eric. "I'll talk to you later."

"But Da-ddy . . . ," Annie began. But even she fell silent under Eric's glare. She pulled off her heavy space boots, wriggled out of her suit, and shot out of the door like a streak of blond lightning. "Bye, George," she muttered as she ran past him.

"As for you . . . ," said Eric in such a menacing tone that George's blood ran cold. But then he realized Eric wasn't talking to him. He was looming over Cosmos, casting threatening looks at the computer screen.

"Master," said Cosmos mechanically, "I am just a humble machine. I can only obey the commands I am given."

"Ridiculous!" cried Eric wildly. "You are the world's most powerful computer! You let two children travel into outer space by themselves. If I hadn't come home when I did, who knows what might have happened? You could have—you *should* have—stopped them!"

"Oh dear, I think I am about to crash," replied Cosmos, and his screen suddenly went blank.

Eric clutched his head in his hands and staggered around the room for a minute. "I can't believe this," he said, as though to himself. "Terrible, terrible!" He groaned loudly. "What a disaster!"

"I'm very sorry," said George timidly.

Eric whipped around and stared at him. "I trusted you, George," he said. "I would never have showed you Cosmos if I'd thought that the minute my back was turned, you would sneak through the doorway into outer space like that. And taking a younger child with you! You have no idea how dangerous it is out there."

George wanted to shout that this was so unfair! It wasn't his fault—it was Annie who had pushed them both through the doorway into outer space, not him. But he kept quiet. Annie, he figured, was in enough trouble already without him making it worse.

"There are things in outer space you can't even imagine," continued Eric. "Extraordinary, fascinating, enormous, amazing things. But dangerous. So dangerous. I was going to tell you all about them, but now . . ." He shook his head. "I'm going to take you home." And then Eric said a terrible thing. "I need to have a word with your parents."

As George found out afterward, Eric had more than just one word with his parents. In fact, he had quite a few, enough to make them feel very disappointed in their son. They were very hurt that despite all their good intentions about bringing up George to love nature and hate technology, he'd been caught red-handed at Eric's house playing with a computer. A valuable and delicate one no less; one that wasn't for kids to touch. Worse, George had invented some kind of game (Eric had become somewhat vague at this point), which he'd persuaded Annie to join in, and this game had been very dangerous and very silly. As a result, the two children were both grounded and not allowed to play together for a whole month.

"Good!" said George when his dad told him what his punishment would be. At that moment he never wanted to see Annie again. She'd got him into so much trouble already, and yet George had been the one to take all the blame.

"And," added George's dad, who was looking very angry and bristly today with his big, bushy beard and his itchy, hairy homemade shirt, "Eric has promised me he will keep his computer locked up so neither of you will be able to get near it."

"*No-o-o!*" yelled George. "He can't do that!"

"Oh yes he can," said George's dad very severely. "And he will."

"But Cosmos will get lonely all by himself!" said George, too upset to realize what he was saying.

"George," said his dad, looking worried, "you do understand that this is a computer and not a living being we're talking about? Computers can't get lonely—they don't have feelings."

"But this one does!" shouted George.

"Oh dear," sighed his dad. "If this is the effect that technology has on you, you see how right we are to keep you away from it."

George ground his teeth in frustration at the way adults twisted everything to make it sound like they were always right, and then dragged his feet up the stairs to his room. The world suddenly seemed a much more boring place.

George knew he was going to miss Cosmos, but what he didn't expect was that he would miss Annie too. At first he was pleased to be banned from seeing her—it was good to have a punishment that stopped him from doing something he didn't want to do anyway. But after a while he found himself looking for the flash of her golden hair. He told himself he was just bored. He was grounded, so he couldn't go and see any of his other friends, and there wasn't much for him to do at home that was any fun—his mom wanted him to weave a rug for his bedroom, and his dad attempted to get him interested in his homemade electricity generator. George tried to be enthusiastic, but he felt rather flat.

The only bright star in his life was that he'd seen a poster at school advertising a science-presentation competition. The first prize was a computer! George desperately wanted to win. He spent ages trying to write a really good talk about the wonders of the Universe and drawing pictures of the planets he'd seen on the comet

ride. But no matter how hard he tried, he just couldn't seem to get the words right. Everything sounded wrong. Eventually he gave up in frustration and resigned himself to a boring life forever and ever.

But then at last something interesting happened. One gray autumn afternoon at the end of October—the slowest and dullest month he had ever lived through—George was loafing around in the backyard when he noticed something unusual. Through a small round hole in the fence he saw something very blue. He went over to it and pressed his eye socket to the fence. From the other side he heard a squeak.

"George!" said a familiar voice. He was eye to eye with Annie.

"We're not supposed to be talking to each other," he whispered through the fence.

"I know!" she said. "But I'm so bored."

"You're bored! But you've got Cosmos!"

"No, I haven't," said Annie. "My dad has locked him up so I can't play with him anymore." She sniffed. "I'm not even allowed to go trick-or-treating for Halloween this evening."

"Me neither," said George.

"I've got such a pretty witch's costume too," said Annie sadly.

"My mom's making pumpkin pie right now," George told her glumly. "I bet it'll be horrible. And when she's finished, I'll have to go and eat a slice of it in the kitchen."

"Pumpkin pie!" said Annie longingly. "That sounds really good. Can I have your slice if you don't want it?"

"Yeah, but you're not allowed in my kitchen, are you? After what happened . . . last time we played together."

"I'm really sorry," said Annie. "About the comet ride and the asteroids and the jets of gas and my dad getting angry with you. And everything. I didn't mean it."

George didn't reply. He'd thought of so many angry things to say to Annie, but now that he was nearly face-to-face with her, he didn't feel like saying any of them.

"Oh dear." Annie sniffed.

From the other side of the fence, George thought he heard the noise of crying. "Annie?" he called quietly. "Annie?"

Brrreeeewwwhhh! George heard a sound like someone furiously blowing their nose.

He ran down the length of the fence. His dad had started to mend the hole where Freddy had broken through into Next Door, but he'd got distracted halfway through and had forgotten to finish the job. There was still a little gap, maybe large enough for a small person to squeeze through.

"Annie!" George poked his head through the space. He could see her on the other side now, wiping her nose on her sleeve and rubbing her eyes. Wearing normal clothes, she no longer looked like a strange fairy child or a visitor from outer space. She just looked like a lonely little girl. Suddenly George felt really sorry for her. "Come on!" he said. "Climb through! We can hide together in Freddy's sty."

"But I thought you hated me!" said Annie, scampering down to the hole in the fence. "Because of—"

"Oh, that!" said George carelessly, as though he'd never given it a moment's thought. "When I was a little kid, I *would* have minded," he said grandly. "But I don't now."

"Oh," said Annie, whose face was blurred by tears. "So, can we be friends?"

"Only if you climb through the fence," teased George.

"But what about your dad?" asked Annie doubtfully. "Won't he be angry again?"

"He's gone out," said George. "He won't be back for hours." In fact, that morning George had been pretty glad to be grounded. Sometimes on Saturdays his dad took George with him when he went on global-warming protest marches. When he was younger, George had loved the marches—he'd thought that walking through the center of town carrying a sign and shouting slogans was great. The eco-warriors were fun and sometimes they would give George piggyback rides or mugs of steaming homemade soup. But now that George was older, he found going on marches a bit embarrassing. So when 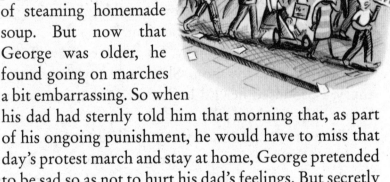 his dad had sternly told him that morning that, as part of his ongoing punishment, he would have to miss that day's protest march and stay at home, George pretended to be sad so as not to hurt his dad's feelings. But secretly he had breathed a sigh of relief.

"Come on, Annie, jump through," he said.

The pigsty wasn't the warmest or the most comfortable place to sit, but it was the one best hidden from angry grown-up eyes. George thought Annie might protest at the smell of pig—which wasn't as strong as people tended to think—but she just wrinkled her nose and then snuggled down in some straw in the corner. Freddy was

asleep, his warm breath coming
out in little piggy snores as
he dozed, his big head
resting on his hooves.

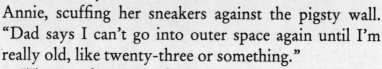

"So, no more
adventures?" George
asked Annie, settling
down next to her.

"Not likely," said
Annie, scuffing her sneakers against the pigsty wall.
"Dad says I can't go into outer space again until I'm
really old, like twenty-three or something."

"Twenty-three? But that's ancient!"

"I know," sighed Annie. "It's forever away. But at
least he didn't tell my mom. She would have been *really*
angry. I promised her I'd look after Dad and stop him
from doing anything silly."

"Where is your mom anyway?" asked George.

"My mom," said Annie, tilting her head in a way he
had come to recognize, "is dancing *Swan Lake* with the
Bolshoi Ballet in Moscow."

In his sleep, Freddy gave a loud snort.

"No, she isn't," said George. "Even Freddy knows
that's not true."

"Oh, all right," agreed Annie. "She's taking care of
Granny, who isn't very well."

"Then why didn't you say so?"

"Because it's much more interesting to say something

else. But it was true about outer space, wasn't it?"

"Yes, it was," said George. "And it was amazing. But . . ." He paused.

"What?" said Annie, who was braiding Freddy's straw.

"Why does your dad go there? I mean, why does he have Cosmos? What's he for?"

"Because he's trying to find a new planet in the Universe."

"What sort of new planet?" asked George.

"A special one. One where people could live. Y'know, in case the Earth gets too hot."

"Wow! Has he found one?"

"Not yet," said Annie. "But he keeps looking and looking, everywhere across all the galaxies in the Universe. He can't stop until he finds one."

"That's amazing. I wish I had a computer that could take me across the whole Universe. Actually, I wish I had a computer at all."

"You don't have a computer?" Annie sounded surprised. "Why not?"

"I'm saving up for one. But it's going to take years and years and years."

"That's not much good, is it?"

"So," said George, "I'm entering a science competition, and the first prize is a computer, a really huge one!"

"What competition?"

"It's a science presentation. You have to give a talk. And the person who gives the best one wins the computer. Lots of schools are taking part."

"Oh, I know!" said Annie, sounding excited. "I'm going to it with my school—it's next week, isn't it? I'm staying at Granny's all next week, but I'll see you at the competition."

"Are you entering?" George asked, suddenly worried that Annie, with her interesting life, scientific know-how, and vivid imagination, would pull off a presentation that made his own sound about as exciting as cold rice pudding.

"No, of course not!" said Annie. "I don't want to win a stupid computer. If it was some ballet shoes, then that would be different . . . What are you going to talk about?"

"Well," said George shyly, "I've been trying to write something about the Solar System. But I don't think it's very good. I don't know very much about it."

"Yes, you do!" said Annie. "You know lots more

than anyone else at school does. You've actually seen parts of the Solar System, like Saturn, Jupiter, asteroids, and even the Earth from outer space!"

"But what if I've got it all wrong?"

"Why don't you get Dad to check it for you?" suggested Annie.

"He's so mad at me," said George sadly. "He won't want to help me."

"I'll ask him this evening," said Annie firmly. "And then you can come by after school on Monday and talk to him."

At that moment there was a gentle tap on the roof. The two children both froze as the door to the pigsty swung open.

"Hello?" said a nice voice.

"It's my mom!" George mouthed silently to Annie.

"Oh no!" she mouthed back.

"Trick or treat?" said George's mom.

"Treat?" said George hopefully. Annie nodded.

"Treat for two?"

"Yes, please," replied George. "For me and, um, Freddy, that is."

"Freddy's a funny name for a girl," said George's mom.

"Oh, please, George's mom!" Annie burst out. She couldn't stay silent any longer. "Don't let George get into more trouble! It isn't his fault!"

"Don't worry," said George's mom in the kind of voice

that they both knew meant she was smiling. "I think it's silly that you can't play together. I've brought you both a snack—some nice broccoli muffins and a slice of pumpkin pie!"

With a squeak of delight, Annie fell on the plateful of lumpy, funny-shaped muffins. "Thank you!" she mumbled through a mouthful of muffin. "These are delicious!"

Chapter Sixteen

Meanwhile, on the other side of town, George's dad was enjoying his environmental protest march. Holding up huge signs and shouting slogans, the campaigners charged across the shopping district, batting the crowds aside. *"The planet is dying!"* they yelled as they marched to the town square. *"Recycle plastic bags! Ban the car!"* they bellowed to surprised passers-by. *"Stop wasting the Earth's resources!"* they yelled.

When they reached the middle of the square, George's dad jumped up onto the base of a statue to give a speech.

"Now is the time to start worrying! Not tomorrow!" he began. No one heard him, so one of his friends handed him a megaphone. *"We don't have that many years left to save the planet!"* he repeated, this time so loudly that

everyone in the area could hear him. "If the Earth's temperature continues to rise," he went on, "by the end of the century, flood and droughts will kill thousands and force over two hundred million people to flee from their homes. Much of the world will become uninhabitable. Food production will collapse, and people will starve. Technology will not be able to save us. *Because it will be too late!*"

A few people in the crowd were clapping and nodding their heads. George's dad felt quite surprised. He'd been coming to these marches for years and years, handing out flyers and giving speeches. He'd got quite used to people ignoring him or telling him he was crazy because he believed that people owned too many cars, caused too much pollution, and relied too heavily on energy-consuming machines. And now, suddenly,

people were listening to the environmental horror story he'd been talking about for so long.

"The polar ice caps are melting, the seas are rising, the climate is getting warmer and warmer," he went on. "The advances in science and technology have given us the power to destroy our planet! Now we need to work out how to save it!"

By now, a little group of Saturday shoppers had stopped to hear what he had to say. A small cheer went up from the people listening.

"*It's time to save our planet!*" yelled George's dad.

"*Save our planet!*" the campaigners shouted back at him, one or two of the shoppers joining in. "*Save our planet! Save our planet!*"

As a few more people cheered, George's dad lifted his arms in the air in a victory salute. He felt very excited.

At last people were taking some notice of the terrible state the planet was in. He suddenly realized that all those years he had spent trying to raise public awareness were not lost after all. It was starting to work. All the eco-friendly groups had not protested in vain. When the cheers trailed off, George's dad was about to speak again when suddenly, out of nowhere, a huge custard pie sailed across the heads of the crowd and hit him right in the face.

There was a moment of shocked silence, and then everyone burst out laughing at the sight of poor George's dad standing there, with runny cream dripping down his beard. Wriggling through the onlookers, a group of boys dressed in Halloween costumes started running away from the square.

"Catch them!" shouted someone in the crowd, pointing to the band of masked figures sprinting away as fast as they could, laughing their heads off as they went.

George's dad didn't really mind—after all, people had been throwing things at him for years while he made his speeches; he'd been arrested, jostled, insulted, and thrown out of so many places in his efforts to make people understand the danger the planet faced, that one more custard pie didn't upset him very much. He just wiped the sticky goo out of his eyes and got ready to continue talking.

A few of the other green campaigners ran after the group of demons, devils, and zombies, but they were soon left behind, staggering and gasping for breath.

When the boys realized that the grown-ups had given up the chase, they came to a halt.

"Ha-ha-ha-ha," snickered one of them, ripping off his zombie mask to reveal the features of Ringo. His real face wasn't much more attractive than the rubber mask.

"That was great!" gasped Whippet, stripping off his black-and-white *Scream* mask. "The way you threw that pie, Ringo!"

"Yeah!" agreed an enormous devil, swishing his tail and waving his pitchfork. "You got him right on the nose!" Judging by his great size, it could be none other than Tank, the boy who just couldn't stop growing.

"I love Halloween," said Ringo happily. "No one will ever know it was us!"

"What should we do next?" squeaked Zit, who was dressed as Dracula.

"Well, we've run outta pies," said Ringo. "So we're going to play some *tricks* now, some good ones. I've got some ideas . . ."

By late that afternoon, the boys had given quite a few people living in their small town a bad fright. They'd shot an old lady with colored water from a toy pistol; they'd thrown purple flour over a group of small kids; and they'd set off firecrackers under a parked car, making its owner think they'd blown it up. Each time, they had caused as much havoc as possible and then scampered away very quickly before anyone could catch them.

Now they had reached the edge of town, where the houses started to spread out. Instead of narrow streets with rows of snug little cottages, the buildings got bigger and farther apart. These houses had long green lawns in front of them, with big hedges and crunchy gravel driveways. It was getting dark, and some of these enormous houses, with their blank windows, columns, and fancy front doors, were starting to look quite eerie in the dim light. Most of them were dark and silent, so the gang didn't even bother ringing their bell. They were just about to give up for the day, when they came to the very last house in the town, a huge rambling place with turrets, crumbling statues, and old iron gates hanging off their hinges. On the ground floor, lights were blazing from every window.

"Last one!" announced Ringo cheerfully. "So let's make it a good one. Tricks ready?"

His band of boys checked their stash of trick weapons and hurried along behind him up the weed-covered driveway. But as they approached the house, they all noticed a strange eggy smell, which grew stronger as they approached the front door.

"Pooo-eeey!" said the huge devil, holding his nose. "Who did that?"

"Wasn't me!" squawked Zit.

"He who smelt it, dealt it," said Ringo ominously. The smell was getting so overpowering now, the boys were finding it hard to breathe. As they edged toward the front door—where the paint was peeling off the woodwork in ribbons—the air itself became thick and gray. Hand over his mouth and nose, Ringo reached forward and pressed the giant round doorbell. It made a sad, lonely clanging noise, as though it wasn't used very often. To the boys' surprise, the door opened a crack and fingers of yellowish gray smoke curled through the narrow gap.

"Yes?" said an unpleasant voice that was somehow familiar.

"Trick or treat?" croaked Ringo, almost unable to speak.

"*Trick!*" cried the voice, throwing the door wide open. For a fleeting second the boys saw a man wearing an old-fashioned gas mask standing in the doorway. Another second, and great clouds of stinky yellow and gray smoke rolled out through the open door and the man vanished from view.

"*Run!*" Ringo yelled. His gang didn't need telling twice—they had already turned tail and were rushing back through the thick smog. Panting and wheezing, they staggered down the drive, through the gates, and onto the pavement. They ripped off their Halloween masks so they could breathe better after choking on the smelly smoke. But Ringo wasn't with them—he had tripped in the driveway and fallen onto the gravel. He was struggling to his feet when he saw the man from the big house walking toward him.

"Help! Help!" he yelled. The other members of his gang stopped and turned, but no one wanted to go back for him. "Quick!" said Zit, who was the smallest. "Go and save Ringo!"

The other two just shuffled awkwardly and mumbled. The spooky man wasn't wearing a gas mask anymore, and the boys could almost make out his features through the clearing smoke. Ringo was standing up now, and the man seemed to be speaking to him, although the other boys couldn't hear what he said.

After a few minutes Ringo turned and waved to his gang. "Hey!" he shouted. "All of you! Get over here!"

Reluctantly the other three straggled toward him. Strangely, Ringo seemed very pleased with himself. Standing next to him, looking just a tiny bit sinister, was none other than Dr. Reeper.

Chapter Seventeen

"Good afternoon, boys," said the teacher. He looked at them, standing there in their Halloween costumes, clutching their masks. "How kind of you to think of including your poor old teacher in your fun Halloween games."

"But we didn't know . . . ," protested Zit. The other two looked too surprised to speak. "We wouldn't have, not if we'd known this was a *teacher's* house."

"Don't you worry!" said Dr. Reeper with a forced chuckle. "I like to see young people enjoying themselves." He waved a hand around to clear a bit of the lingering smelly smoke. "I'm afraid you interrupted me just as I was in the middle of something. That's why it's a little foggy around here."

"Ugh! Were you cooking?" said Whippet unhappily. "It stinks here."

"No, not cooking—well, not food, anyway," said Dr. Reeper. "I was doing an experiment. I should get back to it. And I shouldn't keep you here—I'm sure you have other people in the neighborhood to delight with your amusing tricks."

"What about . . . ?" said Ringo, trailing off deliberately.

"Oh yes!" said Dr. Reeper. "Why don't you boys come and wait on the doorstep while I go get something. I'll only be a moment."

The boys followed him as far as the open front door, where they hovered while Dr. Reeper went in.

"What's going on?" Whippet hissed to Ringo as they waited.

"Listen up, gang," said Ringo importantly. "Gather round. Greeper wants us to do something for him. And he's gonna pay us."

"Yeah, but what does he want us to do?" asked Tank.

"Relax, chill," replied Ringo. "It's nothing. He just wants us to deliver a letter—to the house with the weirdo in the space suit."

"And he'll pay us for that?" squeaked Zit. "Why?"

"I dunno," admitted Ringo. "And I don't really care. It's money, isn't it? That's what matters." They waited for a little longer. The minutes ticked by, and there was still no sign of Greeper. Ringo peeked through the front door. "Let's go in," he said.

"We can't do that!" exclaimed the others.

"Yeah, we can," said Ringo, his eyes sparkling with mischief. "Just think—at school we can tell everyone we've been inside Greeper's house! Let's see if we can take something of his. Come on!" He tiptoed into the house, stopped, and beckoned furiously for the others to follow. One by one they sidled through the front door.

Inside, they saw a hallway with several doors leading off it. Everything in the hallway was covered with dust, as though no one had touched it for a hundred years.

LUCY & STEPHEN HAWKING

"This way," ordered Ringo, snickering with glee. He set off down the hallway, stopping in front of one of the doors. "I wonder what the old doc keeps in here." He pushed it open. "Well, well, what's all this?" he said, a sly smile spreading across his face as he peered in. "Seems like there's more to the doc than meets the eye." The other boys crowded around him to see what lay in the room beyond, their eyes widening as they took in the strange scene before them.

"Wow!" said Zit. "What's in there?"

But before anyone could answer, Dr. Reeper had reappeared in the hallway behind them.

"I asked you," he said in the scariest voice imaginable, "to wait outside."

"Sorry sir, sorry sir," said the boys quickly, whipping around to face him.

"Did I invite you into my house? I don't think so. Perhaps you could explain why you have behaved so very badly? Or I will be forced to give you extra detention at school for disobedience."

"Sir, sir," said Ringo very fast, "we were waiting outside, but we were so interested to know . . . the experiment you talked about earlier . . . we wanted to come in and see."

"You were?" said Dr. Reeper suspiciously.

"Oh yes, sir!" chorused the boys enthusiastically.

"I wasn't aware that any of you were interested in science," said Dr. Reeper, sounding a little happier.

"Oh, sir, we love science!" Ringo assured him feverently. "Tank here wants to be a scientist. When he grows up." Tank looked rather startled but then tried to compose his face into what he hoped was an intelligent expression.

"Really?" said Dr. Reeper, perking up considerably. "This is wonderful news! You must all come into my laboratory—I've been longing to show someone what I've been working on, and you seem like the perfect boys. Come in, please. I can tell you all about it."

"What've you gotten us into now?" muttered Whippet to Ringo as they followed Dr. Reeper into the room.

"Shut up," Ringo replied out of the corner of his mouth. "It was this or detention. So look sharp, all right? I'll get us out as soon as I can."

Chapter Eighteen

Dr. Reeper's laboratory was clearly divided into two parts. On one side, a strange-looking chemistry experiment was in progress. Lots of glass balls were linked to others via glass tubes. One of the balls was connected to what looked like a miniature volcano. Most of the volcano fumes funneled upward into the glass ball, but from time to time little wisps of them leaked out. Gases poured from one glass ball to the next, eventually ending up in one large ball in the center. There was a cloud inside this last ball, and now and then they saw sparks flying around.

"So, who wants to go first with the questions?" asked Dr. Reeper, excited to have an audience.

Ringo sighed. "Sir, what's that?" he said, pointing to the large chemistry experiment.

"Aha!" said Dr. Reeper, grinning and rubbing his hands. "I'm sure you remember the wonderful rotten-egg stink you smelled when you entered the house. Well, do you know what it is?"

"Rotten eggs?" piped up Tank, feeling happy he knew the answer.

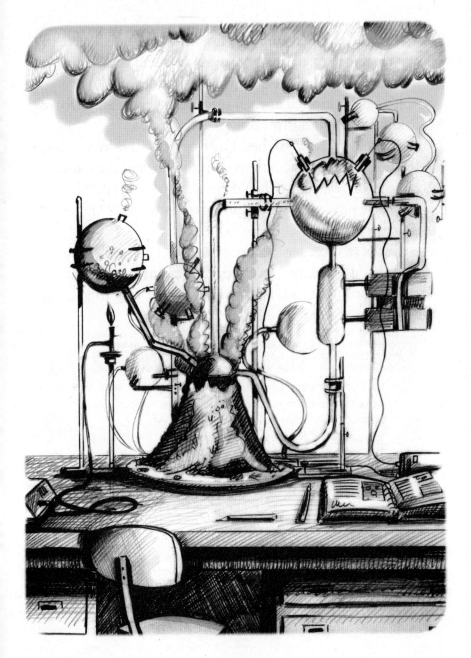

"Stupid child," grumbled Dr. Reeper. "You'll have to try harder than that if you want to become a scientist. Think! What could it be? Such an easy answer."

The boys looked at each other and shrugged. "Don't know," they all murmured.

"Dear, oh dear," sighed Dr. Reeper. "Children today, they really do know nothing. It is the smell of the Earth—billions of years ago, when there was no life on it."

"Well, how were we supposed to know that?" moaned Whippet.

But Dr. Reeper ignored him. "This isn't a real volcano, obviously," he continued, pointing at the small homemade volcano, which had smoke erupting from the crater at its top.

THE EARLY ATMOSPHERE

- The Earth's atmosphere hasn't always been as it is today. Were we to travel back 3.5 billion years (to when the Earth was about 1 billion years old), we would not be able to breathe.

- Today, our atmosphere is made of approximately 78% nitrogen, 21% oxygen, and 0.93% argon. The remaining 0.07% is mostly carbon dioxide (0.04%) and a mixture of neon, helium, methane, krypton, and hydrogen.

- The atmosphere 3.5 billion years ago contained no oxygen. It was mostly made of nitrogen, hydrogen, carbon dioxide, and methane, but the exact composition is not known. What is known, however, is that huge volcanic eruptions occurred around that period, releasing steam, carbon dioxide, ammonia, and hydrogen sulphide in the atmosphere. Hydrogen sulphide smells like rotten eggs and is poisonous when used in large amounts.

"Yeah, like, obviously,"
murmured Ringo. "I
mean, like we hadn't
noticed that."

"It's just a little
chemical reaction
that emits the same
kind of fumes,"
Dr. Reeper enthused,
seemingly unaware of
Ringo's rudeness. "So,
I made it look like a little
volcano with mud from the garden. I very much like it."

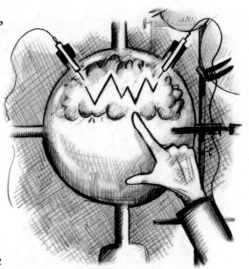

The fumes from the volcano puffed upward into
a glass ball, where they mixed with water vapor. This
came from another glass ball, in which water was being
heated over a gas burner. When they mixed together, the
fumes and vapor formed a little cloud inside the large
ball. Dr. Reeper had built a device inside that cloud that
produced electrical sparks.

As the mini-volcano puffed dark smoke upward, a
little crackle of lightning shot across the cloud inside
the ball. Dr. Reeper tapped the glass gently.

"You see, when lightning strikes clouds of gas, strange
reactions occur, and scientists have discovered that
these reactions can sometimes lead to the formation of
the most basic chemicals that life on Earth needs. These
chemicals are called amino acids."

MILLER & UREY'S EXPERIMENT

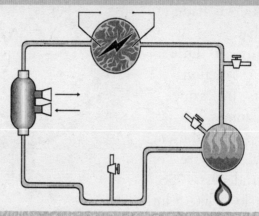

In 1953 two scientists named Stanley Miller and Harold Urey were working on the origin of life on Earth. They believed the ingredients for life could appear out of completely natural phenomena in the Earth's early atmosphere.

At that time (the 1950s) scientists had an idea about the kinds of chemical compounds the early atmosphere probably contained. They also knew that lightning was frequent. So Miller and Urey conducted an experiment in which they stroked these chemical compounds with electric sparks (to mimic lightning). Astonishingly, they discovered that they had created special organic compounds.

Organic compounds are molecules that contain carbon and hydrogen. Some of these molecules, like the ones called amino acids, are necessary for life. Miller and Urey's experiment produced amino acids and gave hope to the scientific community that it may be possible to create life in a laboratory.

Today, however, more than fifty years after Miller and Urey, such a creation has yet to be achieved, and we still do not know how life appeared on Earth. But we have been able to create, under special circumstances that mimic conditions on Earth a long time ago, more and more of the basic chemical building blocks of life.

"But why?" said Whippet. "What do you want them for?"

"Because," said Dr. Reeper, a sinister look crossing his face, "I am trying to create life itself."

"What a load of garbage," said Ringo under his breath.

But Zit sounded more intrigued than his leader did. "Sir," he said thoughtfully, "there's lots of life around us. Why would you need to make some more?"

"There is on *this* planet," replied Dr. Reeper, giving him an approving look. "But what about on another planet? What about another planet where life has not yet emerged? What would happen if we went there and took life with us?"

"Sounds a bit stupid to me," said Ringo. "If we go to a new planet, there won't be anything there, so there'll be nothing to do."

"Oh, unimaginative boy!" cried Dr. Reeper. "We would be masters of the planet! It would be all ours."

"But hang on a minute," said Whippet, somewhat suspiciously. "Where is this planet? And how are we gonna get there?"

"All good questions," said Dr. Reeper. "Come and have a look over here."

He walked over to the other side of the room, which was covered with a huge picture of space and stars. In one corner there was a red circle around a couple of little white dots with lots of arrows pointing at it. Near the red circle was another circle drawn in green — except that the green circle seemed to be empty. Next to the map were white boards covered with diagrams and crazy-looking scribbles. There seemed to be some kind of link between the scribbles and the star poster.

Dr. Reeper cleared his throat as the boys gathered around him. "This, children, is the future!" he said, waving his hands toward the crazy scribbles. "*Our* future! I expect," he continued, "you have never given a moment's thought to what I do when I'm not teaching you at school."

The group nodded, agreeing that no, they hadn't.

"So let me save you the trouble. I" — Dr. Reeper drew himself up to his full height so he towered over the

boys—"am an expert on planets. I have worked all my
life on planets, trying to find new ones."

"Did you find any?" asked Whippet.

"I found many," replied Dr. Reeper proudly.

"But don't we know them all, like Mars or Saturn or
Jupiter?" asked Whippet again.

The other boys nudged each other. "Oooh," whispered
Tank. "Who'd have thought it? Whippet's trying to be
teacher's pet."

"No, I'm not," huffed Whippet. "It's just interesting,
that's all."

"Aha!" said Dr. Reeper. "You are right! We know
all the planets that are around the star closest to the
Earth, the star that we call the Sun. But I am looking
for other ones! I am looking for planets that are around
other stars, planets that are very far away. You see," he
continued, enjoying having his class—or a few of them,
anyway—actually listen to what he said for a change,
"a planet is not an easy thing to find. I have spent years
collecting data from telescopes, and I have looked at
hundreds of planets in space. Unfortunately, most of the
planets we have found so far are too close to their sun,
making them too hot to support life and be habitable."

"That's not gonna help then, is it?" said Whippet,
sounding disappointed.

Dr. Reeper pointed at his star map. "But wait," he said,
"I haven't told you everything yet. Out there in space
are extraordinary, fantastic things, things that until now

EXOPLANETS

- An exoplanet is a planet that revolves around a star other than the Sun.
- So far, more than 240 exoplanets have been detected in space, and new ones are discovered every month. This may not sound like a lot in comparison to the hundreds of billions of stars that are known to exist within the Milky Way alone, but this small number is mostly due to the difficulty of detecting them. A star is easy to detect because it is huge and emits light, whereas a planet is much smaller and only reflects the light of its star.
- Most of the techniques used to detect exoplanets are indirect, meaning that the exoplanet is not seen directly but the effects of its existence are. For instance, a big exoplanet will attract its star via gravity and will make the star move a bit. This star movement can be detected from Earth. One hundred sixty-nine exoplanets

we have only been able to dream about. But the time is coming when all that will change, when man will go out across the cosmos and inhabit the whole Universe. Just imagine, boys, if we were the first to discover a whole new planet."

"That's like that TV show," said Zit cheerfully, "where everyone gets on a spaceship and goes to a new planet, where they get eaten by green aliens."

"No, it's not like that at all!" snapped Dr. Reeper. "You must learn to distinguish between science fiction and science fact. This planet here that I have found"— his finger traced the red circle drawn in the corner of the map around the white dots—"could be the new Planet Earth."

"But it looks like this new planet is pretty far away," said Whippet doubtfully.

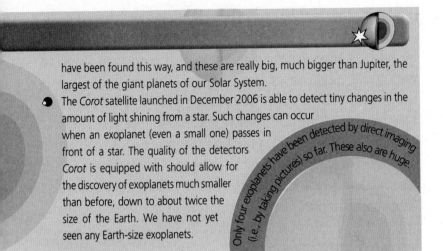

have been found this way, and these are really big, much bigger than Jupiter, the largest of the giant planets of our Solar System.

The *Corot* satellite launched in December 2006 is able to detect tiny changes in the amount of light shining from a star. Such changes can occur when an exoplanet (even a small one) passes in front of a star. The quality of the detectors *Corot* is equipped with should allow for the discovery of exoplanets much smaller than before, down to about twice the size of the Earth. We have not yet seen any Earth-size exoplanets.

Only four exoplanets have been detected by direct imaging (i.e. by taking pictures) so far. These also are huge.

"Yes, it is," agreed the teacher. "It is very, very, very far. So far away that if I had a phone conversation with someone there, I would need to wait several years between the time I ask a question and the time they reply, just because of the time it would take my question to travel there and their reply to travel back again."

"Did you talk with them on the phone?" the four kids said in unison.

"No, no, no!" said Dr. Reeper in an annoyed voice. "I said *if* I had. Don't you understand anything?"

"But *is* there anyone out there?" Zit persisted, hopping from foot to foot in excitement.

"That's hard to tell," said Dr. Reeper. "So I need to get out there and have a look."

"How are you going do that?" asked Ringo, who was feeling interested now in spite of himself.

Dr. Reeper gazed into the distance over their heads. "I have been trying all my life to get into outer space," he said. "Once, I nearly made it. But someone stopped me, and I have never been able to forgive him. It was the greatest disappointment of my life. Ever since then, I've been looking for a way. And now I've got another chance. That's where you boys come in." Dr. Reeper reached for the letter in his pocket. "Here is the letter that we spoke about in the driveway. Take it to George's friend. His name is Eric. Drop it in his mailbox and make sure no one sees you," said the teacher as he handed the letter over to Ringo.

"What's in it?" asked Ringo.

"Some information," replied Dr. Reeper. "Information

is power, boys. Always remember that." Facing his star map and pointing with his burned hands toward the red circle drawn around the bright dots, he said, "And the information contained in this letter is the space location of this amazing new planet Earth number two."

Whippet opened his mouth to speak, but Dr. Reeper interrupted him.

"Drop off the letter *tonight*," he said, cutting short any questions. "And now it's time for you to go," he added, hurrying them back out into the hallway.

"What about the cash?" asked Ringo sharply. "When do we get our money?"

"Come and see me on Monday at school," said Dr. Reeper. "If you've delivered the letter, I will pay you handsomely. Now go."

Chapter Nineteen

At lunchtime on Monday, George was sitting quietly in the school cafeteria, minding his own business. He got out his lunchbox and looked inside it, wishing he could have bags of chips or chocolate bars or orange soda like the other kids. Instead, he had a spinach sandwich, a hard-boiled egg, yet more broccoli muffins, and some apple juice pressed by his mother. He took a large bite of his sandwich and sighed. He wished his parents would understand that he wanted to save the planet as much as they did, but he wanted to do it in his own way. It was all very well for his parents to lead their alternative lifestyles because they only hung around with their friends, who were just like them. They didn't

have to go to school every day with people like Ringo and his gang laughing at them because they wore funny clothes and ate different food and didn't know what happened yesterday on the television. He tried to explain this to his dad, but all he heard back was, "We all have to do our part, George, if we're going to save the Earth."

George knew this was true; he just thought it was unfair and rather pointless that his *part* meant him being a laughingstock at school and not having a computer at home. He had tried to explain to his parents how useful a computer could be.

"But, Dad," he had pointed out, "there's stuff you could do on a computer too, stuff that would help you with your work. I mean, you could get lots of information from the Internet and organize your marches with e-mail. I could set it all up for you and show you how." George had gazed hopefully at his dad. He thought he saw a spark of interest in his dad's eyes, but it flickered and died.

"I don't want to talk about it anymore," his dad had said. "We're not getting a computer and that's final."

That, thought George as he tried to swallow his lump of spinach sandwich, was why he had liked Eric so much. Eric had listened to George's questions and given him honest replies—ones that made sense to George. George wondered if he dared stop by and see Eric later that afternoon. There was so much he wanted to ask him, and also he really wanted Eric to check his talk for the competition.

Just before lunch he had finally summoned up the courage to sign up on the board for the science competition, the one with a computer as the first prize. Under "Topic" he had written, *My Amazing Rock from Outer Space*. It looked great as a title, although George still wasn't sure his talk was any good. He'd taken his lucky rock from outer space out of his pocket while he stood in front of the bulletin board, but to his horror had found it was crumbling into dust! It was his lucky charm—the little piece of the Solar System he had picked up near Saturn. The principal had been delighted to see George writing his name on the board.

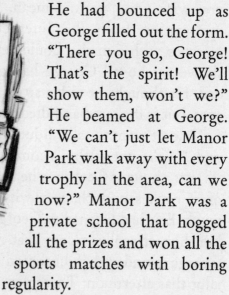

He had bounced up as George filled out the form. "There you go, George! That's the spirit! We'll show them, won't we?" He beamed at George. "We can't just let Manor Park walk away with every trophy in the area, can we now?" Manor Park was a private school that hogged all the prizes and won all the sports matches with boring regularity.

"Yes, sir," said George, trying to stuff his outer-space rock back into his pocket. But the sharp-eyed principal spotted it.

"Oh dear, a handful of dirt," he said, grabbing a nearby trash can. "Toss it in here, George. We can't have you going off to lunch with a pocket full of dust." When George just stood there, rooted to the spot, the principal rattled the can impatiently under his nose. "I was just the same as a boy," he said, a claim George doubted. As far as he was concerned, the principal had never been a boy; he'd been born wearing a suit and making enthusiastic comments about the Under-12 Football League. "Pockets full of nonsense. Drop it in and off you go."

Reluctantly George dropped the gray, crumbly remains of his most treasured possession into the can. He promised himself he would come back later and try and save it.

As George munched his way through his sandwich, he thought about Eric and outer space and the competition the next

day. While he was thinking, a hand crept over his shoulder and snatched a mufin out of his lunchbox.

"Yum! This looks good!" said Ringo's voice behind him. "Georgie's famous muffins!" Ringo took a large bite, then made a spluttering sound as he spat it out.

George didn't need to look around to know that the whole dining room would be staring in his direction and snickering.

"Ugh, that's gross," said Ringo, making fake gagging sounds behind him. "Let's see if the rest is just as horrible." His hand made another dive for George's lunch, but George had had enough. As Ringo's big paw rooted inside the handmade wooden box in which he kept his sandwiches, George slammed the lid down on his fingers.

"*Ow!*" squealed Ringo. "Ow! Ow! Ow!" George opened the box again, allowing Ringo to pull out his hand.

"What's all this noise?" said the teacher on lunchroom duty, walking over. "Can't you boys manage to do anything without causing trouble?"

"Sir, Doctor Reeper, sir!" screeched Ringo, who was

cradling his damaged hand. "I was just asking George what he had for lunch when he attacked me, sir! You better give him double detention, sir, for the rest of term! He's broken my hand, sir!" Ringo smirked at Dr. Reeper, who gave him a cool glance.

"Very well, Richard," he said. "Go and see the school nurse and come to my room when she's looked at your hand. I'll deal with George." He ordered him away with a point of his finger, and Ringo slouched away, grinning to himself.

The rest of the dining room had fallen silent while they waited for Dr. Reeper to announce George's punishment. But Dr. Reeper surprised them. Instead of giving George an earful, he just sat down next to him on the long bench. "Go on!" He waved a red hand at the rest of the room. "Get on with your lunches. The

bell will ring soon enough, you know." After a couple of seconds, the usual hubbub started up again as everyone lost interest in George and went back to his or her conversations.

"So, George . . . ," said Dr. Reeper chummily.

"Yes, Doctor Reeper?" asked George nervously.

"How *are* you?" Dr. Reeper sounded as though he really wanted to know.

"Oh, um, fine," said George, somewhat taken aback.

"How are things at home?"

"They're . . . well . . . okay," said George cautiously, hoping Greeper wasn't going to ask him about Cosmos.

"And how about your neighbor?" said Dr. Reeper, trying and failing to sound casual. "Have you seen him lately? Is he around at the moment? Or perhaps he has gone away . . ."

George tried to figure out what answer Dr. Reeper wanted so he could give him the opposite one.

"Perhaps people on the street are wondering where he's gone," went on Dr. Reeper, sounding spookier and spookier. "Maybe it seems that he has just disappeared! Vanished from view! No idea where he might be! Is that it?" He peered hopefully at George, who was now convinced that there was something very wrong with Dr. Reeper. "Almost as though"—Dr. Reeper sketched a shape in the air with his hands—"he just flew off into outer space and never came back. Hmm? What about that, George? Is that what's happened, would you say?" The teacher was gazing at George, obviously wanting to hear that Eric had somehow melted away into thin air.

"Actually," said George, "I saw him this morning." He hadn't, but it seemed very important to tell Dr. Reeper he had.

"Drat," muttered Dr. Reeper angrily, suddenly getting to his feet. "Miserable boys." He walked off without even bothering to say good-bye.

George closed up his lunchbox and decided to head back to the bulletin board so that he could look for his rock in the trash can. As he hurried down the corridor, he passed Dr. Reeper's office. He heard raised voices and stopped to listen through the door for a second.

"I told you to deliver the note!" rasped the familiar voice of Dr. G. Reeper.

"We did?" whined a boy's voice, which sounded all too like Ringo's.

"You couldn't have," insisted Dr. Reeper. "You just couldn't have."

George would have stayed to listen longer, but then the bell rang and he desperately wanted to find his special outer-space rock before class began. However, when he got back to the can, it had been emptied. There was only a clean plastic liner inside it. Saturn's mini-moon had gone.

Chapter Twenty

It was pouring when George walked home that afternoon. Cold splats of water hurtled down from the dark gray sky as he trudged along. Cars dived through the big puddles at the edge of the road, sending tidal waves of dirty water swooshing over the pavement. By the time George reached his own street, he was shivering with cold. He got as far as Eric's door and hovered anxiously on the doorstep. He was longing to ring the bell and ask the scientist to help him with his talk for the next day. And he also wanted to find out why

Dr. Reeper might think he had disappeared. But he was worried Eric would still be angry with him and send him away. To ring or not to ring? What to do? The skies were getting darker and darker, and suddenly he heard a huge clap of thunder. The rain got even heavier, and George made up his mind. It was important to ask Eric about his talk and tell him about Dr. Reeper. He decided to be brave and ring the bell.

Bing-bong! He waited for a few seconds and nothing happened. Just as he was wondering whether to ring again, the door flew open and Eric's head popped out.

"George!" he said in delight. "It's you! Come in!" He reached out a long arm and whisked George inside, shutting the front door with a brisk slam. To his great surprise, George found himself standing in Eric's hallway, his wet coat dripping onto the bare floorboards.

"I'm so s-sorry," he stammered.

"What for?" said Eric, looking a little startled. "What have you done?"

"About Annie . . . and the comet . . . and Cosmos," George reminded him.

"Oh, that!" said Eric. "I'd forgotten all about it! But now that you mention it, don't worry. Annie told me that it was her idea, not yours, and that she made you go into outer space. I take it that's true?" He looked at George over his heavy glasses, his bright eyes twinkling.

"Um, yes, actually, it is," said George with relief.

"So really," continued Eric, "I should be saying sorry to *you*, for jumping to the wrong conclusion. Instead of considering all the evidence, I just applied some common sense—otherwise known as prejudice—and came up with a totally wrong answer."

George didn't really understand all of this, so he just nodded. From the library he could hear the sound of voices.

"Are you having a party?" he asked.

"Well, yes, a kind of party," said Eric. "It's a party of scientists, so we like to call it a conference. Why don't you come in and listen? You might be interested. We're talking about Mars. Annie's had to miss it, I'm afraid, as she's still at her granny's. You can tell her about it if you stay."

"Oh yes, please!" said George, forgetting in his excitement to ask about his talk or tell Eric about Dr. Reeper. As he took off his wet coat and followed Eric into the library, he could hear a woman's voice.

"...this is the reason why my colleagues and I strongly advocate a thorough search of our closest neighbor. Who knows, in the end, what we may find by digging underneath the red surface..."

Eric and George tiptoed into the library. It looked quite different from the last time George had seen it. All the books were neatly arranged on shelves, pictures of the Universe hung on the wall in frames, and in the corner lay a pile of carefully folded space suits. In the middle of the room, on rows of chairs, sat a group of scientists who were all different shapes and sizes and looked like they had come from all over the world. Eric showed George to a seat, a finger pressed to his lips to show that George should keep very quiet.

Standing at the front of the room was the speaker, a tall, beautiful woman with a braid of thick red hair so long it reached right down past her waist. Her green eyes glittered as she smiled at the scientists gathered for

the conference. Just above her head, Cosmos's window portal was showing a red planet. The red-haired speaker continued her talk.

"Isn't it highly probable that evidence of life, had life existed on Mars in long-ago times, is not there for us to find on the surface? We should never forget that every now and then, sandstorms radically alter the planet's surface, burying deeper and deeper beneath layers of inorganic dust the entire past of our red neighbor."

As she spoke, they all saw through Cosmos's window an enormous sandstorm that took over the whole surface of the red planet.

Eric bent his head toward George and whispered, "What she means is that even if there was once life on

Mars, we wouldn't see it on the surface today. In fact, I can tell you, this scientist strongly believes there was life on Mars at some stage. She sometimes even declares that there still *is* life there. That would be one of the most amazing discoveries of all time. But we can't say much more than that at this stage. We need to get onto this beautiful red planet ourselves to find out."

George was about to ask why Mars was red, but realized that the speaker was finishing her talk.

"Do you have any questions before we have a short break?" she asked her audience. "After that we will discuss our last and most important issue."

George felt very sad that he had only heard the end of the talk, so he raised his hand to ask something.

Meanwhile all the scientists were murmuring, "Ooh, snacks!" None of them wanted to ask a question.

"So let's have our well-deserved break then," said Eric, who hadn't spotted George's raised hand.

The scientists rushed over to the tea cart in the corner of the room, anxious to nab all the jelly doughnuts before the others could grab them.

But the red-haired speaker had noticed George's thin arm waving in the air. "Well, well," she said, looking at George. "Colleagues, we do have a question after all, and it's from our new fellow down here."

The other scientists turned and looked at George. When they saw how small he was, they all smiled and brought their coffee and pastries back to their seats.

"What would you like to know?" asked the speaker.

"Um . . . please . . . if you don't mind," said George, suddenly feeling very shy. He wondered if his question was a really stupid one and whether everyone would laugh at him. He took a deep breath. "Why is Mars red?" he asked.

"Good question!" said one of the other scientists, blowing on his tea. George breathed a sigh of relief. Professor

Crzkzak, the red-haired speaker, whose name no one ever managed to pronounce, nodded and started to give George an answer.

"If you walk through the hills and mountains here on Earth, you can sometimes see red patches of ground that are not covered with any plants. This is true, for instance, in the Grand Canyon in the United States. But there are many other places where this is also the case. The ground is this red color because there is iron there that has rusted. When iron becomes oxidized, which is another way of saying that it has rusted, it becomes red. It is because of the presence of oxidized iron, I mean rusted iron, that the surface of Mars is red."

"Do you mean that Mars is made of iron?" asked George.

"Well, not quite. Since we sent some robots to Mars, we know that it is just a thin layer of rusted iron powder that gives Mars its red color. It seems that underneath the layer of red dust, the surface of Mars may be quite similar to the surface of the Earth—without the water, that is."

"So, there is no water on Mars?"

"There is, but the water we know of is not liquid. On Mars it's far too hot during the day—any water turns into vapor and is lost. So, the only places where water can remain are those where the temperature always

MARS

 Mars is the fourth closest planet to the Sun.

Average distance to the Sun: 141.6 million miles (227.9 million km)
Diameter at equator: 4,228.4 miles (6,805 km)
Surface area: 0.284 x Earth's surface area
Volume: 0.151 x Earth's volume
Mass: 0.107 x Earth's mass
Gravity at the equator: 37.6% of Earth's gravity at Earth's equator

Mars is a rocky planet with an iron core. In between its core and its red crust, there is a thick rocky layer. Mars also has a very thin atmosphere mostly made of carbon dioxide (95.3%), which we cannot breathe. The average temperature on Mars is very cold: around -76°F (-60°C).

The largest volcanoes in the Solar System are on the surface of Mars.

The largest one of all is called Olympus Mons. From one side to the other, it spreads over a disc-shaped area 403 miles (648 km) wide and is 15 miles (24 km) high. On Earth the largest volcano is on Hawaii. It is called Mauna Loa and reaches 2.54 miles (4.1 km) in height from sea level—though if one measures it from where its base starts at the bottom of the ocean, it rises 10.5 miles (17 km) high.

remains cold, day and night, so that water can freeze and remain frozen. This happens at the poles. At the north pole of Mars we have found large quantities of frozen water: ice. It is the same on Earth, where large ice reservoirs can be found at the poles, in the Arctic and the Antarctic. Does that answer your question?"

Since Mars has an atmosphere, one can talk about Martian weather. It very much resembles what the weather would be like on a very cold desert-covered Earth. Sandstorms are common, and huge cyclonic storms of water-ice clouds measuring more than ten times the size of the United Kingdom have been observed.

○ Mars is believed to have once been at the right temperature for liquid water to flow on its surface and carve the channels we can now see there. Today, the only confirmed water presence there is in the ice caps at the poles, where ice-water is mixed with solid carbon dioxide.

○ In December 2006, however, scientists looking at pictures of newly formed gullies on the Martian surface suggested a striking possibility: liquid water may still be present on Mars, buried deep down under its surface.

Mars has two small moons: Phobos and Deimos.

"Yes, thank you!" said George. He was just busy thinking up another question when Eric stood up at the front of the room, next to the speaker.

"Thank you, Professor Crzkzak," he said, "for your very interesting paper on Mars."

Professor Crzkzak bowed and went to take her seat.

"Dear friends and colleagues," continued Eric. "Before we move on to the last and most important issue we have to discuss, let me thank you all for making the effort to get here. Some of you have come from far across the globe, but I know the talks we have heard today have made the journey worthwhile. I'm sure I don't need to remind you how important it is that the existence of Cosmos stays a closely guarded secret."

The group nodded its agreement.

"Now," continued Eric, "the question we all came to answer is a question of fundamental interest for everyone who is involved in science. We all know far too well how it can be used for evil purposes, and that is why we have all taken the Oath of the Scientist, so that science is used only for the good of humanity. But we are now facing a dilemma. As you heard in the news and saw at the evironmental march on Saturday, more and more people are concerned about the state of the Earth. So, the question we now have to answer is: Should we concentrate on finding ways to improve life on Earth and face its problems, or should we try to find another planet for humanity to inhabit?"

All the scientists in the room were silent and looked very serious. George watched them as they wrote an answer on a little piece of paper. Eric then collected the papers in a hat. In total, including Eric and the red-haired speaker, eight scientists had voted. Eric then started to open up the papers one by one.

"The Earth."

"The Earth."

"Another planet."

"Another planet."

"Another planet."

"The Earth."

"The Earth."

"Another planet."

"Well, well," said Eric. "It seems we have a split vote."

The red-haired Professor Crzkzak put up her hand. "May I make a suggestion?" she asked. Everyone else nodded. She got to her feet. "George," she said, addressing the boy directly, "we may lack a bit of perspective on this matter, because we are all specialists in our fields. So you could maybe tell us what you think about it."

All the scientists were looking at him now. George felt very shy and stayed silent for a few seconds.

"Say what you really think," whispered Professor Crzkzak.

Twisting his fingers in his lap, George thought about his parents and the green campaigners. He then thought about the excitement of traveling in space and trying to find another home out there. And then he heard himself say to the scientists, "Why can't you do both?"

Chapter Twenty-one

"George, you are absolutely right," Eric said as they waved good-bye to all the scientists, who were leaving now that the conference had come to an end. George and Eric went back into the library, which was covered in cake crumbs, half-drunk cups of coffee, old pens, and conference papers folded into airplane shapes. "We need to work on saving this planet *and* looking for a new one. We don't have to do one or the other."

"Do you think you will?" asked George. "You and your friends? Do both, I mean?"

"Oh, I think so, yes," said Eric. "Maybe we could invite your parents to our next conference? Do you know, George, I heard your father's talk at the climate-change protest march the other day. Maybe he has some good ideas we could use?"

"Oh no, don't do that!" said George, panicking. He wasn't at all sure that his father would approve of Eric and his friendly scientists. "I don't think he'd like that."

"He might surprise you," said Eric. "We all need to

work together to save the planet if we're to get anything done." He started to clear up some of the mess the scientists had made. They seemed to have left behind an extraordinary number of things: jackets, hats, sweaters — even a shoe.

"It was very nice of you to drop by to apologize," said Eric, gathering together a great armful of abandoned clothing.

"Well, actually," admitted George, "that's not quite why I came around." Eric dumped the clothes in a corner of the room and turned back to look at him. "I signed up for a science competition," the boy continued

nervously. "It's sort of like your conference, except it's kids giving the talks. And there's a big computer as first prize. I've tried to write something to say, but I'm really worried I've made lots of mistakes and everyone will laugh at me."

"Yes, Annie told me about your competition," said Eric, looking serious. "And I've got something that might help you. Funnily enough, I had an idea after your comet ride. I decided to start writing a book about the Universe for you and Annie—I've made some notes. They might help you with your science presentation." He picked up a plate of cookies. "Have one of these. Brain food."

George helped himself to what was left of the cookies.

"How about this for an idea?" said Eric thoughtfully. "If you could just give me a hand to get my library straightened up a bit—Annie's left me strict instructions that I'm not to make the house messy while she's away— then we can talk about your science presentation and I'll go through the notes I made for you. Does that sound like a fair deal?"

"Oh yes!" said George, delighted by Eric's promise. "What would you like me to do?"

"Oh, perhaps a little sweeping or something like that," said Eric vaguely. He leaned casually on a wobbly pile of chairs as he spoke, accidentally pushing them over with a loud crash.

George burst out laughing.

"You can see why I need help," said Eric apologetically, but his eyes were twinkling with laughter. "I'll pick up these chairs, and maybe you could brush a bit of this mud off the floor? Would you mind?"

The carpet was covered in footprints left by the scientists, none of whom ever remembered to wipe their feet on the doormat.

"Not at all," said George, stuffing the last cookie into his mouth and running off to the kitchen, where he found a dustpan and brush. He came back into the library and started to swish away at some of the worst bits of dirt. As he worked, a piece of paper stuck to his brush. He picked it off the bristles and was about to throw it away when he realized it was a letter, addressed to *Eric*. There was something strangely familiar about the handwriting.

"Look at this!" He passed the note to Eric. "Someone must have dropped it." Eric took the piece of paper and unfolded it while George kept on sweeping. Suddenly he heard a great shout.

"Eureka!" cried Eric. George looked up. Eric was just standing there, piece of paper in hand, a joyous look on his face.

"What's going on?" George asked him.

"I've just been given the most amazing piece of information!" cried Eric. "If this is correct . . ." He peered at the piece of paper again, holding it up very close to his thick glasses. He muttered a long string of numbers to himself.

"What is it?" asked George.

"Hang on." Eric seemed to be calculating something in his head. He ticked off a series of points on his fingers, scrunched up his face, and scratched his head. "Yes!" he said. "Yes!" He stuffed the paper into his pocket, then picked George up off his feet and whirled him around. "George, I've got the answer! I think I know!" Suddenly dropping him again, Eric went over to Cosmos and started typing.

"What do you know?" said George, who was a little dizzy.

"Great shooting stars! This is fantastic!" Eric was frantically tapping on the computer's keyboard. A huge flash of light shot out of Cosmos's screen into the middle of the room, and George saw that the great computer was once more making a doorway.

"Where are you going?" George asked. Eric was struggling into a space suit, but he was in such a hurry that he put both feet into one pant leg and fell over. George

LUCY & STEPHEN HAWKING

hauled him up again and helped him on with the suit.

"So *exciting*!" said Eric as he buckled it up.

"What is?" said George, who was now feeling rather alarmed.

"The letter, George. The letter. This might be it! This might be what we've all been looking for."

"Who was the letter from?" asked George, who had a bad feeling in his stomach, although he didn't know why.

"I'm not sure," admitted Eric. "It doesn't really say."

"Then you shouldn't trust it!" said George.

"Don't be silly, George," said Eric. "I expect it was written by someone at the conference who wanted me to check out the information using Cosmos. I expect they wanted to know it was correct before they announced it to the whole scientific community."

"Then why didn't they just ask you directly? Why write a letter?" persisted George.

"Because, because, because," said Eric, sounding a little annoyed. "They probably had a good reason, which I'll find out when I get back from my trip."

George saw that Cosmos's screen was now covered in long strings of numbers. "What are those?" he asked.

"Those are the coordinates of my new journey," said Eric.

"Are you going now?" asked George sadly. "What about my science presentation?"

Eric stopped in his tracks. "Oh, George, I am

sorry!" he exclaimed. "But I really have to go. It's too important to wait. Your talk will be fine without me! You'll see . . ."

"But—"

"No *buts*, George," said Eric, putting on his glass space helmet and speaking in his funny space voice once more. "Thank you so much for finding that letter! It has given me a vital clue. Now I must go. G-o-o-o-d-b-y-e-e-e-e!"

Eric leaped through the portal doorway and was gone into outer space before George had time to say another word. The portal slammed shut behind him, and George was left alone in the library.

Chapter Twenty-two

After the door to outer space closed, there was a moment of deathly silence in the library. It was broken by the sound of a tune playing very faintly in the background. George looked around to see who might be humming, but then he realized it was Cosmos, singing a little song to himself as he crunched the long strings of numbers that were flashing across his screen.

"*Ba-ba-ba-ba,*" tooted Cosmos.

"Cosmos," said George, who wasn't feeling very happy about Eric's sudden departure. He certainly didn't feel like whistling a merry tune.

"*Tum-ti-tum-tum,*" said Cosmos in reply.

"Cosmos," repeated George, "where has Eric gone?"

"*Tra-la-la-la,*" Cosmos went on cheerfully, rolling reams of endless numbers across his screen.

"Cosmos!" said George once more, this time with more urgency. "Stop singing! *Where has Eric gone?*"

The computer stopped mid-hum. "He has gone to find a new planet," he said, sounding rather surprised. "I'm sorry you don't like my music," he continued. "I

was just singing while I worked. *Pom-pom-pom-pom*," he started again.

"*Cosmos!*" yelled George. "*Where is he?*"

"Well, that's hard to say," replied Cosmos.

"How come you don't know?" said George, surprised. "I thought you knew everything."

"Unfortunately not. I don't know what I have not been shown."

"Do you mean Eric is lost?"

"No, not lost. His travels uncover new places for me. I follow him and I map the Universe."

"All right," said George, relieved to know Eric wasn't lost. "Fine. I suppose it must be something very special that he's gone to see, for him to rush off like that—"

"No, no," interrupted Cosmos. "Just another undiscovered part of the Universe. All in a day's work."

George felt a bit confused. If that was the case, why had Eric just shot off into outer space in such a great hurry? He'd thought that Eric was his friend and that, unlike other adults, he would explain what he was up to and why. But he hadn't. He had just gone.

For a split second George wondered about grabbing a space suit, asking Cosmos to open the portal, and joining Eric. But then he remembered how furious Eric had been after he and Annie had gone into outer space without his permission. He realized sadly that he would just have to go home now. Maybe Eric wasn't really his friend at all but just another grown-up who didn't think it mattered whether George understood stuff or not. He picked up his wet coat and school bag and made for the door; Cosmos was still humming his little melody in the background.

George opened Eric's front door to leave. He was just about to step out into the street when he had a sudden flash of memory. There had been *two* reasons he had come to see Eric today, and he'd only managed to tell him about one of them: the science competition. In all the excitement he'd completely forgotten to warn Eric about Dr. Reeper and his strange questions.

The letter, George now remembered. It's Greeper! George had overheard him asking the bullies to deliver a note! *That must be the letter Eric received! And Reeper asked if Eric had disappeared!* George turned and rushed straight back into the house, leaving the door wide open behind him.

In the library, Cosmos was still at work. On the desk in front of him, George spotted the letter that Eric had read with such joy. He read the whole thing, his hands shaking as he realized who had written it.

LUCY & STEPHEN HAWKING

Dear Eric,

I understand that your longstanding quest to find new planets to inhabit isn't yet over.

I wanted to draw your attention to a very particular planet I happen to have found. It is roughly the size of the Earth and lies at about the same distance from its star as the Earth is from the Sun. As far as I know, there has never been such a strong candidate planet for humans to settle on. I am pretty sure it has an atmosphere like ours. An atmosphere we could breathe.

I'm not in a position to verify this information, but I very much look forward to hearing what you think of it. Please see below for the coordinates of that planet, or rather, a way to reach it.

Scientifically yours,

G.R.

George knew perfectly well who "G.R." was. The handwriting was all too familiar to him—he recognized it from his school reports, which usually said things like, *George will amount to nothing unless he learns to pay attention in class and stop daydreaming.* It was without doubt written by Dr. Reeper.

And Greeper knows Cosmos exists! It must be a

trap! George thought. "Cosmos!" he said out loud, interrupting the computer, who was now humming "Twinkle, Twinkle, Little Star." "You have to take me to Eric right now! Can you find him?"

"I can try," replied Cosmos. A succession of images appeared on his screen. The first one looked like a starfish, with long arms twisted into some sort of spiral. Above it was written, OUR GALAXY, THE MILKY WAY.

"Our galaxy, the Milky Way, is made of approximately two hundred billion stars," Cosmos started. "Our star, the Sun, is only one of them—"

Chapter Twenty-three

"No!" howled George. "Not another lecture! I haven't got time—this is an emergency, Cosmos."

The picture of the Milky Way zoomed inside the spiral very quickly, as if Cosmos was offended by George's lack of interest. George could see that the spiral was indeed made of countless stars. The image whizzed past these until it reached a place where there didn't seem to be anything anymore. The picture stopped moving. The screen looked as if it had been cut in two. The bottom half of the screen was full of stars, the other half completely empty except for a thin line that was moving up toward the top edge of the screen. The empty part of the screen seemed to correspond to an unknown part of the Universe—an unknown part that the thin line seemed to be unraveling as it moved.

Pointing at the upper end of the line was a moving arrow with a little tag attached to it. The writing was so small, George could hardly read it.

"What does it say?" he asked Cosmos.

Cosmos didn't reply, but the tag grew bigger, and George saw the word ERIC written on it.

"*There he is!* Open the portal for me! Near that arrow," commanded George, pressing the ENTER key on Cosmos's keyboard.

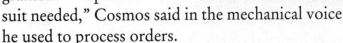

"George is a member of the Order. Authorization granted. Space suit needed," Cosmos said in the mechanical voice he used to process orders.

George rummaged through the pile of space suits but he couldn't see the one he'd worn before. Eric's old space suits were all huge, so he reluctantly ended up wearing Annie's old pink one. It was a bit tight and he felt very silly, but as the only person he was going to see in outer space was Eric, he figured it didn't matter. Once George was snugly buckled into the sequined suit, Cosmos drew the doorway into outer space.

George reached forward and opened the door.

Holding onto the portal frame with his hands, he leaned out to have a look around, his feet still anchored inside Eric's library. This part of outer space seemed very similar to the one he had seen before, but this time he didn't see any planets around him. It didn't look much like the image on Cosmos's screen—it wasn't cut in two at all. There were stars shining everywhere. Eric, however, was nowhere to be seen.

"*Eric!*" George shouted. "*Eric! Can you hear me?*"

There was no reply.

Maybe he was in the wrong place.

George looked back into the library, toward Cosmos's screen; the ERIC arrow was still there. Next to it he saw a new one that had GEORGE written on it. He realized that what he saw out of the doorway wasn't yet on Cosmos's screen. Cosmos had to process the information and only after he had done so, would it appear on the screen.

George leaned through the door into outer space once more, making sure not to fall. "*Eric! Are you there? Can you hear me?*" he yelled.

"Who's calling me?" replied a faint voice through the transmitter fitted inside George's space helmet.

"*Eric! Where are you? Do you see the door?*"

"Oh, hello! George! Yes, I can see you. Stop shouting now, you're hurting my ears. I'm coming straight toward you from your left."

George looked to his left and there it was, a little asteroid, gently traveling through space. Sitting on it

was Eric, holding in each hand a rope attached to spikes he had planted in the rock. He looked very relaxed.

"What are you doing?" he asked.

"Come back!" cried George, trying to sound urgent without shouting. "It's Greeper who sent you the letter! It's my fault! I spoke to him about Cosmos!"

"George," replied Eric firmly, "right now I'm working, so we'll have to talk about this later. You definitely shouldn't have mentioned Cosmos to anyone. Close the portal, George, and go home!"

"You don't understand!" said George. "Greeper is horrible! I know him, he's my teacher! It must be a trap! Come back now! Please! This morning he asked me if you had disappeared!"

"That's enough! And stop being silly! Look around— there's nothing dangerous at all," said Eric impatiently. "Now go home and forget about Cosmos. I'm not sure I should have shown you my computer after all."

George looked over at Eric's rock. In a few seconds it was going to be close enough for him to jump onto it. He took a few steps back into the library, paused for a second, and then ran toward the doorway, leaping through it as far toward the rock as he could.

"Holy planet!" he heard Eric say. "*George! Grab my hand!*"

Chapter Twenty-four

As George flew through space, he just managed to hold on to Eric's hand. Eric hauled him onto the rock, sitting him down beside him. Behind them, the doorway back into Eric's library vanished.

"*George, are you crazy?!* If I hadn't caught your hand, you could have been lost in space forever!" said Eric, sounding furious all over again.

"But—," said George.

"*Silence!* I'm sending you back! *Now!*"

"*No!*" shouted George. "*Listen to me! This is really important.*"

"What is?" said Eric, suddenly aware that there was something very wrong in George's voice. "What is it, George?"

"*You have*

to come back with me!" babbled George. "I'm really, really sorry, and it's all my fault, but I told my teacher from school about Cosmos—I told Doctor Reeper and then he sent you the letter about the planet!" Before Eric could say anything, George rushed on, "And this morning he asked me if you'd disappeared! He did! It's true! It's a trick, Eric! He's out to get you!"

"Greeper . . . Reeper! . . . I see!" said Eric. "So the letter is from Graham! He found me again."

"Graham?" asked George, astonished.

"Yes, Graham Reeper," Eric replied calmly. "We used to call him Grim."

"You *know* him?" George gasped with shock underneath his space helmet.

"Yes, I do. A long, long time ago we used to work together. But we had an argument that led to an awful accident. Reeper got very badly burned, and after that he went off on his own. We stopped him being a member of the order in the end because we were so worried about what he might do. But do you know what he sent me in that letter?"

"Yeah," said George, remembering how Eric left without saying good-bye. "Just another planet."

"*Just* another planet? George, you must be joking! The planet Graham told me about is one where humans could live! I've been looking for such a place for ages, and there it is!" Pointing toward two little dots in front of him—one big and bright, the other smaller and less bright—Eric added, "*It's right there!* The big bright dot there is a star, and the smaller dot is the planet we're heading for. It doesn't actually shine on its own—it just reflects the light of its star, like the Moon reflects the light of the Sun at night."

"But Greeper is horrible!" objected George, who really couldn't understand why Eric and Cosmos always had to be in lecturing mode in times of danger. "He would never have given you the coordinates of that planet just like that! There *must* be a trick."

"Oh, come on, George," said Eric. "You know that I can get Cosmos to open up the portal to take us home again any time I want. We're quite safe. It's true that your teacher and I had our differences in the past, but I expect he's decided to put it behind him and join in the efforts we're making to explore and understand the Universe. And I have installed new antennae on our helmets. We can now communicate with Cosmos even if they get damaged."

"Why didn't you ask Cosmos to just send you there directly? Let's do just that—let's get back to your library."

"Aha!" said Eric. "We can't do that. Cosmos doesn't know what lies ahead of us, and that's my job—to go where computers cannot. After I've been somewhere new, then we can use Cosmos to go there again, like you just did to find me here. But the first trip I always need to do myself."

"Are you sure it's safe?" asked George.

"Positive," said Eric confidently.

George and Eric fell silent for a few moments, and George started to feel a bit better. He managed to stop thinking about Greeper and look around him to see where he was. In all his eagerness to warn Eric, he had quite forgotten he was on a rock in outer space!

To be fair to Eric, everything around them seemed calm. They could see clearly in all directions, and the star with its planet was growing bigger and bigger as their rock approached it.

But then something started to go wrong with the path of the rock. Just as George's comet had changed direction when it flew past the giant planets and the Earth, their rock seemed to be switching course. But this time there didn't seem to be any planets around them. The rock was now heading in a completely different direction, away from the distant planet Eric so much wanted to see.

"What's going on?" George asked Eric.

"I'm not sure!" replied Eric. "Look around and let me know if you see any place in the sky where there is no star! And Cosmos, open the portal, just in case."

Cosmos didn't seem to have heard Eric's request since no portal appeared nearby.

George and Eric looked in the direction the rock was heading. Everywhere, all around them, were stars— except for an area on their right, where there was a small patch of sky containing no stars, which was becoming larger and larger all the time.

"Over there!" George said to Eric, pointing toward the growing dark patch. The stars around it were moving in a very strange way, as if space itself were being distorted by it.

"*Oh, no!*" shouted Eric. "*Cosmos, open the portal now! Now!*"

But no portal appeared.

"*What is it?*" asked George, who was becoming scared.

The dark area now covered more than half the space they were looking at, and all the stars they could see outside it were moving erratically, even though they were far behind it.

"*Cosmos!*" shouted Eric once more.

"Trying . . . ," Cosmos replied in a very faint voice, but nothing happened.

George's mind was starting to spin! In front of them, the dark area was becoming enormous. All the space around George and Eric was warped, and some dark patches started to appear to their left and right. George could no longer tell up from down or right from left. All he knew for sure was that the dark patch was getting bigger and bigger, from all sides, as if it wanted to eat them up.

"*Cosmos! Hurrrrryyyy!*" Eric yelled.

A very faint doorway started to appear in front of them. Eric grabbed George by the belt of his space suit and threw him toward it. As he flew through, George saw Eric trying to reach it too. He was shouting something, but his voice was distorted and it was hard to make sense of it.

Just before landing on Eric's library floor, just before the portal door shut and the view of outer space disappeared, George saw the dark patch engulf Eric entirely. It was only then that he understood what Eric had been saying.

"*Find my new book!*" Eric had shouted. "*Find my book on black holes!*"

© NASA/SCIENCE PHOTO LIBRARY

Jupiter is the largest planet in the Solar System. The black dot on the right is the shadow of one of Jupiter's moons. The Great Red Spot (on the left) is a storm that has been observed from Earth for more than three hundred years.

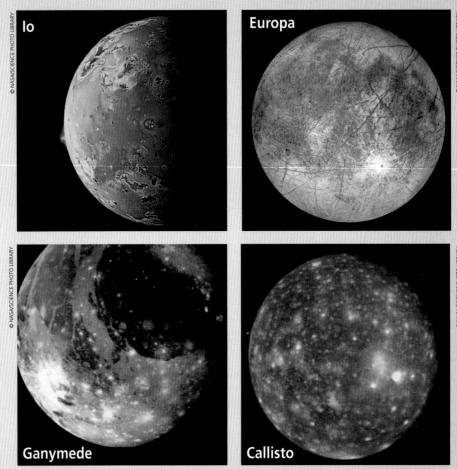

© NASA/SCIENCE PHOTO LIBRARY

The largest moons of Jupiter. Io is known to have intense volcanic activity. Europa is thought to hide an ocean of liquid water more than 60 miles (100 km) deep underneath an icy crust. There are ancient impact craters on Ganymede, and erosion processes have been detected on Callisto.

Mars. The orange area in the center is a large dust storm, and the bluish white areas at the top and left are water ice clouds.

This panorama of Mars is from the top of Husband Hill, a peak in the Columbia Hills, which are named in memory of the astronauts who died in the space shuttle *Columbia*. It was taken in August 2005 by the exploration rover *Spirit*.

Computer artwork of the Solar System. Shown here are a section of the Sun (on left); the eight planets (l–r): Mercury, Venus, Earth, Mars, Jupiter, Saturn, Uranus, and Neptune; and the three dwarf planets, in red boxes (l–r): Ceres, Pluto, and Eris. The distance between the objects is not to scale or nothing would be seen except the Sun; however, the relative sizes are correct.

© ROBERT GENDLER/SCIENCE PHOTO LIBRARY

True-color image of the Andromeda galaxy. It is the closest major galaxy to our own and the largest in terms of the number of stars it contains. Like the Milky Way, it is a spiral galaxy. Light takes about 150,000 years to travel across Andromeda, and 2.5 million years to reach the Earth.

Chapter Twenty-five

George fell back through the door and landed on the floor with a heavy *thump*. This time the journey back from outer space to Eric's library had seemed to suck all the breath out of him, and he had to lie on the floor for a few seconds, panting, before he could get up. When he staggered to his feet, he hoped he would see Eric hurtling through the doorway behind him. But instead, all he saw was the outline of the door, which had become faint and wavy. It seemed to be fading into nothing. He yelled out, *"Eric!"* but got no reply. A millisecond later, the door vanished entirely.

"Cosmos!" shouted George, undoing his glass space helmet. "Quick! Cosmos, we have to get—"

But as he turned around to face the mighty computer, he had his second great shock. Where Cosmos should have been, there was just a spaghetti tangle of colored wires and an empty space. Looking wildly around the room, George saw that the library door was ajar. He ran through it and into the hallway, to find the front door wide open and the cold night air blowing in. With

no time to take off his space suit, he dashed into the street, where he could make out the shapes of four boys running along the road. One of them was carrying a bulky backpack with a few wires sticking out of the top of it. George hurried after them as fast as he could in his heavy suit. As he stumbled along, familiar voices drifted back to him on the wind.

"Be careful with that!" George heard Ringo shout.

"Beep! Beep!" came a noise from the backpack. "Unlawful action! Unauthorized command!"

"When's it going to shut up?" shouted Tank, who was carrying the backpack. "How come it can speak when it isn't even plugged in?"

"Help! Help!" came the mechanical voice from the backpack. "I am being kidnapped! I am the world's most amazing computer! You cannot do this to me! Alarm! Alarm!"

"It'll run out of batteries soon," said Whippet.

"Unhand me, you villains!" said the voice inside the backpack. "This bouncing around is bad for my circuits."

"I'm not carrying it any farther!" said Tank, coming to a sudden halt. George immediately stopped in his tracks.

"Someone else can take over," he heard Tank say.

"All right," said Ringo in a menacing voice. "Give it to me. Listen up, little computer. *You* will *shut up* for the rest of the journey or I will take you to pieces bit by bit until you are just a big pile of microchips."

"Eek!" said the computer.

"Do you understand?" said Ringo in fierce tones.

"Of course I understand," said the computer snootily. "I am Cosmos, the world's most amazing computer. I am programmed to understand concepts so complex that your brain would explode if you were even to—"

"*I said*," snarled Ringo, opening the top of the backpack and speaking down into it, "*shut up!* Which part of those two words don't you get, you moron?"

"I am a peaceful computer," replied Cosmos in a small voice. "I am not used to threats or violence."

"Then be quiet," replied Ringo, "and we won't threaten you."

"Where are you taking me?" whispered Cosmos.

"To your new home," said Ringo, shouldering the backpack. "C'mon, gang, let's get there." The boys set off at a run once more.

George staggered after them as fast as he could, but he was unable to keep up. After a few more minutes, he lost them in the foggy, dark night. There was no point in running any farther—he couldn't tell which way they had gone. But even so, he felt sure he knew who had asked Ringo and his friends to break in and steal Cosmos. And knowing that was the first step to finding the super computer again.

As Ringo and the boys ran off into the night, George turned and walked back to Eric's house, where the front door was still wide open. He went in and headed straight for Eric's library. Eric had told him to look for the book—but which book? The library was full of books—they stretched from floor to ceiling on the shelves. George picked out a large, heavy volume and looked at the cover. *Euclidean Quantum Gravity*, it said on the front. He flicked through the pages. He tried to read a little:

> *. . . because the retarded time coordinate goes to infinity on the event horizon, the surfaces of constant phase of the solution will pile up near the event horizon.*

It was hopeless. He had no idea what any of it meant. He tried another book, this one called *Unified String Theories*. He read a line from it: *The equation for a conformal . . .*

His brain hurt as he tried to make out what it meant. In the end he decided it meant he hadn't yet found the right book. He carried on looking around the library. *Find the book*, Eric had said. *Find my new book.* George stood in the middle of the library and thought very hard. With no Cosmos, no Eric, and no Annie, it seemed terribly empty in that house. The only link George had to them now was a pink space suit, some tangled wires and these huge piles of science books.

Suddenly, he missed them all so terribly that he felt a sort of pain in his heart: he realized that if he didn't do something, he might never see any of them again. Cosmos had been stolen, Eric was fighting with a black

hole, and Annie would certainly never want to speak to him again if she thought George had anything to do with her dad getting lost forever in outer space. He had to think of something.

He concentrated very hard. He thought of Eric and tried to imagine him with his new book in his hand—to picture the front cover so that he could remember what the book had been called. Where would he have put it? Suddenly George knew.

He ran into the kitchen and looked next to the teapot. Sure enough, there, covered in tea stains and rings where hot mugs had been rested on top of it, was a brand-new book called *Black Holes*, which, George now realized, was actually written by Eric himself! There was a sticker on it that read, in what must be Annie's handwriting: *Freddy the pig's favorite book!* with a little cartoon drawing of Freddy next to the words. That's it! thought George. This must be the new book Eric was so happy to find when Freddy stormed through the house! This *must* be the one.

There was just one more thing he needed from Eric's house—it was another book, a large one with lots and lots of pages. He grabbed it from beside the telephone, stripped off Annie's pink space suit, and, shoving the two books into his school bag, rushed back to his own house, closing Eric's front door carefully behind him as he went.

• • •

That evening George scarfed down his supper very quickly and then shot upstairs to his room, claiming he had lots of homework to do. First of all he got the very big book out of his bag. On the front it said, TELEPHONE DIRECTORY. As his parents didn't have a phone, George had thought it was unlikely they would have the phone book, which was why he had borrowed Eric's. He searched through the alphabetical lists under *R*. Using his finger to go down the long column of names, he came to REEPER, DR. G., 42 FOREST WAY. George knew Forest Way—it was the road that led out of town, to the woods where his parents took him in autumn to gather mushrooms and blackberries. He figured he couldn't go there tonight—it was too late and his parents would never let him out at this time. And anyway, he still had work to do with the *Black Holes* book. First thing in the morning, though, he'd go to Dr. Reeper's house on his way to school. By then he hoped he would have a plan.

He put down the phone book and got Eric's *Black Holes* book out of his bag, desperately hoping it would hold the information he needed to rescue Eric. Every time he thought about Eric—which was about once every three minutes—he felt awful. He imagined him alone and frightened in outer space, not knowing how to get back, with a black hole trying to drag him into its dark belly.

George opened the book and read the first sentence of

page one. *We are all in the gutter, but some of us are looking at the stars*, he read. It was a quote from the famous Irish writer Oscar Wilde. George felt it was written specially for him: he was indeed in the gutter, and he knew for sure that some people were looking at the stars. So he kept on reading, but that first sentence was the only one he understood. Next he read: *In 1916 Karl Schwarzschild found the first ever analytic black hole solution to Einstein's equation . . .*

Aarrgghh! he groaned to himself. The book was in a foreign language again! Why had Eric told him to look for this book? He didn't understand it at all. And Eric had written it! Yet every time Eric had told him about science, he had made it sound so simple, so easy to understand.

George felt his eyes tearing up. He'd failed them: Cosmos, Annie, and Eric. He lay down on his bed with the book in his hand as hot tears ran down his cheeks. There was a knock at the door, and his mom came in.

"Georgie," she said, "you look very pale, honey. Are you feeling ill?"

"No, Mom," he said sadly. "I'm just finding my homework really difficult."

"Well, I'm not surprised!" His mom had picked up the *Black Holes* book, which had fallen out of George's hand and onto the floor. She looked through it. "It's a very difficult textbook for professional researchers! Honestly, I'm going to write to the school and tell them this is ridiculous." As she spoke, a few pages fluttered out from the back of the book.

"Oh dear," said George's mom, collecting them up, "I'm dropping your notes."

"They're not—" *Mine*, George was about to say when he stopped himself. At the top of one of the pages, George read, *My Difficult Book Made Simple for Annie and George.*

"Thanks, Mom," he said quickly, grabbing the pages

from her. "I think you've just found the part I need. I'll be fine now."

"Are you sure?" said his mom, looking very surprised.

"Yes, Mom." George nodded furiously. "Mom, you're a star. Thank you."

"A star?" said his mom, smiling. "That's a nice thing to say, George."

"No, really," said George earnestly, thinking of Eric telling him that they were all the children of stars. "You are."

"And don't you work too hard, my little star," George's mom told him, kissing him on the forehead. George was smiling now so she went off downstairs to put another batch of lentil cakes in the oven, feeling a lot happier about him.

As soon as his mom left the room, George jumped off his bed and gathered together all the bits of paper that had fallen out of the back of the *Black Holes* book. They were covered in spidery handwriting and little doodles, and numbered pages 1 to 7. He started to read.

Chapter Twenty-six

My Difficult Book Made Simple for Annie and George *(version 3),* it began.

WHAT YOU NEED TO KNOW
ABOUT BLACK HOLES

1

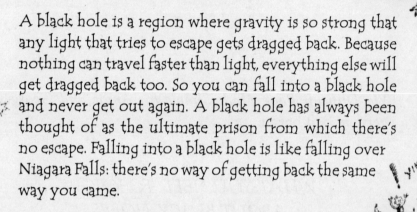

SECTION 1

What Is a Black Hole?

A black hole is a region where gravity is so strong that any light that tries to escape gets dragged back. Because nothing can travel faster than light, everything else will get dragged back too. So you can fall into a black hole and never get out again. A black hole has always been thought of as the ultimate prison from which there's no escape. Falling into a black hole is like falling over Niagara Falls: there's no way of getting back the same way you came.

YIKE!

over

doomed!

The edge of a black hole is called the "horizon." It is like the edge of a waterfall. If you are above the edge, you can get away if you paddle fast enough, but once you pass the edge, you are doomed.

pulled faster + faster

RIP

As more things fall into a black hole, it gets bigger and the horizon moves farther out. It is like feeding a pig. The more you feed it, the larger it gets.

gets bigger and BIGGER

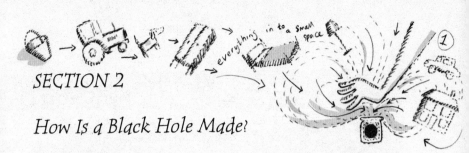

SECTION 2

How Is a Black Hole Made?

To make a black hole you need to squash a very large amount of matter into a very small space. Then the pull of gravity will be so strong that light will be dragged back, unable to escape.

One way black holes are formed is when stars that have burned up their fuel explode like giant hydrogen bombs called supernovas. The explosion will drive off the outer layers of the star in a great expanding shell of gas, and it will push the central regions inward. If the star is more than a few times the size of our Sun, a black hole will form.

Much larger black holes are formed inside clusters and in the center of galaxies. These regions will contain black holes and neutron stars as well as ordinary stars. Collisions between black holes and the other objects will produce a growing black hole that swallows anything that comes too near it. Our own galaxy, the Milky Way, has at its center a black hole several million times the mass of our Sun.

NEUTRON STAR

When stars much more
massive than the Sun run
out of fuel, they usually
expel all their outer layers
in a giant explosion called a
supernova. Such an explosion
is so powerful and bright it can
outshine the light of billions
and billions of
stars put together.

 But sometimes not everything is expelled in such an explosion. Sometimes the core of the star can remain behind as a ball. After a supernova explosion, this remnant is very hot: around 180,000 degrees Fahrenheit (100,000 degrees Celsius), but there is no more nuclear reaction to keep it hot.

 Some remnants are so massive that under the influence of gravity they collapse in on themselves until they are only a few dozen miles across. For this to happen, these remnants need to have a mass that is between around 1.4 and 2.1 times the mass of the Sun.

The pressure is so intense inside these balls that they become liquid inside, surrounded by a solid crust about 1 mile (1.6 km) thick. The liquid is made of particles that normally remain inside the core of the atoms—the neutrons—so these balls are called neutron stars.

There are also other particles inside neutron stars, but they really consist mostly of neutrons. To create such a liquid on Earth is beyond our present technology.

Stars like the Sun do not explode in supernovae but become red giants whose remnants are not massive enough to shrink under their own gravity. These remnants are called white dwarfs. White dwarfs cool down over a period of billions of years, until they are not hot anymore.

Many neutron stars have been observed by modern telescopes. Since the cores of stars are made of the heaviest elements forged inside stars (like iron), although white dwarfs can be quite small (about the size of the Earth) they are extremely heavy (about the mass of the Sun).

Star remnants that are less heavy than 1.4 times the mass of the Sun become white dwarfs. Neutron stars are born from supernovae remnants that have between 1.4 and 2.1 times the mass of the Sun. Remnants more massive than 2.1 times the size of the Sun never stop collapsing on themselves and become black holes.

SECTION 3

How Can You See a Black Hole?

The answer is, you can't, because no light can get out of a black hole. It is like looking for a black cat in a black cellar. But you can detect a black hole by the way its gravity pulls on other things. We see stars that are orbiting something we can't see but that we know can only be a black hole.

We also see discs of gas and dust rotating around a central object that we can't see, but that we know can only be a black hole.

SECTION 4

Falling into a Black Hole

gas

dust

normal astronaut

You can fall into a black hole just as you can fall into the Sun. If you fall in feetfirst, your feet will be nearer to the black hole than your head and will be pulled harder by the gravity of the black hole. So you will be stretched out lengthwise and squashed in sideways.

TO DO!
must buy for Conference

tea
eggs
vanilla
cookies
doughnuts
Jelly
sugar
spaghetti
→ napkins
ginger cookies

must call prof CAS
CRZKZAK

BLACK HOLE

4

This stretching and squeezing is weaker the bigger the black hole is. If you fall into a black hole made by a star only a few times the size of our Sun, you will be torn apart and made into spaghetti before you even reach the black hole.

falling in

spaghetti.

astronaut falling in a black hole →

stretched and squeezed until

fatally

But if you fall into a much bigger black hole, you will pass the horizon—the edge of the black hole and the point of no return—without noticing anything particular. However, someone watching you fall in from a distance will never see you cross the horizon because gravity warps time and space near a black hole. To them you will appear to slow down as you approach the horizon and get dimmer and dimmer. You get dimmer because the light you send out takes longer and longer to get away from the black hole. If you cross the horizon at 11:00 according to your wristwatch, someone looking at you would see the watch slow down and never quite reach 11:00.

spaghettified

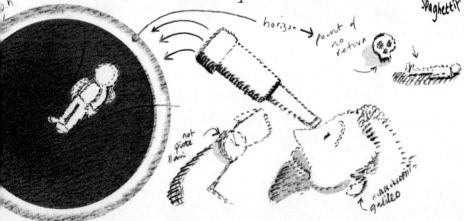

horizon → *point of no return*

not quite 11:00

galileo

SECTION 5

Getting Out of a Black Hole

People used to think nothing could ever get out of a black hole. After all, that's why they were called black holes. Anything that fell into a black hole was thought to be lost and gone forever; black holes would last until the end of time. They were eternal prisons from which there was no hope of escape.

LOST

DOOMED

But then it was discovered that this picture wasn't quite right. Tiny fluctuations in space and time meant that black holes couldn't be the perfect traps they were once thought; instead they would slowly leak particles in the form of Hawking Radiation. The rate of leakage is slower the bigger the black hole is. *the smaller a black hole gets, the quicker it evaporates...*

b.h.

large black holes evaporate slowly.

The Hawking Radiation would cause black holes to gradually evaporate. The rate of evaporation will be very slow at first, but it will speed up as the black hole gets smaller. Eventually, after billions and billions of years, the black hole will

6

disappear. So black holes aren't eternal prisons after all. But what about their prisoners—the things that made the black hole or that fell in later? They will be recycled into energy and particles. But if you examine what comes out of the black hole very carefully, you can reconstruct what was inside. So the memory of what falls into a black hole is not lost forever, just for a very long time.

YOU *CAN* GET OUT OF A BLACK HOLE!

Chapter Twenty-seven

The next day was the day of the big science competition at school. George left home early. He said good-bye to his pig, kissed his mother, put Eric's book on black holes into his school bag, and scooted out of the door, breakfast in hand. His dad offered to take him to school on the back of his bicycle-made-for-two, but George just yelled, "No thanks, Dad," and was gone, leaving his parents feeling like a small tornado had just swept through the house.

George ran up the road, and when he got to the main intersection, he looked back to see if either of his parents was waving at him from the front door. When he saw they weren't, he turned left at the corner instead of right, the direction he would have taken to go to school. He knew he didn't have much time, so he hurried along as fast as he could. As he ran, thoughts streamed through his head.

He thought about Eric, who, by now, would be swallowed up by the great dark menace of the black hole, the strongest force in the Universe. He thought about Cosmos and whether George would find him in the place where he was headed. He thought about Annie, whom he would see later at the competition. Would she believe him when he told her that her dad had been tricked by an evil former colleague into taking a journey across outer space that had plunged him into great danger?

Now George understood why Annie told such extraordinary stories — after the wonders of the Universe, real life did seem pretty dull. He couldn't imagine a life without Annie or Cosmos or Eric now. Or at least he could, but he didn't want to. He had to save Eric, he *had* to!

George didn't know and couldn't imagine why Dr. Reeper wanted to throw Eric into a black hole and steal his amazing computer. But he could guess that whatever Dr. Reeper was up to, it wasn't for the good of mankind, science, Eric, or anyone else. Whatever Dr. Reeper's aim was, George felt sure it was a horrible one.

The other thing that went through George's head as he ran on toward Dr. Reeper's house was the science competition later that day. If he won the competition by giving a great talk about the Solar System, even his dad wouldn't be able to say no to George having the computer in the house. The problem was that the awesome plan George had cooked up to save Eric from being eaten up by a black hole meant he wouldn't actually *be* at the competition. So he had no hope of winning. It wasn't easy for George to give up the idea of entering, but he knew he had no choice if he wanted to get Eric back. There was no other way to do it.

George reached 42 Forest Way and took a few moments to get his breath back. As he panted quietly, he looked at the house in front of him. The driveway led through some dilapidated gates to a huge, old building with weird-looking turrets sticking out of the roof.

George crept up the driveway to the house and stared in through a large window. Through the grimy glass, he saw a room full of furniture covered in yellowing sheets, and cobwebs hanging from the ceiling. Picking his way through a bed of nettles, he tiptoed to the next set of windows. One of the windows was slightly open at the bottom. Looking in, George saw a familiar sight.

In the middle of a crazed mess of pipes, cables, and narrow glass tubes holding brightly colored bubbling liquids, was Dr. Reeper, with his back to him, standing in front of a computer screen that was glowing with green light. Even from behind, George could tell that Dr. Reeper was not at all happy. He watched as his teacher struck the computer keyboard wildly, using all his

fingers at once, as though playing a very difficult piano solo. The window was open just enough for George to hear what he was saying.

"*See!*" Dr. Reeper yelled at the computer screen. "I can keep doing this all day! Eventually I'll find the secret key, you just see if I don't! And when I do, you'll have to let me into the Universe! You'll have to!"

"Negative," replied Cosmos. "You have entered an incorrect command. I cannot process your request."

Dr. Reeper tried some different keys.

"Error," said Cosmos. "Error type two-nine-three."

"Grrrrrrr!" cried Dr. Reeper. "I will crack you, Cosmos. I will!" At that moment his phone rang. He snatched it

up. "Yes?" he barked into the receiver. "Ahhh," he went on in a more polite voice. "Hello—you got my message?" He coughed in a very fake way. "I'm not feeling so good today . . . No, just a bad cold . . . I think I'll have to take the day off . . . Such a shame about the competition . . ." He coughed a few more times. "Sorry! Have to run—I'm feeling really foggy. *Byyyeee!*" He slammed the phone down and turned back to Cosmos. "See, little computer!" he said, rubbing his hands. "Now I have all *day!*"

"I do not operate for anyone who is not a member of the order," replied Cosmos, sounding very brave.

"Ha-ha-ha-ha!" Dr. Reeper laughed crazily. "So the old order still exists, does it? Those silly busybodies who think they can save the planet and humanity! The fools," he went on. "They should save themselves while there is still time. That's what *I* intend to do. Forget humanity! Humans don't deserve to be saved." He spat on the floor. "Look what they've done so far to this beautiful planet. I'm going to start again somewhere else, with a new life form. Those silly little boys think I'll be taking them with me. But I won't! Ha-ha-ha-ha! I'll leave them here to die, like the rest of the human race. I'll be the only one left in the Universe, me and my new life form, which will obey my every word. All I need is to get out there, into outer space. You, Cosmos, are going to help me."

"Negative," replied Cosmos. "I refuse to operate for a nonmember of the order."

"I was a member once," claimed Dr. Reeper.

"Your membership was canceled," replied Cosmos firmly. "After you—"

"Yes, yes, yes," said Dr. Reeper quickly. "Let's not talk about that. Don't bring up bad memories now, Cosmos. Surely it's time to forgive and forget?" He spoke in a horrible, syrupy voice.

"Negative," said Cosmos, causing Dr. Reeper to rise up in a fury in front of the computer and bring his hands crashing down once more on the keyboard.

"Ouch," said Cosmos, a few bright sparks flying out from the keyboard.

George couldn't bear to watch any longer. As much as he wanted to break in and stop Dr. Reeper from hurting poor Cosmos any more, he knew it was vital to get him out of the house and away from the great computer as quickly as possible. To do that, George needed to get to school.

He ran back until he reached the school gates. Big buses sat in the road outside, hordes of children wearing different-colored school uniforms climbing out of them. These were the other kids from nearby schools arriving to take part in the science competition. George weaved through the crowds, saying, "'Scuse me, sorry, 'scuse me, sorry." He was searching for someone.

"George!" He heard his
name and looked around
but couldn't see who
was shouting at him.
Then he spotted
her—a tiny figure in
a dark blue uniform,
jumping up and down
and waving at him.
He scrambled over
to her as quickly as
he could.

"Annie!" he said when he
reached her. "I'm so glad to see
you! Come on, we haven't got a minute to spare."

"What's up?" said Annie, wrinkling her nose. "Is
something wrong with your talk?"

"Is that your boyfriend?" A much older boy in the
same school uniform as Annie interrupted them.

"Oh, go away," Annie snapped at the bigger boy.
"And say stupid things to someone else." George held
his breath in fear, waiting to see what the bigger boy
would do. But he just turned away meekly and got lost
in the crowd.

"Where've you been?" George asked Annie.

"I told you," replied Annie. "At Granny's house.
Mom dropped me back at the school, so I haven't even
been home yet. What's wrong, George? What is it?"

"Annie," said George very seriously, "I've got something awful to tell you." But he didn't get the chance. A teacher blew a whistle very loudly, forcing everyone to be quiet.

"Okay everybody!" the teacher announced. "I want you all to line up in your school groups, ready to go into the great hall, where the science competition will begin. *You*"—he pointed at George in his dark green uniform among a crowd of kids in blue—"are with the wrong school! Kindly go and find your own group before you confuse people anymore!"

"Meet me just outside the hall!" George hissed to Annie. "It's really important, Annie! I need your help!" With that he left her and joined his own school group. He started walking toward the hall, looking now for someone—or rather several someones—else. When he saw them—Ringo and his group of friends hovering in the hallway—George knew what he had to do. He grabbed the nearest teacher and started speaking in a very loud voice.

"Sir!" he yelled. "*Sir!*"

"What is it, George?" said the teacher, backing off a little at the unexpected volume.

"Sir!" shouted George again, making sure everyone around had stopped what they were doing and was listening to him. "I need to change the topic of my talk!"

"I'm not sure that's possible," said the teacher. "And do you mind not shouting?"

"But I have to!" bellowed George. "I've got a new title!"

"What's the title?" said the teacher, who was now worried that the boy had gone a little crazy.

"It's *Cosmos, the World's Most Amazing Computer, and How He Works*."

"I see," said the teacher, thinking George was definitely insane. "I'll ask the judging panel what they think."

"Oh good, thank you, sir!" George yelled even louder than before. "Did you catch the whole title? It's *Cosmos, the World's Most Amazing Computer, and How He Works*."

"Thank you, George," said the teacher quietly. "I'll do my best for you."

As he walked off, sighing deeply to himself, George noticed that Ringo had taken out his cell phone and was making a call. All he could do now was wait.

George stood by the entrance to the hall, watching the long lines of schoolchildren file in past him. He didn't

have to wait long before, out of breath and trembling with excitement, Dr. Reeper rushed up to him.

"George!" he exclaimed, smoothing his hair down with one scaly hand. "Did you manage? To change the topic of your talk, that is?"

"I think so," George told him.

"I'll check for you," said Dr. Reeper. "Don't worry, you go ahead and give the talk on Cosmos and how he works, and I'll make sure it's okay with the judging panel. Good idea for a talk, George. Brilliant!"

Just then the principal came by. "Reeper?" he said curiously. "I heard you were ill today."

"I'm feeling *much* better," stated Dr. Reeper firmly. "And very much looking forward to the competition."

"That's the spirit!" said the principal. "I'm so glad you're here, Reeper! One of the judges has had to drop out, so you're just the man to take his place."

"Oh no no no no no no no no," said Dr. Reeper hurriedly. "I'm sure you can find someone much better."

"Nonsense!" said the principal. "You're just the ticket! Come along, Reeper, you can sit with me."

Grimacing, Reeper had no choice but to follow the principal and take a seat next to him at the front of the hall.

George waited by the door until at last he saw Annie again, coming toward him in a great gaggle of kids in blue uniforms. As she walked past him, he grabbed her sleeve and pulled her out of the great river of children flowing into the hall.

"We've got to go!" he whispered in her ear. *"Now!"*

"Where?" asked Annie. "Where have we got to go?"

"Your dad's fallen into a black hole!" said George. "Follow me—we have to rescue him . . ."

Chapter Twenty-eight

Annie hurried along the hallway after George.

"But, George," she said, "where are we going?"

"Shush," he said over his shoulder. "This way." He was taking Annie toward the side door, which led out onto the road. It was strictly forbidden for pupils to go out of that door by themselves during school hours. If George and Annie were caught leaving school without permission, they would be in deep trouble. Worse—much worse—they would forfeit their only chance to reach Cosmos, which would mean that Eric would be lost inside a black hole forever. It was vital that they leave the school as fast as possible.

They walked along stiffly, trying to look completely natural and innocent, as though they had every reason in the world to be going in the opposite direction from everyone else. It seemed to be working—no one paid any attention to them. They were just approaching the side door when George saw a teacher walking toward them. He crossed his fingers, hoping they wouldn't be spotted, but it didn't work.

"George," said the teacher. "And where might you be going?"

"Oh, sir!" said George. "We, um, we are just, um . . ." He faltered and ran out of steam.

"I left something for the science presentation in my coat pocket, sir," Annie's clear voice cut in. "So my teacher asked this boy to show me the way back to the coatrooms."

"Carry on, then," said the teacher, letting them pass. But he stood watching them until they disappeared into the coatrooms. When they peered back down the hallway, he was still standing there, guarding the school

exit. The last children were straggling into the science presentation, which was due to start any minute now.

"Rats," said George, retreating back into the coatroom. "We won't get out through that door." They looked around. In the wall above the rows of coat pegs was a long, thin, rectangular window.

"Do you think you can squeeze through?" George asked Annie.

"It's the only way out, isn't it?" she said, looking up at the window.

George nodded grimly.

"Then I'll just have to," said Annie with great determination. "I'm not letting a black hole eat my dad, I'm not, I'm not, I'm not!"

George could tell by the way she scrunched up her face that she was trying not to cry. He wondered if he'd done the right thing in telling her—maybe he should have tried to rescue Eric all by himself? But it was too late for these kinds of thoughts. He had Annie with him now, and they needed to get on with it.

"Come on," he said briskly.

"I'll give you a leg up." He hoisted her up so she could undo the catch, push the window open, and slither through the narrow gap; she gave a small squeak as she vanished from view. George pulled himself up onto the ledge and tried to slide through as Annie had done, but he was a lot bigger than her and it wasn't easy. He got halfway through but then couldn't go any farther! He was stuck, one side of him dangling out of the window over the street outside his school, the other still inside the coatroom.

"George!" Annie reached up and grabbed his foot.

"Don't pull!" he said, gently easing himself through the gap, sucking in his breath as much as he could. With another wriggle, he pulled himself free of the tight frame and landed in a crumpled heap on the pavement. He staggered to his feet and grabbed Annie's hand. "Run!" he panted. "We've got to get out of sight."

They sped around the corner and stopped so that George could catch his breath. "Annie—," he started to say, but she waved at him to be quiet. She'd got out her cell phone and was making a call.

"Mom!" she said urgently into the phone. "It's an emergency . . . No, I'm fine, it's not me . . . Yes, I'm at the school where you dropped me this morning, but I've got to . . . No, Mom, I haven't done anything . . . Mom, listen, *please*! Something's happened to Dad, something awful, and we've got to rescue him . . . He's gone into outer space and got lost, and we have to get him back . . . Can you come and pick us up us? I'm with my friend George and we're just near his school. Quickly, Mom, quickly, hurry up, we haven't got long . . . okay, bye."

"What did your mom say?" asked George.

"She said, *When will your father learn to stop doing silly things and behave like an adult?*"

"What does she mean by that?" said George, perplexed.

"I don't know," said Annie. "Grown-ups have funny ideas."

"Is she coming?"

"Yes. She won't be long—she's coming in her Mini."

Sure enough, just a few minutes later a little red car with white stripes pulled up next to them. A sweet-faced lady with long brown hair wound down the window and stuck out her head.

"Well, whatever next!" she said cheerfully. "Your father and his adventures! I don't know. And what are you two doing out of school?"

"George, this is my mom. Mom this is George," said Annie, ignoring her mother's question and wrenching

open the passenger door. She held the front seat forward so that George could climb in. "You can go in the back," she told him. "But be careful, don't break anything." The backseat was covered in recorders, cymbals, triangles, mini-harps, and string drums.

"Sorry, George," said Annie's mom as he clambered in. "I'm a music teacher—that's why I have so many instruments."

"A music teacher?" echoed George in surprise.

"Yes," said Annie's mom. "What did Annie tell you I was? President of the United States?"

"No," said George, catching her eye in the rear-view mirror. "She said you were a dancer in Moscow."

"That's enough talking about me as though I wasn't

LUCY & STEPHEN HAWKING

here," said Annie, putting on her seat belt. "Mom—drive the car! We *need* to rescue Dad, it's really important."

Annie's mom just sat there with the engine off. "Don't panic, Annie," she said mildly. "Your father's been in all sorts of difficult situations before. I'm sure he's going to be fine. After all, Cosmos wouldn't let anything terrible happen to him. I think you two should go back to school and we won't say any more about it."

"Um, that's the thing," said George, who wasn't quite sure what to call Annie's mom. "Eric hasn't got Cosmos—he's been stolen! Eric's in outer space all by himself. And he's near a black hole."

"By himself?" repeated Annie's mom. She suddenly turned quite pale. "No Cosmos? But then he can't get back! And a black hole . . . ?"

"Mom, I keep telling you it's an emergency!" pleaded Annie. "Now do you believe me?"

"Oh my goodness gracious me! Fasten your seat belt, George!" exclaimed Annie's mom, starting the car. "And tell me where I need to go."

George gave her Dr. Reeper's address, and she put her foot down on the accelerator so hard that the little car shot forward with a great lurch.

As the red Mini zoomed through the heavy traffic toward Greeper's house, George explained as best he could what had happened over the past twenty-four hours. While the little car wove through the traffic across town, cutting in and out—much to the annoyance of people in bigger cars—he told Annie and her mom (who asked him to call her Susan) all about going to see Eric yesterday to ask for his help with his science presentation. He told them about the mysterious note that he hadn't trusted and about Eric leaping through the portal into outer space and having to follow him. And how both of them had got sucked toward an invisible force and how when the doorway appeared to save them, it was too faint and only George had managed to get through.

He told them about landing in the library and looking around to find that Eric wasn't there, and how Cosmos had been stolen; how George had run after the thieves but had lost them in the dark; how he had gone back to Eric's to look for the book that Eric had told him to find; how he'd tried to read it but couldn't understand it and then had found the notes in the back that explained that it *was* possible to escape from a black hole; how he needed to find Cosmos because although someone *could* escape from a black hole, he would need Cosmos to make it happen; and how he'd realized where Cosmos must be and had gone there that morning and seen Dr. Reeper—

"Reeper? Do you mean Graham Reeper?" Susan interrupted him as she swerved the little car around a corner.

"Yes," replied George. "Greeper. He's my teacher. Do you know him?"

"I did once, a long time ago," said Susan in a dark voice. "I always told Eric that he shouldn't trust Graham. But he wouldn't listen. Eric always thought the best of people. Until. . ." She trailed off.

"Until what?" piped up Annie. "Until what, Mom?"

"Until something terrible happened," said Susan, her mouth set in a grim line. "Something none of us have ever forgotten."

"None of who?" said Annie, gasping with excitement at the prospect of a thrilling family story she hadn't heard before. But she didn't get to find out, because right then, her mom turned into Greeper's driveway and parked the car in front of his house.

Chapter Twenty-nine

It wasn't easy to break into Greeper's house. Even though the place was old, scruffy, and unloved, Greeper had locked every single window and door. They went around the house, trying everywhere, but nothing would budge. When they reached the window of the room where George had seen Cosmos only that morning, it looked like the great computer was no longer there.

"But I saw him!" protested George. "In that room!"

Annie and Susan looked at each other. Susan bit her lip to try and hide her disappointment. A fat tear snaked down Annie's cheek.

"If we can't find Cosmos . . . ," she whispered.

"Hang on a minute!" exclaimed Susan. "Shush, you two! Listen!" They all strained their ears as hard as they could.

From somewhere inside the room they heard the faint tinny mechanical sound of someone singing: "*Hey diddle diddle the cat and the fiddle . . . the cow jumped over the moon . . .* although technically that would not be possible without a space suit because the cow would freeze," the voice added.

"It's Cosmos!" cried George. "He's singing so that we know where to find him! But how are we going to get to him?"

"Wait there!" said Susan mysteriously. She vanished off around the corner, but a few minutes later appeared inside the room where Cosmos was singing. She opened the ground-floor window very wide so that Annie and George could climb through.

"How did you do that?" asked George in wonder.

"I should have thought of it before," said Susan. "Graham had left his spare key under a flowerpot by the front door. It's what he always used to do. So I let myself in."

Meanwhile Annie had followed the sound of brave Cosmos's singing and was rooting around in a big cupboard. She pulled out a cardboard box full of old blankets, threw them out, and, at the bottom, found Cosmos himself. Unfolding his screen, she covered it in kisses. "Cosmos, Cosmos, Cosmos!" she squealed. "We found you! Are you all right? Can you rescue my dad?"

"Please plug me in," gasped Cosmos, who was a bit the worse for wear. At Eric's house, he had been sleek, silver, and shiny — a glossy, well-looked-after computer. Now he was scratched and battered, with marks and smudges all over him. "I am exhausted. My batteries are nearly dead."

George looked at the spot where he had seen Cosmos earlier that day and, sure enough, there was the computer's cable. He attached Cosmos to the cable and heard him take big, thirsty gulps, as though he were drinking down a huge glass of cold water.

"That's better!" sighed Cosmos. "Now, would someone like to tell me what the microchip is going on around here?"

"Eric's fallen into a black hole!" George told him.

"And we need you to get him out," pleaded Annie. "Dear Cosmos, please say you know how."

Cosmos made a whirring noise. "I am checking my disks for information," he said. "I am searching for files on how to rescue someone from a black hole . . . Please wait . . ." He made more whirring noises and then stopped and went silent.

"Well?" said Annie, sounding worried. "Can you?"

"Um, no," said Cosmos reluctantly. "Those search terms have produced zero information."

"You don't know how? But, Cosmos, that means—" Annie couldn't finish the sentence. She threw her arms around her mom and started to cry.

"No one has provided me with information about escaping from black holes," explained Cosmos apologetically. "I only know how to get into a black hole and not how to get out again. I am not sure it is possible. Eric would have told me if he knew. I am accessing my archive on black holes, gravity, and mass, but I fear none of these files holds the data I need." His drives whirred again, but then he fell silent—unusually, for Cosmos, lost for words . . .

"So Eric's lost," said Annie's mom, wiping her eyes. "He told me a long time ago that nothing can come out of a black hole once it has fallen in."

"No!" said George. "That's not right! I mean, Eric's changed his mind about black holes. That's what he says in the notes he wrote for Annie and me."

"What notes?" asked Cosmos.

"The ones I found in the back of his new book."

"What did the notes say?"

Searching in his bag, George tried to remember Eric's exact words. "Eric wrote that black holes are not eternal," he said. "They somehow spit out everything that falls in . . . takes a long time . . . radiator something."

"Radiation," corrected Cosmos. "Do you have the book? Maybe I can download the information from it and work something out."

"Yeah! Radiation! That's it!" George had found Eric's big book on black holes and handed it over to Annie. "But, Cosmos, we've got to be quick—as soon as Greeper sees I'm not at school to give my talk, he'll come right back here."

"We'd be a lot quicker if Eric had bothered to update my system properly in the first place." Cosmos sniffed.

"Perhaps he meant to but forgot?" said George.

"Typical!" said Cosmos.

"Do you mind?" said Annie angrily. "Could we hurry up?"

"Of course," said Cosmos, sounding serious again. "Once I have the new information, I can start right away. Annie, attach the book to my book port."

As quickly as she could, Annie pulled out a clear plastic tray from Cosmos's side and adjusted it until it stood upright. She propped the book on it and pressed a button on the computer. "Ready?" she said.

The humming noise of the computer grew louder and louder and the pages of the book started to glow. "Rebooting my memory files on black holes!" said Cosmos. "Finished! You were right, George. It *is* all in Eric's new book. I *can* do it. I can rescue Eric from a black hole."

"Then *do it!*" George, Annie, and her mom shouted in unison.

Annie pressed the ENTER key on Cosmos's keyboard and the portal window appeared in the middle of the room. On the other side of it was a very distorted view of somewhere in outer space. In the middle was a black patch.

269

"That's the black hole!" cried George.

"Correct," replied Cosmos. "That's where I left you and Eric."

The view seemed very still, as though nothing was happening.

"Cosmos, why aren't you doing anything?" asked Annie.

"It takes time," replied Cosmos. "I need to pick up all the little things that come out of the black hole. Most of them are so small, you can't even see them. If I miss one, I may not be able to reconstruct Eric. I will have to filter out Eric from every single object that ever fell in the black hole."

"What do you mean *reconstruct*?" asked Annie's mom.

"The black hole expels particles one by one. Each time a particle gets out, the black hole expels more the next time, so it gets quicker and quicker all the time. I'm fast forwarding time by billions of years. Please let me work. I need to pick up everything."

George, Annie, and her mom fell silent and stared through the window, each willing Cosmos to get it right. After a few minutes the black hole still looked exactly the same as it had before. But then, as they watched, it started to shrink, and the space around it became less and less distorted. Once the black hole had begun shrinking, it got smaller and smaller faster and faster. Now they could see an enormous number of particles that seemed to be coming from the black hole itself.

Cosmos was making a whirring noise that was getting louder and louder as the black hole shrank. The lights on his screen—so bright just a minute ago—started to flicker and grow dim. The whirring noise suddenly went crunchy and a high-pitched alarm rang out from Cosmos's keyboard.

"What's wrong with Cosmos?" George whispered to Annie and Susan.

Susan looked worried. "It must be all the effort he's making with the calculations. Even for Cosmos, they must be very difficult."

"Do you think he'll be able to do it?" squeaked Annie.

"We just have to hope," said Susan firmly.

Through the window, they saw that the black hole was now the size of a tennis ball. "Don't look!" cried Susan. "Cover your eyes with your hands!" The black hole became very bright and then suddenly exploded, disappearing in the most powerful explosion the Universe could withstand. Even with their eyes closed, George, Annie, and her mom could see its light.

"Hold on, Cosmos!" shouted Annie.

Cosmos gave a horrible groan and shot a green blaze of light from his screen as some white smoke rose from his circuits. "*Eu-re-k—!*" Cosmos started to shout, but his voice was cut off before he reached the end of the word.

The light suddenly vanished, and when George opened his eyes, he saw that the window was no longer there. Instead, the portal doorway had appeared. It burst open and the room in Dr. Reeper's house was flooded with the fading flash of brilliant light from the explosion. Standing in the middle of the doorway was the figure of a man in a space suit. Behind him, the portal doorway opened on a quiet place in space where the black hole was no more.

Chapter Thirty

Eric took off his helmet and shook himself, like a dog after a swim.

"That's better!" he said. He looked around. "But where am I? And what happened?" A pair of eyeglasses with yellow lenses slid off his nose, and he looked at them in bemusement. "These aren't mine!" He glanced at Cosmos, but Cosmos's screen was blank and black smoke drifted from the keyboard.

Annie rushed forward and hugged him. "Dad!" she squealed. "You fell into a black hole! And George had to rescue you—he was so smart, Dad. He found out from the notes you left him that you could escape from the black hole, but first he had to find Cosmos—Cosmos was stolen by a horrible man who—"

"Slow down, Annie, slow down!" said Eric, who seemed rather dazed. "You mean I've been inside a black hole and come back again? But that's incredible! That means I've got it right—that means all the work I've done on black holes is correct. Information that goes into a black hole is *not* lost forever—I know that now! That's amazing. Now, if I can come out of—"

"Eric!" said Susan sharply.

Eric jumped. "Oh, Susan!" he said, looking rather sheepish and embarrassed. He handed over the yellow glasses. "I don't suppose," he said apologetically, "you have a spare pair of my glasses with you? I seem to have come out of the black hole wearing someone else's."

"These two have been running around all over town to try and save you," said Susan, digging into her handbag and pulling out a pair of Eric's usual glasses. "They've cut school, and George is missing the science competition he wanted to enter, all for your sake. I think the least you could do is say thank you, especially to George. He figured it all out by himself, you know—about Graham and the black hole and everything else. And don't lose this pair!"

"Thank you, Annie," said Eric, patting his daughter gently and putting his glasses onto his nose at their familiar crooked angle. "And thank you, George. You've been very brave and very smart."

"That's all right." George stared at his feet. "It wasn't me, really—it was Cosmos."

"No, it wasn't," said Eric. "Cosmos couldn't have got me back without you—otherwise I'd be here already, wouldn't I?"

"S'pose so," said George gruffly. "Is Cosmos all right?" The great computer was still silent and black screened.

Eric untangled himself from Annie and went over to Cosmos. "Poor old thing," he said, unplugging the computer, folding him up, and tucking him under his

arm. "I expect he needs a bit of a rest. Now, I'd better get home right away and write up my new discoveries. I must let all the other scientists know immediately that I've made the most astonishing—"

Susan coughed loudly and glared at him.

Eric looked at her, puzzled. "What?" he mouthed.

"George!" she mouthed back.

"Oh, of course!" said Eric out loud, striking his hand against his forehead. He turned to George. "I'm so sorry! What I meant to say was that first of all, I think we should go back to your school and see if you're still in time to enter the science competition. Is that right?" he asked Susan, who nodded and smiled.

"But I'm not sure . . . ," protested George.

"We can go through your presentation in the car," said Eric firmly. He started clanking toward the door in his space suit. "Let's get moving." He looked around to find that no one was following him.

"What now?" he asked, raising his eyebrows.

"Dad!" said Annie in a disgusted tone. "You're not going to George's school dressed like that, are you?"

"I don't think anyone will notice," said Eric. "But if you insist . . ." He peeled off his space suit to reveal his ordinary everyday clothes below, then ruffled his hair. "And anyway, where are we? I don't recognize this place."

"This, Eric," said Susan, "is Graham Reeper's house. Graham wrote you that note to send you into outer space, and while you were there, he stole Cosmos, thinking this would mean you could never come back."

"No!" Eric gasped. "Graham did it deliberately? He stole Cosmos?"

"I told you he'd never forgive you."

"Oh dear," said Eric sadly, struggling to pull off his space boot. "That is very unhappy news."

"Um, Eric," piped up George, "what did happen with you and Greeper? I mean, why did he want you to be eaten by a black hole? And why won't he ever forgive you?"

"Oh, George," said Eric, shaking off the space boot, "it's a long story. You know that Graham and I used to work together?" He reached into the inside pocket of his jacket for his wallet. From it he took out a crumpled old photo and handed it to George. In the picture George saw two young men; standing in between them was an older man with a long white beard. Both the young men were wearing black gowns with white fur–lined hoods, and all three were laughing at the camera. The man on the right had thick dark hair and heavy-framed glasses that, even then, were sitting at a slightly strange angle.

"But that's you!" said George, pointing at the photo. He examined the face of the other young man. It was strangely familiar. "And that looks like Greeper! But he looks really nice and friendly, not scary and weird like he is now."

"Graham," said Eric quietly, "was my best friend. We studied physics together at the university, the one here in this town. The man you see in the middle was our tutor—a brilliant cosmologist. He invented the concept of Cosmos, and Graham and I worked together on the early prototypes. We wanted a machine that would help us to explore outer space so that we could extend our knowledge of the Universe.

"At the beginning, Graham and I got along very well together," Eric continued, gazing into the distance. "But after a while he became strange and cold. I started to realize he wanted Cosmos all for himself. He didn't want to go on a quest for knowledge to benefit humanity— he wanted to use Cosmos to make himself rich and powerful by exploiting the wonders of space for his own good. You have to understand," he added, "that in those days, Cosmos was very different. Back then he was a gigantic computer—so big he took up a whole basement. And yet he wasn't even half as powerful as he is now. Anyway, one evening when Graham thought he was alone, I caught him. He was trying to use Cosmos for his own terrible plans. I was there and I tried to stop him and . . . it was . . . dreadful. Everything had to change after that." Eric fell silent.

"What—after the terrible thing happened?" asked Annie.

Susan nodded. "Yes, honey," she said. "Don't ask your father any more questions about it. That's enough for now."

Chapter Thirty-one

Back at George's school, the pupils in the hall were getting restless and bored. Kids were shifting around in their seats, whispering and giggling as a series of nervous, solemn-faced competitors from the different schools battled to gain their attention. However, no one was more agitated or jumpy than Dr. Reeper, who was sitting in the front row with the principal and the other judges.

"Sit still, Reeper! Good heavens, man!" hissed the principal out of the side of his mouth. He was feeling very irritated with Dr. Reeper for behaving so badly in front of the teachers and principals from the other schools. So far he hadn't bothered to listen to any of the presentations and hadn't asked a single question. All he had done was anxiously check the order in his program and crane his neck around to look at the hallway behind him.

"I'll just go and make sure George is up to speed with his speech," Reeper whispered back to the principal.

"*You will not!*" spluttered the principal. "George will do perfectly well without you. Try and show some interest, would you? You're letting the school down."

The boy on stage finished his speech on dinosaur remains. "So that," he concluded brightly to his tired audience, "is how we know that dinosaurs first walked the Earth two hundred and thirty million years ago." The teachers dutifully clapped as he clambered down from the stage and went back to join his school group.

The principal stood up. "And now," he said, reading from his notes, "we have our last contestant, our own George Greenby, from this very school! Can we give a big welcome to George, whose topic today is . . ." The principal paused and read his notes again.

"No, no, that's correct," said Dr. Reeper hurriedly. He stood up. "George's talk will be on the subject of Cosmos, the world's most amazing computer, and how he works. Hurray for George!" he cheered, but no one joined in. Then a long silence followed as everyone waited for George to appear. When he didn't, the noise level in the room rose as the kids, sensing the prospect of a swift end to the school day, rumbled with excitement.

The principal looked at his watch. "I'll give him two minutes," he said to the other judges. "If he hasn't shown up by then, he'll be disqualified, and we'll get on with the prizes." Just like the pupils, the principal was thinking how nice it would be to get home early for once, so he

could put up his feet with no pesky kids getting in the way.

The clock ticked but still there was no sign of George. With just seconds to go, the principal turned to the judges and was about to announce the competition closed, when a flurry of activity at the back of the hall caught his attention. A group of people seemed to have come in—two adults, one with a laptop computer under his arm; a blond girl; and a boy.

The boy ran straight up to the front of the hall and said, "Sir, am I still in time?"

"Yes, George," said the principal, relieved that he had shown up after all. "Get yourself onto the stage. Good luck! We're relying on you!"

George climbed onto the big school stage and stood right in the very middle.

"Hello, everyone," he said in a thin voice. The crowds in the hall ignored him and carried on pushing and pulling and pinching each other. "Hello," George tried again. For a moment he felt sick with nerves and very foolish, standing there by himself. But then he remembered what Eric had said to him in the car on the way there, and he felt more confident. He pulled himself up straight, threw his arms out to either side, and yelled, *"Good afternoon, Alderbash School!"*

The kids in the audience fell silent in surprise.

"I said," bellowed George again, *"Good afternoon, Alderbash School!"*

"*Good afternoon, George!*" the room shouted back at him.

"Can you hear me at the back?" asked George in a loud voice. Leaning on the wall at the back of the hall, Eric gave him a thumbs-up.

"My name," continued George, "is George Greenby. And I am here today to give a talk. The title of my talk is *My Secret Key to the Universe.*"

"Noooooo!" cried Dr. Reeper, jumping out of his seat. "That's wrong!"

"*Hush!*" said the principal angrily.

"I'm leaving!" said Dr. Reeper in a furious temper. He tried to storm out of the hall but got halfway down the center aisle when he saw Eric standing at the back. Eric gave him a little wave, smiled, and patted Cosmos, whom he was carrying under his arm. Reeper turned a shade of light green and slunk back to his seat at the front, where he sat down quietly once more.

"You see," George carried on, "I've been really lucky. I found a secret key that's unlocked the Universe for me. Because of this secret key, I've been able to find out all sorts of things about the Universe around us. So I thought I'd share some of the stuff I learned with you. Because it's all about where we came from—what made us, what made our planet, our Solar System, our Galaxy, our Universe—and it's about our future. Where are we going? And what do we need to do to survive centuries into the future?

"I wanted to tell you about it because science is really important. Without it, we don't understand anything, so how can we get anything right or make any good decisions? Some people think science is boring, some people think it's dangerous—and if we don't get interested in science and learn about it and use it properly, then maybe it *is* those things. But if you try and understand it, it's fascinating, and it matters to us and to the future of our planet."

Everyone was listening to George now. When he stopped talking, there was complete silence.

He started again. "Billions of years ago, there were clouds of gas and dust wandering in outer space. At first these clouds were very spread out and scattered, but over time, gravity helping, they started to shrink and become denser and denser . . ."

EARTH

- Earth is the third closest planet to the Sun.
- Average distance to the Sun: 93 million miles (149.6 million km)

A total of 70.8% of the surface of the Earth is covered with liquid water and the rest is divided into seven continents. These are: Asia (29.5% of the land surface of the Earth), Africa (20.5%), North America (16.5%), South America (12%), Antarctica (9%), Europe (7%), and Australia (5%). This definition of continents is mostly cultural since, for instance, no water expanse divides Asia from Europe. Geographically, there are only four continents that are not separated by water: Eurasia-Africa (57% of the land surface), Americas (28.5%), Antarctica (9%), and Australia (5%). The remaining 0.5% is made up of islands, mostly scattered within Oceania in the central and South Pacific.

- A day on Earth is divided into 24 hours, but in fact it takes Earth 23 hours, 56 minutes, and 4 seconds to rotate around itself. There is a 3-minute-and-56 second mismatch. Over a year this adds up to the one turn the Earth makes by going around its orbit.
- An Earth-year is the time it takes for the Earth to complete one revolution around the Sun. It may vary very slightly over time, but remains about 365.25 days.
- So far, the Earth is the only known planet in the Universe to harbor life.

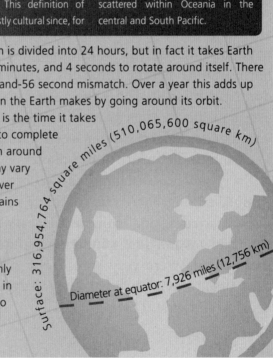

Surface: 316,954,764 square miles (510,065,600 square km)

Diameter at equator: 7,926 miles (12,756 km)

Chapter Thirty-two

"*So what?* you might think," continued George. "What's a cloud of dust got to do with anything? Why do we care or need to know what happened billions of years ago in outer space? Does it matter? Well, yes, it does. Because that cloud of dust is the reason we are here today.

"Now we know that stars are formed from giant clouds of gas in outer space. Some of these stars end their lives by becoming black holes that slowly, very slowly, let things escape until they vanish in a huge explosion.

"Other stars explode before they become black holes and send all the matter inside them through space. We know that all the elements we are made of were created inside the bellies of these stars that exploded a long time ago. All the people on Earth, the animals, the plants, the rocks, the air, and the oceans are made of elements forged inside stars. Whatever we might think, we are all the children of stars. It took billions and billions of years for Nature to make us out of these elements."

George paused for a second.

"So, you see, it took an incredibly long time to make us and our planet. And our planet isn't like any other planet in the Solar System. There are bigger ones and more impressive ones but they aren't places you could think of as home. Like Venus, for example, which is really  hot. Or Mercury, where one day lasts for fifty-nine of our Earth days. Imagine that, if one day at school lasted fifty-nine days! That would be pretty awful."

George paused for a moment and then continued to speak, the whole hall hanging on his every word as he described some of the wonders of the Solar System. Finally he came to what he thought was probably the most important part, at the end of his presentation.

"Our planet is amazing and it's ours," he summed up. "We belong to it—we're all made of the same stuff as the planet itself. We really do need to look after it. My dad's been saying this for years, but I've just felt embarrassed by him. All I could see was how different he was from other parents. But I don't feel that way now—he's right to say we have to stop messing up the Earth. And he's right that we can all try just a little bit harder. I feel proud of him now for wanting to protect something as unique and beautiful as the Earth. But we all need to do it or it won't work, and our awesome planet will be ruined.

"Of course, we can also work on finding another planet for us to live on, but it isn't going to be easy. We know there isn't one close to us. So if there is another Earth out there—and there might be—it's a long, long way away. It's exciting, trying to discover new planets and new worlds out there in the Universe. But that doesn't mean that home isn't the place you still want to come back to. We've got to make sure that in a hundred years' time, we've still got an Earth to return to.

"So, you might wonder how I know all this. Well, the other thing I wanted to say to you is that you don't need to find an actual secret key, like I did, to unlock the Universe and help the Earth. There's one that everyone can use, if they learn how. It's called 'physics.' That's what you need to understand the Universe around you. Thank you!"

The hall burst into applause as everyone rose to his or her feet to give George a standing ovation. Wiping a tear from his eye, the principal sprang onto the stage to clap George on the back, and said, "Well done, George! Well done!" He pumped George's arm up and down in a very vigorous handshake. George blushed. He was embarrassed by the clapping and wished it would stop.

Down in the audience, Dr. Reeper also appeared to be crying, but not from pride or happiness, like the principal.

He was weeping for quite a different reason. "Cosmos!" he raged under his breath. "So close! I had you in my hands! And now he's stolen you away from me!"

The principal helped George down off the platform and had a very brief consultation with his fellow judges—all except Dr. Reeper, that is, who was hunched in his seat, whispering to himself and casting nasty looks at George. Borrowing the gym teacher's whistle and blowing it sharply several times, the principal brought the hall to order again.

"A-hem!" he said, clearing his throat. "I would like to announce that this year's winner of the interschool science presentation is, by—almost!—a unanimous vote on the part of the judges, *George Greenby*!" The school hall cheered. "George," the principal continued, "has given us a wonderful presentation, and I am delighted to award him the first prize, which is this truly amazing computer, kindly donated by our sponsors." One of the other judges produced a large cardboard box from under the table and handed it to George.

"Thank you, sir, thank you!" said George, who was rather overwhelmed, both by the experience and by the size of the box he had just been given. He staggered down the center aisle toward the exit, clasping his prize in both hands. Everyone smiled as he passed—except for one group of boys sitting at the end of the row, who were deliberately not clapping. They sat there with their arms folded, glaring at George.

"You haven't heard the last of this," hissed Ringo as George passed him.

George ignored him and hurried on until he reached Eric, Annie, and Susan.

"You did it, George! I'm so proud!" said Eric, trying to hug George around the huge cardboard box.

"George! You were great," said Annie shyly. "I never thought you would be so good on stage. And your science was pretty amazing too."

"Did I get it all right?" George asked her, feeling worried as Eric took the large box from him. "I mean, when I said 'billions,' should I have said 'tens of millions'? And when I talked about Jupiter, I thought maybe I should have said—"

"No!" said Annie. "You got everything right, didn't he, Dad?"

Eric nodded and beamed at George. "Especially the last part. You got that really, really right. And you won first prize as well. You must be very happy."

"I am," said George, "but there's just one problem. What are my parents going to say when I come home with a computer? They're going to be *so* angry."

"Or they might be *so* proud," said a voice.

George looked around and saw his dad, standing next to Susan. His jaw dropped. "Dad?" he said. "Were you here? Did you hear my speech about science?"

"I did," said his dad. "Your mother wanted me to come and pick you up from school—she was worried about you this morning—and I got here in time to hear your talk. I'm very glad I did, George. Because you're right, we shouldn't be scared of science. We should use it to help us save the planet and not close our minds to it."

"Does that mean I can keep my computer?" squeaked George.

George's dad smiled. "Well, I think you deserve it. Only an hour a week, though, or my homemade generator won't be able to keep up."

There was a sudden commotion behind them, and their little group was rudely pushed to one side by Dr. Reeper, who was charging through the crowd in a great hurry. Following him were Ringo and the other members of his gang. They all looked mad.

George watched them go and turned to Eric. "Aren't you going to do something about Greeper? Like punish him?"

"Um, no," said Eric sadly. "I think Graham's punished himself quite enough already. Best leave him alone. I doubt our paths will cross again."

"But . . . but . . . ," said George. "Eric, I wanted to ask you—how did Greeper know where to find you? I mean, you could have gone anywhere in the world, but he was waiting for you here, and he was right. How did he know?"

"Ah well. The house next door to you," said Eric. "It belonged to my old tutor, the man in the photo with the beard."

"But he disappeared!" said George.

"He only sort of disappeared," replied Eric. "I got a letter from him some time ago, saying he was going away on a very long journey, and he didn't know if or when he'd be back. He told me he wanted me to have his house, in case I ever needed somewhere to work on Cosmos. He couldn't have imagined that Graham would lie in wait for me here, for all these years."

"Where did the old man go?" asked George.

"He went . . . ," Eric started.

"Home," said Susan very firmly. "Can I give you a lift?" she asked George's dad.

"Oh no!" he said. "I've got my bike. I'm sure we can balance the computer on the handlebars to get it home."

"Dad!" huffed George. "Please! We might drop it."

"I don't mind running George home," said Susan. "It might be cramped, but it's amazing what you can fit inside a Mini."

Back at George's house that night, Eric, Susan, and Annie all stayed for a delicious supper of home-grown vegetables eaten by candlelight at the kitchen table. Eric and George's dad got into a long and very enjoyable argument about whether it was more important to look for a new planet or to try and save this one, while Susan helped George to set up his shiny new computer.

Annie went out into the garden and fed Freddy, who was looking rather lonely in his sty. When she came back from chatting to the pig, she spent the evening dancing around George's mom, showing her all her ballet steps and telling her lots of tall stories, which George's mom pretended to believe.

After they went home, leaving with lots of promises of eco-warriors talking to scientists at their conferences and trips to *The Nutcracker* together, George went upstairs to his room. He was very tired. He got into his pajamas but he didn't close the curtains—he wanted to look out of the window as he lay under his comforter.

It was a clear evening, and the night sky was studded with brilliant, twinkling stars. As he watched, a shooting star fell across the dark background, its long, shiny tail blazing with light for a few seconds before it melted into nothing.

Perhaps the shooting star is a piece of the comet's tail, thought George as he fell asleep. As a comet passes the Sun, it warms up and the ice on it starts to melt . . .

George's Secret Key to the Universe

★ BONUS MATERIAL ★

Q: What gave you the idea for the book?

A: I came up with the idea of George and his journey through physics and the Universe a couple of years ago. My son was nine years old at the time and I thought it would be wonderful if my father and I could write something together that would explain to my son the work of his grandfather. In the time that we've been working on the book, my father has gained a second grandson so the book is for him as well. In order to explain physics for kids, we decided to tell a story and use the events in that story to illustrate concepts of physics. When I looked around for inspiration, it was clear to me that there was a wealth of science fiction available for children but not very much "science fact" for kids to read. Science fiction can be exciting and very gripping, but it doesn't tell us anything about the Universe in which we live. We wrote an adventure story in which the adventures were based on real science rather than on fantasy. I thought it was very important to weave the science into a story line because I wanted to make it entertaining and creative so that *George's Secret Key* might appeal to children who wouldn't otherwise pick up a book on physics. Obviously, we hope it will appeal to their parents, too!

Q: How did working on this book change your relationship with your father?

A: Working on this book together gave us the chance to form a relationship as adults, which was a great gift. In working on the George book, we got to spend a lot of time kicking ideas around, we learned so much about each other, and we had a lot of fun. It gave us something really special.

Q: What was it like growing up as the daughter of the world's most famous physicist?

A: When I was young, he wasn't the world's most famous physicist—the fame didn't arrive until the publication of *A Brief History of Time*, by which time I was in my late teens. When I was a child, he was well known among physicists, but they are a fairly select, serious bunch, not much given to celebrity idolizing. As a young child, what was more striking about my father in terms of the way the public reacted to him, was the high level of attention his electric wheelchair attracted. I suppose that in the 1970s, it was quite unusual to see a disabled person drive themselves around in a wheelchair, and people really did stop and stare. He did drive his chair extremely fast and sometimes in a rather perilous fashion so I expect it did look rather eye-catching. Even so, as a kid, I used to stare back really hard at those people, to see how they liked it, but I don't suppose they noticed that for a second. I'm so glad that these days, disabled access is so much better than it was then and that disabled people are given more dignity by the general public than they were. I think that one big contribution my father has made is to show that having a disability does not bar you from leading a full and eventful life. Many people who have been through difficult times themselves have told me what an inspiration he has been to them. His recent zero gravity flight and plans to go into space show that the sky is literally the limit, as far as he is concerned!

Q: Did you feel any pressure to become a scientist yourself?

A: No, I didn't. From an early age, it was very clear that my interests lay in the arts subjects. My earliest ambition was to be a ballerina, but I was a bit small and round and prone to giggling too much—I lacked the necessary elegance to pull that one off! I think my dad would have been pleased if I had turned out a scientist because he truly believes that is the most interesting career open to anyone. But he also believes that you have to follow your own path in life and so he certainly wasn't going to push me toward theoretical physics when it didn't look like I was going in that direction naturally.

PROFESSOR STEPHEN HAWKING, AUTHOR

Q: You have just written a science book for children that will explain the Universe—and black holes. What made you write this book, and how are you going to explain black holes in a way that even children can understand?

A: Children ask how things do what they do, and why. Too often they are told that these are stupid questions to ask, but this is said by grown-ups who don't know the answers and don't want to look silly, by admitting they don't know. It is very important that young people keep their sense of wonder and keep asking why. I'm a child myself, in the sense I'm still looking. Children are fascinated by black holes and ask me questions. I find they soon get the idea if it is explained in nontechnical language.

Q: Will we ever be able to travel through time?

A: We are all traveling forward in time anyway. We can fast-forward by going off in a rocket at high speed and returning to find everyone on Earth much older or dead. Einstein's general theory of relativity seems to offer the possibility that we could warp space-time so much that we could travel back in time. However, it is likely that the warping would trigger a bolt of radiation that would destroy the spaceship, and maybe the space-time itself.

Q: What were you like as a child? What were your interests?

A: As a child, I wanted to know how things worked and to control them. With a friend, I built a number of complicated models that I could control. It was a natural next step to want to know how the Universe works. If you understand the Universe, you control it, in a way. I was never top of the class at school, but my classmates must have seen potential in me, because my nickname was Einstein.

Q: Do you believe we need to spread into space in order for the human race to survive? Will you travel into space yourself?

A: I think the human race doesn't have a future if we don't go into space. We need to expand our horizons beyond planet Earth if we are to have a long-term future. We cannot remain looking inward at ourselves on a small and increasingly polluted and overcrowded planet. We need to look outward to the wider Universe. This will take time and effort, but it will become easier as our technology improves. I therefore want to encourage public interest in space. I have never let my condition stop me. You only live once.

Q: In your children's book, you describe the Universe without a creator. Does this reflect your personal beliefs?

A: The lesson of the book is that the Universe is governed by the laws of science. One could regard these laws as the work of God, but discussion of such theological issues is not appropriate in a children's adventure story.

Q: Did you enjoy your zero gravity experience?

A: Being confined to a wheelchair doesn't bother me as my mind is free to roam the Universe, but it felt wonderful to be weightless.

CURRICULUM GUIDE

PREREADING ACTIVITIES

Before having students read *George's Secret Key to the Universe*, use the following activities to build background knowledge and to activate student interest.

1. Have students make a list of questions they have about the planet, the Universe, and outer space. Record their questions on the board. As they read, encourage students to check off the questions that the book answers.
2. Make sure students are familiar with the scientific method (testing a hypothesis through repeated observation and experimentation). You may want to demonstrate the scientific method with a short experiment, such as attracting or repelling various objects with a magnet.
3. Engage students in a discussion of favorite movies or video games that take place in space. Ask students to identify the elements of such movies or games that are most interesting to them. Tell them that this book is an adventure story that takes place in outer space. Ask students to make predictions as to what this story may be about and what George's "secret key" could be.

VOCABULARY

Throughout the reading of the book, discuss the meanings of the vocabulary words below as they come up. Have students use context clues from the page where the word first appears as well as from a dictionary or other reference sources to determine the word's meaning. Students may want to keep a list of these words in a notebook as they read.

toxins (p. 4)	parched (p. 72)
additives (p. 4)	portal (p. 83)
phenomena (p.4)	rubble (p. 95)
squatters (p. 11)	droughts (p. 144)
dense (p.12)	consuming (p. 144)
nanosecond (p. 38)	
oath (p. 40)	
quelled (p. 60)	
rebel (p. 60)	
random (p. 67)	
curdled (p. 67)	

DISCUSSION QUESTIONS

During and after reading, use these questions to stimulate scientific inquiry and literary analysis. These questions cover various subject areas, from language arts to chemistry, making them perfect prompts for cross-curricular lessons. Most of them relate to a specific page in the book and assume that students have read at least up to that page.

1. George's family lives without a lot of modern inventions and appliances (p. 4). Why do they choose to live this way? How does George feel about this way of life? What inventions or appliances do you most rely on? What could you live without?

2. George's mother tells him he asks too many questions (p. 10). What are you curious about? Could you find the answers through research, through scientific experimentation, or another way? Write down three questions you've always wondered about. Then write down what you think would be the best ways to find the answers.

3. Who is Annie and how is she different from George (p. 18)?

4. How does Eric introduce George to science (p. 26)? Do you agree with Eric's definition of science? Why or why not?

5. Eric discusses physics (p. 26). What are some of the other types of natural science? What questions do they try to answer?

6. Why isn't Eric upset at the damage the pig has caused (p. 31)? What does his reaction suggest about what scientists can learn from unexpected events? What would happen if every science experiment worked as planned?

7. Who is Cosmos (p. 37)? Describe Cosmos's "personality." Would you like to have a computer like Cosmos? Why or why not?

8. Cosmos shows George a view of billions of stars in the Universe (p. 45). How are stars made?

9. What is an atom (p. 47)? Why isn't it an elementary particle? How do you think a particle can carry light?

10. What is matter (pp. 50–51)? What is the structure of atoms?

11. Do you agree with Reeper that life is not fair (p. 63)? Why or why not?

12. What is the average temperature where you live (p. 79)? How do you convert degrees Fahrenheit to degrees Celsius?

13. Read the following passage:
    "We're not doing nothing," squealed Ringo.
    "I think you mean, 'We are not doing anything,'" corrected Dr. Reeper in a teacherly voice (p. 92).
    Why does Reeper correct Ringo? Give another example of a double negative.

14. Why is outer space cold (p. 94)?

15. Why aren't mass and weight the same thing (p. 99)?
16. What does Einstein's equation $E = mc^2$ mean (p. 99)? What does each letter stand for?
17. When will Halley's Comet be visible from Earth again (p. 104)? What other comets will be visible from Earth before 2100? Why do some comets not orbit the Sun?
18. Jupiter takes 11.86 Earth-years to circle around the Sun (p. 122). Why does the book give orbits in Earth-years? How long is a year on Jupiter? (Hint: Multiply 365 × 11.86. Remember that the answer will be in Earth-days, because days are also determined by planetary motion.)
19. Reeper tells the rebel boys they must "learn to distinguish between science fiction and science fact" (p. 166). What is science fiction? How is it different from other types of fiction, like historical fiction? Have you read any other books that could be classified as science fiction? How were they similar to or different from this book?
20. What are exoplanets (pp. 166–167)? Why are they so difficult to detect? Do you think scientists will ever detect any Earth-size exoplanets? Why or why not?

ACTIVITIES

These activities encourage reading and writing development and scientific exploration, either through research or through experimentation. Where possible, encourage students to collaborate in order to complete the activities. Remind them that collaboration is central to science. Many scientists work together, building on one another's results so they can advance their knowledge more than any individual could working alone.

Research

The following activities involve student research. Direct students to appropriate Internet and library resources to complete the activities.

1. Have students observe the night sky from where they live (p. 8). (If safety is a concern, arrange a field trip to the school playground.) Have students create a sky map, in which they diagram and label the constellations they can see. *Follow-up:* Constellations seem to move across the sky, just as the Sun does. Why might that be? One star, the North Star, is said to be "fixed" — its position in the night sky doesn't change. Why doesn't its position change? Does it appear to be in the same part of the sky from every place on Earth?
2. Imagine that scientists have announced the discovery of a new object in the solar system. It has a diameter of about 4,500 miles, and it is almost

round. It orbits the sun, and its orbit contains many rocks and asteroids. Is this object a planet or a dwarf planet? Why? (Hint: See p. 87.)

3. How do scientists determine the surface area of planets? Have students find the formula for the surface area of spheres. What would be the surface area of a planet with an equatorial diameter of 15,640 miles?

4. Have students research discoveries that have come about from unexpected events or chance observations, such as the discovery of penicillin or Galileo's discovery of pendulum motion.

5. Have students find and read news stories from August 2006 about Pluto (p. 87). Encourage students to write fictional news stories of their own about a scientific finding. Compile students' stories into a fictional newspaper. Have students create illustrations or stage photographs to accompany their stories. Distribute copies of the completed student paper to other members of the school community.

6. Explore the idea that "mass and energy curve space, creating gravity" (p. 99). What does this mean? How can mass curve space?

7. Have students look at the discussion of temperature on page 79. Point out that one of the earliest thermometers was invented by Galileo. Galileo's thermometer worked on the principle that water expands when it gets hotter. How could that principle have helped him design a thermometer? Before thermometers, scientists could only talk about temperature in relative terms—for example, "This cocoa is hotter than that rock." Why might it be more useful for scientists to talk about temperature in terms of degrees? Why do we have several different temperature scales (Fahrenheit, Celsius, Kelvin)?

8. George can't talk to Annie when the antenna on her helmet is broken (p. 123). Why? How do antennas work? Find out!

9. Have students do research on global warming (p. 145). What causes it? What might happen because of climate change? Ask students to find three different scientific scenarios for the future.

Experiment

The activities below will provide students with hands-on experience in using science to understand the world around them.

1. How do comparisons help writers describe places and things to readers? Select an object in the room (a book, a piece of classroom equipment), and have students write two descriptions of it, both assuming that the audience has never seen such an object before. The first description must be literal: Students must describe the object as accurately as possible. They may not compare it to anything else. In the second description, they may use comparisons (it's the color of ___; it's about the size of ___; it has a nozzle like ___). How do comparisons help them get the

point across? In science, what might be a danger of using comparisons to describe something?

2. Have students duplicate Eric's demonstration with the plastic ruler and static electricity (p. 23). How does it work? What is static electricity?

3. Observe the Moon for a month. Chart its phases, as well as when and where it rises and sets in the sky. Try to observe it in relation to some stationary landmark, such as a tall building or a steeple. How do you think early scientists figured out how the Moon moved?

4. Eric shouts "Eureka!" when he finds the note about the new planet (p. 197). *Eureka* comes from a Greek word meaning "I have found it!" Supposedly, the ancient mathematician Archimedes exclaimed "Eureka!" when he figured out how to measure a solid's volume by water displacement. Provide students with several different irregular solids (for example, a key, an apple, a small toy, a fork). Fill a large, clear graduated container, such as a glass measuring cup, with water. Discuss the formula for calculating volume (V = length × width × height). Ask: How can you find the volume of these objects, when their length and width and height are so irregular? Have students find the volume of each solid by measuring the amount of water it displaces.

COSMOS'S PICTURE FILES

Cosmos, Eric's superintelligent cmputer, is the smartest computer in the world! His picture files on outer space can be found throughout *George's Secret Key to the Universe*. Use Cosmos's photographs as you go through the following questions and activities.

1. Why can't the far side of the Moon ever be seen from Earth?
2. What is infrared light? What is ultraviolet light?
3. Why might the photo of Titan resemble photos of Earth?
4. What does "geologically active" mean?
5. Why do you think the captions talk about "water ice," not just "ice"? What other kinds of ice are there?
6. Compare images of the Great Red Spot with satellite photos of large hurricanes, such as Katrina. How do the planets' rotations shape weather patterns?
7. Look at the map of the solar system. Note that the distances between the planets and the Sun are not to scale. How big would the book have to be to include a scale map of the distances? Have students first figure out the scale of this map, using the planet fact charts in the text. Then have students go through the book to find the outermost planet's distance from the Sun. On the diagram's scale, what would that distance be?

QUESTIONS FOR FURTHER THOUGHT

1. Eric says that Galileo discovered that the Earth goes around the Sun (p. 32). What did people believe before Galileo? Have students research medieval, Galilean, Copernican, and modern models of the solar system. Have them draw each model on a large sheet of paper. Display their drawings side by side to compare and contrast. Ask: Do you think today's model of the solar system is accurate? Why or why not?

2. Have students read the oath of the scientist (pp. 40–41) out loud. Discuss why such an oath might be necessary. Ask students to create their own oaths, either for scientific inquiry or for another pursuit they value highly. Encourage them to write their oaths in cursive or to use calligraphy pens.

3. George tells his father he could use computers and the Internet to organize his ecological work (p. 171). Have students think of a social or ecological cause they would like to help. Then have them list three ways they could use computers to raise awareness or make their activism more effective. Invite students to share their ideas with one another or the school community.

4. This book deals mainly with modern physics, the branch of inquiry that began with Einstein. Advanced students may be interested in exploring classical or Newtonian physics. Encourage them to search for information about inertia and motion using library resources.

5. Many planets and constellations have names that come from Greek and Roman mythology. Have students pick a planet or constellation and write and illustrate a short version of the related myth. Compile students' myths into a class anthology, pairing each myth with a drawing or photo of the related planet or constellation.

HERE'S A LOOK AT GEORGE'S NEXT ADVENTURE!

It hadn't been easy to decide what to wear. "Come as your favorite space object," he'd been told by Eric Bellis, the scientist next door, who had invited George to his costume party. The problem was, George had so many favorite outer-space objects, he hadn't known which one to pick.

Should he dress up as Saturn with its rings?

Perhaps he could go as Pluto, the poor little planet that wasn't a planet anymore?

Or should he go as the darkest, most powerful force in the Universe—a black hole? He didn't think too long or hard about that—as amazing, huge, and fascinating as black holes are, they didn't really count as his favorite space objects. It would be quite hard to get fond of something that was so greedy, it swallowed up anything and everything that came too close, including light.

In the end George had his mind made up for him. He'd been looking at images of the Solar System on the Internet with his dad when they came across a picture

sent back from a Mars rover, one of the robots exploring the planet's surface. It showed what looked like a person standing on the red planet. As soon as he saw the photo, George knew he wanted to go to Eric's party as the Man from Mars. Even George's dad, Terence, got excited when he saw it. Of course, they both knew it wasn't really a Martian in the picture—it was just an illusion caused by a trick of the light that made a rocky outcrop look like a person. But it was exciting to imagine that we might not be alone in this vast Universe after all.

"Dad, do you think there *is* anyone out there?" asked George as they gazed at the photo. "Like Martians or beings in faraway galaxies? And if there are, do you think they might come to visit us?"

"If there are," said his dad, "I expect they're looking

at us and wondering what we must be like—to have this beautiful, wonderful planet and make such a mess of it. They must think we're really stupid." He shook his head sadly.

Both George's parents were eco-warriors on a mission to save the Earth. As part of their campaign, electrical gadgets like telephones and computers had been banned from the house. But when George had won the first prize in the school science competition—his very own computer—his mom and dad didn't have the heart to say he couldn't keep it.

In fact, since they'd had the computer in the house, George had shown them how to use it and had even helped them put together a very snappy virtual ad featuring a huge photo of Venus. WHO WOULD WANT TO LIVE HERE? it said in big letters. *Clouds of sulfuric acid, temperatures of up to 878 degrees Fahrenheit (470 degrees Celsius) . . . The seas have dried up and the atmosphere is so thick, sunlight can't break through. This is Venus. But if we're not care-*

ful, this could be Earth. Would you want to live on a planet like this? George was very proud of the poster, which his parents and their friends had e-mailed all around the world to promote their cause.

VENUS

Venus is the second planet from the Sun and the sixth largest in the Solar System.

Venus is the brightest object in the sky, after the Sun and the Moon. Named after the Roman goddess of beauty, Venus has been known since prehistoric times. Ancient Greek astronomers thought it was two stars: one that shone in the morning, Phosphorus, the bringer of light; and one in the evening, Hesperus, until Greek philosopher and mathematician Pythagoras realized they were one and the same object.

Venus is often called Earth's twin. It is about the same size, mass, and composition as the Earth.

But Venus is a very different world from the Earth.

It has a very thick, toxic atmosphere, mostly made of carbon dioxide with clouds of sulfuric acid. These clouds are so dense that they trap heat, making Venus the hottest planet in the Solar System, with surface temperatures of up to 878 degrees Fahrenheit (470 degrees Celsius)—so hot that lead would melt there. The pressure of the atmosphere is ninety times greater than Earth's. This means that if you stood on the surface of Venus, you would feel the same pressure as you would at the bottom of a very deep ocean on Earth.

The dense spinning clouds of Venus don't just trap the heat. They also reflect the light of the Sun, which is why the planet shines so brightly in the night sky. Venus may have had oceans in the past, but the water was vaporized by the greenhouse effect and escaped from the planet.

Venus is thought to be the least likely place in the Solar System for life to exist.

Some scientists believe that the runaway greenhouse effect on Venus is similar to conditions that might prevail on Earth if global warming isn't checked.

Since *Mariner 2* in 1962, Venus has been visited by space probes more than twenty times. The first space probe ever to land on another planet was the Soviet *Venera 7*, which landed on Venus in 1970; *Venera 9* sent back photos of the surface—but it didn't have long to do it: The space probe melted after just sixty minutes on the hostile planet! The U.S. orbiter, *Magellan*, later used radar to send back images of the surface details of Venus, which had previously been hidden by the thick clouds of its atmosphere.

Venus rotates in the opposite direction from the Earth! If you could see the Sun through its thick clouds, it would rise in the west and set in the east. This is called *retrograde* motion; the direction in which the Earth turns is called *prograde*.

A year on Venus takes less time than a day there! Because Venus turns so slowly, it revolves all the way around the Sun in less time than it takes to rotate once on its axis.

> One year on Venus = 224.7 Earth days

Venus passes between the Earth and the Sun about twice a century. This is called the *transit of Venus*. These transits always happen in pairs eight years apart. Since the telescope was invented, transits have been observed in 1631 and 1639; 1761 and 1769; and 1874 and 1882. On June 8, 2004, astronomers saw the tiny dot of Venus crawl across the Sun; the second in this pair of early twenty-first-century transits will occur on June 6, 2012.

> Venus spins on its axis once every 243 Earth days.

Given what he knew about Venus, George felt pretty sure that there wasn't any life to be found on that smelly, hot planet. He didn't even consider going to Eric's party dressed as a Venusian. Instead, he got his mom, Daisy, to help him with an outfit of dark-orange bobbly knitted clothes and a tall pointy hat so he looked just like the photo of the "Martian" they'd found.

Wearing his costume, George waved good-bye to his parents—who had a big evening planned helping

some eco-friends make organic treats for a party of their own—and squeezed through the gap in the fence between his garden and Eric's. The gap had come about when George's pet pig (given to him by his gran), Freddy, had escaped from his pigsty, barged through the fence, and broken into Eric's house via the back door. Following the trail of hoofprints that Freddy had left behind him, George had ended up meeting his new neighbors, who had only just moved into the empty house next door. This chance encounter with Eric and his family had changed George's life forever.

Eric had shown George his amazing computer, Cosmos, who was so smart and so powerful that he could draw doorways through which Eric; his daughter, Annie; and George could walk, to visit any part of the known Universe.

But space can be very dangerous, as George found out when one of their space adventures ended with Cosmos exploding from the sheer effort of mounting the rescue mission.

Since Cosmos had stopped working, George hadn't had another chance to step through the doorway and travel around the Solar System and beyond. He missed Cosmos, but at least he had Eric and Annie. He could see them anytime he wanted, even if he couldn't go on adventures into outer space with them.

George scampered up the garden path to Eric's back door. The house was brightly lit, with chatter and music pouring out. Opening the door, George let himself into the kitchen.

He couldn't see Annie, Eric, or Annie's mom, Susan, but there were lots of other people milling about: one grown-up immediately pushed a plate of shiny silver-iced muffins under his nose. "Have a meteorite!" he said cheerfully. "Or perhaps I should say, have a meteoroid!"

"Oh . . . um, well, thanks," said George, a bit startled. "They look delicious," he added, helping himself to one.

"If I did this," continued the man, tipping some of the muffins onto the floor, "then I could say, 'Have a meteorite!' because then they would have hit the ground. But when I offered them to you, suspended in the air, they were — technically — still meteoroids." He beamed at George and then at the muffins that were lying in a pile on the floor. "You get the distinction — a meteoroid is a chunk of rock that flies through the air; a meteor*ite* is what you call that piece of rock if it lands on the Earth. So now I've dropped them on the floor, we can call them meteor-ites."

With the muffin in his hand, George smiled politely, nodded, and started backing away slowly.

"Ouch!" He heard a squeak as he trod on someone behind him.

"Oops!" he said, turning around.

"It's okay, it's only me!" It was Annie, dressed all in black. "You couldn't have seen me, anyway, because I'm invisible!" She swiped the muffin out of George's hand and stuffed it into her mouth. "You only know I'm here because of the effect I have on objects around me. What does that make me?"

"A black hole, of course!" said George. "You swallow anything that comes near you, you greedy pig."

"Nope!" said Annie triumphantly. "I knew you'd say that, but that's wrong! I am"—she looked very pleased with herself—"dark matter."

"What's that?" asked George.

"No one knows," said Annie mysteriously. "We can't see it, but it seems to be absolutely essential to keep galaxies from flying apart. What are you?"

"Um, well," said George. "I'm the Man from Mars— y'know, from the pictures."

"Oh yeah!" said Annie. "You can be my Martian ancestor. That's cool."

Around them, the party was buzzing. Groups of the most oddly dressed grown-ups stood eating and drinking and talking at the tops of their voices. One man had come dressed as a microwave oven, another as a rocket. There was a lady wearing a badge shaped like an exploding star and a man with a mini satellite dish on his head. One scientist was bouncing around in a bright green suit, ordering people to "Take me to your leader"; another was blowing up an enormous balloon stamped with the words THE UNIVERSE IS INFLATING. A man dressed all in red kept standing next to people and then stepping away from them, daring them to guess what he was. Next to him was a scientist wearing lots of different-sized hula hoops around his middle, each one with a different-sized ball attached to it. When he walked, his hula hoops all spun around him.

"Annie," said George urgently, "I don't understand any of these costumes. What have these guests come as?"

"Um, well, they've all come as things you'd find in space, if you know how to look for them," said Annie.

"Like what?" asked George.

"Well, like the man dressed in red," explained Annie. "He keeps stepping away from people, which means he's pretending to be the redshift."

"The what?"

"If a distant object in the Universe, like a galaxy, is moving away from you, its light will appear more red than otherwise. So he's dressed in red, and he is moving *away* from people to show them he's come as the redshift. And the others have come as all sorts of cosmic stuff that you'd find out there, like microwaves and faraway planets."

LIGHT AND HOW IT TRAVELS THROUGH SPACE

One of the most important things in the Universe is the *electromagnetic field*. It reaches everywhere; not only does it hold atoms together, but it also makes tiny parts of atoms (called *electrons*) bind different atoms together or create electric currents. Our everyday world is built from very large numbers of atoms stuck together by the electromagnetic field. Even living things, like human beings, rely on it to exist and to function.

Jiggling an electron creates waves in the field. This is like jiggling a finger in your bath and making ripples in the water. These waves are called *electromagnetic waves*, and because the field is everywhere, the waves can travel far across the Universe, until stopped by other electrons that can absorb their energy. They come in many different types, but some affect the human eye, and we know these as the various colors of visible light. Other types include radio waves, microwaves, infrared, ultraviolet, X rays, and gamma rays. Electrons are jiggled all the time by atoms that are constantly jiggling too, so there are always electromagnetic waves being produced by objects. At room temperature the waves are mainly infrared, but in much hotter objects the jiggling is more violent, and produces visible light.

Light travels at 186,000 miles per second. This is very fast, but light from the Sun still takes eight minutes to reach us; from the next nearest star it takes more than four years.

Very hot objects in space, such as stars, produce visible light, which may travel a very long way before hitting something. When you look at a star, the light from it may have been moving serenely through space for hundreds of years. It enters your eye and, by jiggling electrons in your retina, turns into electricity that is sent along the optic nerve to your brain. Your brain says, "I can see a star!" If the star is very far away, you may need a telescope to collect enough of the light for your eye to detect, or the jiggled electrons could instead create a photograph or send a signal to a computer.

The Universe is constantly expanding, inflating like a balloon. This means that distant stars and galaxies are moving away from Earth. This stretches their light as it travels through space toward us—the farther it travels, the more stretched it becomes. The stretching makes visible light look redder, which is known as the redshift. Eventually, if light traveled and redshifted far enough, the light would no longer be visible and would become first infrared, and then microwave (as used on Earth in microwave ovens), radiation. This is just what has happened to the incredibly powerful light produced by the Big Bang. After thirteen billion years of traveling, it is detectable today as microwaves coming from every direction in space. This has the grand title of *cosmic microwave background radiation*, and is nothing less than the afterglow of the Big Bang itself.

Annie said all this matter-of-factly, as though it was quite normal to know this kind of information and be able to rattle it off at parties. But once again George felt a little jealous of her. He loved science and was always reading books, looking up articles on the Internet, and pestering Eric with questions. He wanted to be a scientist when he grew up, so he could learn everything there was to know and maybe make some amazing discovery of his own. Annie, on the other hand, was much more casual about the wonders of the Universe.

When George had first met Annie, she'd wanted to be a ballerina, but now she'd changed her mind and decided on being a soccer player. Instead of spending her time after school in a pink-and-white tutu, she now charged around the backyard, hammering a soccer ball past George, who always had to be goalie. And yet she still seemed to know far more about science than he did.

Annie's dad, Eric, now appeared, dressed in his normal clothes and looking no different from usual.

"Eric," cried George, who was bursting with questions. "What have you come as?"

"Oh, me?" Eric smiled. "I'm the only intelligent life-form in the Universe," he said modestly.

"What?" asked George. "You mean you're the only intelligent person in the whole Universe?"

Eric laughed. "Don't say that too loudly around here," he told George, gesturing to all the other scientists.

"Otherwise people will get very upset. I meant, I've come as a human being, which is the only intelligent form of life in the Universe that we know about. So far."

"Oh," said George. "But what about all your friends? What have they come as? And why does red light mean something is going away? I don't understand."

"Well," said Eric kindly, "you'd understand if someone explained it to you."

"Can *you* explain it to me?" pleaded George. "All about the Universe? Like you did with the black holes? Can you tell me about red thingies and dark matter and everything else?"

"Oh dear," said Eric, sounding rather regretful. "George, I'd love to tell you all about the Universe, but the problem is, I'm just not sure I'll have time before I have to . . . Hang on a second . . ." He trailed off and gazed into the distance, the way he did when he was having an idea. He took off his glasses and polished them on his shirt, setting them on his nose at the same off-kilter angle as before. "I've got it!" he cried, sounding very excited. "I know what we need to do! Hold on, George, I've got a plan."

With that, he picked up a soft hammer and struck a huge brass gong, which rang out with a deep, humming chime.

"Right, gather round, everyone," said Eric, waving

everyone into the room. "Come on, come on, hurry up! I've got something to say."

A ripple of excitement went through the crowd.

"Now then," he went on, "I've gathered the Order of Science here today for this party—"

"Hurray!" cheered someone at the back.

"And I want us to put our minds to some questions my young friend George has asked me. He wants to know all sorts of things! For a start, I'm sure he'll want to know what your costume is!" He pointed to the man wearing the hula hoops.

"I've come to the party," piped up the cheerful-looking scientist, "as a distant planetary system where we might find another planet Earth."

"Annie," whispered George, "isn't that what Doctor Reeper did? Find new planets?"

Dr. Reeper was a former colleague of Eric's, who wanted to use science for his own selfish purposes. He had told Eric he'd found an exoplanet—that is, a planet in orbit around a star other than the Earth's Sun—that might be able to support human life. But the directions he'd given Eric had been bogus—in fact, in his search for the planet, they had sent Eric dangerously close to a black hole. Dr. Reeper had been trying to get rid of Eric so he could control Cosmos, Eric's supercomputer. But his evil trick hadn't worked, and Eric had returned safely from his trip inside a black hole.

No one knew where Dr. Reeper was now. He had

fled after his master plan backfired. At the time, George had begged Eric to do something about him, but Eric had just let him go.

"Doctor Reeper knew how to *look* for planets," said Annie, "but we don't know whether he ever actually found one. After all, that planet he wrote about in the letter to Dad? We never got to see whether it really existed or not."

"Thank you, Sam. And how many planets have you

found so far?" Eric questioned the hula hoop man.

"So far," replied Sam, shaking his hoops as he spoke, "three hundred and thirty-one exoplanets—more than a hundred of them in orbit around stars quite nearby. Some of these stars have more than one planet going around them." He pointed to his hula hoops. "I'm a nearby system with planets in orbit around its star."

"What does he mean by 'nearby'?" George whispered to Annie, who passed the message on to Eric. Her father whispered back to her, and she then relayed the answer to George.

"He means, maybe, like, about forty light-years away. So, like, about two hundred and thirty-five trillion miles," said Annie. "Nearby for the Universe!"

"Have you seen anything that might be like the Earth? A planet we could call home?"

"We've seen a few that might—and only might—be like a second Earth. Our planet-hunting search continues."

"Thank you, Sam," said Eric. "Now, what I want us to do is answer George's questions—all of us. Each of you"—he handed out pens and paper—"can write me a page or two by the end of the party about what you think is the most interesting part of the science you work on. You can send or e-mail it to me later if you don't have time to finish it now."

The scientists all looked really happy. They *loved* talking about the most interesting parts of their work.

"And," added Eric quickly, "before we get back to

the party, I've got one more brief announcement to make—one of my own this time. I'm very excited and pleased to tell you all that I have a new job! I'm going to work for the Global Space Agency, looking for signs of life in our Solar System. Beginning with Mars!"

"Wow!" said George. "That's amazing!" He turned to Annie, but she didn't meet his eye.

"So," continued Eric, "in just a few days' time, my family and I will be packing up . . . and moving to the headquarters of the Global Space Agency in the United States of America!"

With that, George's universe imploded.

WHAT ARE YOU WAITING FOR?

Read all the books by
New York Times bestseller
STUART GIBBS!

Praise for *George's Secret Key to the Universe*

★"What better way to interest young readers in science—and specifically in its relevance to the long-term survival of humankind—than for one of the world's most renowned theoretical physicists to put his subject at the center of a children's book? Stephen Hawking, his novelist daughter, and French physicist Galfard create two inquisitive, middle-school heroes, then send them on wondrous adventures through time and space. . . . [A] true beginner's guide to *A Brief History of Time*."
—*Publishers Weekly*, starred review

"People who know real scientists will appreciate Eric's enthusiasm, naïve idealism, and tendency to lecture. The book gets points for tackling the recurrent tension between environmentalism and science, but it succeeds first and foremost as a good old-fashioned adventure tale."   —*Natural History*

Praise for *George's Cosmic Treasure Hunt*

"[E]mbeds actual facts, current research, and working scientific theories into this story, giving me a very real experience of space adventures from my own chair. He includes special articles by other famous scientists about planets, robotic space travel, and satellites in space, and there are some amazing photographs of space exploration."
—*New Mexico Kids!*

"The plot is very exciting. . . . I enjoyed how many real facts and events are woven into the story, like global warming, space shuttles, real planets, and accurate facts about space."   —*Time for Kids*

Also by
Lucy & Stephen Hawking

George's Secret Key to the Universe

Find out about Stephen Hawking's books for adult
readers at hawking.org.uk.

To hear Lucy and Stephen Hawking talk
about George and his adventures, visit
georgessecretkey.com.

GEORGE'S COSMIC TREASURE HUNT

Lucy & Stephen HAWKING

Illustrated by Garry Parsons

SIMON & SCHUSTER BOOKS FOR YOUNG READERS
NEW YORK LONDON TORONTO SYDNEY

SIMON & SCHUSTER BOOKS FOR YOUNG READERS

An imprint of Simon & Schuster Children's Publishing Division

1230 Avenue of the Americas, New York, New York 10020

Originally published in Great Britain in 2009 by Doubleday, an imprint
of Random House Group Ltd.

First U.S. Edition 2009

For information about special discounts for bulk purchases, please contact Simon & Schuster
Special Sales at 1-866-506-1949 or business@simonandschuster.com.

The Simon & Schuster Speakers Bureau can bring authors to your live event. For more
information or to book an event, contact the Simon & Schuster Speakers Bureau at
1-866-248-3049 or visit our website at www.simonspeakers.com.

Also available in a Simon & Schuster Books for Young Readers hardcover edition.

Book design by Clair Lansley

The text for this book is set in Stempel Garamond.

The illustrations for this book are rendered in pencil that was digitally edited.

Manufactured in the United States of America

0718 MTN

First Simon & Schuster Books for Young Readers paperback edition May 2011

10

The Library of Congress has cataloged the hardcover edition as follows:

Hawking, Lucy.

George's cosmic treasure hunt / Lucy & Stephen Hawking ; illustrated by Garry Parsons.

1st U.S. ed.

299 p., [32] p. of col. plates : ill. ; 23 cm.

Summary: George is heartbroken when his neighbor Annie and her space-scientist father move to Florida,
but when Annie sends him a secret message telling him she has been contacted by aliens with a terrible
warning, he joins her in a galaxy-wide search for answers. Includes scientific essays on space travel

ISBN 978-1-4169-8671-3 (hc)

[1. Extraterrestrial beings—Fiction. 2. Astronauts—Fiction. 3. Space flight—Fiction. 4. Outer space—
Exploration—Fiction.] 1. Title.

PZ7.H3134 Gd 2009

[Fic] 22

2009008413

ISBN 978-1-4424-2175-2 (pbk)

ISBN 978-1-4169-9057-4 (eBook)

For Rose

GEORGE'S COSMIC TREASURE HUNT

THE LATEST SCIENTIFIC THEORIES!

There are a number of fabulous science essays that appear within the story to give readers a fascinating real insight into some of the latest theories. These have been written by the following eminent scientists:

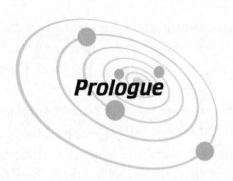

Prologue

"T minus seven minutes and thirty seconds," said a robotic voice. *"Orbiter access arm retracted."*

George gulped and shifted around in the commander's seat on the space shuttle. This, finally, was it. In just a few short minutes—minutes that were ticking by far faster than the endless ones of the last class at school—he'd be leaving planet Earth behind and flying into the cosmos.

Now that the orbiter access arm, which formed the bridge between his spacecraft and the outside world, had been taken away, George knew he'd missed his final chance to leave. This was one of the last stages before lift-off. It meant the connecting hatches were closing. And they weren't just closing—they were being *sealed*. Now, even if he hammered on the hatches and begged to be let out, there

1

would be no one on the other side to hear him. The astronauts were alone with their mighty spacecraft. There was nothing to do now but wait for the countdown to reach zero.

"T minus six minutes and fifteen seconds. Perform APU prestart." The APUs—the Auxiliary Power Units—helped to steer the shuttle during launch and landing. They were powered by three fuel cells, which had already been running for hours. But the command to prestart the APU made the shuttle hum with life, as though the spaceship knew its moment of glory was not far off now.

"T minus five minutes," said the voice. *"Go for APU start."*

George's stomach quivered with butterflies. Above all things in the Universe, he wanted to fly through space again. And now here he was, on board a real spaceship with astronauts inside it, waiting on a launchpad for liftoff. It was exciting but scary at the same time. What if he did something wrong? He was in the commander's seat, which meant he was in charge of operating the shuttle. Next to him sat his pilot, who was there as the commander's backup. "So, you're all astronauts on some kind of star trek?" he muttered to himself in a silly voice.

"What was that, Commander?" came a voice over George's headset.

"Oh, er, um . . . ," said George, who'd forgotten that launch control could hear every word he said. "Just wondering what aliens might say to us, if we run into any."

Someone at launch control laughed. "You be sure to tell them we all said hi."

"T minus three minutes and three seconds. Engines to start position."

Vroom vroom, thought George. The three engines and the two solid rocket boosters would provide the speed during the first few seconds of liftoff, when the shuttle would be moving at one hundred miles per hour before it even cleared the launch tower. It would only take eight and a half minutes to reach a speed of seventeen thousand five hundred miles an hour!

"T minus two minutes. Close visors." George's fingers itched to flip a couple of the thousands of switches in front of him, just to see what would happen, but he didn't dare. In front of him was the joystick that he, the commander, would use to steer the shuttle once they got into space, and then to dock with the International Space Station. It was like the steering wheel of a car,

except that the joystick moved in all sorts of directions rather than just left and right. It could go backward and forward as well. He put one finger on the top of the joystick, just to see what it felt like. One of the electronic graphs in front of him shivered very slightly as he did so. He snatched his hand back and pretended he hadn't touched anything.

"*T minus fifty-five seconds. Perform solid rocket*

booster lockout." The two solid rocket boosters would blast the space shuttle off the pad and up to around 230 miles above the Earth. They didn't have an off switch. Once they were ignited, the space shuttle was going up.

Good-bye, Earth, thought George. *I'll be back soon.* He felt a twinge of sadness at leaving his beautiful planet, his friends, and his family behind. In just a short time he would be orbiting over their heads when the shuttle docked with the International Space Station. He would be able to look down and see the Earth as the ISS whizzed overhead, completing a full orbit once every ninety minutes. From space, he would be able to see the outlines of continents, oceans, deserts, forests and lakes, and the lights of big cities at night. Looking up from Earth, his mom and dad and his friends—Eric, Annie, and Susan—would only see him as a tiny bright dot moving fast across the sky on a clear night.

"*T minus thirty-one seconds. Ground launcher sequencer go for auto sequence.*"

The astronauts wriggled slightly in their seats, wanting to get comfortable before their long journey. It felt surprisingly small and cramped inside the cockpit. Just getting into position for takeoff had been a squeeze, and George had needed the help of a space engineer to clamber into his seat. The space shuttle stood upright for liftoff, so everything in the cockpit seemed as though it had been turned upside down. The seat was tilted back so that George's

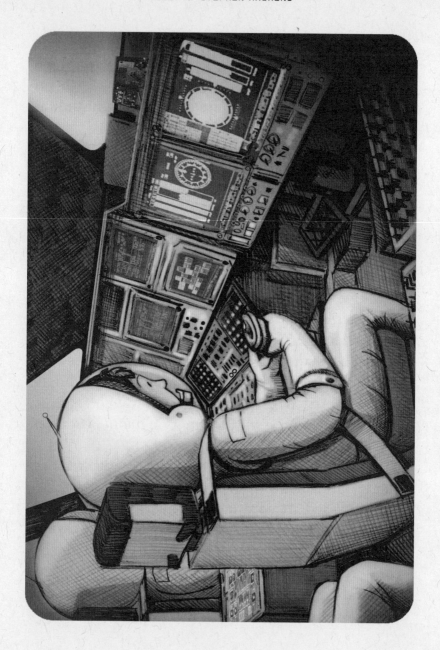

feet were pointing up toward the nose of the shuttle and his spine was aligned with the ground underneath.

The shuttle was in rocket mode, waiting to go vertically through the sky, clouds, and atmosphere, way up into the cosmos itself.

"*T minus sixteen seconds,*" the robotic voice said very calmly. "*Activate sound suppression water. T minus fifteen seconds.*"

"Takeoff minus fifteen seconds, Commander George," said the pilot in the seat next to George's. "The space shuttle launches in fifteen seconds and counting."

"Woo hoo!" cheered George. *Yikes!* he thought.

"Woo hoo to you too, Commander," replied launch control. "Have a good flight."

George shivered with excitement. Every breath he took counted down toward the great launch itself.

"*T minus ten seconds. Free hydrogen burn-off system ignition. Ground launcher sequencer go for main engine start.*"

This was it! It was really happening!

Looking out of the window, George could see a strip of green grass and, above it, the blue sky where birds wheeled about. Lying on his back in his astronaut's seat, he tried to feel calm and in control.

"*T minus six seconds,*" said the announcer. "*Main engine start.*" George felt an incredible shaking as the three main engines started, even though the shuttle

7

wasn't yet moving. He heard launch control again through his headset.

"*We are go for launch at T minus five seconds and counting. Five, four, three, two, one. You are go for launch.*"

"Yes," said George very calmly, although inside he was screaming. "We are go for launch."

"*T minus zero. Solid rocket booster ignition.*"

The shaking increased. The two rocket boosters ignited underneath George and the other astronauts. It was like being kicked sharply in the backside. With a huge roar, the rockets broke through the silence, propelling the space shuttle off the launchpad and up into the skies. George felt as though he had blasted off from Earth while strapped to an enormous firework. Anything could happen now—it could explode, it could veer off course and crash back to Earth, or head up into the skies and spin out of control. And there would be nothing George could do about it.

Through the window, he saw the blue of the Earth's atmosphere all around the spaceship, but he could no longer see the Earth itself. He was leaving his own planet! A few seconds after launch, the shuttle performed a roll, so that the astronauts were upside down, under the big orange fuel tank!

"Arrrgggghhh!"
yelled George. "We're
upside down! We're fly-
ing into space the wrong
way up! Help! Help!"

"It's okay, Commander!"
said the pilot. "We always do
it this way."

Two minutes after launch George
felt a huge jolt that rocked the whole
spacecraft.

"What was that?" he cried.

Out of the window, he saw first one and then the
second rocket booster detach and fly away from the
shuttle in a great big arc.

It was suddenly quiet now that the rocket boosters
had gone; so quiet it was nearly silent inside the orbiter.
He looked through the window and wanted to fill the
silence with cheering. The shuttle rolled around again
so that the orbiter was once more on top of the big
orange fuel tank rather than underneath it.

After eight minutes and thirty seconds in the air—
George felt like entire centuries could have passed by
and he wouldn't have noticed—the three main engines
shut down and the external fuel tank detached.

"There she goes!" whistled his pilot, and through the
window George saw the huge orange fuel tank disappear
from view to burn up in the atmosphere.

Outside, they passed the boundary line, where the blue of the earthly sky turns into the black of outer space. Distant stars shone around them. They were still climbing higher, but they didn't have much farther to go before they reached their maximum height.

"All systems are good," said George's pilot, checking all the flashing lights on the panels. "Heading for orbit. Commander, will you take us into orbit?"

"I will," said George confidently, now speaking to mission control in Texas. "Houston"—he said the most famous word in the history of space travel—"we are go for orbit. Do you read me, Houston? This is *Atlantis*. We are go for orbit."

In the darkness outside, the stars suddenly looked very bright and very close. One of them seemed to be zooming toward him, shining a bright light directly into his face, so close and so brilliant that—

George woke up with a start and found himself in an unfamiliar bed with someone shining a flashlight in his face.

"George!" the figure hissed. "George! Get up! It's an emergency!"

Chapter 1

It hadn't been easy to decide what to wear. "Come as your favorite space object," he'd been told by Eric Bellis, the scientist next door, who had invited George to his costume party. The problem was, George had so many favorite outer-space objects, he hadn't known which one to pick.

Should he dress up as Saturn with its rings?

Perhaps he could go as Pluto, the poor little planet that wasn't a planet anymore?

Or should he go as the darkest, most powerful force in the Universe—a black hole? He didn't think too long or hard about that—as amazing, huge, and fascinating as black holes are, they didn't really count as his favorite space objects. It would be quite hard to get fond of something that was so greedy, it swallowed up anything and everything that came too close, including light.

In the end George had his mind made up for him. He'd been looking at images of the Solar System on the Internet with his dad when they came across a picture

sent back from a Mars rover, one of the robots exploring the planet's surface. It showed what looked like a person standing on the red planet. As soon as he saw the photo, George knew he wanted to go to Eric's party as the Man from Mars. Even George's dad, Terence, got excited when he saw it. Of course, they both knew it wasn't really a Martian in the picture—it was just an illusion caused by a trick of the light that made a rocky outcrop look like a person. But it was exciting to imagine that we might not be alone in this vast Universe after all.

"Dad, do you think there *is* anyone out there?" asked George as they gazed at the photo. "Like Martians or beings in faraway galaxies? And if there are, do you think they might come to visit us?"

"If there are," said his dad, "I expect they're looking

at us and wondering what we must be like—to have this beautiful, wonderful planet and make such a mess of it. They must think we're really stupid." He shook his head sadly.

Both George's parents were eco-warriors on a mission to save the Earth. As part of their campaign, electrical gadgets like telephones and computers had been banned from the house. But when George had won the first prize in the school science competition—his very own computer—his mom and dad didn't have the heart to say he couldn't keep it.

In fact, since they'd had the computer in the house, George had shown them how to use it and had even helped them put together a very snappy virtual ad featuring a huge photo of Venus. WHO WOULD WANT TO LIVE HERE? it said in big letters. *Clouds of sulfuric acid, temperatures of up to 878 degrees Fahrenheit (470 degrees Celsius) . . . The seas have dried up and the atmosphere is so thick, sunlight can't break through. This is Venus. But if we're not care-*

ful, this could be Earth. Would you want to live on a planet like this? George was very proud of the poster, which his parents and their friends had e-mailed all around the world to promote their cause.

VENUS

Venus is the second planet from the Sun and the sixth largest in the Solar System.

Venus is the brightest object in the sky, after the Sun and the Moon. Named after the Roman goddess of beauty, Venus has been known since prehistoric times. Ancient Greek astronomers thought it was two stars: one that shone in the morning, Phosphorus, the bringer of light; and one in the evening, Hesperus, until Greek philosopher and mathematician Pythagoras realized they were one and the same object.

Venus is often called Earth's twin. It is about the same size, mass, and composition as the Earth.

But Venus is a very different world from the Earth.

It has a very thick, toxic atmosphere, mostly made of carbon dioxide with clouds of sulfuric acid. These clouds are so dense that they trap heat, making Venus the hottest planet in the Solar System, with surface temperatures of up to 878 degrees Fahrenheit (470 degrees Celsius)—so hot that lead would melt there. The pressure of the atmosphere is ninety times greater than Earth's. This means that if you stood on the surface of Venus, you would feel the same pressure as you would at the bottom of a very deep ocean on Earth.

The dense spinning clouds of Venus don't just trap the heat. They also reflect the light of the Sun, which is why the planet shines so brightly in the night sky. Venus may have had oceans in the past, but the water was vaporized by the greenhouse effect and escaped from the planet.

Venus is thought to be the least likely place in the Solar System for life to exist.

Some scientists believe that the runaway greenhouse effect on Venus is similar to conditions that might prevail on Earth if global warming isn't checked.

Since *Mariner 2* in 1962, Venus has been visited by space probes more than twenty times. The first space probe ever to land on another planet was the Soviet *Venera 7*, which landed on Venus in 1970; *Venera 9* sent back photos of the surface—but it didn't have long to do it: The space probe melted after just sixty minutes on the hostile planet! The U.S. orbiter, *Magellan*, later used radar to send back images of the surface details of Venus, which had previously been hidden by the thick clouds of its atmosphere.

Venus rotates in the opposite direction from the Earth! If you could see the Sun through its thick clouds, it would rise in the west and set in the east. This is called *retrograde* motion; the direction in which the Earth turns is called *prograde*.

A year on Venus takes less time than a day there! Because Venus turns so slowly, it revolves all the way around the Sun in less time than it takes to rotate once on its axis.

> One year on Venus = 224.7 Earth days

Venus passes between the Earth and the Sun about twice a century. This is called the *transit of Venus*. These transits always happen in pairs eight years apart. Since the telescope was invented, transits have been observed in 1631 and 1639; 1761 and 1769; and 1874 and 1882. On June 8, 2004, astronomers saw the tiny dot of Venus crawl across the Sun; the second in this pair of early twenty-first-century transits will occur on June 6, 2012.

> Venus spins on its axis once every 243 Earth days.

Given what he knew about Venus, George felt pretty sure that there wasn't any life to be found on that smelly, hot planet. He didn't even consider going to Eric's party dressed as a Venusian. Instead, he got his mom, Daisy, to help him with an outfit of dark-orange bobbly knitted clothes and a tall pointy hat so he looked just like the photo of the "Martian" they'd found.

Wearing his costume, George waved good-bye to his parents—who had a big evening planned helping

some eco-friends make organic treats for a party of their own—and squeezed through the gap in the fence between his garden and Eric's. The gap had come about when George's pet pig (given to him by his gran), Freddy, had escaped from his pigsty, barged through the fence, and broken into Eric's house via the back door. Following the trail of hoofprints that Freddy had left behind him, George had ended up meeting his new neighbors, who had only just moved into the empty house next door. This chance encounter with Eric and his family had changed George's life forever.

Eric had shown George his amazing computer, Cosmos, who was so smart and so powerful that he could draw doorways through which Eric; his daughter, Annie; and George could walk, to visit any part of the known Universe.

But space can be very dangerous, as George found out when one of their space adventures ended with Cosmos exploding from the sheer effort of mounting the rescue mission.

Since Cosmos had stopped working, George hadn't had another chance to step through the doorway and travel around the Solar System and beyond. He missed Cosmos, but at least he had Eric and Annie. He could see them anytime he wanted, even if he couldn't go on adventures into outer space with them.

George scampered up the garden path to Eric's back door. The house was brightly lit, with chatter and music pouring out. Opening the door, George let himself into the kitchen.

He couldn't see Annie, Eric, or Annie's mom, Susan, but there were lots of other people milling about: one grown-up immediately pushed a plate of shiny silver-iced muffins under his nose. "Have a meteorite!" he said cheerfully. "Or perhaps I should say, have a meteoroid!"

"Oh . . . um, well, thanks," said George, a bit startled. "They look delicious," he added, helping himself to one.

"If I did this," continued the man, tipping some of the muffins onto the floor, "then I could say, 'Have a meteorite!' because then they would have hit the ground. But when I offered them to you, suspended in the air, they were — technically — still meteoroids." He beamed at George and then at the muffins that were lying in a pile on the floor. "You get the distinction — a meteoroid is a chunk of rock that flies through the air; a meteor*ite* is what you call that piece of rock if it lands on the Earth. So now I've dropped them on the floor, we can call them meteorites."

With the muffin in his hand, George smiled politely, nodded, and started backing away slowly.

"Ouch!" He heard a squeak as he trod on someone behind him.

"Oops!" he said, turning around.

"It's okay, it's only me!" It was Annie, dressed all in black. "You couldn't have seen me, anyway, because I'm invisible!" She swiped the muffin out of George's hand and stuffed it into her mouth. "You only know I'm here because of the effect I have on objects around me. What does that make me?"

"A black hole, of course!" said George. "You swallow anything that comes near you, you greedy pig."

"Nope!" said Annie triumphantly. "I knew you'd say that, but that's wrong! I am"—she looked very pleased with herself—"dark matter."

"What's that?" asked George.

"No one knows," said Annie mysteriously. "We can't see it, but it seems to be absolutely essential to keep galaxies from flying apart. What are you?"

"Um, well," said George. "I'm the Man from Mars—y'know, from the pictures."

"Oh yeah!" said Annie. "You can be my Martian ancestor. That's cool."

Around them, the party was buzzing. Groups of the most oddly dressed grown-ups stood eating and drinking and talking at the tops of their voices. One man had come dressed as a microwave oven, another as a rocket. There was a lady wearing a badge shaped like an exploding star and a man with a mini satellite dish on his head. One scientist was bouncing around in a bright green suit, ordering people to "Take me to your leader"; another was blowing up an enormous balloon stamped with the words THE UNIVERSE IS INFLATING. A man dressed all in red kept standing next to people and then stepping away from them, daring them to guess what he was. Next to him was a scientist wearing lots of different-sized hula hoops around his middle, each one with a different-sized ball attached to it. When he walked, his hula hoops all spun around him.

"Annie," said George urgently, "I don't understand any of these costumes. What have these guests come as?"

"Um, well, they've all come as things you'd find in space, if you know how to look for them," said Annie.

"Like what?" asked George.

"Well, like the man dressed in red," explained Annie. "He keeps stepping away from people, which means he's pretending to be the redshift."

"The what?"

"If a distant object in the Universe, like a galaxy, is moving away from you, its light will appear more red than otherwise. So he's dressed in red, and he is moving *away* from people to show them he's come as the red-shift. And the others have come as all sorts of cosmic stuff that you'd find out there, like microwaves and faraway planets."

LIGHT AND HOW IT TRAVELS THROUGH SPACE

One of the most important things in the Universe is the *electromagnetic field*. It reaches everywhere; not only does it hold atoms together, but it also makes tiny parts of atoms (called *electrons*) bind different atoms together or create electric currents. Our everyday world is built from very large numbers of atoms stuck together by the electromagnetic field. Even living things, like human beings, rely on it to exist and to function.

Jiggling an electron creates waves in the field. This is like jiggling a finger in your bath and making ripples in the water. These waves are called *electromagnetic waves*, and because the field is everywhere, the waves can travel far across the Universe, until stopped by other electrons that can absorb their energy. They come in many different types, but some affect the human eye, and we know these as the various colors of visible light. Other types include radio waves, microwaves, infrared, ultraviolet, X rays, and gamma rays. Electrons are jiggled all the time by atoms that are constantly jiggling too, so there are always electromagnetic waves being produced by objects. At room temperature the waves are mainly infrared, but in much hotter objects the jiggling is more violent, and produces visible light.

Light travels at 186,000 miles per second. This is very fast, but light from the Sun still takes eight minutes to reach us; from the next nearest star it takes more than four years.

Very hot objects in space, such as stars, produce visible light, which may travel a very long way before hitting something. When you look at a star, the light from it may have been moving serenely through space for hundreds of years. It enters your eye and, by jiggling electrons in your retina, turns into electricity that is sent along the optic nerve to your brain. Your brain says, "I can see a star!" If the star is very far away, you may need a telescope to collect enough of the light for your eye to detect, or the jiggled electrons could instead create a photograph or send a signal to a computer.

The Universe is constantly expanding, inflating like a balloon. This means that distant stars and galaxies are moving away from Earth. This stretches their light as it travels through space toward us—the farther it travels, the more stretched it becomes. The stretching makes visible light look redder, which is known as the redshift. Eventually, if light traveled and redshifted far enough, the light would no longer be visible and would become first infrared, and then microwave (as used on Earth in microwave ovens), radiation. This is just what has happened to the incredibly powerful light produced by the Big Bang. After thirteen billion years of traveling, it is detectable today as microwaves coming from every direction in space. This has the grand title of *cosmic microwave background radiation*, and is nothing less than the afterglow of the Big Bang itself.

Annie said all this matter-of-factly, as though it were quite normal to know this kind of information and be able to rattle it off at parties. But once again George felt a little jealous of her. He loved science and was always reading books, looking up articles on the Internet, and pestering Eric with questions. He wanted to be a scientist when he grew up, so he could learn everything there was to know and maybe make some amazing discovery of his own. Annie, on the other hand, was much more casual about the wonders of the Universe.

When George had first met Annie, she'd wanted to be a ballerina, but now she'd changed her mind and decided on being a soccer player. Instead of spending her time after school in a pink-and-white tutu, she now charged around the backyard, hammering a soccer ball past George, who always had to be goalie. And yet she still seemed to know far more about science than he did.

Annie's dad, Eric, now appeared, dressed in his normal clothes and looking no different from usual.

"Eric," cried George, who was bursting with questions. "What have you come as?"

"Oh, me?" Eric smiled. "I'm the only intelligent lifeform in the Universe," he said modestly.

"What?" asked George. "You mean you're the only intelligent person in the whole Universe?"

Eric laughed. "Don't say that too loudly around here," he told George, gesturing to all the other scientists.

"Otherwise people will get very upset. I meant, I've come as a human being, which is the only intelligent form of life in the Universe that we know about. So far."

"Oh," said George. "But what about all your friends? What have they come as? And why does red light mean something is going away? I don't understand."

"Well," said Eric kindly, "you'd understand if some-one explained it to you."

"Can *you* explain it to me?" pleaded George. "All about the Universe? Like you did with the black holes? Can you tell me about red thingies and dark matter and everything else?"

"Oh dear," said Eric, sound-ing rather regretful. "George, I'd love to tell you all about the Universe, but the problem is, I'm just not sure I'll have time before I have to . . . Hang on a second . . ." He trailed off and gazed into the distance, the way he did when he was having an idea. He took off his glasses and polished them on his shirt, setting them on his nose at the same off-kilter angle as before. "I've got it!" he cried, sounding very excited. "I know what we need to do! Hold on, George, I've got a plan."

With that, he picked up a soft hammer and struck a huge brass gong, which rang out with a deep, humming chime.

"Right, gather round, everyone," said Eric, waving

27

everyone into the room. "Come on, come on, hurry up! I've got something to say."

A ripple of excitement went through the crowd.

"Now then," he went on, "I've gathered the Order of Science here today for this party—"

"Hurray!" cheered someone at the back.

"And I want us to put our minds to some questions my young friend George has asked me. He wants to know all sorts of things! For a start, I'm sure he'll want to know what your costume is!" He pointed to the man wearing the hula hoops.

"I've come to the party," piped up the cheerful-looking scientist, "as a distant planetary system where we might find another planet Earth."

"Annie," whispered George, "isn't that what Doctor Reeper did? Find new planets?"

Dr. Reeper was a former colleague of Eric's, who wanted to use science for his own selfish purposes. He had told Eric he'd found an exoplanet—that is, a planet in orbit around a star other than the Earth's Sun—that might be able to support human life. But the directions he'd given Eric had been bogus—in fact, in his search for the planet, they had sent Eric dangerously close to a black hole. Dr. Reeper had been trying to get rid of Eric so he could control Cosmos, Eric's supercomputer. But his evil trick hadn't worked, and Eric had returned safely from his trip inside a black hole.

No one knew where Dr. Reeper was now. He had

fled after his master plan backfired. At the time, George had begged Eric to do something about him, but Eric had just let him go.

"Doctor Reeper knew how to *look* for planets," said Annie, "but we don't know whether he ever actually found one. After all, that planet he wrote about in the letter to Dad? We never got to see whether it really existed or not."

"Thank you, Sam. And how many planets have you

found so far?" Eric questioned the hula hoop man.

"So far," replied Sam, shaking his hoops as he spoke, "more than seven hundred exoplanets in orbit around stars quite nearby. Some of these stars have more than one planet going around them." He pointed to his hula hoops. "I'm a nearby system with planets in orbit around its star."

"What does he mean by 'nearby'?" George whispered to Annie, who passed the message on to Eric. Her father whispered back to her, and she then relayed the answer to George.

"He means, maybe, like, about forty light-years away. So, like, about two hundred and thirty-five trillion miles," said Annie. "Nearby for the Universe!"

"Have you seen anything that might be like the Earth? A planet we could call home?"

"We've seen a few that might—and only might—be like a second Earth. Our planet-hunting search continues."

"Thank you, Sam," said Eric. "Now, what I want us to do is answer George's questions—all of us. Each of you"—he handed out pens and paper—"can write me a page or two by the end of the party about what you think is the most interesting part of the science you work on. You can send or e-mail it to me later if you don't have time to finish it now."

The scientists all looked really happy. They *loved* talking about the most interesting parts of their work.

"And," added Eric quickly, "before we get back to

the party, I've got one more brief announcement to make—one of my own this time. I'm very excited and pleased to tell you all that I have a new job! I'm going to work for the Global Space Agency, looking for signs of life in our Solar System. Beginning with Mars!"

"Wow!" said George. "That's amazing!" He turned to Annie, but she didn't meet his eye.

"So," continued Eric, "in just a few days' time, my family and I will be packing up . . . and moving to the headquarters of the Global Space Agency in the United States of America!"

With that, George's universe imploded.

Chapter 2

Georget hated watching his next-door neighbors pack up their house and get ready to leave. But he wanted to spend as much time with them as he could before they vanished from his life. So day after day, he went there and saw how the house got bigger and bigger inside as

more and more of the Bellises' things were swallowed up—first by big cardboard boxes marked with Global Space Agency stickers and then by the trucks that kept arriving to take them all away.

"It's so exciting!" Annie kept exclaiming. "We're going to America! We're going to be movie stars! We're going to eat huge burgers! We're going to see New York! We're going . . ." On and on she went about her fabulous new life and how much better everything would be when she was living in a different country. Sometimes George tried to suggest that

maybe it wouldn't be quite as amazing as she thought. But Annie was too carried away by her fantasy life in the United States to pay him much attention.

Eric and Susan tried a little harder to mask their excitement about the big move, so as not to hurt George's feelings. But even they couldn't hide it from him entirely. One day, when the house was nearly empty, George sat in Eric's library, helping him wrap his precious scientific objects in old newspaper and put them carefully into big boxes.

"You'll come back, won't you?" pleaded George. All the pictures had come off the walls now, and the shelves were nearly bare of the books that had lined the room. The house was starting to feel as empty and desolate as it had when they'd first moved in.

"That depends!" said Eric cheerfully. "Maybe I'll hitch a lift on the next mission into space and go out there forever." He caught sight of George's desolate face. "No, no, I don't mean that," he added hastily. "I couldn't leave you all behind. I'd make sure I had a way back to planet Earth."

"But will you come back and live here?" persisted George. "In your house?"

"It's not really my house," said Eric. "It's just a place I was given, where I could work on Cosmos without anyone finding out. But unfortunately, someone—or rather, Graham Reeper—was here already, lying in wait for me."

34

"How did Doctor Reeper know that you'd come here?" asked George, wrapping up an old telescope.

"Ah, well, looking back, of course I realize this place was a far more obvious choice than I realized," replied Eric. "You see, this house belonged to our former tutor, one of the greatest scientists who ever lived. No one knows where he is right now—he seems to have disappeared. But before that happened he wrote me a letter, offering me this house as a safe place to work on Cosmos. It was so important to keep Cosmos away from harm, but in the end, I just couldn't do that." He looked really sad.

George put down the telescope and reached for his schoolbag. He got out a package of sandwich cookies, ripped them open, and passed them over. Eric smiled at the sight of his favorite cookies. "I should really make us a cup of tea to go with your cookies," he said. "But I think I've packed the kettle."

George crunched the cookie between his teeth. "What I don't understand," he said, realizing this might be his last chance to ask, "is why you don't just build another Cosmos."

"If I could," said Eric, "I would. But my tutor, Graham Reeper, and I built the prototype of Cosmos together, many years ago. The modern version of Cosmos still has some of the original features from that first computer. That's why it's not possible for me to simply build another one. Without the other two, I'm not sure I know how. One of them has vanished and the other, Reeper—well, we know all about him. In a way"—Eric licked the cream out of the center of the cookie—"Cosmos breaking down has changed all our lives. Now that I don't have him, I have to look for other ways to continue my work on space. And it means I'm not always worrying that someone will find out about my supercomputer and try to steal him. We moved so many times in order to keep Cosmos out of danger. Poor Annie, she's lived in so many different houses. But this is the one where she's been happiest."

"You wouldn't know it," said George darkly. "She doesn't seem sad to be going."

"She doesn't want to leave you. You're her best friend," Eric told him. "She's going to miss you, George, even if she doesn't show it. She won't find another friend like you in a hurry."

George gulped. "I'll miss her, too," he muttered, turning bright red. "And you. And Susan."

"We'll see one another again," said Eric gently. "You won't be missing us forever. And if you ever need me, you know that you just have to let me know. I'll do anything I can for you, George."

"Um, thanks," murmered George. A thought struck him. "But is it safe for you to go?" he said, clutching at a ray of hope. "Shouldn't you stay here? What if Reeper follows you to the United States?"

"I don't think there's much poor, old Reeper can do to me now," said Eric sadly.

"'Poor, old Reeper'?" exclaimed George hotly. "He tried to throw you into a black hole! I don't understand why you feel sorry for him! I don't get it. Why didn't you do something about him when you had the chance?"

37

LUCY & STEPHEN HAWKING

"I've ruined enough of Reeper's life already," said Eric. George opened his mouth to speak, but Eric cut him off. "Look, George," he said firmly, "Reeper's confronted me already, and I expect that's enough for him. He's had his revenge, and I don't think I'll be hearing from him again. Anyway, Cosmos doesn't work anymore, so I don't have anything that Reeper would want. I'm safe, my family is safe, and now I want to go to the Global Space Agency. They've offered me the chance to work on finding signs of life on Mars and in other places in the Solar System. You do understand I couldn't refuse?"

"S'pose so," said George. "Will you tell me if you find anyone out there in space?"

"I most certainly will," promised Eric. "You'll be among the first to know. And, George . . . I want you to keep this telescope." He pointed to the bronze cylinder that George had been carefully wrapping in paper. "It's to remind you to keep looking at the stars."

"Really?" said George with wonder, unwrapping the telescope again and feeling the cool, smooth metal under his hand. "But isn't it very valuable?"

"Well, so are you. And so are the observations you'll make when you use it. To help you, I've got another special good-bye present for you." Eric dived into a nearby pile of books and finally—triumphantly—came up with a bright yellow volume that he waved in the air at George. On the front in big letters it said: *The User's Guide to the Universe*.

38

"Do you remember," he asked George, "when I asked all my science friends at the party to write a page for me, answering some of the questions you posed? Well, I made their answers into a book—one for you and one for Annie. Here it is! When you read it, remember that I wanted you to understand something about being a scientist. I wanted to show you that me and my friends love to read one another's work and talk about it. We exchange our theories and our ideas, and that's one of the really important—and fun—parts of being a scientist: having colleagues who help, inspire, and challenge you. That's what this book is all about. I thought maybe you'd like to look at the first few pages with me. I wrote them myself," he added modestly.

Eric started to read.

39

WHY DO WE GO INTO SPACE?

Why do we go into space? Why go to all that effort and spend all that money just for a few lumps of Moon rock? Aren't there better things we could be doing here on Earth?

Well, it's a bit like Europe before 1492. Back then, people thought it was a big waste of money to send Christopher Columbus off on a wild-goose chase. But then he discovered America, and that made a huge difference. Just think—if he hadn't, we wouldn't have the Big Mac. And lots of other things, of course.

Spreading out into space will have an even greater effect. It will completely change the future of the human race; it could decide whether we have a future at all.

It won't solve any of our immediate problems on planet Earth, but it will help us look at them in a different way. The time has come when we need to look outward across the Universe rather than inward at ourselves on an increasingly overcrowded planet.

Moving the human race out into space won't happen quickly. By that I mean it could take hundreds, or even thousands, of years. We could have a base on the Moon within thirty years, reach Mars in fifty years, and explore the moons of the outer planets in two hundred years. By *reach*, I mean with manned—or should I say *personed*?—flight. We have already driven rovers on Mars and landed a probe on Titan, a moon of Saturn, but when we're dealing with the future of the human race, we have to go there ourselves and not just send robots.

But go where? Now that astronauts have lived for months on the International Space Station, we know that human beings can survive away from planet Earth. But we also know that living in zero gravity on the Space Station doesn't just make it difficult to have a cup of tea! It's not very good for people to live in zero gravity for a long time, so if we're to have a base in space, we need it to be on a planet or moon.

So which one shall we choose? The most obvious is the Moon. It is close and quite easy to get to. We've already landed on the Moon, and driven across it in a buggy. On the other hand, the Moon is small and without an atmosphere or a magnetic field to deflect the solar wind particles, like on Earth. There is no liquid water, but there may be ice in the craters at the north and south poles. A colony on the Moon could use this as a source of oxygen, with power provided by nuclear energy or solar panels. The Moon could be a base for travel to the rest of the Solar System.

What about Mars? That's our next obvious target. Mars is farther from the Sun than planet Earth is, so it gets less warmth from the sunlight, making temperatures much colder. Once, Mars had a magnetic field, but that decayed four billion years ago: It was stripped of most of its atmosphere, leaving it with only 1% of the pressure of the Earth's atmosphere.

In the past, the atmospheric pressure—which means the weight of the air above you in the atmosphere—must have been higher because we can see what appear to be dried-up channels and lakes. Liquid water cannot exist on Mars now, as it would just evaporate.

However, there is lots of water in the form of ice at the two poles. If we went to live on Mars, we could use this. We could also use the minerals and metals that volcanoes have brought to the surface.

So the Moon and Mars might be quite good for us. But where else could we go in the Solar System? Mercury and Venus are way too hot, while Jupiter and Saturn are gas giants, with no solid surface.

We could try the moons of Mars, but they are very small. Some of the moons of Jupiter and Saturn might be better. Titan, a moon of Saturn, is larger and more massive than our Moon, and has a dense atmosphere. The Cassini-Huygens mission of NASA and ESA, the European Space Agency, has landed a probe on Titan, which sent back pictures of the surface. However, it is very cold, being so far from the Sun, and I wouldn't like to live next to a lake of liquid methane.

What about beyond our Solar System? From looking across the Universe, we know that quite a few stars have planets in orbit around them. Until recently we could see only giant planets the size of

Jupiter or Saturn. But now we are starting to spot smaller Earth-like planets, too. Some of these will lie in the Goldilocks Zone, where their distances from the home star is in the right range for liquid water to exist on their surfaces. There are maybe a thousand stars within ten light-years of Earth. If 1% of these have an Earth-size planet in the Goldilocks Zone, we have ten candidate new worlds.

At the moment we can't travel very far across the Universe. In fact, we can't even imagine how we might be able to cover such huge distances. But that's what we should be aiming to do in the future, over the next two hundred to five hundred years. The human race has existed as a separate species for about two million years. Civilization began about ten thousand years ago, and the rate of development has been steadily increasing. We have now reached the stage where we can boldly go where no one has gone before. And who knows what we will find and who we will meet?

Good luck on all your cosmic journeys, and I hope you find this book useful.

Interstellar best wishes,

Eric

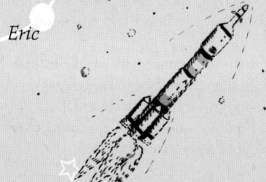

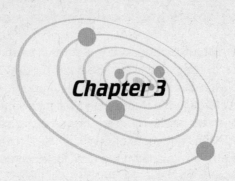

Chapter 3

Finally, the day came when the doors slammed on the last vanload of Eric, Annie, and Susan's belongings, and they were standing in the street, saying goodbye to George and his parents.

"Don't worry!" said George's dad. "I'll keep an eye on the house for you. Might tidy up the garden a bit." He gave Eric a firm handshake, which made the scientist turn rather pale and rub his hand afterward.

George's mom hugged Annie. "Who's going to kick a ball over my fence now?" she said. "My vegetable patch is going to find life very quiet."

Annie whispered something in her ear. Daisy smiled. "Of course you can." She turned to George. "Annie would like to say good-bye to Freddy," she told him.

George nodded, not wanting to speak, in case his voice wobbled. In silence, the two of them went through George's house and out into the backyard.

"Good-bye, Freddy," cooed Annie, leaning over the pigsty. "I'm going to miss you so much!"

George took a deep breath. "Freddy's going to miss you too," he said, his voice squeaking from the effort of holding back the tears. "He really likes you," he added. "He's had a really great time since you've been here. It isn't going to be the same once you're gone."

"I've had a great time as well," said Annie sadly.

"Freddy hopes you don't find another pig in America that you like as much as him," said George.

"I'll *never* like another pig as much as Freddy," declared Annie. "He's my best pig ever!"

"Annie!" they heard Susan calling through the house. "Annie, we have to go!"

"Freddy thinks you're the best," said George. "And he'll be waiting for you when you get back."

"Bye, George," said Annie.

"Bye, Annie," said George. "See you in space."

Annie walked slowly away. George climbed into the pigsty and sat on the warm straw. "It's just you and me now, Freddy, my cosmic pig," he said sadly. "Just like it was before."

After Eric, Susan, and Annie had left, it seemed horribly quiet in the backyard. The days stretched on and on, each one pretty much the same as the last. There was nothing particularly wrong with George's life these days. The horrible Dr. Reeper had left the school, and now that George had won the big science competition, he had found some friends to spend his lunch breaks with. The bullies who had given him such a hard time when Dr. Reeper was around tended to leave him alone these days. At home, George had his computer, so he could find out interesting stuff for his homework—or about science in general, in which he was more and more interested—and send e-mails to his friends. He regularly logged on to the various space sites to read about all the new discoveries. He loved looking at the pictures taken by space-based observatories, like the Hubble Space Telescope, and reading accounts of space journeys by astronauts.

But although this was all really fascinating, it wasn't the same without Annie and her family to share these discoveries with. Each night, George looked up into the sky with the hope of seeing a shooting star fall toward Earth, as a sign that his cosmic adventures were not yet over. But one never came.

Then one day, just as he had given up hope, he got a very surprising e-mail from Annie. He'd written to her lots of times, and in return received rambling messages full of long, boring stories about kids he'd never met.

But this message was different. It read:

George, Mom and Dad have written to your parents to ask you to come and stay over summer vacation. YOU MUST COME! The fact is, I need you. Have COSMIC mission! Do not chicken out!! Elderly loons are useless, so say nothing of space adventures to them. Even Dad says NO, which is situation serious. So pretend is normal trip. SPACE SUITS AT THE READY! YRS IN THE UNIVERSE, xxx A

George e-mailed her right back.

What?? When?? Where??

But her reply was short.

Can say no more for now. Make plans to come. Raid bank for ticket and get here, xx A

George just sat there, staring at the screen, in shock. There was nothing he wanted more than to go and see Annie and her family in Florida. He would go in a heartbeat even if there wasn't an adventure. But how? How would he get there? What if his parents said no? Would he have to run away from home and hide on an ocean liner to get there? Or sneak onto an airplane when no one was looking? He'd slipped out into space through a computer-generated portal when he wasn't supposed to. But getting to America suddenly seemed far more complicated than fishing someone out of a black hole. *Life on Earth . . .* , he thought. *Much trickier than life in space.*

Then he had a good idea. *Gran. That's who I need.* He e-mailed her.

Dear Gran. Must go to America. Have been invited to stay with a friend but need to go SOON! Is very very important. Sorry can't explain. Can you help me?

The answer pinged back in just a few seconds.

On my way over, George. Sit tight, all will be well. Love Gran

Sure enough, just an hour later, there was a ferocious banging on the front door. George's dad went to open it, but as soon as he did, he was barged out of the way by his mother, who was waving a cane and looking very angry.

"Terence, George must go to America to stay with his friends," she announced, without so much as a hello. She brandished her walking stick at George's dad.

"Mother," he said, looking furious, "how dare you interfere?"

"I can't hear you—I'm deaf, you know," she said, thrusting a notebook and pen at him.

"Mother, I am very well aware of that," he said through gritted teeth.

"You'll have to write it down!" said Gran. "I can't hear you! I can't hear a word you say."

George going to Florida—or not—is none of your business, he wrote in her notepad.

Gran looked over at George and winked craftily at him. He flashed a quick smile back.

George's mom had come in from the garden and was wiping her muddy hands on a towel. "That's very odd, George," she said quietly, "because it was only this morning that we opened a letter from Susan and Eric, inviting you to visit during your summer vacation. How does your gran know about this already?"

"Um, perhaps Gran is psychic?" said George quickly.

"I see," said his mom, giving him a funny look. "The thing is, George, Eric and Susan told me they were asking us first, before you knew about the invitation, in case it wasn't possible for you to come. They didn't want you to be disappointed if it didn't work out. And, you see, we just can't afford the fare, George."

"Then I'll pay for him to go," retorted Gran.

"Oh, you heard that, did you?" said George's dad, who was still scribbling away in the notebook.

"I lip-read," said Gran hastily. "I can't hear a thing. I'm deaf, you know!"

You can't afford to send George to America! George's mom wrote in her notepad.

"Don't you tell me what I can and can't do!" said Gran. "I've got pots of money, all hidden under the floorboards. More than I know how to spend. And if you silly people won't let him go by himself, then I'll fly out with him. I've got some friends in Florida whom I haven't seen in years." She grinned at George. "What do you say, George?" she asked.

With a huge smile on his face, George nodded at her so many times, his head looked like it might fall off. But then he turned to his parents to see how they were taking it. He couldn't believe they would agree to any of this, especially since it meant traveling on an airplane—something his mom and dad didn't approve of, in theory.

But Gran had thought of that problem already. "You know," she said airily, "I don't see why it should be just George and I who get to go away. After all, Terence, you and Daisy haven't been anywhere exciting for a very long time. There must be somewhere you'd like to go—somewhere in the world you could do some good; somewhere you could really make a difference, if only you had the time and the ticket to get there."

George's dad gasped, and George realized that clever Gran had spoken right to his heart.

"Isn't there something you'd love to do?" she persisted.

Her son wasn't looking angry anymore but hopeful instead. "You know," he said to George's mom, "*if* George did go to Florida for summer vacation and Mother would help us out with the airfares, it would mean that we could go on that other trip ourselves— the eco-mission to the South Pacific."

She looked thoughtful. "I suppose we could," she mused. "I'm sure Eric and Susan would take good care of George."

"Excellent!" piped up Gran, intent on closing the deal before anyone could change their minds. "It's a plan. George goes to Florida and you can have a vacation—I mean, save the world," she corrected herself quickly. "I'll buy the tickets for everyone and we'll be off."

George's dad shook his head at his mother. "Sometimes I think you only hear what you want to hear."

Gran just smiled regretfully and pointed to her ears. "Didn't catch that," she said firmly. "Not a word."

George felt the laughter bubbling up inside him. Because of Gran, he might be going to America! Where Annie was waiting for him with some hot news about her discovery. He felt a bit guilty about his mom and dad. They thought they were sending him off for a nice, safe, quiet vacation in a different country. But George knew enough about Annie's way of working to suspect it was going to be anything but safe and quiet. And she'd mentioned the space suits in her message—the ones they'd worn to fly around the Solar System. It must mean she had uncovered a secret that had to do with space, and she wanted him to travel out there with her once more. He held his breath while he waited for his mom to speak.

"All right, then," she said, after the longest pause. "If Gran is offering to take you to Florida, and Eric and Susan will meet you the minute your plane touches down and take care of you the whole time, I suppose I have to say *yes*!"

"YES!" said George, punching the air. "Thanks, Mom, thanks, Dad, thanks, Gran. Better go pack!" With that, like a little whirlwind, he was gone.

* * *

It was so exciting to be packing to go on a journey rather than watching other people fill their suitcases. George had no idea what to take with him so he just threw things around his room for a while and made an incredible mess.

He didn't know much about America, just what he'd seen on TV shows when he'd been at friends' houses. That didn't give him much of a clue to what he might need in Florida. A skateboard? Some cool clothes? He didn't have either. He packed some of his books and clothes and put his precious copy of *The User's Guide to the Universe* in his schoolbag, which he was using as his carry-on luggage for the plane. As for packing for a trip into space, George knew that astronauts only took a change of clothes and some chocolate with them, but then they went up in spaceships, and he doubted even Annie had managed to arrange for one of them.

As George got ready to leave, so did his parents. They had decided they would go on the eco-mission while he was in the United States. They were going to join a ship in the South Pacific that was helping some islanders whose lives were being threatened by rising seawater.

"We'll be in touch as often as we can from the sinking islands—by e-mail or phone," George's dad told him. "Find out how you're doing. Eric and Susan have promised to look after you. And Gran"—he sighed—"will be nearby, if you need her." Even Freddy the pig got to take a vacation—he was going to spend the summer at a local children's farm.

George couldn't sleep at all the night before the flight. He was off to America to see his best friend and maybe, just maybe, go out into space again. He'd flown around the Solar System before, but he'd never actually been on an airplane, so that was exciting too. Before, he'd been far away in outer space, but this time he would be flying through the Earth's atmosphere. He would be traveling through the part where the sky is still blue, before it turns to the black of space.

On the plane, he looked out of the window at the white, fluffy clouds below. Above them, he could see the Sun, the star at the center of our Solar System, radiating down heat and energy. Below was his planet, which he saw in snatches when the clouds parted.

Gran slept for most of the journey, giving out tiny gentle whooshes of air, just like Freddy did when he was dozing. While she slept, George got out *The User's Guide to the Universe* and read about another voyage—this one not just across our planet but across our whole Universe.

* * *

A VOYAGE ACROSS THE UNIVERSE

We will now go on a voyage across the Universe.

Before setting out we must understand what we mean by the terms *voyage* and *universe*. The word *universe* literally means "everything that exists." However, the history of astronomy might be regarded as a sequence of steps, at each of which the Universe has appeared to get bigger. So what we mean by "everything" has changed.

Nowadays most cosmologists accept the Big Bang theory, according to which the Universe started in a state of great compression around fourteen billion years ago. This means that the farthest we can see is the distance that light has traveled since the Big Bang. This defines the size of the *observable* Universe.

So what is meant by a *voyage*? First we must distinguish between *peering* across the Universe and *traveling* across it. *Peering* is what astronomers do and, as we will see, involves looking back in time. *Traveling* is what astronauts do and involves crossing space. This also involves another kind of voyage. For as we travel from the Earth to the edge of the observable Universe, we are essentially retracing the history of human thought about the scale of the Universe. We will now discuss these three journeys.

The Voyage Back Through Time

The information astronomers receive comes from electromagnetic waves that travel at the speed of light (186,000 miles per second). This is very fast, but it is finite and astronomers often measure distance by the equivalent light travel time. Light takes several minutes to reach us from the Sun, for instance, but years from the nearest star, millions of years from the nearest big galaxy (Andromeda), and many billions of years from the most distant galaxies.

This means that as one peers across greater *distances*, one is also looking farther into the *past*. For example, if we observe a galaxy ten million light-years *away*, we are seeing it as it was ten million years *ago*. A voyage across the Universe in this sense is therefore not only a journey through *space*; it is also a journey back through *time*— right back to the Big Bang itself.

We cannot actually observe all the way back to the Big Bang. The early Universe was so hot that it formed a fog of particles that we cannot see through. As the Universe expanded, it cooled and the fog lifted about four hundred thousand years after the Big Bang. However, we can still use our theories to speculate what the Universe was like before then. Since the density and temperature increase as we go back in time, our speculation depends on our theories of high energy physics, but we now have a fairly complete picture of the history of the Universe.

One might expect that our voyage back through time would end at the Big Bang. However, scientists are now trying to understand the physics of creation itself and any mechanism that can produce our Universe could, in principle, generate others. For example, some people believe the Universe undergoes cycles of expansion and re-collapse, giving us universes strung out in time. Others think that our Universe is just one of many "bubbles" spread out in space. These are variants of what is called the *multiverse* proposal.

The Voyage Across Space

Physically *traveling* across the Universe is much more challenging because of the time it would take. Einstein's special theory of relativity (1905) suggests that no spaceship could travel faster than the speed of light. This means it would take at least one hundred thousand years to cross the Galaxy and ten billion years to cross the Universe—at least as judged by someone who stays on Earth. But special relativity also predicts that time flows more slowly for moving observers, so the trip could be much quicker for the astronauts themselves. Indeed, if one could travel at the speed of light, no time at all would pass!

No spaceship can travel as fast as light, but one could still approach this maximum speed. The time experienced would then be much shorter than that on Earth. For example, a journey across the Galaxy at nearly the speed of light would seem to take only thirty years, while much more time would have passed on Earth. One could therefore return to Earth in one's own lifetime, although one's friends would have died long ago. If one continued to accelerate beyond the Galaxy for a century, one could, in principle, travel to the edge of the currently observable Universe!

Einstein's general theory of relativity (1915) could allow even more exotic possibilities. For example, maybe astronauts could one day use wormholes or space warp effects—just like in *Star Trek* and other popular science-fiction series—to make these journeys even faster and get home again without losing any friends. But this is all very speculative.

The Voyage Through the History of Human Thought

To the ancient Greeks, the Earth (*geos*) was the center of the Universe (*cosmos*), with the planets, the Sun (*helios*), and the stars being relatively close. This *geocentric* view was demolished in the sixteenth century, when Copernicus showed that the Earth and other planets move around the Sun. However, this *heliocentric* picture did not last very long. Several decades later, Galileo used his newly invented telescope to show that the Milky Way—then known only as a band of light in the sky—consists of numerous stars like the Sun. This discovery not only diminished the status of the Sun, it also vastly increased the size of the known Universe.

By the eighteenth century it was accepted that the Milky Way is a disk of stars (the Galaxy) held together by gravity. However, most astronomers still assumed that the Milky Way comprised the whole Universe, and this *galactocentric* (*galactos* = milk) view persisted well into the twentieth century. Then, in 1924, Edwin Hubble measured the distance to our nearest neighboring galaxy (Andromeda) and showed that it had to be well outside the Milky Way. Another shift in the size of the Universe!

Within a few more years, Hubble had obtained data on several dozen nearby galaxies, which showed that they are all moving away from us at a speed that is proportional to their distance from us. The easiest way to picture this is to think of space itself as expanding, just like the surface of an inflating balloon onto which the galaxies are painted. This expansion is known as Hubble's Law, and it has now been shown to apply up to distances of tens of billions of light-years, a region containing hundreds of billions of galaxies. Yet another huge shift of scale!

The *cosmocentric* view regards this as the final shift in the size of the Universe. This is because the cosmic expansion means that as one goes back in time the galaxies get closer together and eventually merge. Before that, the density just continues to increase—back to the Big Bang fourteen billion years ago—and we can never see *beyond* the distance traveled by light since then. However, recently there has been an interesting observational development. Although one expects the expansion of the Universe to slow down because of gravity, current observations suggest that it is actually *accelerating*. Theories to explain this suggest that our observable Universe could be a part of a much larger "bubble." And this bubble could itself be just one of many bubbles, as in the multiverse proposal!

What Next?

So the end point of all three of our journeys—the first back through time, the second across space, and the third retracing the history of human thought—is the same: those unobservable universes that can only be glimpsed through theories and visited in our minds!

I wonder what tomorrow's astronomers will discover. . . .

Bernard

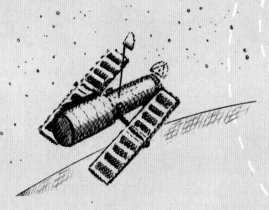

When the plane landed, George and Gran joined the line to get through immigration and customs. Eric and Annie were waiting in the arrivals area. Annie shrieked and jumped up and down on the other side of the barrier as soon as she saw him.

"George!" she hollered. "George!" She ducked under the rail and grabbed him. She was taller and more tan than he remembered. She hugged him and whispered in his ear, "It is sooooo good you are here! Can't tell you now, but we are in an emergency! But remember, shush!

Say nothing." She took his cart and careered off with it toward Eric. Gran and George hurried after her.

George had a shock when he saw Eric. He looked so tired, with some strands of white in his dark hair. But he smiled when he saw George, and his face lit up just like it used to.

They said their hellos, and Gran shook hands with Eric and got him to write down comments in her notebook. Then she gave him an envelope marked *George's Emergency Fund*, hugged her grandson, grinned at

Annie, and went off to greet her friends, who had come to the airport to meet her. "A bunch of old rogues and rebels from my past, who live near Eric and Susan," she had told George. "Nice chance for us to relive some of our hijinks."

But the people who came to pick up Gran were so old and wobbly-looking, George couldn't imagine them ever being young, let alone having an adventure. Gran tottered off into the distance with them, and he felt his stomach shrink as he watched her leave. It seemed very big and bright here in America—everything was much shinier and larger and louder than it was at home. A wave of homesickness struck him. But not for long.

A smaller boy with thick glasses and a very peculiar

hairstyle had appeared from behind Eric.

"Greetings, George," he said earnestly. "Annie"—he shot her a look of total disgust—"has told me all about you. I have been eagerly anticipating interfacing with you. You sound a most interesting person."

"Back off, Emmett," said Annie fiercely. "George is *my* friend, and he's come to see *me*, not you."

"George, this is Emmett," Eric told him calmly, while Annie glared at Emmett and Emmett looked away with pursed lips. "He is the son of one of my friends. Emmett is staying with us for a while this summer."

"He's the son of doom, more likely," Annie whispered in George's ear.

Emmett snuck around to George's other side and hissed in his other ear, "The girl humanoid is a total moron."

"As maybe you can tell," continued Eric lightly, "there's been a small falling-out between these two."

"I told him not to touch my Girl's World action doll!" Annie exploded. "And now it only speaks Klingon."

"I didn't ask her to cut my hair," Emmett bleated. "And now I look stupid."

"You looked stupid before," muttered Annie.

"Better to speak Klingon than just garbage like you," retorted Emmett. His big eyes, magnified by his glasses, looked very shiny.

"George has had a long journey," said Eric firmly. "So we are going to take him to the car and drive home, and everyone is going to be nice to everyone else. Do you hear me?" He sounded quite stern.

"Yes!" said George.

"It's all right, George," said Eric. "You're always nice. It's the other two I'm worried about."

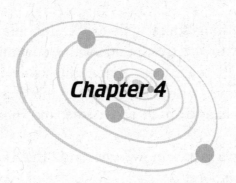

Chapter 4

Eric drove them to the big white wooden house where his family now lived. The sun was beating down from the perfectly blue sky, and the heat rose up from the ground to smack George in the face as he got out of the car. Annie scrambled out after him. "Come on," she said as Eric unloaded George's bag from the trunk. "We've got work to do. Follow me." She took him around to the back of the house, where a huge tree shaded a veranda with a table and chairs on it.

"Up the tree!" Annie instructed him. "It's the only place we can talk!" She shinned up to a large overhanging branch. George slowly clambered after her. Susan had come out onto the veranda, carrying a tray. She stood underneath Annie and George, with Emmett close behind her.

"Hello, George!" she called up into the tree. "It's nice to see you! Even if I can't actually see you."

"Hello, Susan," George called back. "Thanks for inviting me."

"Annie, don't you think George might like a rest?

And something to eat and drink after his journey?"

"Give it to the tree," said Annie, sticking her head out through the papery green-and-white leaves. She reached down with an arm and grabbed a juice box, which she handed back to George, and then a load of cookies.

"Okay, we're good now!" she sang. "Bye, other people! You can vamoose!"

Emmett just stood there, looking longingly up into the tree.

"Can Emmett come up and join you?" asked Susan.

"Quite literally," said Annie, "no. He might fall out of one of the brancheroonies and damage his amazing brain cell count. Better stay safely on the ground. Ciao, you guys! George and I are busy."

From the tree, they heard Susan sigh. "Why don't you sit here?" she said to Emmett, arranging a chair for him under the branches. "I'm sure they'll come down soon."

Emmett made a small snuffling noise, and they heard Susan comforting him.

"Ignore him—he's a total crybaby!" Annie whispered to George. "And don't start feeling sorry for him—that's lethal. The minute you show weakness, he pounces. I felt sorry for him the first time he cried. And then he bit me. My mom's too sappy—she just can't see it."

Susan's footsteps tapped away into the house.

"Okay, hold on to that branch," ordered Annie, "in case you faint away in shock at what I have to tell you."

"What is it?" said George.

"Huge news," confirmed Annie. "So huge-ously huge, your bottom will fall through your pants in surprise." She looked at him expectantly.

"Well, tell me," said George patiently.

"Promise you won't think I've gone bananas?"

"Um, well, I pretty much thought you were already," admitted George. "So that won't change anything."

Annie swatted him with her free hand.

"Ouch!" he said, laughing. "That hurt."

"George, are you okay?" came a little voice from below. "Do you need protection from the renegade one? She can be really evil."

"Shut up, Emmett!" Annie shouted down. "And stop listening to our conversation."

"I'm not trying to listen!" came Emmett's high-pitched whine. "It's not my fault that you're sending a stream of useless vibrations into the atmosphere."

"Then go somewhere else!" yelled Annie.

"No!" said Emmett obstinately. "I'm staying here in case George needs my superintelligent assistance. I don't want him to waste his bandwidth on your rudimentary communication."

Annie rolled her eyes up to heaven and sighed. She inched along the branch toward George and whispered in his ear: "I've had a message from aliens."

"Aliens!" said George loudly, forgetting about Emmett below. "You've had a message from aliens!"

"Shush!" said Annie frantically. But it was too late.

"Does the young female humanoid really believe that a life-form intelligent enough to send a message across the vast expanse of space would pick her to receive it?" said Emmett, standing up and looking into the tree. "And anyway, there are no aliens. We have no proof of another intelligent life-form in the Universe at this moment. We can only calculate the probability that on some other planets, there are conditions suitable for forms of extremophile bacteria. Which would have the approximate IQ level of Annie herself. Or probably a bit more. I can calculate the probability of intelligent life for you, if you like, using the Drake Equation.'

THE DRAKE EQUATION

The Drake Equation isn't really an equation. It's a series of questions that helps us to work out how many intelligent civilizations with the ability to communicate there might be in our Galaxy. It was formulated in 1961 by Dr. Frank Drake of the SETI Institute, and is still used by scientists today.

This is the Drake Equation:

$$N = N^* \times f_p \times n_e \times f_l \times f_i \times f_c \times L$$

N^* represents the number of new stars born each year in the Milky Way Galaxy

Question: What is the birthrate of stars in the Milky Way Galaxy?
Answer: Our Galaxy is about twelve billion years old, and contains roughly three hundred billion stars. So, on average, stars are born at a rate of three hundred billion divided by twelve billion, equaling twenty-five stars per year.

f_p is the fraction of those stars that have planets around them

Question: What percentage of stars have planetary systems?
Answer: Current estimates range from 20% to 70%.

n_e is the number of planets per star that are capable of sustaining life

Question: For each star that does have a planetary system, how many planets are capable of sustaining life?
Answer: Current estimates range from 0.5 to 5.

f_l is the fraction of planets in n_e where life evolves

Question: On what percentage of the planets that are capable of sustaining life does life actually evolve?
Answer: Current estimates range from 100% (where life can evolve, it will) down to close to 0%.

f_i is the fraction of habitable planets with life where intelligent life evolves

- -

Question: On the planets where life does evolve, what percentage evolves intelligent life?

Answer: Estimates range from 100% (intelligence has such a survival advantage that it will certainly evolve) down to near 0%.

f_c is the fraction of planets with intelligent life capable of interstellar communication

- -

Question: What percentage of intelligent races have the means and the desire to communicate?

Answer: 10% to 20%.

L is the average number of years that a communicating civilization continues to communicate

- -

Question: How long do communicating civilizations last?

Answer: This is the toughest of the questions. If we take Earth as an example, we've been communicating with radio waves for less than one hundred years. How long will our civilization continue to communicate with this method? Could we destroy ourselves in a few years, or will we overcome our problems and survive for ten thousand years or more?

When all of these variables are multiplied together, we come up with:

N, the number of communicating civilizations in the galaxy.

"Well, thanks for that, Professor Emmett," said Annie. "Your Nobel Prize is in the mail. So now why don't you bacteria off yourself? Go find some of your own species to hang out with? Actually, George, there *are* aliens on Earth, and Emmett is one of them."

"No, no, rewind," said George urgently. "You've had a message from some aliens? Where? How? What did it say?"

"They sent her a text message to say they would be beaming her up to the mother ship at twenty-one hundred hours," said Emmett. "We live in hope."

"Shut up, Emmett." This time it was George's turn to feel annoyed. "I want to hear what Annie has to say."

"Okay, here's the scoop!" said Annie. "Settle down, friends and aliens, and prepare to be amazed."

Below them, Emmett was hugging the tree in an attempt to get closer to them.

George smiled. "I'm prepared, agent Annie," he said. "Go for it."

"My amazing story," began Annie, "starts one ordinary evening when no one could have predicted that for the first time ever in the history of this planet we would finally hear from an ET.

"Me, my family, and I—," she continued grandly.

"And me!" squeaked Emmett from below.

"And him," she added, "had just come back from watching a robot land on Mars. Just your everyday family outing. Nothing special. Except that . . ."

* * *

A few weeks back, Eric, Susan, Annie, and Emmett had gone to the Global Space Agency to watch a new type of robot attempt to land on the red planet. The robot, Homer, had taken nine months to travel the 423 million miles to Mars. He was the latest in a series of robots sent by the agency to explore the planet.

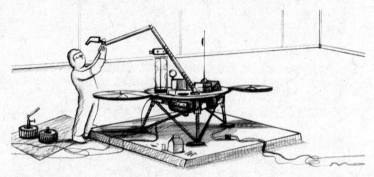

Eric was very excited about Homer touching down on Mars because he had special equipment on board that would help him find out whether there had ever been any life on our nearest neighbor. Homer would be looking for water on Mars: Using a special scoop at the end of his long robotic arm, he would scrabble through the icy surface of Mars to pick up handfuls of mud, which he would then bake in a special oven. As Homer heated up the samples of soil, he would be able to discover whether Mars, now a cold desert planet, had once, in its distant, warmer, wetter past, been flowing with water.

ROBOTIC SPACE TRAVEL

A space probe is a robotic spacecraft that scientists send out on a journey across the Solar System in order to gather more information about our cosmic neighborhood. Robotic space missions aim to answer specific questions such as: "What does the surface of Venus look like?" "Is it windy on Neptune?" "What is Jupiter made of?"

While robotic space missions are much less glamorous than manned spaceflight, they have several big advantages:

- Robots can travel for great distances, going much farther and faster than any astronaut. Like manned missions, they need a source of power: Most use solar arrays that convert sunlight to energy, but others traveling long distances away from the Sun take their own onboard generator. However, robotic spacecraft need far less power than a manned mission, as they don't need to maintain a comfortable living environment on their journey.

- Robots don't need supplies of food or water, and they don't need oxygen to breathe, making them much smaller and lighter than a manned spacecraft.

- Robots don't get bored or homesick or fall ill on their journey.

- If something goes wrong with a robotic mission, no lives are lost in space.

- Space probes cost far less than manned spaceflights, and robots don't want to come home when their mission ends.

Space probes have opened up the wonders of the Solar System to us, sending back data that has allowed scientists to far better understand how the Solar System was formed and what conditions are like on other planets. While human beings have, to date, traveled only as far as the Moon—a journey averaging 234,000 miles (376,000 kilometers)—space probes have covered billions of miles and shown us extraordinary and detailed images of the far reaches of the Solar System.

In fact, almost thirty space probes reached the Moon before mankind did! Robotic spacecraft have now been sent to all the other planets in our Solar System, they have caught the

dust from a comet's tail, landed on Mars and Venus, and traveled out beyond Pluto. Some space probes have even taken information about our planet and the human race with them. Probes *Pioneer 10* and *11* carry engraved plaques with the image of a man and a woman on them and also a map, showing where the probe came from. As the *Pioneer*s journey onward into deep space, they may one day encounter an alien civilization!

The *Voyager* probes took photographs of cities, landscapes, and people on Earth with them, as well as a recorded greeting in many different Earth languages. In the incredibly unlikely event of these probes being picked up by another civilization, these greetings assure any aliens who manage to decode them that we are a peaceful planet and we wish any other beings in our Universe well.

There are different types of space probes, and the type used for a particular mission will depend on the question that the probe is attempting to answer. Some probes fly by planets and take pictures for us, passing by several planets on their long journeys. Others orbit a specific planet to gain more information about it and its moons. Another type of probe is designed to land and send back data from the surface of another world. Some of these are rovers, others remain fixed wherever they land.

The first rover, *Lunokhod 1*, was part of a Russian probe, *Luna 17*, which landed on the Moon in 1970. *Lunokhod 1* was a robotic vehicle that could be steered from Earth, in much the same way as a remote control car.

NASA's Mars landers, *Viking 1* and *Viking 2*, which touched down on the red planet in 1976, gave us our first pictures from the surface of the planet, which had intrigued people on Earth for millennia. The *Viking* landers showed the reddish-brown plains scattered with rocks, the pink sky of Mars, and even frost on the ground in winter. Unfortunately, it is very difficult to land on Mars, and several probes sent to the red planet have crashed onto the surface.

ROBOTIC SPACE TRAVEL (continued)

Later missions to Mars sent the two rovers, *Spirit* and *Opportunity*. Designed to drive around for at least three months, they lasted for far longer and also, like other spacecraft sent to Mars, found evidence that Mars had been shaped by the presence of water. In 2007, NASA sent the Phoenix Mars Mission. Phoenix could not drive around Mars, but it had a robotic arm to dig into the soil and collect samples. It had an onboard laboratory to examine the soil and work out what it contains. Mars also has three operational orbiters around it—the *Mars Odyssey*, *Mars Express*, and *Mars Reconnaissance Orbiter*, showing us in detail the surface features.

Robotic space probes have also shown us the hellish world that lies beneath the thick atmosphere of Venus. It was once thought that dense tropical forests might lie under the Venusian clouds, but space probes have revealed the high temperatures, heavy carbon dioxide atmosphere, and dark brown clouds of sulfuric acid. In 1990 NASA's *Magellan* entered orbit around Venus. Using radar to penetrate the atmosphere, *Magellan* mapped the surface of Venus and found 167 volcanoes more than seventy miles wide! ESA's *Venus Express* has been in orbit around Venus since 2006. This mission is studying the atmosphere of Venus and trying to find out how Earth and Venus developed in such different ways. Several landers have returned information from the surface of Venus, a tremendous achievement given the challenges of landing on this most hostile of planets.

Robotic space probes have braved the scorched world of Mercury, a planet even closer to the Sun than Venus. *Mariner 10*, which flew by Mercury in 1974 and again in 1975, showed us that this bare little planet looks very similar to our Moon. It is a gray, dead planet with very little atmosphere. In 2008 the MESSENGER mission returned a space probe to Mercury and sent back the first new pictures of the Sun's nearest planet in thirty years.

Flying close to the Sun presents huge challenges for a robotic spacecraft, but probes sent to the Sun—*Helios 1*, *Helios 2*, *SOHO*, *TRACE*, *RHESSI*, and others—have sent back information that helped scientists to develop a far better understanding of the star at the very center of our Solar System.

Farther away in the Solar System is Jupiter, first seen in detail when the probe *Pioneer 10* flew by in 1973. Pictures captured by *Pioneer 10* also showed the Great Red Spot in great detail, a feature seen through

telescopes from Earth for centuries. After *Pioneer*, the *Voyager* probes revealed the surprising news about Jupiter's moons. Thanks to the *Voyager* probes, scientists on Earth learned that Jupiter's moons are all very different from one another. In 1995 the *Galileo* probe arrived at Jupiter and spent eight years investigating the giant gas planet and its moons. *Galileo* was the first space probe to do a flyby past an asteroid, the first to discover an asteroid with a moon, and the first to measure Jupiter over a long period of time. This amazing space probe also showed the volcanic activity on Jupiter's moon, Io, and found Europa to be covered in thick ice, underneath which may lie a gigantic ocean that could even harbor some form of life!

NASA's *Cassini* was not the first to visit Saturn—*Pioneer 11* and the *Voyager* probes had flown past on their long journey and sent back detailed images of Saturn's rings and more information about the thick atmosphere on Titan. But when *Cassini* arrived in 2004 after a seven-year journey, it showed us many more features of Saturn and the moons that orbit it. *Cassini* also released a probe, ESA's *Huygens*, which traveled through the thick atmosphere to land on the surface of Titan. The *Huygens* probe discovered that Titan's surface is covered in ice and that methane rains down from the dense clouds.

Voyager 2 flew by Uranus, even farther from Earth, and showed pictures of this frozen planet, tilted on its axis! Thanks to *Voyager 2*, we also know much more about the thin rings circling Uranus, which are very different to the rings of Saturn, as well as many other details of its moons. *Voyager 2* carried on to Neptune and revealed this planet is very windy—Neptune has the fastest moving storms in the Solar System. *Voyager 2* is now ten billion miles from Earth and *Voyager 1* is eleven billion miles away. They should be able to continue communicating with us until 2020.

The Stardust mission, during which a probe caught particles from a comet's tail and returned them to Earth in 2006, taught us far more about the very early Solar System from these fragments. Capturing these samples from comets, which formed at the center of the Solar System but have traveled to its very edge, has helped scientists to understand more about the origin of the Solar System itself.

"Where there is water," Eric had told the kids, "as we know from our planet Earth, there could be life!"

Even more important, Homer was to help prepare for a mission to Mars, which would take human beings to a new planet. For the first time ever, the Global Space Agency was getting ready to send a spacecraft with people on board to explore Mars and see if it would be possible to start a colony out there.

So Homer mattered a lot—not just because he was expensive or had fancy technology or, as Annie put it, looked like he had a personality, with his beady little camera eyes, stick legs, and round tummy where the onboard oven lived.

Homer mattered because he was the first step into space for the human race—he was the front-runner for a whole new type of space exploration that might lead to people living on another planet.

On the day of Homer's descent to the red planet, the big round control room was crammed with people eagerly reading the information from the banks of computer screens. As Homer traveled, he sent back signals to Earth with progress reports. These arrived at the Global Space Agency in code, which the terrestrial computers then turned into words and pictures. Because of the time it took for Homer's signal to reach Earth, in the control room they were only discovering now what had happened on Mars. Had Homer landed—or had he crashed? They were about to find out.

On the overhead screens, Annie and Emmett watched an animation of what was happening to Homer as he approached Mars. The atmosphere in the room was electric: groups of people stood nervously by, hoping that their robot had made it to the start of his mission.

It is very difficult to land on Mars, Eric explained. Mars has a thin atmosphere, which means it doesn't provide the natural braking that the Earth's atmosphere gives returning spacecraft. This meant Homer would be hurtling toward the surface of Mars at a great speed, and they would have to hope that all his systems worked properly to help him slow down; otherwise he would just crash down and end up as a pile of broken parts millions of miles away, with no one to fix him.

As Homer approached Mars's atmosphere, everyone was glued to the screens. To one side was a digital clock

counting the time Homer had spent in space. Next to it, another time was displayed in UTC, the time system used by all space agencies to coordinate with one another and with their missions in space.

"We're watching the EDL now," called out a serious-looking man wearing a headset.

"What's that?" asked Annie.

"Entry, descent, and landing," Emmett told her in a rather superior voice. "Really, Annie, I thought you would have done some reading before we came, to get the most out of the experience."

In reply, Annie stomped firmly on Emmett's foot.

"Ouch! Ouch! Susan!" he cried. "She's hurting me again!"

Susan gave her daughter a fierce look. Annie moved quietly away from Emmett to stand next to her dad. She slipped her hand into his. He was chewing his lip and frowning.

"Do you think Homer's landed?" she whispered.

"Hope so," he said, smiling down at her. "I mean, he's only a robot, but he could send us some really useful information."

"Atmospheric entry!" said the control operator.

When Homer—shaped a bit like an upside-down spinning top—broke through Mars's atmosphere, they saw the bright stream of flames erupting in his wake. The room burst into applause.

"Peak heating rate in one minute and forty seconds,"

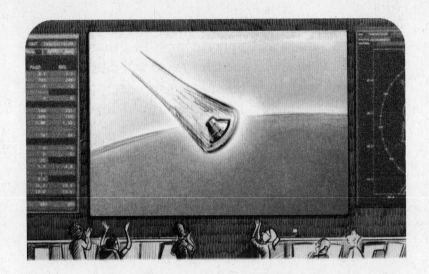

warned the controller. "Possible plasma blackout." The room seemed to tense up automatically, as if everyone was holding their breath.

"Plasma blackout!" said the controller. "We have plasma blackout! Expect signal to resume after two minutes."

Annie squeezed her dad's hand.

He squeezed back. "Don't worry," he said. "We know this happens sometimes. It's due to friction in the atmosphere."

The clock on the wall ticked away as everyone in the room stared at it, waiting for contact to resume. Two minutes went by, then three, then four. People started to mutter to one another as the anxiety in the room mounted.

"We are receiving no signal from Homer," said the

Laika, the first living
Earth-born creature
in orbit.

Launch of the first U.S. manned
space flight, May 1961.

Yuri Gagarin.

Launch of the Soviet spacecraft, *Vostok I*,
carrying Yuri Gagarin, April 1961.

© NASA/SCIENCE PHOTO LIBRARY

Footprint of Neil Armstrong's first step on the Moon, July 21, 1969.

© NASA/SCIENCE PHOTO LIBRARY

Apollo II astronaut Buzz Aldrin walking on the moon.

Apollo 15 astronaut James B. Irwin and lunar rover, July 1971.

© NASA/SCIENCE PHOTO LIBRARY

Above: Space shuttle simulator cockpit, 1999.

© NASA/SCIENCE PHOTO LIBRARY

First space shuttle launch, 1981. The shuttle was called *Columbia*.

Astronaut floating in the International Space Station (ISS).

Below: ISS astronaut with fresh fruit in microgravity conditions.

Astronauts making burgers aboard the ISS.

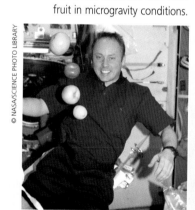

ISS with new solar panels, 2006.

Image of the Chasma Boreale canyon on Mars.

Mercury

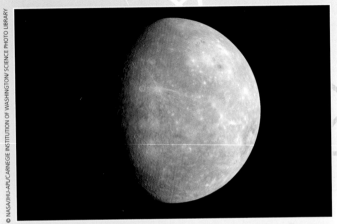

The cratered surface of the planet Mercury.

Below: Craters on Mercury.

controller. The screens showing Homer's descent had frozen as well. "We have lost the signal to Homer!" said the controller. Red lights started flashing around the room.

"What's going on?" whispered Annie.

Her dad shook his head. "I'm worried now," he replied. "There's a possibility that Homer's communication system melted during entry."

"Does that mean Homer is dead?" asked Emmett loudly. Several people turned around to glare at him.

The controller had taken off his headset and was mopping his brow miserably. If Homer had no communication system, they had no way of knowing what had happened to their clever robot. He might have landed, he might have crashed. He might find evidence of life on Mars, but no one on Earth would ever know because he would never be able to send a signal to tell them.

"The Mars monitoring satellite shows no trace of Homer!" someone shouted, sounding like they were beginning to panic. "The monitoring satellite cannot locate Homer. Homer has vanished from all systems."

But then, just a few seconds later, Homer was back again. "We have a signal!" exclaimed another man as his computer came to life. "Homer approaching the surface of Mars. Homer deploying his parachute."

On the TV screen they saw a parachute billowing out

from behind Homer as the little robot swayed down to the planet's surface.

"Homer has landing legs prepared for touchdown. Homer has landed! Homer has reached the north polar region of Mars."

Some people cheered—but Eric didn't. He looked puzzled.

"That's good, isn't it?" Annie whispered to him. "Homer is okay."

"Good, but weird," said Eric, frowning. "It doesn't make sense to me. Why did Homer lose the signal completely for so long and then bring it back? And why wasn't he showing up on the monitoring satellite? It's like he just disappeared for a few minutes. It's very strange. I wonder what is happening right now. . . ."

"So," said George, who was now lying across the branch, "what's this got to do with aliens?"

"Nothing," said Emmett from below. "She doesn't realize it was just a normal technical malfunction and she is making it into too big a deal."

"That's because you don't know the rest of the story," said Annie darkly. "You don't know what happened next."

"What?" said Emmett. "What happened next?"

"It's not for crybabies and sneaks," said Annie grandly. "It's a story for big kids. So why don't you go inside and write some computer code while I talk to my friend."

"Can you do that?" George asked Emmett. "Can you really write computer code?"

"Oh yeah!" said Emmett enthusiastically. "Anything you need on a computer, I can do it. I'm the code wizard. I applied for a job at a software firm a few months ago—I sent them some more information for an online version of my space shuttle simulator. They were going to give me a job. But then they found out I'm only nine years old. So they didn't."

"So you're some kind of genius?" said George.

"Yup," agreed Emmett happily. "You can try my simulator if you like. It shows you what it's like to go up in a spaceship. It's really cool. If you tell me the story about aliens, I'll let you both play."

"We don't want to," said Annie, just as George was

thinking he'd love to have a try. "So get lost!"

At the foot of the tree, Emmett burst into noisy sobs just as Susan and Eric came out onto the veranda.

"Tree time is over," called Susan. "And you three are coming in for dinner."

Chapter 5

George was so tired after his long journey that he nearly fell asleep while brushing his teeth. He staggered into the room he was sharing with Emmett, who was messing around on his computer, launching spaceships on his simulator.

"Hey, George," he said. "Do you want to fly the space shuttle? Look, it's really just like it is. I've put in all the time commands too, and it tells you what's happening."

"*T minus seven minutes and thirty seconds,*" said a robotic voice from Emmett's computer. "*Orbiter access arm retracted.*"

George was so exhausted he could hardly speak. "No, Emmett," he said. "I think I'll just . . ." And he fell asleep to the countdown of a spaceship launch.

The commands from the space-shuttle launch must have wormed their way into George's brain because he had a strange dream. He dreamed he was in the commander's seat on the shuttle, responsible for flying the huge great spacecraft into space. It felt like being strapped to the top of an enormous rocket and sent up into the heavens. As they flew into the darkness of space, he thought he saw stars flashing at him through the shuttle window. In the darkness outside, they suddenly looked very bright and very close. One of them seemed to be zooming toward him, shining a bright light directly into his face, so close and so brilliant that—

He woke up with a start and found himself in an unfamiliar bed with someone shining a light in his face.

"George!" the figure hissed. "George! Get up! It's an emergency!"

It was Annie in her pajamas.

"Bleeeuurgh!" exclaimed George, shielding his eyes from the light as she threw back his duvet and grabbed him by the arm.

"Downstairs," she said. "And super quietly. It's our only chance to escape Emmett! Come on!"

George blundered after her, his mind still reeling from his strange dream about flying the space shuttle. He tiptoed down the stairs to the kitchen, where Annie opened the door and led him out onto the veranda. She shone her flashlight on a piece of paper.

The piece of paper had drawings all over it. It looked like this:

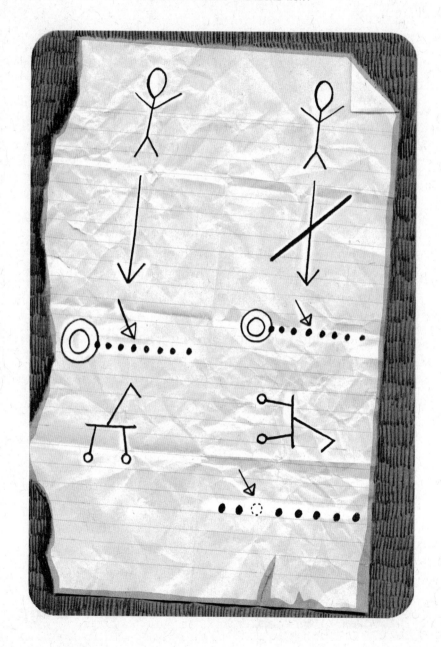

"This is it?" said George, blinking. "This is the alien message? They sent it to you on a piece of school notebook paper?"

"No, twit," Annie told him. "Of course they didn't. I got this through Cosmos! I copied it from his screen."

"Cosmos?" George exclaimed. "But he doesn't work."

"I know!" said Annie. "But I didn't finish the story."

After Homer had landed on Mars, the robot was supposed to start doing all sorts of things, like taking readings of the Martian weather, looking for water in the soil samples and other signs that there might be some form of bacterial life on Mars.

But he wouldn't do any of them. The robot seemed to have gone crazy. He refused to respond to any signals from Earth; he just drove around in circles or threw scoopfuls of mud into the air.

Even though he wasn't replying to their signals, Homer continued sending messages, which turned out to be pictures of his tires and other useless information. From

Earth, they could see the robot—but only sometimes— via the monitoring satellite that orbited Mars and sent back pictures. Once, Annie said, her dad had been watching Homer and he'd picked up something really odd on the satellite pictures. He said that if he hadn't known better, he would have sworn that Homer was waving his robotic arm at him. It was almost like Homer was trying to attract his attention.

Eric, Annie said, was getting really stressed out by all this. Lots of people wanted to know what Homer had found on Mars and what he was doing up there. But so far they had nothing to show except a robot behaving in a very silly fashion.

It was putting the Global Space Agency in an awkward position. Homer was an extremely expensive robot, and it took many people to build, launch, and operate him. He was an important part of the new space program, since he was meant to blaze the trail for human beings to go out and live on a different planet. So the fact that he didn't seem to work properly meant that those who weren't in favor of the space program or sending astronauts far out into space could argue that this was all a big waste of time.

Homer's bad behavior also meant that Eric wasn't getting the information he was hoping for about possible life on Mars. It was breaking his heart to see his robot mess around on the red planet. Day by day he looked sadder and sadder. If Homer didn't start cooperating soon, the mission would be abandoned and the robot would become just a pile of metal on a distant planet.

Annie couldn't bear it. Her dad had been so excited and happy at the prospect of receiving Homer's findings. She hated seeing him so upset. So she had a brilliant idea: She decided to get Cosmos out of retirement, just to see if she could make him work again.

"I realized that if we had Cosmos," she told George as they stood outside under the starry sky, "we could just go off to Mars, fix the robot, and come home again without anyone even knowing. If we went when the monitoring satellite was on the other side of Mars, no one would even see us. I mean, we'd have to be careful not to leave a footprint or drop anything. That would be a bit of a disaster."

"Hmm," said George, still affected by his weird dream. "So what did you do?"

"I got Cosmos out of his secret hiding place."

"Not that secret if you knew about it," said George.

"And," Annie went on, ignoring him, "I started him up."

"And he actually worked?" George was wide awake now.

"Not really," admitted Annie. "At least, only for a few seconds, and he didn't say anything. But this is what I saw on his screen." She waved the paper at George. "It was there—honest, it was. It was a message. I checked the sender ID and it said: *unknown*. For message location, it said: *extraterrestrial*. Then Cosmos died and I couldn't start him up again."

"Wow!" said George. "Did you tell Eric?"

"Of course," said Annie. "And he tried to start

95

Cosmos up again but couldn't. I showed him the message, but he didn't believe me." She pouted. "He said I was making up stories—but I'm sure Homer really is waving to us and has something he wants to tell us. But my dad just insisted that Homer doesn't work because he had a bad atmospheric entry and that this message— if Cosmos received it at all— is just something to do with Cosmos being broken."

"But that's really boring of him!" remarked George.

"No, he's just being a scientist. It's like Emmett said," admitted Annie. "Most people believe there

is only some form of bacteria out there and no real aliens. But I think . . ."

"What do you think?" asked George, looking up at the stars.

"I think," said Annie firmly, "that someone out there is trying to get in touch with us. I think someone is using Homer to attract our attention, and because we're just ignoring him, they've started sending us messages instead. Only we can't pick them up because Cosmos isn't working."

"What are we going to do?"

"We've got to go out there," said Annie, "and see for ourselves. But first we have to fix Cosmos. We need to see if the aliens are sending us any more messages! And then, maybe, we can send one back . . ."

"How would we do that?" asked George. "I mean, how can we send a message that they will understand? And even if we knew how to send it, what would we say? And in what language? They've sent us the message in pictures—it must be because they don't know how to speak to us."

"I think we're going to say, *Leave our lovely robot alone, you pesky aliens!*" said Annie, looking fierce. "*You're messing with the wrong civilization! Pick on someone else!*"

"But we want to know who they are and where they come from," protested George. "We can't just say, *Get lost, aliens,* and never find out who sent the message."

"What about, *Come in peace and then go home?*" said Annie. "So we find out who they are, but they're not allowed to come to Earth if they have evil intentions."

"Yeah?" said George. "Who's going to stop them? They could land here and be like huge scary machines who stamp us into the ground, just like we do with ants."

"Or," said Annie, her eyes shining in the light from the flashlight, "they might be teeny-weeny, like little wriggly bacteria under a microscope. Only they don't realize how large we are and so we don't even notice when they arrive."

"They might have fourteen heads and dribble slime," said George ghoulishly. "We'd notice that!"

They heard a creaking noise, followed by footsteps on the stairs. A bleary-eyed Eric came out onto the veranda.

"What's going on here?" he asked.

"George couldn't sleep," said Annie quickly. "Because of the jet lag. So I was just, um, getting him a glass of water."

"Hmm," said Eric, his hair sticking up all over the place. "Upstairs with you both now."

George sneaked into the room he shared with Emmett and hopped back into bed, but not before he'd taken Annie's flashlight from her. He was wide awake now, so he got out his copy of *The User's Guide* and turned to the chapter, "Getting in Touch with Aliens."

GETTING IN TOUCH WITH ALIENS

If aliens are really out there, will we ever get to meet them?

The distances between the stars are staggeringly great, so we still can't be sure that a face-to-face encounter will someday take place (assuming the aliens have faces!). But even if extraterrestrials never visit our planet or receive a visit from us, we might still get to know one another. We might still be able to talk.

One way this could happen is by radio. Unlike sound, radio waves can move through the empty spaces between the stars. And they move as fast as anything *can* move—at the speed of light.

Almost fifty years ago some scientists worked out what it would take to send a signal from one star system to another. It surprised them to learn that interstellar conversation wouldn't require superadvanced technology like you often see in science-fiction movies. It's possible to send radio signals from one solar system to another with the type of radio equipment we could build today. So the scientists stood back from their chalkboards and said to themselves: If this is so easy, then no matter what aliens might be doing, they'd surely be using radio to communicate over large distances. The scientists realized that it would be a perfectly logical idea to turn some of our big antennae to the skies to see if we could pick up extraterrestrial signals. After all, finding an alien broadcast would instantly prove that there's someone out there, without the expense of sending rockets to distant star systems in the hope of discovering a populated planet.

Unfortunately, this alien eavesdropping experiment, called SETI (the Search for Extraterrestrial Intelligence), has so far failed to find a single, sure peep from the skies. The radio bands have been discouragingly quiet wherever we've looked, aside from the natural static caused by such objects as quasars (the churning, high-energy centers of some galaxies) or pulsars (rapidly spinning neutron stars).

Does that mean that intelligent aliens, able to build radio transmitters, don't exist? That would be an astounding discovery, because there are surely at least a million million planets in our Milky Way Galaxy—and there are one hundred thousand million *other* galaxies! If no one is out there, we are stupendously special—and dreadfully alone.

Well, as SETI researchers will tell you, it's entirely too soon to conclude that we have no company among the stars. After all, if you're going to listen for alien radio broadcasts, not only do you have to point your antenna in the right direction, but you also need to tune to the right spot on the dial, have a sensitive enough receiver, and be listening at the right time. SETI experiments are like looking for buried treasure without a map. So the fact that we haven't found anything so far isn't surprising. It's like digging a few holes on the beach of a South Pacific island and coming up with nothing but wet sand and crabs. You shouldn't immediately conclude that there's no treasure to be found.

Fortunately, new radio telescopes are speeding up our search for signals, and it's possible that within a few dozen years we could hear a faint broadcast from another civilization.

What would they be saying to us? Well, of course we can only guess, but one thing the extraterrestrials will surely know: They'd better send us a long message, because speedy conversation is simply impossible. For example, imagine that the nearest aliens are on a planet around a star that's one thousand light-years away. If we pick up a signal from them tomorrow, it will have taken one thousand years to get to us. It will be

an old message, but that's okay. After all, if you read Sophocles or Shakespeare, those are old "messages" too, but they're still interesting.

However, if we choose to reply, our response to the aliens will take one thousand years to get to them, and another one thousand years will pass before their answer gets back to us! In other words, even a simple "Hello?" and its alien response, "Zork?" would take twenty centuries. So while talking on the radio is a lot faster than traveling in rockets for a meet-and-greet, it's still going to be a very relaxed conversation. That suggests that the aliens might send us books and books of stuff about themselves and their planet, knowing that we won't be doing a lot of chatting.

But even if they do, even if they send us *The Alien Encyclopedia*, will we be able to read it? After all, unlike in the movies and TV, the extraterrestrials aren't going to be fluent in English or any other earthly language. It's possible that they may use pictures or even mathematics to help make their message understandable, but we won't know until or unless we pick up a signal.

No matter what they send us, detecting a radio squeal coming from a distant world would be big news. Indeed, imagine what it was like five centuries ago when explorers first discovered that there were entire continents, filled with inhabitants, that were completely unknown in Europe. Finding the New World changed everything.

Today, we've replaced the wooden sailing ships of those early explorers with giant aluminium-and-steel antennae. Someday soon they may tell us something extraordinarily interesting: namely, that in the vast expanses of space, humans are not the only ones watching the Universe.

And today's young people may be those who will be there to listen—and to respond. This could be *you*!

Seth

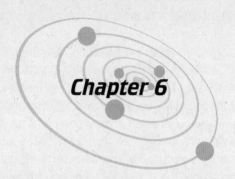

Chapter 6

The next morning at breakfast, George's eyelids were very heavy, and he felt confused to be eating breakfast at the time he'd usually be having lunch. However, that felt like nothing compared to Annie's revelations from the night before. He didn't know what to make of what she'd told him.

Once before, George hadn't believed her: When he first met Annie and she had told him she went on journeys around the Solar System, he had laughed at her and said she was lying. But that had turned out to be true in the end, so he wondered what to make of this latest story.

It worried him that, according to Annie, Eric didn't seem to be taking the alien message seriously. On the other hand, if it meant he might get a trip out to space, just to check it out, he felt he would probably go along with Annie's version. Anything to fly through the cosmos again, even if it was on a fruitless quest for an alien life-form!

Susan suddenly spoke up. "I thought we'd show

George the neighborhood today," she said. "Take him around and maybe go to the beach."

Annie looked stricken. "Mom!" she said. "George and I have stuff to do here."

"And I've got my theories on the information-loss paradox to work on," said Emmett rather sourly. "Not that anyone cares."

"Don't be silly," said Susan firmly. "George has come a long way to see us, and we can't expect him to just sit in a tree, chatting to you all day." The phone rang and she answered it. "George, it's for you," she said, passing over the receiver.

"George!" came the crackly voice of his dad, sounding like he was shouting from a very long way away. "Just wanted to let you know we've arrived in Tuvalu! We're just about to get on the ship and sail for the atolls. How's it going in Florida?"

"It's fine!" said George. "I'm here with Eric and Susan and Annie and this other boy called Emmett who is—"

But the connection cut off. George handed the phone back to Susan.

"I'm sure he'll call again," she reassured him. "And your mom and dad know you are okay. Now we're going to go out and have lots of fun!"

Annie rolled her eyes at George, but there was no getting out of it. Her mom had made plans to take them to the theme park, to the pool, to a dolphin sanctuary, to the beach. They were out all day and all evening for several days. There was no opportunity for them to get Cosmos out of his secret hiding place and work on him. And with Emmett constantly trailing their every move, they hardly even had a chance to look at Annie's alien message—only once, when they locked themselves into the bathroom and studied the piece of paper.

"So, that's a person," said Annie. "And that arrow must mean the person is going somewhere. But where?"

"Um, the person is going to . . . ," said George. "A series of small dots moving around a bigger dot. I know! What if the dots are the planets in orbit around the Sun, which is at the center? The arrow points to the fourth dot, so it means the person is going to the fourth planet from the Sun, which is—"

"Mars!" said Annie. "I *knew* it! There *is* a link to Homer. This message means we have to go to Mars and—"

"But what does the rest mean?" said George. "What does all this mean—a person with an arrow crossed out?"

"Perhaps that's what will happen if the person *doesn't* go to Mars?"

"If the person doesn't go to Mars," said George, looking down the column, "then the funny-looking stick insect falls over."

"Funny-looking stick insect . . . ," said Annie. "What if that's Homer? If the person doesn't go to Mars, maybe something terrible will happen to Homer. We have to get out there and save Homer! It's really important!"

"Look, Annie," said George doubtfully. "I know your dad's upset about Homer, but he is just a robot. They could send another one. I just don't know that these messages are enough to prove anything."

"Look at the last line," said Annie in a spooky voice. "And be afraid."

"If the person doesn't go to Mars and doesn't save Homer, then . . . ," said George.

"No planet Earth," said Annie.

"No planet Earth?" exclaimed George.

"No planet Earth," confirmed Annie. "That's what the message means. We have to go to Mars to save Homer, because if we don't, something terrible will happen to this planet."

"We have to tell your dad," said George urgently.

"I've tried," said Annie. "See what you can do."

At that moment they heard a banging on the bath-room door.

"Come out!" shouted Emmett. "Resistance is futile!"

"Can I flush his head down the toilet?" said Annie longingly.

"No!" said George sharply. "You can't. He's not a bad kid. He's really nice if you actually try to talk to him. . . ."

Emmett started bashing on the door again.

At last Annie's mom decided they all needed a quiet day at home. The next day was to be the great highlight of George's visit. Eric had got them tickets to see the launch of the space shuttle! They were going to the launchpad to watch the mighty spacecraft blast off from Earth. Even Emmett got thoroughly overexcited. He kept muttering space-shuttle commands to himself and reciting facts about orbital velocity.

George and Annie were both thrilled for different reasons. George was gripped by the idea of the enor-mous rocket that gave the space shuttle the power it needed to zoom upward into space. In the past, he had walked through Cosmos's doorway to travel through space; now he was going to watch a real spacecraft begin its great journey!

As for Annie, she was fizzing with secretive joy over the idea of the launch. "My plan is coming together," she whispered to George. "We will uncover the aliens!

We will!" Annoyingly, she refused to explain to George quite how she meant to do this. When he asked her, she got a faraway look in her eyes. "It's all in the plan," she told him. "And when you need to know, then I will tell you. For now, you must believe." It was very irritating for George, and he much preferred talking to Emmett than to Annie when she was in full-on mystery mode.

Even so, the more she stalked about, impersonating a secret agent working on extraterrestrial activity, the more George racked his brains as to what the alien message might mean and where it had come from. He had tried talking to Eric about it, but he hadn't got far.

"George," Eric said patiently. "I'm sorry that I don't believe that an evil alien life-form is messing around with my robot or wanting to destroy the Earth, but I don't. So please drop it. I've got other things on my mind. Like how to send another robot out to Mars to take over the work that Homer should have done. This has been a terrible time for us at the Global Space Agency. Not everyone is as excited about space travel as you and Annie. Some people don't accept that it has any use at all."

"But what about all the inventions that have come from space?" said George hotly. "If we hadn't gone into space, there's so much stuff we wouldn't have now on Earth."

SPACE INVENTIONS

There are many things we use on Earth that have been improved or developed because of advances in space technology. Here are just some of them:

- air purification
- anti-fog ski goggles
- automatic insulin pumps
- bone-analyzer technology
- car brake linings
- cataract-surgery tools
- composite golf clubs
- corrosion protection coating
- Dustbuster
- earthquake prediction system
- energy-saving air-conditioning
- fire resistant materials
- fire/flame detectors
- flat-panel televisions
- food packaging
- freeze-dried technology
- high-density batteries
- home security systems
- lead poison detection
- miniaturized circuits
- MRI imaging

- noise reduction
- pollution measuring devices
- portable x-ray devices
- programmable pacemakers
- protective clothing
- radioactive-leak detectors
- robotic hands
- satellite navigation
- school bus design
- scratch-resistant lenses
- sewage treatment
- shock-absorbing helmets
- smokestack monitors
- solar energy systems
- storm warning services (Doppler radar)
- studless winter tires
- swimming-pool purification systems
- toothpaste tubes

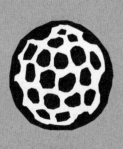

"And," continued Eric gently, "even if we could get Cosmos working, after all that computer has been through, I don't think it's safe to use the portal. What if he broke down when someone was out there in space and we couldn't get him started again in time to rescue them? Homer is only a robot, George. It isn't worth the risk."

"But what about the end of the message?" persisted George. "With the Earth crossed out?"

"It probably comes from some crank," said Eric. "And there are plenty of them. Don't think about it anymore. I will get Homer sorted out—somehow. And the planet isn't coming to an end, not for several billions of years, when our Sun comes to the end of its life. So there's no panic."

"Finally!" said Annie when her dad went to work, her mom popped out for a few minutes, and Emmett seemed safely absorbed with his online simulator. "We can work on Operation Alien Life-form. We don't have long. And we *have* to get Cosmos working before tomorrow. It's crucial. Come on, George!" She ran up the stairs to her parents' room.

George followed her, grumbling as he went. "Are you actually going to tell me what we're doing?" he demanded from outside her parents' bedroom. "I'm sick of you saying, 'It's on a need-to-know basis and you don't need to know.' I came over because you said you needed my help. So far you've hardly told me anything about your plan."

Annie emerged beaming from her parents' room, holding a metal box. "I'm sorry!" she whispered. "But I didn't want you to tell Emmett about us going into space to chase aliens."

"I wouldn't!" said George, feeling hurt that she didn't trust him.

Annie barged her way into her bedroom and put the metal box down on her desk. "Cosmos," she announced, "is in here. And I have the key." She produced a tiny little key on a chain around her neck, then opened the box and pulled out the familiar silver computer. She locked the box again and took it back to the wardrobe in her parents' room.

"How did you get the key?" asked George when she returned.

"I borrowed it," said Annie mysteriously. "After I got Cosmos out and received the alien message, Dad decided to lock him away. But he doesn't realize how smart I am."

113

"Or how sneaky?" commented George.

"Whatever," said Annie. "Let's get going."

She opened up Cosmos and plugged him in. She pressed ENTER—the secret key to the Universe—but nothing happened. She pressed it again, but the screen stayed blank.

Suddenly her bedroom door inched open and a nose poked around it.

"What are you doing?" said Emmett.

"Nothing!" said Annie, jumping up to try to block his view. But Emmett had already edged his way in.

"If you don't tell me what you're doing with that computer," he said slyly, "I'll tell your mom and dad."

"Tell them what?" said Annie.

"I'll tell them whatever it is you're doing that you don't want me—or them—to know about."

"But you don't know what I'm doing," said Annie.

"Yes, I do," said Emmett. "That computer is the one you think is really powerful. The one you're not supposed to use by yourselves. I've been listening to you and George when you don't think I can hear you."

"You little worm!" screamed Annie, throwing herself at Emmett.

"I hate you!" he yelled back, tussling with her. "I never wanted to come here! I wanted to go to Silicon Valley with my mom and dad. This is the

worst summer of my life!"

"JUST SHUT UP, BOTH OF YOU!" shouted George.

Annie and Emmett let go of each other and gazed at the normally mild-mannered George with surprise.

"Now look here," he said. "You're both being ridiculous. Emmett's having a horrible summer and he's really bored. But you're a computer genius, right, Emmett?"

"Affirmative," said Emmett sulkily.

"And, Annie—you've got a computer problem you can't solve. So why don't you ask Emmett—nicely—if he'll take a look at Cosmos and see if he knows what to do with him? He might enjoy doing it and we might be able to stop fighting. Okay?"

"S'pose so," grumbled Annie.

"Right," said George. "Annie, you explain."

She pointed to the silver laptop lying on her bed. "This is a computer—"

"I can see that." Emmett scowled.

She ploughed on. "—that can do special things. Like open doorways to places in space."

Emmett looked down his nose. "I doubt that."

"No, it can," said George. "The computer has a name—he's called Cosmos and when he works, he's amazing. Eric invented him but we blew him up by mistake last year. Now Eric really needs Cosmos and we need you to get him working again. Emmett, do you think you could try to fix him?"

"I'll get my emergency computer kit!" said Emmett, who was now beaming from ear to ear. He dashed out of the door.

"He's not so bad," said George to Annie. "Just give him a chance."

"Just *one*," muttered Annie.

Emmett came back with a collection of hardware, CDs, and screwdrivers of different sizes. He arranged them all in neat piles and started fiddling around with Cosmos. The others watched him in silence, noticing how the smug look on his face faded as he grappled with their old friend. A frown crept over his brow.

"Wow!" he remarked. "I have never seen anything like this! I didn't think they could make a computer I didn't understand!"

"Can you save him?" whispered Annie.

Emmett looked baffled. "This hardware is mega-cool,"

he said. "And I thought quantum computing was just a theory." He twiddled a bit more, biting his lip in concentration.

The noise of cicadas buzzing in the garden floated in from the window. But suddenly they heard another sound. It was very faint and none of them could be absolutely sure they'd really heard it.

"Wasn't that—?"

"Shush!" said Annie. They heard it again. A very quiet *beep*. When they looked closely at the great computer, they realized that a tiny yellow light on one side of him had come on. In the middle of his screen, which until now had been blank, they saw a thin line appear.

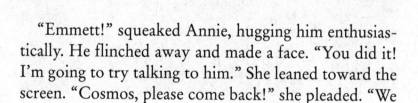

"Emmett!" squeaked Annie, hugging him enthusiastically. He flinched away and made a face. "You did it! I'm going to try talking to him." She leaned toward the screen. "Cosmos, please come back!" she pleaded. "We *need* you."

The screen flickered and then went dull. But then Cosmos beeped again—once, and then twice. And another line appeared across the center of his screen. The line turned into a squiggle for a few seconds, and then a circle, and then disappeared.

"This is weird," said Emmett slowly. He punched in a few commands. He pressed a few more keys and sat back.

There was a whirring noise. And then, finally, Cosmos spoke.

"1010111110000010," he said.

George and Annie were stunned into silence. It had never occurred to them that they might get Cosmos working but then not understand what he said.

"11000101001," Cosmos continued.

Annie tugged Emmett's shirt.

"What have you done to him?" she asked him, her face a picture of panic. "Where's the alien message?"

"Holy supersymmetric strings!" exclaimed Emmett. "He's speaking Base Two!"

"What's that?" said George.

"It's a positional notation with a radix of two," said Emmett. "It's binary—the system used internally by all computers."

George tried typing a command on the screen but jumped back as Cosmos screeched, "101000101011 101010100010101010101101010000010010101!"

"What?" said Annie. "What's happening to Cosmos? Why can he speak but we don't know what he's saying?"

"So this computer, like, it speaks to you in English and you understand it . . . ?" said Emmett slowly. "Because now he's speaking the underlying system, the one underneath a computer language. Like a prelanguage."

"1101011!" wailed Cosmos.

"Oh my gosh!" Annie gasped. "What if it's like he's become a little baby computer, and he's speaking baby language?"

Cosmos gurgled. And then laughed.

"So he could just be saying ''Poon! Dada! Mama,'" Annie continued.

"I think you're right," said Emmett, who was too busy staring at the screen to notice he'd just agreed with Annie. "I'll try him on something. Let's see if he knows BASIC."

"GOTO GOTO GOTO GOTO," said Cosmos.

Emmett inserted a disk into the supercomputer. "I'll try to update him on something harder," he said. "Something more up-to-date. It's like he's in an ancient computer world right now. I'll try FORTRAN 95."

BINARY CODE

Our normal numerical system works with a base of 10. There are numbers from 1 to 9 and then the number 1 moves into the next "column" to show that there is one group of 10s. After 99 (9 x 10 plus 9 x 1), a new column is needed to show the amount of 100s (10 x 10); then again for 1000s (10 x 10 x 10) after 999 is reached. And so on.

With binary, the base is 2 instead of 10, so that the columns will represent multiples of 2, i.e.: 2, 4 (2 x 2), 8 (2 x 2 x 2), etc. The number 3 therefore appears as 11 (1 x 2 plus 1 x 1). And counting 1 to 10 becomes 1, 10, 11, 100, 101, 110, 111, 1000, 1001, 1010.

Early computer programmers decided to use binary code because it is simpler to design a circuit with either on or off positions than one with many alternative states. Binary code works on the principle that the early computers were constructed using electrical systems that recognized on or off positions only—which could be represented by using 0 for *off* and 1 for *on*. In this way complicated calculations could be translated into on/off circuits throughout the computer.

"REAL. NOT. END. DO," replied the supercomputer.

Emmett tried once more, and Cosmos's screen dimmed and his circuits fizzed. "He is gobbling up these disks," said Emmett. "Spooky, huh?"

Finally Cosmos spoke in a language they could understand. "What's up?" he asked.

"Cosmos!" said Annie excitedly. "You're back. That's great news! Now I need you to open up the portal, quick as you can. I need to have a look—"

"Yo," said Cosmos lazily.

George jumped in. "Cosmos!" he pleaded. "We're in deep trouble. We really need you to help us."

"Dude, I'm chillin'," replied the world's most intelligent computer.

"You're doing what?" said George slowly, bending down to take a closer look at him.

"Don't look at my screen!" shouted Cosmos suddenly.

George tried again. "We've got a big problem—," he began.

"Dude," Cosmos interrupted him. "I'm busy. Don't look at my screen."

"Cosmos . . . ," cooed Annie gently. "Why are you so annoyed?"

"Because I don't want to roll with these losers," he replied. "But you're cool."

"Thanks!" said Annie. "But, Cosmos, things are really messed up right now. My dad's freaking out because someone's, like, jacked his robot."

"Word!" exclaimed Cosmos, finally sounding interested.

George and Emmett listened in complete bewilderment as Annie chatted to the computer.

"Cosmos, you rock!" said Annie. "Can you help us find out who's been messing with our robot?"

"Word," replied Cosmos. "I'm on it."

As he whirred away, Annie turned to face the others with a smug grin on her face.

"He said I was cool!" she exclaimed happily. "And look . . . ," she said, breathlessly. "The door to the Universe!"

A little beam of light had shot out from Cosmos's screen, and on the other side of the room, he was drawing the doorway through which George and Annie had once walked into the Universe. The door swung open, and behind it they saw a dark sky peppered with stars that shone much more brightly than when they were seen from Earth.

A red planet was coming into view.

George took a step toward the portal, but before he could get any closer, the door slammed shut in his face. On it was pinned a large poster with the words KEEP OUT scrawled in big letters. They all jumped as loud electronic music blared from behind the door.

"Annie, what's going on?" asked George.

"Well, I'm not really sure," she said. "But Cosmos sounds like the older kids at my school back home. I mean, he's speaking the way they do when they think they're really cool."

"How old are these kids?" asked George.

"Oh, about fourteen, I suppose," said Annie. "Why?"

"Because," said George, who had worked it out, "Cosmos started out with baby computer language when we first got him going. And Emmett moved him on but couldn't update him totally. So that means that now—"

Annie finished the sentence for him: "Cosmos," she said with fear and wonder, "is a *teenager*."

"What's your dad going to say?" asked George.

"I think we'd better not tell him. At least, not yet."

They heard the front door open downstairs. "Quick!"

said Annie. "Emmett, close Cosmos down!"

Emmett shut down the computer, and they shoved Cosmos under Annie's bed. Footsteps came up the stairs, and when Eric opened the door to Annie's bedroom, he found the three kids sitting in a row, looking at a book he had written.

"Nice to see you all getting along," he remarked.

Annie slung an arm around Emmett's shoulders. "Oh yes," she said. "We're friends now, aren't we?" She poked him lightly. "Speak," she whispered in his ear.

"Yes, I can confirm that," said Emmett mechanically. He hadn't yet recovered from seeing Cosmos open up the portal.

"Good, good," said Eric. "I see you're reading one of my books. *The Large-scale Structure of Space-time.* How are you finding it?"

"It's very interesting," said George politely. He hadn't understood a word of it.

Emmett came back to life. "You've made an error on page one hundred and thirty-six," he said helpfully.

"Is that so?" said Eric, smiling. "No one's ever spotted that before, but that doesn't mean you're wrong."

"I have a suggestion as to how to rectify it," said Emmett.

Annie groaned, but George gave her a stern look. "I mean, well done, Emmett," she said.

"Okay, good," said Eric slowly. "I was going to

suggest we all go out for ice cream. But if you're all absorbed, then I won't disturb you any further—"

"Ice cream!" Annie and George jumped up. Emmett stayed sitting on the bed, his eyes still glued to the book.

"Earth to Emmett!" said Annie. "Ice cream! You know, the cold sweet stuff that kids like! Let's go have some!"

Emmett looked up, unsure. "Do you actually want me to come too?" he said.

"Yes!" said Annie and George. "We do!"

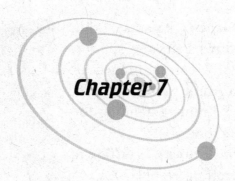

Chapter 7

The next day dawned beautiful and calm, the perfect day to set off into space. Annie woke George and Emmett up early.

"It's space-shuttle day!" she shrieked into George's ear. He groaned and turned over beneath his duvet. "Get up, get up!" she said, pulling the duvet off him and dancing around the room with it. "This is the most exciting day of our lives!"

Emmett had sat bolt upright in bed. "I'm so happy I might be—" He jumped out of bed and ran into the bathroom.

Annie grabbed one of George's hands and pulled him to his feet as he blearily tried to wake up. Emmett tottered back in, looking rather pale.

"Tree!" Annie said to both of them. "Now! We've got planning to do."

Still in their pajamas, they scrambled downstairs and out onto the veranda. George shinned up the tree and Annie swiftly followed him, leaving Emmett standing forlornly at the foot.

"Come on, Emmett," said Annie. "Get up here!"

"I can't," said Emmett miserably.

"Why not?"

"I've never climbed a tree," he admitted. "I don't know how."

"Oh, for heaven's sakes!" exclaimed Annie. "What have you been doing with yourself?"

"Writing computer programs," said Emmett sadly. "By myself."

Annie sighed noisily, but George dropped out of the tree in one single fluid movement, grabbed Emmett, and hoisted him up. George pushed from below and Annie pulled from above, and with some squeaking and scraping, they propelled the smaller boy onto the big branch. Emmett looked down nervously.

"Now then," Annie told him sternly. "We are going to have an

adventure today. We are going to be brave and amazing. And hopefully we are going to save planet Earth. And that means no crying or whining or running to my mom. Do you understand, Emmett?"

Emmett nodded while clinging tightly to the branch. "Yes, Annie," he said meekly.

"You're our friend now," Annie told him. "So if you have something to say, you tell me or George—you don't go charging off to a grown-up."

"Yes, Annie," he agreed, giving her a little smile. "I've never had a friend before."

"Well, now you've got two," said George.

"And we're going to need you," added Annie. "You are super important to the master plan, Emmett. Don't let us down."

He gasped. "I won't!" he said. "I absolutely totally and utterly will not!"

"Okay, great!" said George. "That's all great! But what, in fact, Annie, *are* we going to do?"

"We are going," she said, "on a great cosmic journey. So listen up, savers of planet Earth, and prepare to meet the Universe. I'm going to tell you the master plan: We're going to change out of our pajamas, pack up Cosmos, find my dad, and get to the Global Space Agency. And that's where it will all begin."

The first step of their cosmic journey, Annie explained, took them to the launchpad at the Global Space Agency, where they would be watching the space-shuttle launch.

MANNED SPACEFLIGHT

"The Eagle Has Landed!"

This is the message U.S. astronaut Neil Armstrong radioed back from the Moon to mission control in Houston, Texas, on July 20, 1969. The *Eagle* was the lunar module, which had detached from the spacecraft *Columbia*, in orbit sixty miles above the surface of the Moon. While astronaut Michael Collins remained on board *Columbia*, the Lunar Excursion Module touched down on an area called the Sea of Tranquility—but there is no water on the Moon so it didn't land with a splash! Neil Armstrong and Buzz Aldrin, the two astronauts inside the *Eagle*, became the first human beings ever to visit the Moon.

 Astronaut Armstrong was the first to step out of the capsule onto the Moon (with his left foot). Buzz Aldrin followed him and looked around—at the totally black sky, the impact craters, the layers of moondust—and commented, "Magnificent desolation.' As they'd been instructed, they quickly put Moon rocks and dust into their pockets, so that they would have some samples of the Moon, even if they had to leave in a hurry.

 In fact, they stayed for nearly a day on the Moon and covered over half a mile on foot. This epic voyage of *Apollo 11* remains one of the most inspirational journeys into the unknown that mankind has ever undertaken, and three craters to the north of the Sea of Tranquility are now named after the astronauts on the mission—Collins, Armstrong, and Aldrin.

Walking on the Moon

Including those on *Apollo 11*, a total of twelve astronauts have now walked on the Moon. But each mission was still a dangerous business, as was clearly shown on the *Apollo 13* mission in April 1970, when an explosion on board the service module meant that not only the astronauts but also the people on the ground had to make heroic efforts to return the spacecraft safely to Earth.

All the Apollo astronauts, including the ones from the harrowing *13* mission, came back safely. Astronauts are highly trained specialists with backgrounds in aviation, engineering, and science. But to launch and operate a space mission, people with a wide variety of skills are needed. The Apollo missions—like all space missions before and since—were the result of work by tens of thousands of people who built and operated the complex hardware and software.

The Apollo missions also brought back 840 pounds of lunar material to be studied on Earth. This allowed scientists on our planet to gain a much better understanding of the Moon and how it relates to the Earth.

The last mission to the Moon was *Apollo 17*, which landed on the Taurus-Littrow highlands on December 11, 1972, and stayed for three days. When they were 18,000 miles from the Earth, the *Apollo 17* crew took a photo of the complete Earth, fully lit. This photo is known as *The Blue Marble* and may be the most widely distributed photo ever. Since then, no human being has been far enough away from the Earth to take such a picture.

The First Man in Space
The Apollo missions were not the first time that man had flown into space. Soviet cosmonaut Yuri Gagarin, who orbited the Earth on April 12, 1961, in the *Vostok* spacecraft, was the first-ever human being in space.

Six weeks after Gagarin's historic achievement, U.S. President John F. Kennedy announced that he wanted to land a man on the Moon within ten years, and the newly created NASA—the National Aeronautics and Space Administration—set to work to see if they could match the Russian manned space program, even though at that time, NASA had only sixteen minutes of spaceflight experience. The space race—to be the first on the Moon—had begun!

Mercury, Gemini—and Walking in Space

Project Mercury, an American single-astronaut program, was designed to see if human beings could survive in space. In 1961 astronaut Alan Shepard became the first American in space with a suborbital flight of fifteen minutes, and the following year, John Glenn became the first NASA astronaut to orbit the Earth.

NASA's Project Gemini followed. Gemini was a very important project, since it taught astronauts how to dock vehicles in space. It also allowed them to practice operations such as space walks—also called EVAs (Extra Vehicular Activity). But the first space walk ever performed was by a Russian cosmonaut, Alexei Leonov, in 1965. The Russians didn't make it to the Moon, however, with this honor going to the United States in 1969.

The First Space Stations

After the race to land on the Moon was over, many people became less interested in space programs. However, both the Russians and the Americans still had big plans. The Russians were working on a supersecret program called Almaz, or Diamond. They wanted to have a manned space station orbiting the Earth. After a doomed first attempt, the next versions, Salyut-3 and then Salyut-5, were more successful, but neither of them lasted for much more than a year.

The Americans developed their own version, Skylab—an orbiting space station that was in operation for eight months in 1973. Skylab had a telescope on board that astronauts used to observe the Sun. They brought back solar photographs, including x-ray images of solar flares and dark spots on the Sun.

A Handshake in Space

At this time on Earth—the mid 1970s—both the USSR and the U.S. were locked into what was known as the Cold War. This meant the two sides were not actually fighting a war, but they disliked and distrusted each other very strongly. However, in space the two countries began to work together. In 1975 the *Apollo–Soyuz* project saw the first "handshake in space" between the two opposing superpowers. *Apollo*, the U.S. spacecraft, docked with *Soyuz*, the Soviet one, and the American astronaut and Russian cosmonaut—who would have had difficulty meeting in person on Earth—shook hands with each other.

The Shuttle

The space shuttle was a new type of spacecraft. Unlike the craft that went before it, it was reusable, designed to fly into space like a rocket but also to glide back to Earth and land like an airplane on a runway. The shuttle was also designed to take cargo as well as astronauts into space. The first U.S. shuttle, *Columbia*, was launched in 1981.

The ISS

In 1986 the Russians launched space station Mir, which means "world" or "peace."

Mir was the first elaborate and large space station ever to orbit the Earth. It was built in space over a span of ten years and designed as a space laboratory so that scientists could carry out experiments in a nearly gravity-free environment. Mir was the size of six buses and was home to between three and six astronauts at a time.

The International Space Station (ISS) was built in space with its construction beginning in 1998. Orbiting the globe every ninety minutes, this research facility is a symbol of international cooperation with scientists and astronauts from many countries involved both in running it and spending time there. The ISS is serviced by a space shuttle from NASA, the *Soyuz* spacecraft from Russia, and the European Space Agency's Automated Transfer Vehicles. The crew also have permanent escape vehicles, in case they need to make an emergency exit!

The Future

In 2010 the space shuttle will go out of service and the ISS will receive supplies and crew from the Russian *Soyuz* and *Progress* spacecraft.

NASA is developing a new type of spacecraft, called *Orion*, which it hopes will take us back to the Moon and possibly beyond—to the red planet, Mars.

But a totally new type of space travel is also becoming a reality. In the future, space tourists may be able to take short, suborbital flights. One day, perhaps, we will all be able to take vacations on the Moon!

The agency had departments in several places in the United States, each one responsible for different aspects of spaceflight. Here in Florida, they ran the launch of space shuttles and robotic probes into the cosmos. In Houston, Texas, they took over control of the manned spaceflights once they had taken off, and in California there was another mission control for the robotic spaceflights. Sometimes Eric went to visit these other offices, but he had decided to base his family in Florida, so they wouldn't have to move around all the time.

Annie told the others that they had to get inside the main building at the Global Space Agency to get their space suits, which Eric had stored there, so that, like the shuttle, they could leave the Earth and travel into space. They couldn't go without their suits because it would be too cold, and they needed air to breathe and a way to communicate with Cosmos.

However, it was pretty much impossible for kids to get into the Global Space Agency by themselves: They had to have special passes, and Eric had to drive them there. They intended to put the master plan into action the minute Eric took his eyes off them.

"When no one is looking—," continued Annie.

"What do you mean, 'when no one is looking'?" interrupted George. "I think your dad will notice if we suddenly disappear."

"No he won't!" said Annie. "He'll be too busy staring up at the spaceship in the sky. So that will be the moment I give the command for us to run. All we need to do is find the space suits, put them on, open up Cosmos, and go through the doorway into space. It's simple, really," she told them. "The greatest plans always are. Just like Einstein said."

"I think he was talking about scientific theories," said George gently. "Not kids traveling around the Solar System by themselves."

"If Einstein was here now," insisted Annie, "he'd be saying, Annie Bellis, you are the coolest cat that ever wore pajamas."

Emmett's face had clouded over. "Am I going into space?" he fretted. "I mean, I really want to, but I'm very allergic to lots of things and I might—"

"No, Emmett," said Annie. "You are the controller of the cosmic journey. You're going to stay on Earth with Cosmos and direct us. So you don't have to worry about meeting a peanut in space. It isn't going to happen."

"Oh, phew," said Emmett with relief. "My mom would never forgive me."

"And what are *we* going to do?" asked George.

"We," said Annie, "you and me, that is, are going to Mars. The truth is out there, George. And *we* are going to find it."

Standing on a wide balcony high up on the Global Space Agency's main building, George, Annie, and Emmett could see all the way across the swampland to where the space shuttle sat waiting, patiently and quietly, for takeoff. Around it was the scaffolding that had been holding it upright—a steel cat's-cradle of joists and supports for the enormous spacecraft. Two railway lines led away from the launchpad to the largest building that George had ever seen.

"You see that place?" said Eric, pointing to the building. "That's where they get the spaceship ready to send it into space. It's called the Vehicle Assembly Building, and it's big enough to stand the spaceship up inside it. It's so tall that it has its own weather systems—sometimes clouds form inside."

"You mean it can rain inside there?" said Annie.

"That's right," Eric told her. "You have to take an umbrella if you work in that building! When the orbiter—that's the spacecraft part of the shuttle—is ready to go, it leaves that building by train and travels to the launchpad, where it's prepared for takeoff."

With its black-and-white nose pointing upward, the orbiter looked quite small against the giant orange fuel tank underneath it. The fuel tank was flanked on either

side by two long white rocket boosters, waiting for ignition.

"See, they've taken the arms of the scaffolding away now," said Eric. "That means they've closed all the hatches, and the crew who've readied the shuttle for launch have left the area."

"Just like on my computer game," boasted Emmett, "which teaches you how to fly the shuttle."

"I'd like to try that," said a voice from behind him. George turned around. A woman in an all-in-one blue Global Space Agency suit stood behind him. George knew this outfit meant she was a real astronaut.

"Okay!" said Emmett happily. "I can let you do that. If you come over to our house this evening, I'll show you how it works." He caught Annie's eye. "Or another day," he added hastily. "We're a bit busy right now, and I might not have time. You could come over tomorrow, if you like. If we're back,

138

that is. Not that we're going anywhere, but—ouch!"

Annie had nudged him quite hard.

"I was just trying to be friendly!" he whispered to her. "I thought you said that was a good thing to do!"

"I did!" she hissed. "But making friends with people doesn't mean you have to tell them everything we're up to the minute you meet them!"

"Then how do I make friends?" asked Emmett plaintively.

"Look, let's just get the planet saved, all right?" said Annie. "And tomorrow I'll teach you about being friends with people and how it works? Okay? Deal?"

"Deal," said Emmett solemnly. "This is turning out to be a mega-cool vacation."

"But don't you know how to fly the space shuttle already?" said George, asking a question to deflect attention away from Emmett. "Aren't you an astronaut?"

"Yes, that's right," she said. "I am an astronaut. I'm what's called a *mission specialist*. That means I'm a scientist who goes up into space to perform experiments, do space walks, and help build parts of the International Space Station. I am trained to fly spacecraft, but that isn't really my job. The commander and the pilot fly the shuttle and dock it at the International Space Station. When we get there, that's when my work begins."

"When you're in the space station," said Annie, "are you all just floating around?"

"We are," said the astronaut. "It's a lot of fun, but

it's difficult to do simple things like eat and drink. We have to drink through straws, and our food comes in packets: We open them, dig our fork in, and hope the food sticks to it and doesn't go flying around all over the place."

"Do you ever have food fights?" asked George. "That would be cool!"

"But how do you go to the toilet?" asked Emmett, looking perplexed. "Isn't that very difficult in a low-gravity scenario?"

"Emmett!" squeaked Annie. "I'm so sorry about him," she said to the astronaut. "He's really embarrassing."

"Oh no!" The woman laughed. "Don't be embarrassed about your brother's question."

Annie's face was a picture of horror at the idea that anyone could think Emmett was her brother.

"Everyone asks about the space toilet," said the astronaut. "And yes, it is quite tricky at first. We have to do special training sessions to learn how."

"You have toilet lessons to be an astronaut!" Emmett's face had turned pink with delight.

"It's just one of the things we have to learn to get by in space," said the astronaut firmly. "We train for several years, learning the tasks we need to carry out during our two-week missions in space. We have to learn how to cope with being weightless and how to operate the shuttle's robotic arm and use all the other complicated electrical and mechanical equipment. Have any of you thought of becoming astronauts when you grow up?"

"I might," said Annie. "It depends. You see, I want to be a physicist *and* a soccer player, so I might not have time for all that extra training."

"What about you two?" the astronaut asked George and Emmett. "Would you like to go into space?"

"Oh yes!" said George. "I'd like that more than anything."

Emmett shook his head. "I have motion sickness."

"We know," said Annie. On the drive over, he had nearly been sick in

her backpack—the one with Cosmos in it. She'd had to snatch it away and push Emmett's head out of the open car window to prevent a disaster. Even then, it hadn't been pleasant.

Eric appeared next to them, looking worried. "Hello!" he said to the astronaut. "I'm Eric—Eric Bellis from the Mars Science Laboratory."

"The famous Eric!" she exclaimed. "I'm Jenna. I've wanted to meet you for ages. It's great, the work you're doing on life in the Universe. We're all very excited about Homer and what he might find on Mars. We can't wait to hear the results!"

"Ah, well . . ." Eric frowned. "Um, yes, we're . . . excited too." But he didn't sound like it. "I see you've met the kids." He was fidgeting with his pager, which let him know if anything important was happening, either on the Earth or on Mars.

"I have!" said Jenna. "Are they all yours?"

"Er, no," said Eric. "Just Annie, the blond one. The rest I seem to have collected somehow." But he smiled as he spoke. "These are her friends, George and Emmett." Suddenly his pager beeped furiously in his hand. "Oh, collapsing stars!" he said to himself and looked up. "I've been sent an urgent alert," he told Jenna. "I've got to get to the control room immediately."

"You can leave the kids with me," she said. "I'm sure nothing will happen to them." The kids shuffled their feet and looked rather guilty. "You can page me when you're done," she continued cheerfully. "I'll let you know where to pick them up."

"Thank you," said Eric, and shot off down the stairs. As he left, the clock on the wall that displayed the time to takeoff had started moving again. From time to time it stopped in order to allow more checks—of everything, from the shuttle launch systems, to the computers on the orbiter, to the weather in different locations around the world—to take place. Once all the checks were completed and everyone was happy, the clock moved on again. This time they were just seconds away from liftoff. George gripped Annie's hand as everyone called out to count down the final seconds together.

"Five . . . four . . . three . . . two . . . *one!*"

The first thing they saw was a great cloud of dust at the bottom of the spaceship, billowing outward in slow, soft, pillowy folds of grayish white. As the spacecraft rose up from the ground, George and Annie could see a brilliant light under the tail. The spaceship moved upward as though pulled by an invisible thread, and the light beneath it was so bright, it was like seeing the skies ripped open to reveal an angel or some other celestial being appear from within. The spaceship climbed higher and higher, the mighty blast beneath it sending it vertically into the heavens.

"It's so quiet," whispered George to Annie. "It's not making any noise."

Until that moment, the spaceship seemed to be starting its cosmic journey in complete silence, as though
they were watching it on television with the sound
turned off. But seconds later the noise rolled over
the intervening miles toward them. First they heard
a strange crackling sound, then the full force of the
boom hit them. The sound seemed to swallow them
whole. It was so loud, it blocked out everything else.
They felt a pounding in their chests so intense that they
thought they might be knocked backward by the wave
of sound.

HOW SOUND TRAVELS THROUGH SPACE

On Earth there are lots of atoms close together and knocking one another around. Giving atoms a kick can make them kick their neighboring atoms, and then those atoms kick other atoms, and so on, so the kick travels through the mass of atoms. Lots of little kicks can create a stream of vibrations traveling through a material. The air covering the Earth's surface consists of a large number of gas atoms and molecules bouncing off one another. The air can carry these vibrations, as can the sea, the rock beneath our feet, and even everyday objects. We call the vibrations that are the right sort to stimulate our ears *sound*.

It takes time for sound to travel through a material, because an atom has to pass each kick on to its neighbors. How much time depends on how strongly the atoms affect one another, which depends on the nature of the material and other things like the temperature. In air, sound travels at around one mile every five seconds. This is about one million times slower than the speed of light, which is why the light from a space shuttle launch is seen almost immediately by the spectators, while the noise arrives a bit later. In the same way a lightning flash arrives before the thunder, which is the kick given to the air molecules by the sudden and intense electrical discharge. In the sea, sound travels at around five times faster than it does in air.

In outer space it is very different. Between stars atoms are very rare, so there is nothing to kick against. Of course, if you have air in your spacecraft, sound inside it will travel normally. A small rock hitting the outside will make the wall of the craft vibrate, and then the air inside, so you might hear that. But sounds created on a planet, or in another spacecraft, would not carry to you unless someone there converted them into radio waves (which are like light and don't need a material to carry them), and you used your radio receiver to convert them back into sound inside your ship.

There are also natural radio waves traveling through space, produced by stars and faraway galaxies. Radio astronomers examine these in the same way that other astronomers examine visible light from space. Because radio waves are not visible, and we are used to converting them into sound using radio receivers, radio astronomy is sometimes thought of as "listening," rather than "looking." But both radio and visible-light astronomers are doing the same thing: studying types of electromagnetic waves from space. There isn't really any sound from space at all.

The roar of the engines rang through their whole bodies as the spaceship curved away, leaving a trail of white smoke behind it. As they stood and watched the craft climb ever upward, they saw the wispy white clouds form into a shape against the blue sky.

"That looks like a heart," said Annie dreamily. "Like it's saying, *From the space shuttle with love.*" But a second later she shook herself back into action again. Looking around, she saw that all the adults were still gazing up at the sky. She grabbed George and Emmett.

"Okay, I'll give the countdown," she said, "and then we run! Are you ready? Five, four, three, two, *one* . . ."

Chapter 8

As the spaceship disappeared into the skies above, the kids also vanished—down the same stairway Eric had taken. They found themselves inside a huge building with long corridors leading in all directions.

"I think it's this way," said Annie, but she didn't sound at all sure. They rushed down the hallway after her, past framed pictures of astronauts and drawings done by the children of astronauts, which hung on the wall to commemorate each mission.

"Um, let's try this door." Annie pushed hard, and they burst into a huge room full of giant pieces of machinery.

"Oops!" she said, backing out rapidly, treading on George and Emmett behind her. "Not that door, then."

"Do you actually know where you're going?" asked George.

"Of course I do!" said Annie huffily. "I just got a little confused because all these places look alike. We need the

Clean Room. That's where they keep the suits. Let's go this way."

George's heart sank at the idea of Annie navigating her way around the Solar System. If she couldn't find her way around the Global Space Agency, which she claimed to have visited many times, could she really be trusted to take them to Mars and back?

But Annie was not to be deterred. She dragged them along to another door, which she shoved open. The room was in darkness, apart from an illuminated screen at the front, where a man was pointing to a picture of Saturn.

"And so we can see that the rings of Saturn," he was saying, "are made up of dust and rocks in orbit around the giant gas planet."

George thought back to the little rock from Saturn he had once pocketed when he and Annie were riding around the Solar System on a comet. Unfortunately a teacher at George's school had thought the precious rock was nothing more than a handful of dust and had made George throw it in the trash can. *If only!* he thought. If only he'd been able to bring that little rock here. What clues about the Universe might they have been able to discover from his fragment of Saturn?

They came to a door marked COMETS, but it was locked.

"*Ping-pong!*" they heard from inside Annie's backpack. Cosmos seemed to have switched himself on.

"Cosmos!" said George. "You have to stay quiet! We're trying to find the Clean Room and we don't want anyone to notice us."

"Do I sound like I care?" came the reply.

"Oh, shush!" said George urgently.

"Emmett, make him be quiet!" ordered Annie.

"Actually," said Emmett, "it would be better to leave him switched on right now. If I close him down and then have to open him up quickly, we might have even more problems."

"Over there!" said George, spotting a sign on a huge pair of double doors. It read, CLEAN ROOM. "Is that where the suits are?"

"That's it!" said Annie. "I remember it now. I've never been inside, but it's where they keep all the equipment that goes into space. It's a super-duper clean environment so that bugs and stuff don't go from Earth into space."

"Oh yes," said Emmett nerdily. "It's very important that microbes don't travel into space with any of the machinery. Otherwise how would we ever know if we've found evidence of life in space or whether we're just seeing fingerprints that we ourselves left out there?"

Annie ran over to the double doors. "Follow me!" she said. "Most of the people should be upstairs, watching the launch."

They went through, expecting to emerge in the Clean Room, but there was a surprise in store for them. They found themselves standing on a moving conveyor belt. Gusts of air started blowing at them from all sides as the belt dragged them along. Brushes emerged from the ceiling as they were sprayed with jets and buffed with a huge piece of fabric.

"What's happening?" shouted George.

"We're being *cleaned*!" Annie called back.

"Arrghh!" shouted Cosmos. "They're messin' with my ports!"

George saw a pair of robotic arms in front of him pick Annie up and drop her into an all-in-one

white plastic suit, pop a hat on her head, a mask on her face, and a pair of gloves on her hands. Before she had time to call out, she was ejected from the conveyor belt through another set of double doors, and it was his turn. George and then Emmett behind him were similarly outfitted by the machine and propelled through the doorway, where they stood, blinking at the incredible whiteness that surrounded them.

It was, thought George, like being inside a set of someone's very white teeth. On one side of the kids was a robot under construction; on the other, what looked like half a satellite. Everything seemed to gleam with an

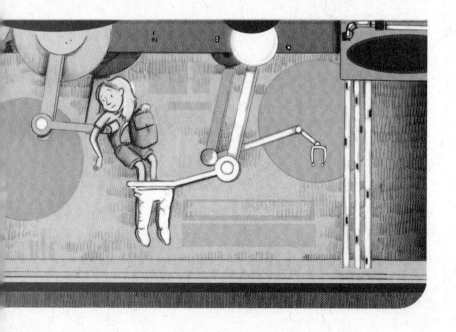

unusual brightness. Even the air felt somehow thinner and more transparent than normal air. On the wall, a sign read: 100,000.

"That's how many particles the air has in here," whispered Emmett through his face mask. "This isn't the cleanest Clean Room. In there, they have a ten thousand rating—that means any cubic foot of air in there has no more than ten thousand particles in it larger than half a micron! And a micron is a millionth of a meter."

"Is it clean enough for us to go to Mars from here?" asked George. "I mean, what if we take some evidence of life on Earth to Mars and then Homer finds it later on? Could we mess up the research program?"

"Theoretically, yes," said Emmett, who was sounding much more confident now that he felt they'd entered his area of expertise. "But that depends on a) whether we can get Cosmos working, b) whether you actually manage to get to Mars, and c) whether Annie's alien message really *is* a threat to destroy the Earth. If she's right—and I have to point out the probability is very low—then if you don't go, there won't be life on Earth, anyway. So it won't matter."

In a corner of the Clean Room, Annie had found some space suits, but they were bright orange and didn't look at all like the ones George remembered from his travels around the Universe in the past.

"These aren't ours!" Annie said in disappointment. "These are the ones they use for the space shuttle—

they're different from the ones me and my dad had." She rooted around a bit farther. "Dad told me he'd put ours in here for safekeeping," she said. "And I said, what if someone else took them by mistake? And he said they wouldn't because he'd labeled them as proto-type suits, not to be used for shuttle missions."

Emmett was tearing at the plastic wrapping that the Clean Room entry machinery had used to cover Annie's backpack. He fished Cosmos out—and at the same time found the bright yellow book, *The User's Guide to the Universe.*

"Okay, little computer," he said, flexing his fingers. "Operation Alien Life-form is underway. Where to, Commander George?"

"See if you can get him to open the doorway," said George. "We need to go to Mars, to the north polar region, destination Homer."

"Bingo!" Annie shouted. "I've got the suits!" She emerged with an armful of white space suits in plastic coverings marked PROTOTYPE—DO NOT USE! She chucked one over to George. "Take off your face mask and then put this on over everything else." She and George ripped the coverings off the suits and started clambering into the heavy space gear.

Meanwhile Emmett had called up some pictures of Mars on Cosmos's screen, zooming closer and closer to the red planet. However, Cosmos himself was being unusually silent.

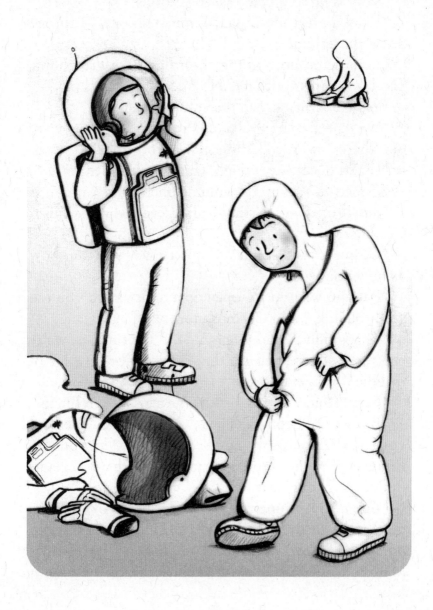

"Why is he so quiet?" asked George.

"I had a great idea," said Emmett simply. "I turned down the volume."

He turned it up, and they heard Cosmos grumbling, "Nobody cares about me. No one understands me."

Emmett turned down the volume again.

"We'll need to be able to talk to Cosmos when we're out there," warned Annie. "We got stuck in space once, and once was enough. Can you handle him?"

Emmett turned up the volume once more.

"*Do this*, *do that*, that's all I ever hear," whined Cosmos.

"Cosmos," said Annie. "I've got a way you can show us how you feel."

"Bet you want me to open up a doorway so you can go through it," said Cosmos morosely.

"That's right," said George. "But the thing is, we're not really allowed to do this. So we'll be in a lot of trouble if we get caught."

"Cool!" said Cosmos, perking up a bit. "Then I'm in."

"But we need you to help us," said George. "We need you to look after us while we're on Mars. And you too, Emmett. If we need to leave quickly, you have to get us out of there immediately."

"But," said Emmett, "if you signal me from Mars, then won't there be a time delay? I mean, it takes four minutes and twenty seconds for light to travel from Mars. Or, if Mars is on the other side of the Sun, it could be twenty-two minutes. So by the time you've said something to me and I've replied, it will have taken either eight minutes and forty seconds or forty-four minutes. And that might be too late."

"No, Cosmos has instant messaging," said Annie. "So you'll hear us and reply immediately."

"Wow! That's some pretty special physics!" said Emmett, looking impressed.

"That is," Annie added, "if Cosmos isn't too chicken to do this—"

"Dude. I'm on it," said Cosmos. A little beam of white light shot out from the great computer. In the middle of the Clean Room, the kids saw the shape of a doorway emerge.

The door swung open. Behind it, they saw a reddish planet coming into view. There was a large dark patch on its middle left-hand side.

"Approaching Mars," said Emmett as the planet drew closer, stars shining brightly in the black sky behind it. "See that dark spot? That's Syrtis Major. That's a huge area of dark, windswept volcanic plain so large, it has been known to science since the first telescope was turned to Mars in the 1600s. The southern polar ice cap is large and visible at this time of year. The bright feature at the lower center is the Hellas Basin, the largest undisputed impact crater on the planet, formed by an asteroid or comet. It is 1,370 miles across. Those four points you see in the equatorial region—they're clouds of water ice crystals over the four largest volcanoes in Tharsis."

"How do you know all this?" asked George, speaking in a strange voice through the voice transmitter in the space helmet he had just put on.

"Actually, I'm getting it from Cosmos's screen," said Emmett almost apologetically. "He's giving me a readout of the conditions on Mars to check that it is safe for you to land. On the way he's giving a bit of tourist advice. It says here that visitors to Mars should remember that gravitational conditions there will be quite different from what you're used to. You'll weigh less than half of what you weigh on Earth, so get ready to bounce."

"Does he say what the weather is like?" Annie asked through her voice transmitter. She sounded rather nervous.

"Let's look . . . ," said Emmett. "Here's today's forecast for the north polar region of Mars: *Today will be mostly clear with an average temperature of minus seventy-six degrees Fahrenheit. Possibility of water ice storms in the area: very low. But dust storms could start from the central region and engulf the planet. I'd better keep an eye on that. It says here that dust storms are common at this time of year and can spread very fast.*"

The doorway got nearer and nearer to Mars, breaking through the thin atmosphere and heading down toward the rocky surface.

George and Annie stood at the threshold, holding hands with their big space gloves, their oxygen tanks plugged in and their transmission devices switched on. As they hovered a few yards above the ground, Annie asked, "Are you ready? Five, four, three, two, one . . . *jump!*"

They disappeared through the doorway and found themselves on Mars—a planet where no human being had ever set foot before.

Emmett saw them vanish; then a spray of red Martian dust floated through the portal before the door slammed shut.

He tried to capture some of the dust as it drifted through the superclean air, but it was quickly sucked away through the Clean Room's contamination control system, designed to immediately dispose of any pollution. Like Annie and George, the Martian dust disappeared completely, leaving Emmett alone in the huge room with Cosmos. He gazed around for a few minutes and then picked up *The User's Guide to the Universe*.

He looked up Mars in the index and turned to the right page.

"*Did Life Come from Mars?*" he read.

DID LIFE COME FROM MARS?

Where and when did life as we know it begin? Did it begin on Earth? Or could it have come from Mars?

A couple of centuries ago most people believed that humans, and other species, had been present since the creation of the Earth. The Earth was thought to be the entire material world, and the creation was described as a sudden event, like the Big Bang that scientists believe in today. This was taught in creation stories, like the one in Genesis, the first book of the Bible, and other cultures throughout the world have similar stories of a single moment of creation.

Although some astronomers did think about the vastness of space, its study only really began after Galileo (1564–1642) made one of the first ever telescopes. His discoveries showed that the Universe contained many other worlds—some of which could, like our own planet, be inhabited. The immensity of the Universe—and the evidence that its creation must have happened *long before* humans arrived on the scene—did not begin to be generally recognized until much later on, in the eighteenth century. During that innovative time the study of rock formation by sedimentation in shallow seas led geologists to understand that such processes must have been going on, not just for thousands or even millions of years, but for thousands of millions of years—what we now call gigayears.

Modern geophysicists now believe our planet Earth—and our Solar System—was formed about 4.6 gigayears ago, when the Universe—now aged about 14 gigayears—was itself just more than 9 gigayears old.

Modern humans appear to have arrived in the rest of the world from Africa fifty thousand years ago, but modern archaeology has shown quite clearly that it was only about six thousand years ago that early human societies began to develop what we call *civilization*—economic systems with the exchange of different kinds of goods. A very important factor in any civilization is the exchange not just of goods but of *information*. But how was this information stored or spread?

Before the invention of paper and ink, one of the earliest methods was to use marks scratched on clay tablets—the distant ancestors of modern computer memory chips. This sharing and collection of knowledge, particularly the kind we now call *scientific*, became an objective in its own right.

The development of civilization depended, of course, on the emergence of what has been called *intelligent life*—beings with a sufficient sense of self-awareness to recognize themselves in a mirror. There are several known examples on our own planet: elephants, dolphins, and, of course, anthropoids—the group that includes chimpanzees and other apes, Neanderthals, and modern human beings like us. So far no signs of intelligent life have been detected elsewhere in the Universe.

How did intelligent life on Earth come into being? Fossils had suggested the idea that modern plants and animals could have arisen from other life-forms present on Earth in earlier times, but people couldn't understand how the various species could be so well adapted without having been designed in advance. The idea of continuous evolution became generally accepted only after Darwin

(in 1859) explained the principle of adaptation by *natural selection*. Understanding how this actually works, however, only became possible in the late 1950s, when Watson and Crick made their discoveries about DNA.

This modern DNA-based understanding of the evolutionary process is supported by the fossil record—as far back as it is dated. The trouble is that the record does not go very far back—less than a gigayear, which is only a fraction of the total age of the Earth.

Early, simple life-forms developed before what is known as the Cambrian era. We can see fairly clearly how (though not precisely why) what we should recognize as intelligent life-forms evolved from them over the last five hundred million years. But there is no proper record of how the pre-Cambrian life-forms evolved in the first place.

One problem is that it is only since the Cambrian era that large bony animals, which turn easily into fossils, have been present. Their largest predecessors are believed to be soft-bodied creatures (like modern jellyfish); farther back in time, the only life-forms seem to have been microscopic single-celled creatures. These don't leave clear fossil records.

Going back even farther, it is evident that evolution must have been very slow. And tricky to achieve. Even if environmentally favorable planets were fairly common in the Universe, the odds against the evolution of advanced life on any single planet would have been very high. This means that it would occur on only a very small fraction of them. Earth must be one of those rare exceptions. And it could still have easily gone wrong. There is a calculation by astrophysicists known as the *solar age coincidence*. This shows that in the time taken by evolution on Earth to lead to intelligent life, a large part of the hydrogen fuel reserves powering our Sun were used up. In a nutshell, if our evolution had been just a little bit slower, we would never have got here at all before the Sun burned itself out!

So which of the essential evolutionary steps would be the hardest to achieve in the available time?

One difficult step on Earth may have been the beginning of what is known as *eukaryotic life*—in which cells have an elaborate structure with nuclei and ribosomes. Eukaryotes include large, multicellular animals like us, as well as single-celled species like the amoeba. The fossil record shows that the first eukaryotic life appeared on Earth at the beginning of the Proterozoic aeon, about two gigayears ago, when the Earth was only about half its present age. Before this period, more primitive *procaryotic* life-forms, such as bacteria (with cells that are too small to contain nuclei), are now thought to have been widespread when the Earth was less than one gigayear old.

There is evidence for the existence of this kind of primitive life right back at the very beginning of this aeon. So we are now faced with a puzzle, because this implies that the whole process by which life actually originated must have occurred during the *preceding* epoch. This is known as the Hadean aeon, the earliest aeon of the Earth's history.

Why should this be a problem? Well, the Hadean aeon was certainly long enough—nearly a gigayear—but conditions on Earth at that time would have been literally infernal, as the name suggests (Hades is the ancient Greek version of hell). This was when debris left over from the formation of the Solar System was crashing into the Moon and forming craters there. And the Earth—with its greater mass and gravitational attraction—would at that time have been subject to even heavier cratering. This bombardment would have caused frequent reheating of our planetary environment. New life-forms could hardly have avoided being nipped in the bud.

The planet Mars, however, has a lesser mass than Earth and is farther away from the Sun, so it has recently been proposed that the bombardment of Mars could have subsided sooner than that of the Earth. Chunks of debris may also have been frequently knocked off Mars and, in some cases, subsequently swept up by the Earth.

This would mean that life may have originated on Mars—before it could have survived here.

Analysis by electron microscope of a meteorite that did reach Earth from Mars (meteorite ALH8400) has shown structures resembling fossil microbes. This proves that *fossil* organisms may have reached the Earth from Mars. But that would still not account for *life* then appearing here unless *living*—not just fossil—organisms could survive the necessary migration by meteor. This is a question that is currently being very hotly debated.

An even more interesting question is whether the environment on Mars at that time really would have been suitable for primitive life.

Nowadays, conditions on Mars are clearly unfavorable, at least on the surface—a cold, dry desert with hardly any atmosphere except for a little carbon dioxide. Probes landing on Mars have, however, confirmed that there is a considerable amount of frozen water at the poles. Additionally, there are many observable features of the kind expected from erosion by rivers or by surf at a seashore. This means that at some stage in the Martian past, there must have been a large amount of liquid water present—exactly what is needed for our kind of life to begin. During that early period the water would have formed an ocean. Initially this could have been several miles deep, with its center near what is now the Martian north pole.

So life could have originated at the edge of this ocean, way back in Martian history.

There are a couple of objections to this theory. One is that the atmosphere would not have contained oxygen. However, primitive life-forms on Earth are believed to have been been able to survive in an atmosphere that was also very deficient in oxygen, so that might not have mattered.

Another objection is that the ancient Martian ocean would have been too salty for known terrestrial life-forms. But maybe Martian life was originally adapted to very salty conditions, or perhaps it developed in freshwater lakes?

Thus life may well have begun on Mars—at the edge of a huge ocean there—then hitched a ride to the Earth on board a meteor. So our ultimate ancestors may, in fact, have been Martians!

Brandon

Chapter 9

As George and Annie jumped through the portal doorway, George twisted around to look back. For a millisecond he saw the Clean Room on planet Earth, and Emmett's worried face peering through the

portal. But then the doorway closed and disappeared entirely, leaving no trace in the dusty Martian sky of where it had once been.

Propelled by the force of their leap through the doorway, George and Annie traveled through the Martian atmosphere without landing for a few yards. They were holding hands tightly, so they didn't lose each other on this strange and empty planet. George touched down, but the impact of his feet on the surface sent them back up again in a great bouncing leap.

"Where are the mountains?" he called to Annie through the transmitter as they landed again and quickly dropped the other one's hand. They were standing on a huge expanse of flat, rubble-strewn, reddish ground. As far as they could see, there was nothing on either side but an endless scattering of red rocks across the desert planet. In the sky the Sun—the same star that shone so brightly on the Earth—seemed more distant, smaller, and colder, its light and warmth coming from farther away than on their home planet. The light looked pink, because of all the red dust floating in the air, but it wasn't the beautiful familiar rosy glow of an earthly sunrise. Instead, it was a luminous color that seemed alien and unwelcoming to the first humanoids ever to complete the journey from Earth to Mars.

"No mountains here," Annie told George. "We're at the north pole of Mars. The volcanoes and valleys are in the middle of the planet."

"How long have we got until sunset?" he asked,

suddenly realizing they wouldn't be able to see anything once the Sun went down. The absolute nothingness of this empty planet was giving him the creeps, and he certainly didn't want to be there in the dark.

"Ages," said Annie. "The sun doesn't set at the north pole in summer. But I don't want to stay that long. I don't like it here." Even though her space suit protected her from the conditions on Mars, she shivered.

It wasn't nice to be so lonely and, like George, Annie suddenly missed being on a planet with people, buildings, movement, noise, and life. Even though they sometimes felt they would love to live on a planet where there was no one to annoy them or order them around, the reality was very different. On an empty planet, there would be nothing to do and no one to play with. They might have dreamed of being masters of their very own world, but when it came down to it, home didn't seem so bad after all.

George jumped into the air again, to see how high he could go. He rose about a couple of feet and landed a second later, not far from where Annie was still standing.

"That was amazing!" he said.

"We'd better try not to leave too many footprints," warned Annie, pointing to the marks George had made on the surface, "or people will see them when the Mars orbiter passes over this place and takes a photo. And then they'll think there really are Martians."

"I can see Homer!" said George, spotting a lonely little figure in the distance. Now separate, they bounced closer. "But what's he doing?" he added in amazement. The robot looked very busy. He was rolling to and fro, chucking bits of rock in the air.

"That's what we're here to find out," said Annie. "I'm going to call Emmett. Emmett!" she said into her voice transmitter. "Emmett? Rats! He's not answering."

They took a few long paces toward Homer and watched as he spun mysteriously—but purposefully—about.

"Keep down!" hissed Annie, crouching. "Otherwise Homer might see us through his camera eyes. And

then my dad will spot us on Mars and he'll know where we are. That would be a disaster!"

"But he won't see us for a few minutes," said George. "Not until the signal gets back to Earth. So even if Homer does take a picture of us, we'd still have time to get away."

"Huh!" Annie snorted. "It's okay for you. If my dad sees us here, all that will happen to you is he'll send you right back to England. But I'll be stuck here—well, not here exactly. Not on Mars, but on Earth, with him being angry with me. And with every kind of boring punishment he can think of."

"Like what?" asked George.

"Oh, I don't know!" said Annie. "No soccer and extra math homework and washing space suits and no allowance for ever and ever and ever, I expect. Honestly, planet Earth won't feel big enough."

"Do we have to be quiet too? Can Homer hear us?" asked George.

"Hmm, don't think so," said Annie. "Mars has the wrong sort of atmosphere for noise to travel, so I don't think he's recording any sound, just pictures." She paused for a second and then shouted into her voice transmitter, "BUT I WISH EMMETT COULD HEAR US!"

"Ouch!" said George, whose space helmet felt like it might explode from the sound of Annie's voice erupting into it.

"Who? What? Where?" Finally, they heard Emmett.

"Emmett, you twit!" said Annie. "Why didn't you answer before?"

"Sorry," came Emmett's voice. "I was just reading something . . . Are you okay?"

"Yes, we are, no thanks to you, ground control," said Annie. "We have landed on Mars and we are approaching Homer. Do you have any further information for us?"

"Just checking," murmured Emmett. "I'll get back to you."

"Can I *boing* right over him?" asked George longingly. He was really enjoying the lower gravity on Mars and wanted to keep jumping higher and higher. "Then I could look down to see what he's doing?" George's white space suit had turned reddish brown from the Martian dust.

"No, you'd crash into him!" said Annie. "You can only go about two and a half times higher on Mars than you can on Earth. So don't try anything silly. We need to get to Homer," she said, "but stay to one side. That way we should miss the camera."

They took a few giant loopy steps nearer to the robot, who was now motionless after his burst of frenzied activity, as though it had worn him out and he needed a rest.

"He's stopped fooling around. Let's creep up on him!" said Annie. It wasn't easy to tiptoe in heavy space boots, but they did their best to approach the robot without him noticing. Homer's legs were splayed firmly against the Martian ground. His solar arrays— the panels that allowed him to collect radiation from the Sun and turn it into energy—were covered in dust. His thick rubber wheels were now still, and his long robotic arm hung limply by his side, but his camera was still flashing its beady eyes.

But as they got near to him, they noticed something else—something they hadn't seen on the pictures Homer had sent back from Mars.

"Over there!" said Annie. "Look!"

Next to Homer on the flat Martian surface they saw a series of marks made in the dust and rubble by Homer's tires.

"It's a message!" yelled George, forgetting not to shout while wearing the voice transmitter. "It's just like the one Cosmos received! It's the same sort of marks! Someone has left us a message on Mars!"

Annie kicked him with her space boot. "Don't shout!" she whispered.

At the same time they heard Emmett's excited voice from planet Earth. "A message? On Mars? What does it say?"

"We're trying to work it out," said Annie. "What if Homer wasn't just messing around? What if all that dancing around he did was because he was writing a message for us?"

They took a careful stride, which landed them right next to the squiggles Homer had drawn in the dust.

"It's going to take a few minutes," George warned, "before we can work it out."

He and Annie bounced together back and forth over the message as they tried to make sense of it.

"Can you tell me anything about the marks?" asked Emmett urgently. "Anything I can enter to see what Cosmos makes of it?"

Just then George and Annie were flying right over the message. "Um, well," said George. "There's a circle surrounded by other circles."

"It could be a planet with rings," said Annie. "It could be Saturn. And look, next to it, all those rocks arranged in a row, that could be the Solar System, like in the other message."

"And over there—there's the planet with rings again, but it's also got lots of little pieces of stone arranged around it."

"Maybe it's the moons of Saturn," came Emmett's voice. "Do you think the message wants you to go to the moons of Saturn? I'm putting the information into Cosmos now, to see if he can give us another clue. Can you count how many little pieces of stone? Saturn has quite a lot—about sixty. But only seven round ones."

The wind, which had been just a breeze, was now starting to blow more strongly, whipping bits of surface rubble up into the air and whirling them around.

"Oh no! Severe weather warning"—Emmett read off Cosmos's screen—"incoming gales from the south. Potential evacuation situation."

"We need more time!" George replied. "We don't know what the message means yet! We're trying to count the moons around the planet with rings."

"But it does have the same ending," pointed out Annie, whose blood had run colder than space itself when she saw the last picture in the row. "It still says no planet Earth." They made another jump and landed right next to Homer. Annie got hold of his legs with her hand to stop herself from falling over in the strong wind; with the other hand, she grabbed on to George.

Emmett came back over the transmitter, sounding panicked. "I don't think you *have* more time," he said urgently. "Cosmos has detected a giant dust storm, which is spreading very fast toward you! We have to get you out of there before you get lost in it! Cosmos says he may not be able to find you in a dust storm—oh!" He broke off abruptly.

"Emmett, what is it?" Annie and George had just seen the huge dust clouds in the far distance, rolling over the empty ground toward them.

"Cosmos is stalled!" Emmett said in despair. "He says: *Reverse portal not available at this moment due to an urgent system update.* Until he's finished updating, he can't bring you back! He can only send you farther out!"

"Em, get us out of here!" shouted Annie, not caring how much noise she made now. "Send us somewhere! Anywhere! But out of this storm! I can't hold on much longer!"

The wind was blowing the surface dust up around them. Homer was already covered in it, his shiny solar arrays blanked out.
George and Annie could only just see each other as the torrent swirled around them. Annie was still hanging on

Venus

© JPL/NASA/SCIENCE PHOTO LIBRARY

Volcanoes on Venus.

Venus's atmosphere.

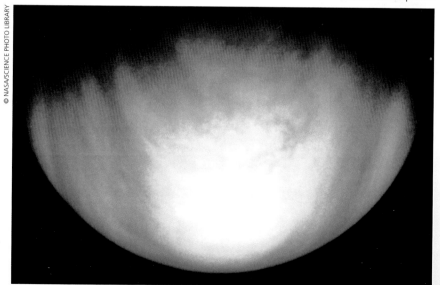

© NASA/SCIENCE PHOTO LIBRARY

Jupiter

© NASA/SCIENCE PHOTO LIBRARY

Voyager 1 image of Jupiter.

Saturn

© NASA/SCIENCE PHOTO LIBRARY

Voyager 1 image of Saturn and its ring system.

© NASA/JPL/SSI/SCIENCE PHOTO LIBRARY

Cassini image of Saturn's largest moon, Titan, in front of Saturn.

Uranus and Neptune

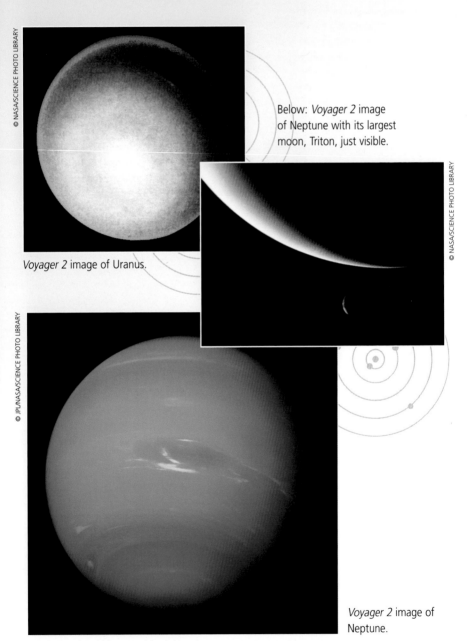

© NASA/SCIENCE PHOTO LIBRARY

Voyager 2 image of Uranus.

Below: *Voyager 2* image of Neptune with its largest moon, Triton, just visible.

© NASA/SCIENCE PHOTO LIBRARY

© JPL/NASA/SCIENCE PHOTO LIBRARY

Voyager 2 image of Neptune.

Deployment of the Hubble Space Telescope (HST) from the space shuttle *Discovery*, 1990.

Colored optical image of the Rosette Nebula.

Optical image of the Tarantula Nebula.

© NASA/SCIENCE PHOTO LIBRARY

Earthrise over Moon, taken by U.S. astronauts on board *Apollo 8*, 1968.

It is one of the first images of the Earth seen from space.

EARTH

Earth from space, in true color,
showing Europe and northern Africa.

to Homer's leg, with George floating out behind her, buffeted by the terrible winds. He wrapped both hands tightly around one of Annie's arms. But they both knew that, at any second, they could be blown away from each other and lost forever on Mars.

"The moons of Saturn!" yelled George into his voice transmitter. "If you can't bring us back, send us farther out! Send us to the next clue!"

Through the gritty cloud, which was growing thicker by the second, they saw the faint outline of a doorway standing right next to them. As it became more solid-looking, George let go of Annie with one arm and grabbed the door frame. Swiveling around, he braced his feet against it, still holding tightly on to Annie, who was in turn still attached to Homer.

"Open the door!" he bellowed to Emmett on Earth. "Annie! When I count down, I'm going to throw you through it! Let go of Homer!"

"I can't!" screamed Annie. "I can't let go!"

George realized she was frozen with fear that she might be blown away if she released her hold on Homer.

"You have to!" he shouted back. "I can't pull you *and* Homer through the doorway! I'm not strong enough!"

The door swung open very fast. Behind it they could see a mysterious orange swirl.

"On my count, Annie, let go!" said George. "Five, four, three, two, *one*." He tried to hurl her through the

door but she was still clinging to Homer. "Close your eyes," he shouted, "and imagine Earth. I'll be right behind you, Annie. I'm coming with you. Try again—you can do this. Five! Four! Three! Two! *ONE!*"

Annie let go of Homer's leg and catapulted through the doorway. George flung himself after her, swinging around the door frame and into another world—one he had never even dreamed of.

The doorway shut behind him as the dust cloud swallowed the whole of Mars, sweeping Homer's message and Annie and George's footprints off the surface and covering the little robot in a blanket of reddish dust. All that was left was the tiny red light on Homer's camera, winking away as he took photos of the Martian storm and sent them back to Annie's dad, so many millions of miles away on friendly planet Earth.

Chapter 10

Far away from the Global Space Agency head-quarters, but really very close in terms of space distances, Daisy, George's mom, had just watched the sun rise over the Pacific Ocean. The sapphire night sky had changed to a light azure wash as the brilliant stars faded from view and the mist rose from the crystal-clear water. Daisy had been watching the sky all night.

As the Sun had set the day before, she had seen Mercury and Venus hang just over the horizon, disappearing as the Moon rose in the east. The night darkened, and a million brilliant stars peppered the sky. Among them were Alpha and Beta Centauri, bright stars that both pointed the way to the Southern Cross, the great constellation that is visible only in the Southern Hemisphere. Daisy had lain back on the sands and looked into the heavens. Above her were the constellations Libra and Scorpius, with the beautiful star and heart of Scorpius, Antares, shining down on her.

As she gazed at the stars, she thought of George at

the space-shuttle launch and imagined his excitement at seeing a real spacecraft lift off into the skies above. Little did she realize, as she sat on the beach and looked upward, that George himself was somewhere out there in the Solar System, traveling between Mars and his next destination on the cosmic treasure hunt!

It was just as well that poor Daisy had no idea her son was, at that moment, lost in space, because George's dad, Terence, was currently lost on Earth, which was why she was sitting on the sand, waiting for the boat he'd taken to reappear. Terence and Daisy had gone to Tuvalu, a group of islands in the Pacific, a beautiful paradise lapped by a gentle blue sea. The sands were white, the palm trees waved, and enormous butterflies and exotic birds fluttered among the thick vegetation.

But they hadn't gone there for a vacation. They had joined a group of their eco-warrior friends who were on a mission to chart the changes affecting these islands, islets, and atolls.

The seas that looked so friendly, warm, and inviting were actually rising, threatening to swallow up some of the tinier islands and leave no trace of life. Soon, all the people might lose their homes as the sea level got higher and higher. The ocean was rising because of a combination of melting land ice in the Antarctic, Greenland, and the glaciers, coupled with the thermal expansion of seawater. As water warms up, it takes up more space,

which all adds up to more water and less land. Some of the islands and atolls were so low-lying that any change to the sea level became obvious very quickly, as homes were flooded and beaches disappeared; the main runway in the capital city was now unusable for much of the year because it was often underwater.

The people could at least leave—even though they didn't want to lose their homes and their lives on those wonderful islands. But all the birds, butterflies, and moths that had become used to that climate and that environment really didn't have anywhere else to go.

The Pacific Islanders had been trying to tell the rest of the world what was happening to them. They'd been to big conferences and made lots of noise about how their homes might not exist in a few years' time if global warming continued to make the sea rise at the same rate. Some people argued that the changes the Tuvaluans were experiencing were just part of a normal cycle of weather patterns that caused big storms to wash over the islands and drown them in monster tides. But others were convinced that what they saw was a sign

of something more sinister that couldn't be explained away so easily.

In a sense, the fact that Tuvalu seemed to be sinking was nothing new. The five atolls that made up the Tuvalu group had been sinking into the sea for a very long time. The famous explorer and naturalist Charles Darwin had sailed across the Pacific in 1835 and come up with an explanation for how atolls, which from above look like flat rings of sand surrounding a lagoon, had formed. New islands were created in tropical waters due to volcanic activity. Over millions of years, coral—organisms that live in warm shallow water—built up along the shoreline of these new volcanic islands as they sank back into the sea. Eventually the volcanic island would disappear altogether, but the coral would carry on growing up to the surface and above the water, forming reefs and beaches.

However, this process had taken place over a very long time—maybe as much as thirty million years. It was the past ten years and the next five that were giving the Tuvaluans serious cause for concern, and it was these rapid recent changes that they wanted to record.

In order to do this, George's dad and a couple of others had left the main atoll by boat to explore the islands. But they hadn't come back when they were expected. They had taken maps for their journey but no GPS system or cell phone. They had said they would navigate by the stars, just as another explorer, Captain

Cook, had done all those years ago when he had sailed across the Southern Seas to record the transit of Venus across the Sun.

Unfortunately for Terence, they had got very lost and had not managed to find their way back to Tuvalu, where Daisy was now horribly worried about them. The other eco-activists had tried sending out boats to find them, but they had come back with no sighting. Daisy and the others were growing frantic with worry. Surely Terence and his friends didn't have enough fresh water on the boat to last long, and by day the sun shines very brightly over the South Pacific. During

that long night, Daisy had made a call to Florida to ask for help. . . .

In another part of the Solar System, as George pushed himself through the doorway from Mars into the swirling dark orange world beyond, he heard Annie scream: "It's all wet!'

George landed behind her on what looked like a sloping patch of frozen ground. He wobbled as he landed and reached back to grab hold of the door frame to steady himself. Annie, who George had thrown through the doorway, seemed to fly slowly through the air, landing just next to a channel of dark liquid that flowed into an enormous black lake. For a second it looked like she might topple over and fall into the black stream. But instead, she bent her knees, whirled her arms, and took off, bounding gracefully over the dark river.

George hung on to the door frame. The actual doorway back to Mars had closed behind him, but the portal was still there, shimmering slightly in the dim light. He tested the ground with one space boot. It looked like it was made of solid ice. He tried to chip a bit off with his heel, but it was as solid as granite. George looked around for something else to hold on to once the portal disappeared, but couldn't reach the rocks behind him and the slope in front was ice all the way down to the mysterious dark river.

"Whatever you do, don't fall in!" called Annie from the other side of the fast-moving liquid. "We don't know what's in it!"

"Where are we?" called George, looking around. The skies above were very low and heavy, full of streaky orange and black clouds. The light was dim, as though it came from some far distant star across many millions of miles of space, and the clouds were so dense that the light struggled to reach the surface of this strange world. "What is this place?"

"I don't know," replied Annie. "It feels like Earth before life began. You don't think Cosmos has sent us back in time by mistake, do you? Maybe he's transported us back to the beginning, to see what it was like before anything happened."

While the wind appeared to be blowing gently, in reality it packed a big punch, and George had to hang on to the portal doorway.

"George, this is ground control"—he heard Emmett's voice, sounding very serious—"Cosmos can't hold the portal doorway in place for much longer. He needs to shut down that application, otherwise he might start malfunctioning."

"Annie, what do I do?" asked George, who was suddenly terrified of tumbling into the stream and getting swept into the lake.

"You'll have to jump," said Annie. "Like I did!" She was now standing on what looked like a tiny, icy beach on the other side of the channel, where it met the shore of the lake. "It's flat here so you can land safely." Beyond the little beach a craggy cliff face overhung the mysterious black lake, its peaks outlined against the glowing tiger-skin sky, like a row of gigantic needles.

"There are too many applications open," George heard Cosmos say. "Portal will shut down instantly. If this has happened in error, please check the box to send a message to the support unit. Your feedback is important to us."

The doorway vanished from view, leaving George and Annie by themselves on the mystery planet. Left with nothing to hold on to, George stumbled down the slope toward the black liquid. He pushed off from the ground, just as he had seen Annie do, which sent him upward and across the stream . . .

"That wind is really strong!" he said, once he'd landed on the other side. All his movements felt as though they were happening in slow motion. "It felt like it was trying to push me over! But it doesn't *seem* to be blowing very hard."

"Maybe it's a thicker atmosphere than we have at home," said Annie. "Perhaps that's why it's like being in soup rather than being in air. And there's not much gravity here—that's why we're not falling very fast. Oh! What *is* that?" The clouds had just parted to allow them a view of this extraordinary world. On the other side of the lake, they saw a huge mountain with a dip where the peak should have been.

"Wow! That looks like a dead volcano," said George.

As they gazed at it, they saw the crater at the top spew out great blobs of bluish liquid.

"I don't think it's dead!" shrieked Annie. The thick liquid was moving slowly down through the atmosphere to land on the slopes of the volcano, where it crept along like huge blind sticky earthworms, snaking down the side of the mountain.

"That looks disgusting!" she squeaked. "What is it? And where are we? What planet are we on?"

"You're not on a planet," Emmett radioed in finally. "You're on Titan, the largest moon of Saturn. You are nearly one billion miles away, near to a cryovolcano, Ganesa Macula, which is currently erupting."

"Is there any danger from the eruption?" asked George. They could see the strange thick lava creeping down channels carved into the rocky landscape.

"Hard to say," replied Emmett cheerfully, "given that no life-form we know of has ever landed on Titan before."

"Thanks a lot, Emmett," said George darkly.

"But the cryovolcanoes emit water—even though it is really cold water. It's mixed with ammonia, which means it can get down to minus one hundred forty-eight degrees Fahrenheit without freezing. So it probably doesn't smell very nice. But that won't bother you, with your space suits on."

"Emmett, there are lakes here! And rivers!" said Annie. "But they are weird and dark. It doesn't look like water.'

TITAN

- Titan is the largest of Saturn's moons and the second largest moon in the Solar System. Only Ganymede—one of Jupiter's moons—is bigger.

- Titan was discovered on March 25, 1655, by Dutch astronomer Christiaan Huygens. Huygens was inspired by Galileo's discovery of four moons around Jupiter. The discovery that Saturn had moons in orbit around it provided further proof for astronomers in the seventeenth century that not all objects in the Solar System traveled around the Earth, as was previously thought.

- Saturn was thought to have seven moons, but we now know there are at least sixty moons in orbit around the giant gas planet.

- It takes fifteen days and twenty-two hours for Titan to orbit Saturn—the same time as it takes for this moon to rotate once on its own axis, which means that a year on Titan is the same length as a day!

- Titan is the only moon we know of in the Solar System that has a dense atmosphere. Before astronomers realized this, Titan itself was thought to be much larger in mass. Its atmosphere is mostly made up of nitrogen with a small amount of methane. Scientists think that it may be similar to the atmosphere of the early Earth and that Titan could have enough material to start the process of life. But this moon is very cold and lacks carbon dioxide, so the chances of life existing there at the moment are slim.

- Titan may show us what conditions on Earth were like in the very distant past and help us understand how life began here.

- Titan is the most distant place on which a space probe has landed. On July 1, 2004, the *Cassini-Huygens* spacecraft reached Saturn. It flew by Titan on October 26, 2004, and the *Huygens* probe detached from the *Cassini* spacecraft and landed on Titan on January 14, 2005.

- *Huygens* took photographs of Titan's surface and found that it rains there!

- The probe also observed dry riverbeds—"traces of once-flowing liquid"—on the surface. *Cassini* imaging later found evidence of hydrocarbons.

- In billions of years' time, when our Sun becomes a red giant, Titan might become warm enough for life to begin!

Artwork of the Cassini spacecraft approaching Saturn

"Why has Cosmos sent us here?" asked George.

"Once you and Annie had realized the clue led to one of the moons, Cosmos calculated that Titan was the most probable location for life of some kind to have existed, due to the chemical composition of its structure and atmosphere. Cosmos thinks you will find the next clue on Titan," Emmett told them. "Although I have to admit, he doesn't seem to know where. He's being a bit of a buzzkill at the moment. Sometimes he's really helpful and then suddenly he starts sulking."

"Dude. Chill out," complained Cosmos.

"Ooh, look!" said Annie, pointing toward the lake. "What is it?" Drifting on the tide toward them, they saw a shape like a lifebuoy or a boat.

"It looks like a machine," said George. "Like something that came from Earth."

"Unless," said Annie, "there's someone here and it

belongs to them . . . Emmett," she went on slowly, "is there anyone out here? And if there is, do we want to meet them?"

"Um," said Emmett, "I'm trying to check on Cosmos, to see what he's got on his files for life on Titan."

"No," snapped Cosmos. "I'm tired now. Go away."

"He's starting to run low on memory," said Emmett. "And we're going to need him to open up the portal to get you back fairly soon. So I'm looking in *The User's Guide* instead. Here we are—'Is There Anyone Out There?' This should tell us."

IS THERE ANYONE OUT THERE?

Will some readers of this book walk on Mars? I hope so. Indeed, I think it is very likely that they will. It will be a dangerous adventure and perhaps the most exciting exploration of all time. In earlier centuries, pioneer explorers discovered new continents, went to the jungles of Africa and South America, reached the North and South Poles, and scaled the summits of the highest mountains. Those who travel to Mars will go in the same spirit of adventure.

It would be wonderful to traverse the mountains, canyons, and craters of Mars, or perhaps even to fly over them in a balloon. But nobody would go to Mars for a comfortable life. It will be harder to live there than at the top of Mt. Everest or at the South Pole.

But the greatest hope of these pioneers would be to find something on Mars that was alive.

Here on Earth, there are literally millions of species of life—slime, molds, mushrooms, trees, frogs, monkeys, and, of course, humans. Life survives in the most remote corners of our planet—in dark caves where sunlight has been blocked for thousands of years, on arid desert rocks, around hot springs where the water is at boiling point, deep underground, and high in the atmosphere.

Our Earth teems with an extraordinary range of life-forms. But there are constraints on size and shape. Big animals have fat legs but still can't jump like insects. The largest animals float in water. Far greater variety could exist on other planets. For instance, if gravity were weaker, animals could be larger and creatures our size could have legs as thin as insects'.

Everywhere you find life on Earth, you find *water*.

There is water on Mars and life of some kind could have emerged there. The red planet is much colder than the Earth, and has a thinner atmosphere. Nobody expects green goggle-eyed Martians like those that feature in so many cartoons. If any advanced intelligent aliens existed on Mars, we would already know about them—and they might even have visited us by now!

Mercury and Venus are closer to the Sun than the Earth is. Both are very much hotter. Earth is the Goldilocks planet—not too hot and not too cold. If the Earth were too hot, even the most tenacious life would fry. Mars is a bit too cold but not absolutely frigid. The outer planets are colder still.

What about Jupiter, the biggest planet in our solar system? If life had evolved on this huge planet, where the force of gravity is far stronger than on Earth, it could be very strange indeed. For instance, there could be huge balloonlike creatures floating in the dense atmosphere.

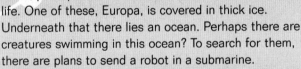

Jupiter has four large moons that could, perhaps, harbor life. One of these, Europa, is covered in thick ice. Underneath that there lies an ocean. Perhaps there are creatures swimming in this ocean? To search for them, there are plans to send a robot in a submarine.

But the biggest moon in the Solar System is Titan, one of Saturn's many moons. Scientists have already landed a probe on Titan's surface, revealing rivers, lakes, and rocks. But the temperature is about minus 274 degrees Fahrenheit (170 degrees Celsius), at which any water is frozen solid. It is not water but liquid methane that flows in these rivers and lakes—not a good place for life.

Let's now widen our gaze beyond our Solar System to other stars. There are tens of billions of these suns in our Galaxy. Even the nearest of these is so far away that, at the speed of a present-day rocket, it would take millions of years to reach it. Equally, if clever aliens existed on a planet orbiting another star, it would be difficult for them to visit us. It would be far easier to send a radio or laser signal than to traverse the mind-boggling distances of interstellar space.

If there was a signal returned, it might come from aliens very different from us. Indeed, it could come from machines whose creators have long ago been usurped or become extinct. And, of course, there may be aliens who exist and have big "brains" but are so different from us that we wouldn't recognize them or be able to communicate with them. Some may not want to reveal that they exist (even if they are actually watching us!). There may be some superintelligent dolphins, happily thinking profound thoughts deep under some alien ocean, doing nothing to reveal their presence. Still other "brains" could actually be swarms of insects, acting together like a single intelligent being. There may be a

lot more out there than we could ever detect. Absence of evidence isn't evidence of absence.

There are billions of planets in our Galaxy and our Galaxy itself is only one of billions. Most people would guess that the cosmos is teeming with life—but that would be no more than a guess. We still know too little about how life began—and how it evolves—to be able to say whether simple life is common. We know even less about how likely it would be for simple life to evolve in the way it did here on Earth. My bet (for what it is worth) is that simple life is, indeed, very common but that intelligent life is much rarer.

There may not be any intelligent life out there at all. Earth's intricate biosphere could be unique. Perhaps we really are alone. If that's true, it's a disappointment for those who are looking for alien signals—or who even hope that some day aliens may visit us. But the failure of searches shouldn't depress us. It is perhaps a reason to be cheerful because we can then be less modest about our place in the great scheme of things. Our Earth could be the most interesting place in the cosmos.

If life *is* unique to the Earth, it could be seen as just a cosmic sideshow—though it doesn't have to be. That is because evolution isn't over. Indeed, it could be closer to its beginning than its end. Our Solar System is barely middle-aged—it will be six billion years before the Sun swells up, engulfs the inner planets, and vaporizes any life that still remains on Earth. Far-future life and intelligence could be as different from us as we are from a bug. Life could spread from Earth through the entire Galaxy, evolving into a teeming complexity far beyond what we can even imagine. If so, our tiny planet—this pale-blue dot floating in space—could be the most important place in the entire cosmos.

Martin

"Is there anyone out there?" said Emmett. "I think probably not—at least, not where you are. So far, I think it's just you and the lakes of methane."

"Ugh! It's raining!" said Annie. She held out one hand to catch a raindrop. Huge drops of liquid, three times the size of raindrops on Earth, were falling from the sky. But they didn't fall fast and straight, like normal rain. They dawdled in the atmosphere, wafting and twirling around like snowflakes.

"Oh no!" said Emmett. "It must be methane rain! I don't know how much pure methane your space suits can withstand before they start to deteriorate."

"Hang on a minute . . ." George peered at the strange boat that was drifting toward the shoreline.

"Huh!" said Annie, rather sharply. "I am just hanging about. There isn't much else to do around here."

"It's got some writing on it!" said George.

"Ooh, spooky!" Annie leaned forward to get a better look as the huge raindrops splashed gently on her space helmet. "It does too. I can see it now . . . Well, bonanza!" she said, staring at the round object, which was now marooned on the shore of the lake. "Look at that! It did come from Earth! It's got human writing on it!"

In big letters on the side of the frozen object they saw the word: HUYGENS.

"Emmett, it says 'Huygens' on it," Annie reported. "What does that mean? It isn't a bomb, is it?"

"No way!" replied Emmett. "It means you've found

the *Huygens* probe—the one they sent to Titan! I don't think it works anymore, but that's still pretty cool. Literally cool. Like minus two hundred seventy-four degrees Fahrenheit cool!"

"But that's not all!" Annie exclaimed. "It's got some other writing on it too! It's got alien letters on it!"

On the other side of her, George now had a clear view. "It's a message in a bottle!" he cried. "Except it isn't! It's a message on a probe."

Painted onto the probe was another row of pictures.

Chapter 11

Back on Earth, Emmett was sitting on the floor in the middle of the Clean Room, with both Cosmos and *The User's Guide to the Universe* open in front of him, when he heard a commotion. The cleaning machines at the entry point suddenly whirred into life and a flashing red sign above the door lit up. DECONTAMINATING, it said, beeping loudly as it flashed. Emmett hadn't noticed the sign on his way in because he was too busy being brushed, buffed, and popped into his white suit by the machine. But he was hardly going to ignore it now. It meant that someone was coming in!

He leaped to his feet, his heart pounding. He didn't want to move Cosmos, who was ready to transfer Annie and George from Titan to wherever they thought they might find the next clue. But neither did he want Cosmos to be interrupted by someone who might mess around with him while he was performing such an important and difficult operation.

Emmett suddenly spotted what looked like a length

of shiny yellow aluminum foil. In fact, it was the covering used to protect probes from overheating in the Sun's rays as they traveled through space. He gently arranged it around Cosmos and then stood in front of the computer, trying to strike a carefree and nonchalant pose, as though he always wandered into Clean Rooms and lurked around large machinery being prepared for space travel. He readjusted his face mask in the hope that whoever came in might not realize that he was, in fact, a kid and would just assume he was a very small Clean Room operative.

A figure was ejected into the Clean Room from the decontamination machine. It staggered a bit, weaving around in its white suit until it had found its feet. It was impossible to guess who it might be—even more so because the decontamination machine seemed to have put the head covering and face mask on backward, so where there should have been eyes and a chin there was just dark hair.

"Youch!" the figure cried, tripping over a half-assembled satellite. "Oh, colliding hadrons!" It hopped from foot to foot. "I've stubbed my toe! Ouch! Ouch!"

Emmett got a sick feeling in his stomach. It felt like it did when he ate too much. There was only one person it could be underneath the white suit, and he was about the last person Emmett wanted to see right now.

The hopping figure stopped dancing around and ripped off his back-to-front face mask and head gear. It was, of course, Eric.

"Ahh," he said, looking down at Emmett, disguised in his white suit. "Do you, by any chance, work here?"

"Er, yes, yes, I do!" said Emmett in his deepest voice. "Absolutely. Have done so for years. Many many many many many many years. I'm really ancient, in fact. You just can't tell because I've got my face mask on."

"It's just that you look, a bit . . . well, a touch, perhaps . . ."

"I was taller," said Emmett in his grown-up voice. "But I got so old I shrank."

"Yes, yes, interesting," said Eric calmly. "Well, the thing is, Mr. . . ."

"Hm, hm . . ." Emmett cleared his throat. "Professor, if you don't mind."

"Of course, Professor . . . ?"

Emmett panicked. "Professor Spock," he said wildly.

"Professor . . . Spock," repeated Eric slowly.

"Er, yes," said Emmett. "That's right. Professor Spock from the University of . . . Enterprise."

"Well, Professor Spock," said Eric, "I wonder if you could help me. I'm looking for some kids who I seem to have lost. And maybe you've seen them somewhere around here? Or, being so wise and so very old, you might have an idea where they've got to? They were seen coming this way by a security camera."

"Kids?" repeated Emmett gruffly. "Can't stand them. Don't have any of them in my Clean Room. No, not never. Not kids."

"The thing is," said Eric gently, "I really do need to find them. For a start, I'm worried about them, and I'd like to know that they're okay. But also because we've got an emergency situation going on, and it involves one of the missing kids."

"It does?" said Emmett, forgetting to use his adult voice.

"Actually it's about his father," Eric told him.

"His father?" Emmett whipped off his face mask. "Is my dad okay? Has anything happened to him?" Tears filled his eyes.

"No, Emmett," said Eric, putting an arm around him and patting him on the back. "It isn't your dad. It's George's."

Eric started to tell Emmett the story of George's dad— where he'd gone and why, and how he'd got lost in the South Pacific—but he was interrupted by the sound of the decontamination machine starting up again. *"Beep! Beep!"* The red light over the door flashed as yet another person entered the machine.

"Get your nasty robot hands off me!" They heard an outraged shout. "I'm an old lady! Show some respect!"

There was a crunching noise, and the machinery seemed to grind to a halt, followed by a stamping of feet as the door was pushed open and an irritated old woman clutching a walking cane and a handbag—both neatly wrapped in plastic—burst through.

The beeping noise had stopped and the red light was frozen in mid-flash.

"What in heaven's name was all that about?" demanded the old woman. She wasn't wearing a white outfit at all—just her usual tweed suit. "I will not be treated like that by some blasted machine. Ah, Eric!" she said as she spotted him.

"I've found you. You can't get away from me, you know."

"I'm starting to realize that," murmured Eric.

"What was that? I'm deaf—you'll have to write it down." She ripped off the plastic covering from her handbag and rummaged around for her notebook.

"Emmett," said Eric in resigned tones, "this is Mabel, George's grandmother. She arrived here today to ask for my help in locating George's dad, Terence— who, as I told you, is lost in the South Pacific. The emergency alert I received earlier—it turned out to be from Mabel, who George's mom, Daisy, had contacted." He took Mabel's notebook and scribbled: *Mabel, this is Emmett. He is George's friend and he is just about to tell me where George and Annie are.*

Mabel looked over at Emmett and smiled, a real smile full of friendliness and warmth. "Oh, Eric!" she said. "What a terrible memory you have! Emmett and I met at the airport so we are old friends already. Remember though, I'm very deaf, so if you want to talk to me you'll have to write it down."

"Live long and prosper," said Emmett, giving her the Vulcan salute with one hand and writing his greeting in her book with the other.

"Thank you, Emmett," replied Mabel. "I have, indeed, lived a very long time and prospered greatly." She saluted him back again.

"But I don't understand. How are you going to

rescue George's dad if he's in the Pacific and you're here?" Emmett asked Eric. "Are you going to send a rocket to pick him up?"

"Ah, well, you forget," said Eric. "I—well, the Global Space Agency actually—have satellites which orbit the Earth. Space missions don't just look outward across the cosmos, they also look back at Earth, so we can see what's happening on our own planet. So I've asked the satellite department to look closely at that part of the Pacific Ocean to see if they can spot Terence. Once we know where he is, we can let Daisy and his friends know, and they can send someone out to rescue him. So fingers crossed, Terence is going to be okay."

SATELLITES IN SPACE

A satellite is an object that orbits—or revolves—around another object, like the Moon around the Earth. The Earth is a satellite of the Sun. However, we tend to use the word *satellite* to mean the man-made objects that are sent into space on a rocket to perform certain tasks, such as navigation, weather monitoring, or communication.

Rockets were invented by the ancient Chinese in around AD 1000. Many hundreds of years later, on October 4, 1957, the Space Age began when the Russians used a rocket to launch the first satellite into orbit around the Earth. *Sputnik*, a small metal sphere capable of sending a weak radio signal back to Earth, became a sensation. At the time, it was known as the *Red Moon* and people all over the world tuned their radios to pick up its signal. The Mark I telescope at Jodrell Bank in the United Kingdom was the first large radio telescope to be used as a tracking antenna to chart the course of the satellite. *Sputnik* was quickly followed by *Sputnik II*, also called *Pupnik* because it had a passenger on board! Laika, a Russian dog, became the first living being from Earth to travel into space.

The Americans tried to launch their own satellite on December 6, 1957, but the satellite only managed to get 4 feet off the ground before the rocket exploded. On February 1, 1958, *Explorer I* was more successful, and soon the two superpowers on Earth—the USSR and the U.S.—were also competing to be the greatest in space. At that time, they were very suspicious of each other and soon realized that satellites were good for spying. Using photographs taken from above the Earth, the two superpowers hoped to learn more about activities in the other country. The satellite revolution had begun.

Satellite technology was originally developed for military and intelligence reasons. In the 1970s the U.S. government launched twenty-four satellites, which sent back time signals and orbital information. This led to the first global positioning system (GPS). This technology, which allows armies to cross deserts by night and long-range missiles to hit targets accurately, is now used by millions of ordinary car drivers to avoid getting lost! Known as *satellite navigation*, or *sat nav*, it also helps ambulances to reach the injured more promptly and coastguards to launch effective search-and-rescue missions.

SATELLITES IN SPACE (continued)

Communication across the world was also changed forever by satellites. In 1962 a U.S. telephone company launched Telstar, a satellite that broadcast the first-ever live television show from the U.S. to Britain and France. The British saw only a few minutes of fuzzy pictures, but the French received clear pictures and sound. They even managed to send back their own transmission of Yves Montand singing "Relax, You Are in Paris!" Before satellites, events had to be filmed and the film taken by plane to be shown on television in other countries. After Telstar, major world events—such as the funeral of U.S. President John F. Kennedy in 1963 and the World Cup in 1966—could be broadcast live across the globe for the first time. Mobile phones and the Internet are other ways in which you might be using a satellite today.

Satellite imaging isn't used only by spies! Being able to look back at the Earth from space has enabled us to see patterns, both on the Earth and in the atmosphere. We can measure land use and see how cities are expanding and how deserts and forests are changing shape. Farmers use satellite pictures to monitor their crops and decide which fields need fertilizer.

And satellites have transformed our understanding of the weather. They have made weather forecasts more accurate and shown the way weather patterns emerge and move around the world. Satellites cannot change the weather but they can track hurricanes, tornadoes, and cyclones, giving us the ability to issue severe weather warnings.

In the late 1990s NASA's *TOPEX/Poseidon* satellite, which maps the oceans, provided enough information for weather watchers to spot the El Niño phenomenon. And *Jason*, a new series of NASA satellites, has recently been launched to gather data about the ocean's role in determining the Earth's climate. This in turn will help us to understand climate change better, showing us detailed images of the melting polar ice caps, disappearing inland seas, and rising ocean levels—information we now need urgently!

Just as satellites can look back at the Earth and transform our understanding of our own planet, so they have also changed our perception of the Universe around us. The Hubble Space Telescope was the first large-scale space observatory. Orbiting the Earth, Hubble has helped astronomers to calculate the age of the Universe and has shown that it is expanding at an accelerated pace.

There are three thousand satellites in orbit around the Earth, with a total coverage of every square inch of the planet. It is getting quite crowded out there and can be dangerous. Satellites in low Earth orbit move very fast—around eighteen thousand miles an hour. Collisions are rare, but when they happen, they make a mess! Even a fleck of paint moving at that speed could cause damage if it hit a spacecraft. There may be a million pieces of space junk orbiting the Earth, but only about nine thousand of these are bigger than a tennis ball.

"Couldn't the satellites also measure the rising sea?" asked Emmett.

"Well, yes, they could," said Eric. "And I would have happily helped them, if only they'd asked me. But even so, human exploration and real experience are still very important. On their journey they will have learned a lot about other things that satellites can't help us with. But we could have worked together on this project. And perhaps we will now. Daisy called Mabel to tell her that Terence was missing, and Mabel came right here to find me. Which was, of course, exactly the right thing to do. Any minute now, we should spot him," he finished, just a touch smugly. "Anyway, where are George and Annie? Have you been playing hide-and-seek?" He smiled, and Emmett's heart leaped into his mouth.

"We are playing a sort of game," he stuttered.

"Oh good!" said Eric. "MABEL, THE KIDS ARE PLAYING A GAME! Tell us—we can all join in. I could do with some fun, what with having missed the launch."

"Y'know, like, a treasure hunt," said Emmett slowly.

"Ye-esss . . . ," said Eric.

"A game?" asked Mabel. "How exciting!"

"Like, where you have clues and you have to follow them to find out where you need to go," continued Emmett, wishing he could blast himself into space at that exact moment and not have to finish what he had to say.

Eric scribbled something in Mabel's notebook.

"A treasure hunt! How splendid!" she exclaimed, reading it. "My, it's not just your memory, Eric! Your handwriting is dreadful too. How ever did you get so far in life?"

"So what's the clue? Where have they gone?"

Eric was still smiling when Cosmos, from under his reflective thermal blanket, said in a loud voice, "*Ping!* Sending is complete! Mission stage three is underway." Eric stopped smiling as soon as he heard Cosmos's voice. He ran over to the shiny pile of crumpled foil and whisked it away to reveal the supercomputer underneath. "THAT'S MY COMPUTER!" he shouted so loudly that even Mabel heard him with no problem. "So where in the Universe are Annie and George?"

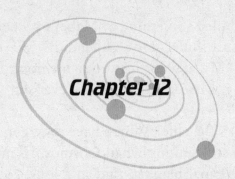

Chapter 12

Eric looked so angry that, for one horrifying moment, Emmett had a vision of him exploding like a supernova in a burst of radiation that was so bright it could outshine a whole galaxy. He glared at Emmett, the full force of nuclear fury blazing in his eyes.

"If you've done what I think you've done . . . ," he said.

Emmett just opened and closed his mouth, like a goldfish. He tried to speak, but he couldn't get any sound out. He made a strange sort of gurgling noise instead.

"Where are Annie and George?" asked Eric quietly but fiercely, his face white with tension.

"A—a—a—" was all Emmett could stutter.

Mabel's bright eyes were flicking from Eric to Emmett as she tried to work out what was going on.

"Tell me," said Eric. "I need to know."

Emmett moved his lips, but he still couldn't make his voice work. He swallowed loudly as tears filled his eyes.

"Okay!" said Eric. "If you refuse to tell me, then I'll ask Cosmos instead." He knelt down on the floor in front of the computer and started tapping away furiously. "How could you!" he muttered. "How could you do this!"

Mabel hobbled over to Emmett and handed him her notepad and pencil.

"If there's something that's too difficult to say," she whispered to him, "perhaps you could write it down instead? Then anything you need to tell Eric, I can say for you."

Emmett looked at her gratefully and took them. He chewed the pencil end, not sure where to start.

"What if I ask you some questions?" said Mabel kindly. "That might get us going. Why is Eric so upset?"

He's mad because we took his special computer, Cosmos, Emmett wrote neatly in Mabel's book.

"What's so special about Cosmos?" asked Mabel.

He can send you across the Universe.

"Have Annie and George gone on a trip?"

Emmett nodded, his big eyes full of fear. But Mabel just smiled at him and motioned for him to carry on writing. He took a big gulp and put pen to paper again. *They were on Titan, but they've just gone through the portal to the nearest star system to us, Alpha Centauri. They think this is where they will find the next clue. The first clue came to them on Earth, they got the second on Mars, and the third on Titan.*

"Ah, the treasure hunt." Mabel nodded understandingly.

Eric was still bashing away on Cosmos, who didn't seem to be helping him. "Bug off! Access denied!" said the supercomputer angrily. Emmett glanced nervously at them.

"Who is leaving these clues for them?" said Mabel.

We don't know, wrote Emmett. *But each message has the same ending—it threatens to destroy planet Earth if we don't follow them.*

"Any more clues about the clues?"

Well, wrote Emmett, doodling a little. *I did work*

something out. But I might be wrong. . . . He drew a series of dots.

"Carry on," said Mabel as Eric let out a howl of frustration. She put a calming hand on Emmett's shoulder. "We'll deal with him in a minute."

The first clue came to them on Earth, where there is already life. The second clue was on Mars, where we think there might have been life in the past. The third clue was on Titan, which is a moon of Saturn. Titan might be like the Earth was just before life began. So we thought the fourth clue might take them to Alpha

Centauri, which is the nearest star system to us and the closest place we would look for signs of life outside the Solar System. And they have to find a planet in a binary star system. That's what the clue says.

"So you think they are following a trail of life in the Universe in order to prevent life on Earth from coming to an end," said Mabel. "You are a very smart boy, Emmett. Eric!" She poked him in the back with her cane.

"Leave. Me. Alone. I. Am. Busy," said Eric as Cosmos blew a loud raspberry at him.

"Oh, grow up!" said Mabel. "I've got something to say. And when you get to my age, you have the right to speak, whether anyone wants to listen to you or not. Eric, you have scared this poor boy so much he can't tell you what he knows. So if you could try and be a bit nicer to him, he will stop feeling so terrified and help you sort this out."

That boy, wrote Eric in Mabel's book, *has put Annie and George in terrible danger. I am incandescent.*

"We can see that," said Mabel. "But you are also wasting valuable time and you need to listen. And stop blaming Emmett."

Eric really did explode this time. "Somehow he managed to repair my computer without telling me," he ranted. "And then he let Annie and George go off across the Universe, chasing after some crank message Annie imagined she'd received through a computer, which at the time didn't even work, from aliens who don't exist. And now Cosmos is malfunctioning again, and we have no idea if we can ever get them back!"

Mabel had clearly heard every word. "Oh, stop it!" she snapped. "This isn't Emmett's fault. This is entirely the work of your daughter and my grandson. It's got their sticky fingerprints all over it. George told me he had to come to Florida because Annie had something important she wanted him to do. And this must be it. They have gone on a mission because they believe the Earth is in danger and they need to do something about it. They received the first clue on Earth, but Emmett here tells me that when they followed it to Mars, they found another clue waiting for them. That clue sent them to Titan. They've just left Titan and gone to look for a planet around"—Mabel checked her notebook—"Alpha Centauri."

"What?" said Eric. "You mean they haven't gone out there just for fun, for messing around? You mean they've actually gone to one location, found a clue, and then gone *farther* out?"

Emmett nodded, his eyes squeezed tight shut.

"How in the name of Einstein could that happen?" asked Eric in disbelief.

"Um, I created a remote portal application when I was updating Cosmos," whispered Emmett, finding a bit of his voice again. "I'm really sorry."

Eric took his glasses off and rubbed his eyes. "And you say they got to Mars and found another clue waiting for them?"

"Yup," said Emmett. "It was drawn on the surface of Mars by Homer's tires."

Eric put his glasses back on and sprang to his feet. "Emmett"—he took the boy by his shoulders—"I'm sorry I shouted at you. I really am. But I need to reach Annie and George immediately. Can you send me out to Alpha Centauri?"

Emmett sagged a little. "I can try," he said nervously. "But Cosmos is being a bit difficult, and I'm worried that he is using too much memory now. I don't know what will happen if I send another person through the portal."

But Eric had already gone to get his space suit.

Emmett plonked himself down cross-legged in front of Cosmos. Mabel stood over him. "My poor old joints won't let me get down that far," she said regretfully.

"Oh!" said Emmett. Immediately he got to his feet, picked up Cosmos, and balanced him on the side of the half-assembled satellite so that George's gran could see the screen. He fetched some spare machinery parts, which he arranged as a sort of chair, so that Mabel could sit down.

"Thank you, Emmett," she said. "That's very considerate of you."

"My pleasure," he said seriously. He tried to arrange some of the shiny yellow foil as a blanket over Mabel's knees, but she batted him away.

"Go on with you!" she said affectionately. "Get to your computer and don't worry about this old dear."

Nervously Emmett entered his personal password, waiting to see if Cosmos would react as badly to him as he had done to Eric. "Access granted," said Cosmos politely. Emmett then typed in a command for locating

the last portal activity, so that he could create another doorway from Earth and send Eric through it to where Annie and George had gone. But this time it wasn't Cosmos's attitude that worried Emmett so much. It was his ability to perform the tasks they so badly needed him to do.

"Planet . . . orbit . . . Alpha Centauri . . . ," said Cosmos slowly. "Seeking coordinates for last portal activity in the Alpha Centauri star system . . . Seeking . . . planet in orbit . . . Seeking information . . . Seeking last portal location . . ." The little hourglass appeared on Cosmos's screen. Emmett pressed a few keys, but Cosmos did not respond. All that happened was that the little hourglass flashed a few times, as though to remind Emmett that Cosmos was busy.

I think he is running out of memory, Emmett wrote in Mabel's notebook as they waited. *He's using so much of it at the moment to operate these portals in distant space. It's really important we don't ask him too many difficult questions right now.*

"What do we need to know?" asked Mabel.

We need to know where Cosmos sent Annie and George. They asked him to find them a planet in the Alpha Centauri star system.

"And how do you find a planet in space . . . ?"

HOW TO FIND A PLANET IN SPACE

Planets don't generate their own energy, leaving them very dim compared to their nuclear-powered home stars. If you use a powerful telescope to take a picture of a planet, its faint light will be lost in the glare of the star it orbits.

However, planets can be detected by the gravitational pull they exert on their star. Planets pull apples, moons, and satellites toward them with gravity, and they also pull on their home star. Just as a dog on a leash can yank its owner around, a planet can pull its home star around, with the leash being gravity.

Astronomers can watch a nearby star, especially a close one such as Alpha Centauri A or B, to see if it is being yanked around by an unseen planet. The responsive motion of a star is a telltale sign of a planet, and that motion can be detected in two ways.

Firstly, the light waves from the star are either compressed or stretched as it approaches or recedes from us on Earth (this is called the Doppler Effect).

Secondly, two telescopes acting as one can combine the light waves from a star to detect the motion of that star.

Planets as small as Earth and as large as Jupiter can be detected using these techniques.

Maybe one day *you* will find a planet that no one has ever spotted before!

 Geoff

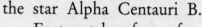

Eeew!" said Annie, shielding her eyes with her arm as they stepped through the portal from Titan onto the planet Cosmos had found for them in orbit around the star Alpha Centauri B. Fortunately, after a few seconds, the special glass in her space helmet visor darkened and her vision started coming back.

"Wow! It's bright," said George, stepping through after her. This time they thought they were better prepared than when they had landed on Mars and Titan. They had gotten out the emergency rope and the metal pegs that came with their space suits, ready to tether themselves to the surface of their new planet. But when they stepped through the doorway, they found that for once they didn't float off. Instead, they felt much heavier than they did on Earth.

They could still walk, but it was an effort to pick up each leg to move forward.

"Oof!" said Annie, dropping the rope and the pegs. "I feel like I'm being squished." It was as though someone was pushing her toward the bleached ground.

"More gravity!" said George. "We must be on a planet similar to Earth but with a greater mass, so we feel the gravity more strongly than we would at home. But it can't be that much greater or we'd be crushed by now."

"I'm going to sit down," puffed Annie. "I'm really tired."

"No! Don't!" said George. "You might never get up again. You shouldn't sit down, Annie, or we'll never get away from here."

Annie groaned and leaned on him. She felt like a ton, and George staggered to stay upright and hold on to her at the same time.

"Annie, we've got to find the next clue and leave," he said urgently. "There's too much gravity here for us—we weren't built to exist in conditions like these. If we were ants, we'd be okay. But we're too big for high-gravity places. And it's too shiny. It hurts my eyes."

Where Mars—and certainly Titan—had been much darker than the Earth, this new planet was blindingly bright. Even with the dark space visors protecting their eyes like superstrength sunglasses, it was still difficult to see. "Don't look directly at the sun," warned

George. "It's even brighter than our Sun at home."

Not that there was much to look at. Around them stretched miles of bald rock, baking in the brilliant light beaming down on this heavy, hot planet. George gazed around anxiously, looking for some sign that would lead them to the fourth clue.

"Whass . . . that . . . over . . . there?" Annie, who was now leaning on him entirely, flapped an arm in one direction. Her speech had become very slow and slurred.

George shook her. "Annie! Wake up! Wake up!" The light and the weight of this weird planet seemed to be drugging her. He tried to call Cosmos or Emmett. The first time he got a busy signal, the second, a recorded message saying: *"Your call is important to us. Press the pound key plus one to be put through to—"* But then he was cut off.

Annie flopped onto him. She was so heavy on this planet that it was like trying to carry a baby elephant. George stood there, Annie's head on his shoulder

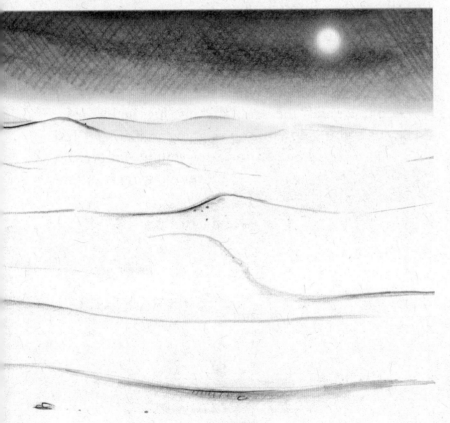

and his arms around her. He started to feel really scared. He imagined that in years to come, when the first interstellar travellers made the journey to this unnamed planet in orbit around one of the nearest stars to Earth, they might find the scorched remains of two human children, frazzled and boiled into fragments on the parched surface. Somewhat dazed himself, he pictured them leaping off their spaceship to claim this new planet, only to find that two kids had once made the four-light-year journey to this infernal place, only to perish under its burning star.

But just as he was giving up hope and starting to sag toward the ground, the light in the sky began to dim a little. It was changing from brilliant white to a softer yellow.

"Look, Annie!" he said, shaking her in his arms. "The sun's going down! You're going to be okay! Just hold on for a few minutes more. It's moving across the

sky pretty quickly—well, quicker than the Sun back home on Earth, anyway. Once it goes down, we'll be able to cool off and find the clue."

"Huh?" said Annie blearily. She raised her head from his shoulder and stared out behind him. "But it's not going down! It's coming up. . . . It's really pretty," she went on dreamily. "Bright shiny star rising in the sky . . ."

"Annie, it's not going up!" said George, who thought she must be hallucinating. "Concentrate! The sun is going down, not up!" The light around them was dimming gently.

"Don't be silly!" Annie sounded annoyed, her voice slightly stronger. George felt relieved—if she could get mad at him, then she was definitely feeling better. "I know up from down, and I tell you it's going up!"

They moved apart by a few inches and stood staring over each other's shoulders.

"It's that way," said Annie, pointing. "Up!"

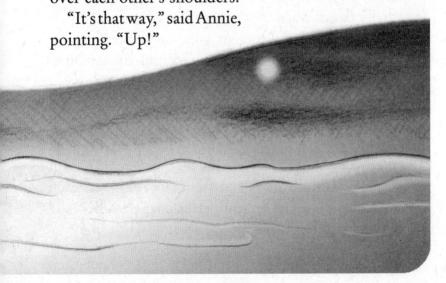

"No, it's over there!" said George. "Down!"

"Turn around," ordered Annie.

George turned around very slowly—it wasn't possible to move fast on the high-gravity planet—and saw she was right. There was a small bright sun in the sky behind him, rising over the rocky planet. It didn't give the same glaring light as the sun setting on the other side of the planet, but it shone a gentle beam on them, meaning that it would not often be dark on this bright, barren planet.

"Of course! We're in a binary star system, just like it showed us in the clue! This planet has two suns!" said George. "I'm sure I've read about this system on the Net. One sun is bigger than the other—that one setting must be Alpha B, the star this planet orbits. It looks bigger because we're closer to it. And the other one must be Alpha A, the other star in the Centauri system. Alpha A is actually larger, but we're farther away from it."

Now that the light was growing softer, they could make out more of the landscape around them. Quite nearby they saw the lip of a huge hole in the ground.

"Let's go and have a look in there," said Annie.

"Because . . . ?" questioned George.

"There isn't anywhere else to look!" She shrugged. "And maybe there's another clue down there. On both Mars and Titan, Cosmos sent us really close to each new clue. Have you got any better suggestions?" She seemed back to her usual difficult self.

"Nope," said George. He tried calling Emmett again but just got the busy signal again.

"Come on," said Annie, "but I'm not walking." She dropped to her hands and knees and started to crawl toward the crater.

George tried to walk, but it was so difficult and slow. He felt like the Tin Man in *The Wizard of Oz*, having to throw each leg forward in order to move. So he too got down on his hands and knees and followed Annie, who was now peering over the edge to see what lay at the bottom.

"There's nothing there," she said in disappointment, looking into the gaping empty crater formed by a collision with a comet or an asteroid.

George wriggled up beside her. "Then where will we find the next cl—?" he started to say. But he stopped. Because just then, at the very bottom of the huge crater, they saw something they definitely weren't expecting. Faintly, but getting more solid by the second, they saw the outline of a doorway. And at the same moment as one space boot and then another stepped through it, the transmission device in George's helmet buzzed into life.

"George!" he heard. "This is your grandmother speaking. Eric is on the way!"

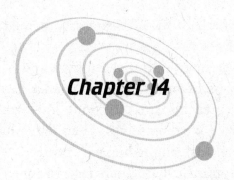

Chapter 14

At the bottom of the crater, Eric stepped quickly through the portal and promptly fell flat on his face. He had prepared his telling-off speech to the kids while he was getting ready to walk through Cosmos's doorway. But once he reached the distant planet, all he came out with was "Nrrgghh!"

"Dad!" cried Annie from the top of the crater, and burst into tears inside her space helmet. She no longer cared whether he was going to be mad at her. She just felt overjoyed to see him. She slithered over the crater's lip and wriggled down toward him on her tummy. As Eric rolled over onto his back, Annie crashed into him and gave him a great big hug.

"Dad!" she sobbed. "It's so nasty here! I don't like this planet."

Eric gave a huge sigh that Emmett and Mabel heard many millions of miles away on planet Earth, and he decided to save his speech about kids who traveled through space by themselves when they shouldn't for another time. Instead, he hugged Annie.

George's gran had no such reservations. "George!" she said sternly over the link from Earth. "I can't believe you roped me into this dangerous scheme without telling me! I'm very angry that you didn't see fit to properly inform me why you wanted to come to America. . . ." She went on and on, and George wished he could turn down the volume, as Emmett had done with Cosmos. But then he looked into the crater and saw Eric beckoning George to come and join them.

"Sorry, Gran!" said George. "I have to go! We'll talk later." And he slid down the side of the enormous hole to join Eric and Annie, ending up in a group hug in space suits at the bottom of the crater on an unnamed planet orbiting Alpha B in the Alpha Centauri star system.

"I've got to close down the portal for a few minutes," came Emmett's voice. "I can't hold the portal and do all the other things I need to with Cosmos. So don't panic when the doorway vanishes. I'll get it back to you right away."

The portal doorway became translucent and started to fade away. George, Annie, and Eric lay back against the curved surface of the crater's wall and gazed at Alpha A, moving across the clear, dark blue sky.

"So, George and Annie," said Eric as they lay on either side of him. "Here we all are, together, once again. Lost in space, once again." By now, the portal had completely disappeared.

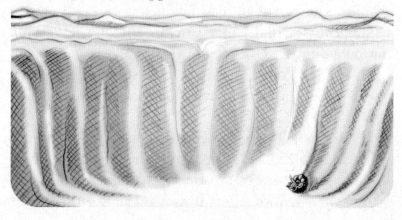

"Can we go home now?" sniffed Annie. "I've had enough of this."

"Soon, very soon," said Eric calmly. "Just as soon as Emmett gets the reverse portal working again."

"What!" exclaimed George, trying to sit up but finding he didn't have the strength left to fight gravity. He lay back down again. "You mean we can't go back to Earth?"

"I'm afraid not," said Eric quietly. "Cosmos is having some problems, but Emmett will sort them out. I wouldn't have left him in charge if I weren't sure he was the best person for the job. He's already done things with Cosmos I couldn't even dream of."

"You mean you came here to find us even though you knew we might not be able to get back?" said Annie. "That we might be stuck here forever?"

"Of course I did," said Eric. "I couldn't leave you out here by yourselves, could I?"

"Oh, Dad!" cried Annie. "I'm so sorry! Now we're going to be burned to a crisp on this horrible planet, and it's all my fault!"

"Don't be silly, Annie. This isn't your fault, and it's going to be okay! We're not going to stay long enough for that to happen," said Eric firmly. "But we do need to leave here before Alpha B rises again. Even with our space suits, it's too hot for us on this planet because it lies too close to its star—that's why there is no water and no life here. But we'll go somewhere else. Somewhere nicer."

"So Cosmos can still send us farther out?" said George hopefully. He didn't want to see the blinding light of Alpha B ever again in his whole life.

"Yes," said Eric, more confidently than he felt. "Sometimes we have to go far, far away in order to be able to get back. So don't worry if it feels like we are traveling in the wrong direction. Think of it as gaining perspective."

"How soon will Alpha B rise again?" asked George.

"I don't know for certain," said Eric, "but we must be gone before its dawn."

"Where are we going?" said Annie.

"Another planet," Eric told her. "Cosmos is looking for another planet to send us to. Emmett tells me that you have been following clues across the Universe—in a sort of cosmic treasure hunt."

"Um, yes," George admitted. "We kept going because in each place we found another clue that sent us to a new location."

"And you came here because the clue you found on Titan told you to go to a binary star system with a planet in orbit around one of the stars?"

"We thought we'd been really smart," said Annie sadly.

"Oh you have!" said Eric. "All three of you. Emmett believes that the clues are taking you on a hunt for signs of life in the Universe. If he's right, then we need to find a planet in what we call the Goldilocks Zone of its star. That means a planet that is not too hot, not too cold, but just right."

"Oh!" said George. "I see—this planet is too hot! So we know this isn't the right planet."

"And I can think of another reason to suspect this isn't the right place. How many stars did the clue show?" asked Eric.

"Two," said George.

"Here," said Eric, "there are three. That fainter star, the one you can only just see over there—that's Proxima Centauri, so called because it's the closest star to Earth. So this is a *triple* system."

"Oh no! Wrong planet, wrong star system," said George. "What do we do now?"

"So, do you believe us now, about the clues and the messages?" interrupted Annie.

"I do, darling," admitted Eric. "And I'm so sorry. I'm sure those messages were left for me, not for you. And if I could send you back to Earth right this second, I would. But I can't do that and I can't leave you here. So I think we're going to have to finish the cosmic treasure hunt together. Are you with me?"

Annie moved closer to him. "I am," she said, "very definitely."

ALPHA CENTAURI

At just over four light-years away, Alpha Centauri is the closest star system to our Sun. In the night sky it looks like just one star, but is, in fact, a triplet. Two Sun-like stars, Alpha Centauri A and Alpha Centauri B—separated by around twenty-three times the distance between the Earth and the Sun—orbit a common center about once every eighty years. There is a third, fainter star in the system, Proxima Centauri, which orbits the other two but at a huge distance from them. Proxima is the nearest of the three to us.

Alpha B is an orange star, slightly cooler and a bit less massive than our Sun. It is thought that the Alpha Centauri system formed around one thousand million years before our Solar System. Both Alpha A and Alpha B are stable stars, like our Sun, and like our Sun may have been born surrounded by dusty, planet-forming disks.

In 2008 scientists suggested that planets may have formed around one or both of these stars. From a telescope in Chile they are now monitoring Alpha Centauri very carefully to see whether small wobbles in starlight will show us planets in orbit in our nearest star system. Astronomers are looking at Alpha Centauri B to see whether this bright, calm star will reveal Earth-like worlds around it.

Alpha Centauri can be seen from Earth's southern hemisphere, where it is one of the stars of the Centaurus constellation. Its proper name, Rigel Kentaurus, means "centaur's foot." Alpha Centauri is its Bayer designation (a system of star-naming introduced by astronomer Johann Bayer in 1603).

Alpha A is a yellow star and very similar to our Sun but brighter and slightly more massive.

Alpha A and Alpha B are binary stars. This means that if you were standing on a planet orbiting one of them, at certain times you would see two suns in the sky!

"Me too," said George. "Let's finish this. And find out who is sending those messages."

"I'm calling the portal," said Eric. On one side of the crater, they could already see the light of dawn as Alpha B hovered below the horizon. "Emmett!" he called. "Any chance of a trip back to Earth?"

"Not just yet," said Emmett. "But I do have some reasonably good news. . . ."

"You've found us a planet that might be just right, a planet about the size of Earth in the Goldilocks Zone?"

"Affirmative," said Emmett rather weakly. "Or at least, we've found something. It's our best guess. It's a moon, not a planet, though."

"How is Cosmos holding up?" asked Eric.

"I just want you to know," Mabel chipped in, "that I promised George's parents I wouldn't let him get into any trouble during his vacation! I'm going to have a very difficult time explaining this to Terence and Daisy. . . ."

"Cosmos is functioning," said Emmett nervously. "I've nearly finished updating the reverse portal. I'll be able to bring you in as soon as I've finished. Can you wait and I'll get you back to Earth?"

Bright rays of light were stealing across the crater, chasing the dark shadows away.

"No, we can't stay here any longer," said Eric. "Send us onward, Emmett. And don't worry, Mabel. We'll be back."

THE GOLDILOCKS ZONE

Our Milky Way Galaxy contains at least one hundred billion rocky planets. Our Sun has four: namely, Mercury, Venus, Earth, and Mars—but only Earth has life.

What makes Earth special?

The answer is *water*, especially in its liquid form. Water is the great mixer for chemicals—breaking them apart, spreading them out, and bringing them back together as new biological building blocks, such as proteins and DNA. Without water, life seems unlikely.

To support life, a planet's temperature must be between 32 and 212 degrees Fahrenheit (0 and 100 degrees Celsius) to keep the water in liquid form.

A planet orbiting too close to its home star will receive so much light energy that it will heat up to scorching temperatures, boiling all the water into steam.

Planets too far from their star will receive very little light energy, keeping the planet so cold that any water will remain as ice. Indeed, Mars has its water trapped as ice at the north and south poles.

There is a certain distance from every star where a planet receives as much *light* as it emits *heat*. That energy balance serves as a thermostat, keeping the temperature lukewarm—just right to keep the water liquid in lakes and oceans. In this "Goldilocks Zone" around a star, any planets would stay warm and bathed in water for millions of years, allowing the chemistry of life to flourish.

Geoff

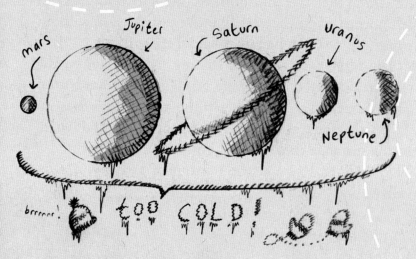

mars

Jupiter

Saturn

Uranus

Neptune

brrrrr!

too COLD!

Chapter 15

Alpha B was rising as they went through the portal, shining brilliantly onto the hot, heavy planet. To avoid having to stand up again, they wriggled feetfirst through the doorway, with Eric hopping up as soon as he was through to pull the two kids after him.

They got to their feet and found they could stand up on the rocky surface of this new place. They didn't float off it, and they weren't squished down toward it. It just felt normal—like they could move easily again, without ropes and without having to crawl around.

The light was pleasant, shining from a star in the sky that looked a bit like the Earth's Sun. It wasn't too bright, but it also didn't seem too cold—there was no ice on the rock as there had been on Mars and Titan. In the distance they heard a gurgling, rushing sound. They seemed to be at the bottom of a rocky valley.

"What's that noise?" said Annie. "And where are we? Are we back on Earth?"

"It sounds like water," said George, "but I can't see it anywhere."

"We're in the 55 Cancri star system," said Eric. "It's a binary star system—the one you see shining in the sky is a yellow dwarf star, just like our Sun. Farther away there is a red dwarf star as well."

Emmett joined in from Earth. "You are on a moon of the fifth planet around 55 Cancri A," he said. "The planet is in the habitable zone—the Goldilocks Zone—of its star, but the planet itself is a gas giant, about half the size of Saturn, so I didn't think you'd want to land there."

"Well done, Emmett," said Eric. "I don't really feel like falling through layers of gas. Not today, anyway. You made a good choice."

55 CANCRI

★ 55 Cancri is a star system forty-one light-years away from us in the direction of the Cancer constellation. It is a binary system: 55 Cancri A is a yellow star; 55 Cancri B is a smaller, red dwarf star. These two stars orbit each other at one thousand times the distance between the Earth and the Sun.

★ On November 6, 2007, astronomers discovered a record-breaking fifth planet in orbit around Cancri A. This makes it the only star other than our Sun known to have as many as five planets!

★ The first planet around Cancri A was discovered in 1996. Named Cancri b, it is the size of Jupiter and orbits close to the star. In 2002 two more planets (Cancri c and Cancri d) were discovered; in 2004 a fourth planet, Cancri e, which is the size of Neptune and takes just three days to orbit Cancri A. This planet would be scorchingly hot, with surface temperatures up to 2,732 degrees Fahrenheit (1,500 degrees Celsius).

★ The fifth planet, Cancri f, is around half the mass of Saturn and lies in the habitable—or Goldilocks—zone of its star. This planet is a giant ball of gas—mostly made of helium and hydrogen, like Saturn in our solar system. But there may be moons in orbit around Cancri f or rocky planets within Cancri's Goldilocks Zone where liquid water could exist on the surface.

★ Cancri f orbits its star at a distance of 0.781 astronomical units (AU). An astronomical unit is the measure of distance that astronomers use to talk about orbits and distance from stars. One AU = 93 million miles, which is the average distance from the Earth to the Sun. Given that there is life on Earth and liquid water on the surface of our planet, we can say that one AU, or 93 million miles, from our Sun is within the habitable zone of our Solar System. So for stars of roughly the mass, age, and luminosity of our Sun, we can guess that a planet orbiting its star at around one AU might be in the Goldilocks Zone. Cancri A is an older and dimmer star than our Sun, and astronomers calculate that its habitable zone lies between 0.5 AU and 2 AUs away from it, which puts Cancri f in a good position!

It is very difficult to spot multiple planets around a star because each planet produces its own stellar wobble. To find more than one planet, astronomers need to be able to spot wobbles within wobbles! Astronomers in California have been monitoring 55 Cancri for more than twenty years to make these discoveries.

Artwork comparing the sizes of the 55 Cancri system (left) with a small brown dwarf star system in the constellation of Chamaeleon (upper right).

The kids stretched out their arms and legs. It felt good to be able to move freely again.

"Can we take our space helmets off now?" asked Annie.

"No, absolutely not!" said Eric. "We have no idea what the atmosphere is made of here. Let me check your oxygen gauge." He looked at her air tank and saw that it was getting close to the red zone—running dangerously low. He looked at George's, but his was still in the green zone—plenty still in there. Eric said nothing but called Emmett again. "Emmett, how long before we can return to Earth?"

"I'm getting hungry," moaned Annie. "Do you think there's anything to eat here?"

"I don't think they have restaurants at the end of Universe," said George.

"We're not at the end of the Universe yet," said Eric, while waiting for Emmett's reply. "We're nowhere near. We're still really quite close to home—only forty-one light-years away! We haven't even left our own Galaxy yet. In terms of the Universe, this is like George coming to the States. A bit of a journey, but hardly an epic voyage."

"What about the clue?" said George. "Don't we need to see if there's another clue here for us? I mean, aren't we supposed to be saving planet Earth from someone who wants to destroy it?"

"Hmm . . ." Eric was looking anxious. Emmett was silent. "I think whoever sent you those messages put that part in to scare you," he said. "I can't think of anything right now that is powerful enough to destroy a whole planet. It would take far more energy than we've ever generated before to blow up the Earth. That was just a threat, to make sure we didn't ignore the messages."

"But what if it came from aliens who have sources of power we can't even dream of?" asked Annie. "How do you know there isn't a superrace out there? Those messages weren't sent by some bacteria, were they?"

"That, I suppose," said Eric, "is what we're trying to find out. Annie"—his tone changed—"why don't you sit down and have a rest? Try not to talk for a few minutes, get your strength back."

"But I don't want to not talk," said Annie. "I like talking. That's what I'm good at. And soccer. I'm good at soccer. And physics. I'm great at that, aren't I, Dad?"

"I know," said Eric soothingly. "But you're running

a bit low on air now. So I need you to be quiet for me, until we know when we're going home."

George looked around. He studied the ravines and mountains of this rocky planet, seeking the source of the rushing noise. Suddenly, at the other end of the valley, he saw something move.

"Over there!" he said quietly to Eric while Annie sat down on a rock.

"It's moving," muttered Eric, spotting it. "But what is it?"

The thing was in shadow so they couldn't even make out its shape. All they could see was that it was coming toward them. It was like a black blob creeping ever closer.

"George," said Eric, "call Emmett *now*! Tell him we've got an ET sighting, and I want him to open the portal and take you and Annie back immediately."

"Emmett . . ." George tried to call him. "Emmett . . . Come in, Emmett . . . Emmett, we need you to beam us up."

The shape was approaching them along the dark side of the ravine, shaded from the rays of the yellow dwarf star, Cancri A. As it crept toward them, they noticed two tiny pinpricks of bright red light shining from its middle, like a pair of very angry eyes.

"Annie," said Eric, "stand up and get behind me. We have an alien approaching."

Annie got to her feet and hurried behind her dad,

peeping around him. The black shape came closer, the red lights in its middle sparkling with demonic fury. As it approached, they could see it was shaped almost like a human being, dressed entirely in black, with scarlet eyes burning out of its stomach.

"Get back," said Eric. "Whatever you are, do not take another step toward us."

The thing took no notice of Eric's warning and continued onward. It stepped out of the shadow and into the light. And then it spoke.

"So, Eric," its voice rasped through all their voice transmitters, "we meet again."

Chapter 16

"OMG! It's Reeper!" shouted Annie and George at the same moment.

Standing in front of them, in a black space suit with a black glass visor on a black space helmet, was none other than Eric's nemesis, Dr. Graham Reeper, the once-upon-a-time friend and colleague who had turned on him and become his deadly enemy.

Not so long ago, Eric had let Dr. Reeper, who had been posing as a teacher at George's school, escape to start a new life somewhere else. Even though he had tried to throw Eric into a black hole and steal his amazing computer, Eric had been convinced that Reeper shouldn't be punished.

And now it seemed that Eric had made a terrible mistake. Reeper was back and—in his black suit on this distant moon—a thousand times scarier than when George and Annie had last seen him.

Reeper wasn't alone, either. In his cupped hands he held what looked like a small animal with glowing bright red eyes. Its little paws scrabbled against the shiny black material of Reeper's space gloves.

"Ahhhh—look!" said Annie. "He's found a lovely little furry pet on this planet!" She took half a step forward, but Eric shot out an arm to stop her from going any closer. The creature in Reeper's hands hissed and bared its teeth. Reeper stroked its head with one hand.

"There, there," he said soothingly. "Don't worry, Pooky. We'll get rid of them very soon."

"You'll never destroy us, Reeper," said Eric defiantly. Behind him, George was desperately trying to radio Emmett.

"Is that the boy?" asked Reeper idly. "Is that the boy who ruined all my plans last time? How kind of you to bring him too. That's so"—the animal made a nasty growling noise—"thoughtful. And your daughter. How charming."

"Reeper, you can do anything you want to me," said Eric, "but don't touch the kids. Let them go."

"Let them go?" said Reeper, as though considering it. "What do you say, Pooky?" He scratched the animal's head. "Shall we let the kids go?" Pooky hissed loudly. "The problem is," he explained, "your children don't have anywhere *to* go. Or any way to get there. I know you're trying to call your dear chum Cosmos to help you out, and it's really very touching how much faith you've put in him. But you might as well save your oxygen because Pooky here is sending out a very powerful blocking signal."

"What!" exclaimed Eric. "What *is* Pooky?"

"Dear little Pooky," said Reeper. "He is my friend. Sweet, isn't he? Twice as powerful as Cosmos and so very much smaller. In fact, you could say Pooky is the nano-Cosmos. I disguised him as a hamster. After all, who would think of looking for a very powerful super-computer inside a hamster's cage?"

"What!" said Eric. "You built a new version of Cosmos?"

"What did you think I'd been up to all this time?" Reeper sneered. "Did you think I would just forget about everything that happened? Or did you think I would *forgive*?" He said the last word in a par-ticularly unpleasant fashion. "Forgiveness is only for lucky people, Eric. People like you. People who get everything they ever wanted. It's easy for you to be forgiving, with your wonderful career and your lovely family and your nice home and your helpful supercomputer. You've always had everything your own way. Until now, that is."

"Reeper, why have you brought us here?" demanded Eric. "It was you, wasn't it, who left those clues?"

"Indeed it was." Reeper sighed. "At last! You guessed. It took a while though. We've been sending messages to Cosmos for ages. We began to think you would never take the bait. It's not like you to be so slow. And yes, before you ask, it was me playing games with your lovely little robot, Homer. Pooky interrupted him on the descent and managed to tamper with his programming. I thought you'd have to notice Homer. But no. Even that took ages. You've been terribly amateur, Eric. I expected better from you."

"It wasn't Eric!" George stepped forward angrily. "It was us! We were the ones who read the clues and came after you."

"Oh, the boy wonder," said Reeper. "Eric's mini-me. Another disciple—how tiring."

"Step back, George," warned Eric. "And keep trying Cosmos. I don't believe that nano-computer is as powerful as Reeper says."

Reeper laughed, a horrible grating sound. "You think you're very clever, don't you, Eric? Looking for signs of life in the Universe. But you're not as clever as me. That's why I brought you here. Finally to prove that to you."

"Prove what?" Eric snorted. "You're proving nothing right now, Reeper. Only that we were right to keep you away from Cosmos all those years ago."

"Always the saint." Reeper sneered back again. "Wanting scientific knowledge to benefit humanity. How have you benefited humanity, Eric? Isn't your precious human race in the process of destroying the beautiful planet it lives on? Why not just help people achieve their goal faster—get rid of Earth and all those morons on it and start again? Somewhere like here. A new planet. This is what I lured you out here to see, Eric. I've completed your mission. I've found a place where life might begin—

a place where intelligent life could thrive. Where, in fact, simple life could already be present." He held up a clear vial of liquid. "I've found *this*," he said. "The elixir of life."

"You don't know that's water!" said Eric. "You don't know what that is."

"I do know that

261

whatever it is, I found it before you. *Me*, not *you*, Eric. *I* found the new planet Earth. I *own* it, and I control access to it. And when the Earth finally goes *boom!* I will be in charge of the whole human race as well."

The cosmic hamster's eyes were now glowing like a burning furnace. It scrabbled excitedly as Reeper spoke.

Eric shook his head. "Reeper," he said sadly, "you are such a loser."

Reeper howled. "I am *not* a loser!" he said angrily. "I am *winning!*"

"No, you're not," said Eric. "So you don't like humanity? So you think we've made a mess of the planet? So you'd prefer to keep all your scientific knowledge to yourself, not share it with anyone else, and perhaps charge people lots of money for the use of it? That makes you a total loser. You've cut yourself off from everything that is good or useful or interesting or beautiful—from everything human, in fact. I mean, look at your version of Cosmos. It's disgusting. And I think Pooky is molting."

Pooky looked outraged. Reeper rocked backward and forward on his space boots in fury.

Behind Eric, Annie was giving George a count-down, using the fingers of her space gloves. Silently she counted down: *Five, four, three, two, ONE!* When she got to *one*, the two kids charged forward, heads lowered, and butted Reeper in the stomach with their space helmets.

George snatched Pooky and dashed away while Annie gave Reeper a swift kick in the stomach. Unbalanced by the sudden attack, Reeper fell backward and lay groaning on the ground, looking like an upturned stag beetle. The vial of liquid flew out of his hand and smashed on a rock, the clear liquid seeping away. Eric ran over and put one heavy boot on Reeper's chest.

"Graham," he said, "this isn't why we went into science. We went into science because it's fascinating and

exciting, because we wanted to explore the Universe and find out the secrets it holds. We wanted to understand, to know, to comprehend, to write another chapter in the story of humanity's search for knowledge. We are part of a great tradition, using the work of those who went before to help us progress farther and yet farther across this amazing Universe in which we live. And to understand why we are here and how it all began. That's what we *do*, Graham. We bring enlightenment by *sharing* our knowledge. We don't keep it to ourselves. We explain, we teach, we seek. We move humanity forward by sharing the secrets we uncover. We aim to create a better world, on whatever planet we live, rather than finding a new world and keeping that planet all to ourselves."

But Reeper didn't seem to care. "Give back Pooky," he rasped. "He's *mine*. You stole Cosmos from me once. Don't take Pooky now. I can't live without him."

"Pooky is only a tool," said Eric. "Just like Cosmos."

"No! It's not *fair*!" ranted Reeper. "You only say that because you have Cosmos! And you don't even need him! You can understand the Universe! I don't! That's why I wanted Cosmos, Eric. You'll never know what it's like! You've always been a genius—you don't know what it's like to be ordinary. Like me." He started sobbing.

George was struggling to hold on to Pooky. "I don't know how to turn him off!" he said to Annie.

"You've got to stroke his head," she said. "Like Reeper was doing. That's where his control panel must be."

"I can't!" said George. "I'll lose him—he's trying to escape! You do it!"

"Eeew!" said Annie, taking a cautious step toward him. She reached out a finger and Pooky promptly bit her. She snatched her hand back. The horrible creature hadn't pierced the space glove, so Annie was still safely sealed into her suit. She moved forward again, and this time waved one hand at Pooky. While he was watching that hand, she used the other to touch his head. She rubbed hard. . . .

The next second they heard Emmett's voice once more.

"Annie! George! Eric!" he said. "I haven't been able to get through!"

"Open the portal, quickly," said George. "We're coming back."

Emmett sounded frantic. "Cosmos doesn't have enough memory," he said. "He needs help. He needs

265

another computer to join up with him to get you back."

"Another computer!" said George. "Where are we going to get another computer? We're on a moon orbiting a planet forty-one light-years away! It's not like they have stores here."

Then the same thought struck George, Annie, and Eric at the same time.

"Pooky!"

Chapter 17

Reeper was still lying underneath Eric's boot, which was firmly pressing him down on the rocky surface.

"Graham," Eric said urgently, "we need you to help us. You must use Pooky to link up with Cosmos so we can open the portal and go back home."

"Send you back to Earth?" cried Reeper. "Never! I won't help you. I've got a much larger tank of oxygen than you. So when yours runs out, I'll get Pooky off you and I'll be gone while you are stuck here forever. By the time I come back, I doubt you'll cause me any trouble."

Even though she knew she didn't have much air left, Annie bravely spoke up:

"Why do you hate everyone so much?" she asked him. "Why do you want to destroy every- thing?"

"Why do I hate everyone, little girl?" asked Reeper. "Because everyone hates me, that's why. Since I was thrown out of the Order of Science to Benefit Humanity all those years ago, nothing—*nothing*—has gone right for me. It's been darkness and despair all this time. And now, at last, I'm calling the shots."

"No, you're not," said George. Pooky had stopped wriggling and was now snuggled up in his hands, as though about to fall asleep. His red eyes no longer glowed with menace. Instead, they had turned a dim shade of yellow. "You're just sad and bitter. And even if you leave us here and we never go home, it won't bring you any happiness. It won't gain you any friends or make you any smarter. You'll just be alone, with your stupid hamster."

Pooky squeaked indignantly.

"Sorry, Pooky . . ." George was growing almost fond of the small furry computer. "Anyway," he added, "you knew what would happen if you broke the rules of the order. It says in the oath."

"Ah, yes," said Reeper dreamily. "The oath. It seems such a long, long time ago. I'd forgotten about that quaint piece of nonsense. How does it go . . . ?"

Annie started to speak, but George shushed her. "No, Annie," he said. "Save your air. It goes like this." He recited the oath he had taken to join the order, the very first time he had met Eric.

"*I swear to use my scientific knowledge for the good of Humanity.*

"*I promise never to harm any person in my search for enlightenment.*

"*I shall be courageous and careful in my quest for greater knowledge about the mysteries that surround us.*

"*I shall not use scientific knowledge for my own personal gain or give it to those who seek to destroy the wonderful Universe in which we live.*

"*If I break this oath, may the beauty and wonder of the Universe forever remain hidden from me.*

"You broke the oath. That's why it's all gone wrong for you."

"Is that so?" said Reeper quietly. "And how did I come to break the oath? Have you ever asked yourself that question? Why would I do that when I knew what I stood to lose?"

"I don't know," whispered Annie.

"Then why don't you ask your father?" he suggested, getting to his knees. Eric had removed his foot from his chest and turned away.

"Dad?" Annie asked. "Dad?"

"It was a long time ago," muttered Eric. "And we were very young."

"What happened?" murmured Annie. She was starting to feel light-headed.

"Why don't you tell her?" said Reeper, getting to his feet. "Or shall I? No one is leaving here until this story is told."

"Graham and I," said Eric slowly, "were students together. Our tutor was the greatest cosmologist who has ever lived. He wanted to find out how the Universe began. With him, Graham and I built the first Cosmos. Cosmos was very different from how he is today. Back then, he was huge—he took up the whole basement of a university building."

"Go on," ordered Reeper, "or no one is going home. Ever."

"Those of us who used Cosmos or worked with him formed the early branch of the Order of Science. We realized what a powerful tool we had. We needed to be careful. Graham took the oath, and at first he and I worked together. But then Graham started to behave very strangely—"

"I did not!" said Reeper angrily. "That is not true!

You wouldn't leave me alone. You followed me everywhere, always trying to get a look at my writing, so you could copy it and pass it off as your own. You wanted to publish my work as yours and take all the glory."

"No, Graham," said Eric. "I didn't. I wanted to work *with* you, but you wouldn't let me. We knew you were hiding your research from other people, and we saw that you were becoming secretive. Our tutor asked me to keep an eye on you."

"Ohhh," said Reeper, in surprise. "I didn't know that."

"That's why I followed you that night—the night you went to use Cosmos all by yourself. We had a rule, then, that no one person could operate Cosmos alone.

But Graham did. He let himself into the university at night and that's when I caught him."

"What was he trying to do?" asked George.

"He was trying," said Eric, "to use Cosmos to view the Big Bang itself. It was too dangerous. We just didn't know what the effects of watching that kind of explosion—even via Cosmos, even from the other side of the portal—might have been. We'd talked about it, but our tutor had said no. Until we knew more about the early Universe—and about Cosmos—we were not to use him to investigate the Big Bang."

"Fools!" Reeper bleated. "You were all fools! We could have found the cornerstone of all knowledge! We could have seen what created the Universe! But you were too scared. I had to try it in secret. It was the only way. I had to know—what happened at the very beginning of everything."

"The risk was too great," said Eric. "Remember, we had sworn to harm no person in our search for enlightenment. But I guessed that was what you were trying to do—witness the first few seconds of time itself. When I followed you that night . . ."

Chapter 18

It had been a cold, clear night in the ancient university town where Eric Bellis and Graham Reeper studied. The air crackled with frost and the wind bit through the thickest garments. They lived in the same college, with rooms overlooking a courtyard where the flagstones were so old that centuries of feet had worn them away. That night, the courtyard was silent, the perfect green grass turned deepest indigo by the brilliant moonlight beaming down through the velvet night sky. The clock in the tower struck eleven as Eric came in through the front gates, which were so strongly fortified, it was like entering a castle rather than a place of learning.

"Good evening, Doctor Bellis," a bowler-hatted porter said to Eric as he passed through the front dorm to pick up his mail. As Eric stood there, leafing through the envelopes, he caught the porter watching him. He looked up and smiled. "You haven't dined in for a while, Doctor Bellis," the porter commented. Fellows of this venerable institution had the right to eat off silver every night in the oak-paneled dining

room, surrounded by portraits of scholars from centuries past.

"It's been a busy time," said Eric. He tucked his mail into his battered old briefcase and wound his scarf more tightly around his neck. It was always freezing in the college, sometimes even colder than it was outside on the street. Eric rarely took off his scarf in winter. In his rooms it was so chilly that he slept wearing his tweed jacket over his pajamas, along with two pairs of socks and a woolly hat.

"Haven't seen that Doctor Reeper much lately either," said the porter, shooting Eric a look. Eric reminded himself that the porters knew everything, saw everything, and heard everything. The reason he hadn't been in college much lately was because he was trying to keep up with Reeper, who was very obviously attempting to give him the slip.

"Is Doctor Reeper in this evening?" he asked casually.

"He is," said the porter heavily. "And funnily enough, he seemed very keen that you should know that. Something going on, Doctor Bellis?"

Eric took off his glasses and rubbed his eyes. He was so tired. Constantly tailing

Reeper as well as doing his own work was becoming exhausting.

"Nothing to worry about," he said firmly.

"We've seen it all before, you know," hinted the porter. "You start off friends but then you get into competition with each other. It never ends well."

Eric sighed. "Thank you," he said, and walked across the main court. He slowly climbed the wooden staircase to his room and let himself in. Switching on the electric heater, he went over to the window.

On the other side of the courtyard, he could see that Reeper's light was still on. Eric wondered if he would get a full night's sleep tonight or whether he would wake up every hour, worried that Reeper had left the college without him. He drew his curtains and sat down in an armchair. Just as he did so, the lightbulb went out, plunging his room into blackness. Eric just sat there for a few minutes, wondering if he could face brushing his teeth in his subzero bathroom. He stood up and, on instinct, peered through a chink in the curtains, just in time to see a dark figure slipping across the courtyard, casting a long shadow in the moonlight.

Wearily, Eric put on an extra tweed jacket and left his room, carefully tailing Graham Reeper as he slipped away out of the college.

Eric didn't need to follow him too closely to know where Reeper was going, but he did want to prevent him from doing too much damage. The handlebars of Eric's bicycle

were covered in frost, and cycling was treacherous and slow on the icy roads. By the time he arrived at the university building where Cosmos was kept, his bare fingers were blue and numb with cold so he could hardly move them. Blowing on them, he fumbled with his set of keys and let himself in.

"What did you find?" asked George, interrupting the story in his eagerness to know what Reeper had done.

"He found me," said Reeper, "on the brink of the greatest discovery in the history of knowledge! And then he ruined it! And blamed me afterward."

Eric's suspicions had been correct. When he ran down the stairs to Cosmos's basement, he had found Reeper attempting to use the computer to watch the Big Bang. The portal doorway was already there, but the door was still closed.

"I had to stop him," said Eric. "The conditions were so extreme at the beginning of the Universe—it was too hot even for hydrogen to form! It could have been so dangerous. I didn't know for sure what was on the

other side of the door, but I had to stop him from opening it."

"But didn't you want to see?" asked George, agog.
"Couldn't you have taken a peek? Like from a long,
long way away?"

"You can't view the Big Bang from a distance,"
replied Eric. "Because it occurs everywhere. What he
should have done is view it with a large redshift."

"A redshift!" exclaimed George. "Like at your party?"

"Exactly! As the radiation emitted shortly after the
Big Bang travels to us on Earth, it becomes much redder and less powerful," explained Eric.

"But that's just what I was trying to do!" cried
out Reeper. "If you had bothered to ask me, instead
of bursting through the door and tackling me to the
ground, I would have told you!"

"Ahh," said Eric slowly. Eric hadn't, in fact, given
Reeper a chance to explain what he was doing. Instead,
he had run into the room where Cosmos was kept and
thrown himself onto Reeper, who was standing near
the portal doorway. In the tussle that followed, Eric
had jabbed wildly with one flailing hand at Cosmos's
keyboard, in the hope of shutting down the portal. But
Reeper had broken free from Eric and run over to the
doorway, which he had wrenched open, only to find
Eric's blind strike at Cosmos's keyboard had accidentally given Cosmos the command to move the portal
location to somewhere very different.

When Reeper opened the door, he found himself staring straight into the Sun. He put his hands up to shield himself from the glare, but the heat burned them horribly. Weeping and moaning, he backed away as Eric got Cosmos to slam the door shut.

Eric tried to help Reeper, but his colleague staggered out of the building alone and disappeared into the darkness. That night, it seemed, Reeper had left the university town, giving Eric no choice, he felt, but to ask their tutor to banish him forever from the Order of Science.

"You ruined me," said Reeper bitterly. "You, Eric. You took everything and left me nothing. I was very embarrassed that you had caught me using Cosmos in secret. And I was in so much pain that night that I didn't really know what I was doing. I staggered out into the road and I ran—I just ran as far as I could. I must have collapsed because when I woke up, I was in the hospital, half blinded by the Sun and with terrible burns on my hands. At first I couldn't even remember who I was. After a while the memories started coming back. I insisted I had to leave the hospital and return to the college to apologize for what I'd done. But when I got there, I found you'd had me banished, with no chance to explain myself. You'd seen to it that I could never walk into the college again."

"I was trying to protect you," raged Eric.

"From what?" said Reeper angrily.

"From yourself!"

"Well, that didn't work, did it?" said Annie woozily. "I mean, you've got to admit, Dad, that even though he shouldn't have been using Cosmos by himself—and we're not allowed to either, Doctor Reeper, just in case you think you're special—you did make him have a nasty accident, you didn't give him a second chance, and you ended his career in science."

"He deserved it!" said Eric. "He knew the rules."

"Well, only sort of," murmured Annie. "I mean, he didn't get to see the Big Bang, did he? After all, he was actually trying to watch it in the way you suggested, but you just didn't bother to find that out! And it was you who made it really dangerous by changing the portal location. So it's at least partially your fault."

"My fault?" said Eric in surprise.

"Yeah," said Annie. "It sounds like it was just a huge

mistake, and if you'd said sorry in the first place, we wouldn't be in this pickle now."

"Say sorry?" said Eric in disbelief. "You want *me* to say sorry to *him*?"

"Yes," said Annie as firmly as she could. "I do. And so does Reeper, don't you? That would make it all better. And then maybe we could get back to Earth."

Eric mumbled something to himself.

"We didn't hear that," George told him.

"All right, all right," said Eric crossly. "Reeper—I mean, Graham, I'm . . . I'm . . ."

"Say it," warned Annie. "And say it nicely."

"I'm s-s-s-s," said Eric through gritted teeth. "I'm s-s-s-s—" He seemed to get stuck on the word.

"You're what? Exactly?" asked Reeper.

"I'm so—so—sor—," said Eric.

"Eric, hurry up!" muttered George. "Annie needs to leave here."

"Graham," said Eric decisively. "Graham, I'm—sorry. I'm sorry for what happened to you and for my part in it. I'm sorry I banished you without giving you the chance to explain. I'm sorry I acted hastily."

"I see," said Reeper. He sounded rather confused.

"You're sorry." He didn't seem to know what to do next.

"Yes, I'm sorry!" said Eric, speaking fast. "You were my best friend once, and my best colleague. Together as scientists we could have been magnificent. We could have done brilliant work, if only you hadn't insisted on trying to grab everything for yourself. And guess what, Graham, you're not the only person who got hurt that evening. I've missed you—at least, I missed the person you once were before you started working against me. And I've had to live with the guilt, too, of what happened that terrible night. You're not the only person who's suffered. So stop being so melodramatic and get us all out of this place and back home again while we can still breathe."

"I lost you once as a friend," said Reeper sadly. "And I lost my life in science. The only way I found the strength to carry on was by hating you and seeking revenge. But now, if you're not my enemy, I have nothing at all."

"That's really silly," said George. "Eric has apologized and said he's sorry. Don't you think you should say something back?"

"Right," said Reeper quietly. "In that case, Eric Bellis, I accept your apology." He gave a little bow.

"Your turn now," whispered Annie.

"What?" exclaimed Reeper.

"Your turn to say sorry. That's how it works. Dad said he was sorry, now you have to apologize too."

"What for?" said Reeper. He sounded like he genuinely didn't know.

"Oh, I don't know . . . ," chipped in George. "For stealing Cosmos, for throwing Eric in a black hole, for making us travel across the Universe because you said you were going to blow up planet Earth if we didn't. I don't know—pick your favorite and say sorry for that."

Eric growled. "Make it quick, Graham."

"No need to go on," said Reeper hastily. "I'm sorry too. I wish I'd been a better person. I wish I hadn't wasted all that time. I wish I could go back to science—proper science . . ." He ended on a wistful, hopeful note.

"Listen, Graham," said Eric urgently. "You want to come back to science—fine. You want me to believe you're a good person after all—fine as well. But just get on with it and get my daughter and George back to Earth before their air runs out. Because if that happens, I can assure you that I would never forgive you and wherever you are in the Universe I will find you."

"Do you mean it?" said Reeper. "Can I really come back to science again?"

"Get us back to planet Earth first and then we'll talk," said Eric.

"George," said Reeper, "you need to stroke Pooky on the head again. You've sent him to sleep, and you need

to wake him up." George gingerly fluffed the top of Pooky's
head, and the hamster stirred in
his hands. "Pooky," continued
Reeper, "I want you to link
with a computer on Earth, the
same computer I ordered you
to block. You're going to work
with him to create a doorway
that can take us all back there
again."

The hamster woke up fully as George called
Emmett.

"Emmett, Gran," he said. "Prepare the portal. We've
found another computer. We need Cosmos to work
with this other supercomputer to make a portal powerful enough to bring us all back."

"You found another computer? Where?" said Emmett
in surprise. "And what on Earth is going on out there?"

"That's just it," said George. "On Earth. It's the final
clue in the cosmic treasure hunt. It takes us back to
where we came from. Get ready—we're coming home.
Over and out."

Pooky sat up straight, and two beams of light shot
out of his eyes and drew a doorway, exactly the way
Cosmos did. While he was forming the portal that
would carry them across the Universe, George asked a
final question:

"Reeper," he said as they waited for the cosmic hamster to complete the portal. "The end of the messages—you said you would destroy planet Earth if we didn't follow them. Did you mean it? Could you really destroy a whole planet?"

"Don't be ridiculous!" said Eric, who was holding Annie as near to the glimmering portal doorway as possible, so he could shove her through it as soon as it opened. "Graham can't destroy the Earth. That would take an explosion of unimaginable power. He was just making empty threats. Weren't you, Graham?"

Reeper fiddled with his space gloves.

"Weren't you?" Eric insisted again.

"The odd thing is," said Reeper, "it could really happen. But it wouldn't actually be my fault. It's just something I heard about on my travels. . . ."

Just then, Pooky's eyes glowed, and he opened the portal doorway for them, back to the Clean Room, back to the Global Space Agency, back to the United States, back to planet Earth once more.

But this time his eyes were no longer yellow but marbled, with patterns of blue, green, and flecks of white.

In his eyes shone the reflection of the most beautiful planet in the Universe—a planet that is not too hot and not too cold; that has liquid water on the surface and where the gravity is just right for human beings and the atmosphere is perfect for them to breathe; where there are mountains and deserts and oceans and islands and forests and trees and birds and plants and animals and insects and people—lots and lots of people.

Where there is life.

Some of it, possibly, intelligent.

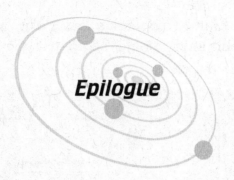

Epilogue

L ive long and prosper!" said Emmett, giving the Vulcan salute as he got into his dad's car to go home at the end of the summer vacation. His dad—a carbon copy of Emmett, except taller—grinned and took one hand off the steering wheel to give the Vulcan salute as well.

Annie and her parents, George and his grandmother all stood outside on the porch to wave good-bye.

"See you next summer!" called George, saluting back.

"Emmett, you rock!" said Annie, waving. "Don't forget us!"

"You are firmly installed in my memory banks," said Emmett, fastening his seat belt. "Forever. It's been the best. I'm going to miss you." He sniffed. "Dad, I made some friends," he said plaintively. "And now I'm going to lose them again!"

"No chance!" called Annie. "I'll be bugging you by e-mail all the time! And so will George!"

"Maybe your friends can come and stay with us

sometime, Emmett?' said his dad. "You know how pleased your mom would be to have your friends come over.'

"Or I could go to England!" said Emmett eagerly. "Annie could come too, and we could see George and check out some university courses over there? They do some really cool stuff."

Eric came over to the car window. "Well done, Emmett," he said. "You saved the day."

"What day?" asked his dad. "What have you been up to?"

"We were playing a game," said Emmett.

"Did you win?" asked his dad.

"No one really won or lost," Emmett tried to explain. "We just progressed to another level."

His dad started the car. "Thanks, Eric," he said. "I don't know what you've done to my son, but it seems like a bit of magic has happened here."

"It's not magic, Dad," said Emmett in disgust. "It's science! And it's friends. It's the two together."

Mabel waved her cane and bellowed, "See you at the final frontier, Emmett!"

The car drove away, and the others turned back to go into the house once more. As they did so, Eric's pager bleeped, giving him news from the Mars Science Laboratory. He read the message and broke into the most enormous smile.

"It's Homer!" he said. "He's working prop-erly again! He's found visual evidence of water on Mars, and we think it won't be long before he can send us the chemical evidence, too!"

"What does that mean?" said George.

"It means," said Eric firmly, "that we need to have another party."

"Are you going to invite Reeper?" asked George. "I bet he hasn't been to a party for years."

After they had gotten back from the 55 Cancri sys-tem, using Cosmos and Reeper's special nano-computer, Pooky, Eric and Reeper had spent quite some time sitting on the veranda, talking. George, Emmett, and Annie had tried to listen in from the tree, but they hadn't caught much of the muttered conversation between the two former colleagues. They'd understood, however, that the conversation had ended well. Reeper had smiled at them when he came to say good-bye. Eric had found him a place at an institute where he could start studying again. It was a nice, quiet place, said Eric, where Reeper would be able to catch up on what he'd missed and get involved with real science again.

The condition of Eric helping Reeper was that Pooky was left behind with Eric. Eric was going to oversee a massive system overhaul of both Cosmos and Pooky, to find out if he could link the two supercomputers together. Right now, both Cosmos and Pooky were in pieces while Eric tried to work out how to do this, so there was no opportunity for any further cosmic adventures for a while.

But Eric, it turned out, wasn't the only person receiving news of life elsewhere. The house phone rang and Susan answered it, passing the receiver over to George. It was his mom and dad, calling from the South Pacific.

The satellites had spotted George's dad, a rescue mission had been dispatched to pick him up, and he had returned safely to the mother ship and been reunited with George's mom.

"George!" she said on the faint, crackly line. "We're all safe, and we'll be seeing you and your gran soon — we're coming back via Florida. And" — she paused, as if wondering whether to continue, then went on in a rush — "we've got some exciting news for you too! We were going to wait until we saw you to tell you, but I just *can't* not tell any longer. You're going to have a baby brother or sister! Isn't that wonderful? It means you're not alone anymore. Are you happy?"

George was rather stunned. All this time they'd been looking for signs of life in the Universe, and now

it turned out there was going to be a brand-new life-form inside his very own home.

"We'll see you in two days!" said his mom.

"Whoa!" George said to the others when he got off the phone. "My mom's having a baby."

"Ahh, how cute," said Annie, smiling.

"Hmph," said George, wondering how she would react if it was her mom and dad.

"No, it's cool!" said Annie, who'd caught the expression on his face. "We'll have another person to join in our adventures!"

"No you won't," said her dad firmly. "No babies in space, Annie. And that's a rule. In fact, no more kids in space."

"But, Dad," complained Annie, "what are we going to do? We're going to be really bored!"

"You're going back to school, Annie Bellis," her dad told her. "So you won't have time to get bored."

"Urrr!" Annie made a face. "Can't I go and live with George?"

"Well," said Eric, "funny that you mention it. I was thinking of taking you back to England. Now that Homer works properly and he's found water on Mars, it might be time for me to take part in another great experiment that's in progress in Europe—in Switzerland. We could all go back to the house in England, and I could join the work from there easily."

"Yeah!" Annie and George celebrated together. They wouldn't have to be apart again.

They all wandered out onto the veranda, wondering what to do with themselves now that all their challenges were over and Emmett had left.

George picked up *The User's Guide to the Universe*, which was lying on the garden table. "Eric," he said thoughtfully. "There's something I've been meaning to ask you, but we haven't had time until now."

"Go on," said Eric.

"When we were"—George lowered his voice—"out there, Reeper said something. He said that you understood the Universe. Is that true?"

"Well, yes, it is," said Eric modestly. "I do."

"But how do you do that?" said George. "How does that happen?"

Eric smiled. "Turn to the last pages in the book, George," he said. "And there you'll find the answer."

HOW TO UNDERSTAND THE UNIVERSE

The Universe is governed by scientific laws. These determine how the Universe starts off and how it develops in time. The aim of science is to discover the laws and to find out what they mean. It is the most exciting treasure hunt of all because the treasure is the understanding of the Universe and everything in it. We haven't found all the laws yet so the hunt is still on, but we have a good idea of what they must be in all but the most extreme conditions.

The most important laws are those that describe the forces.

So far we have discovered four types of forces:

1) The Electromagnetic Force
This holds atoms together and governs light, radio waves, and electronic devices, such as computers and televisions.

2) The Weak Force
This is responsible for radioactivity and plays a vital role in powering the Sun, and in the formation of the elements in stars and the early Universe.

3) The Strong Force

This holds the central nucleus of an atom together and provides the power for nuclear weapons and the Sun.

4) Gravity

This is the weakest of the four forces, but it holds us to the Earth, the Earth and the planets in orbit around the Sun, the Sun in orbit around the center of the Galaxy, and so on.

We have laws that describe each of these forces, but scientists believe that there is one key to the Universe, not four. We think that this division into four forces is artificial and that we will be able to combine the laws that describe those forces into a single theory. So far we have managed to combine the electromagnetic and weak forces. It should be possible to combine these two with the strong force, but it is much more difficult to combine the three with gravity because gravity bends space and time.

Nevertheless we have a strong candidate for the single theory of all forces that would be the key to understanding the Universe. It is called *M-theory*. We haven't completely worked out what M-theory is, which is why some people say the M stands for "mystery." If we do, we will understand the Universe from the Big Bang to the far distant future.

Eric

INDEX TO SPECIFIC FACTUAL SECTIONS

There is lots of science within this book, but there are also a number of separate sections where facts and information are provided on specific subjects. Some readers may wish to refer back to these pages in particular.

Acknowledgments

This book comes with our grateful thanks to:

Jane and Jonathan, without whose kindness and support this book would not exist. William, for his sweetness and good humor about his mom and grandad writing another book.

Garry Parsons, for his illustrations, which capture the story line, the adventure, and the characters so perfectly.

Geoff Marcy, for his amazing lecture at the Institute of Astronomy in Cambridge, which inspired the theme of this book.

The distinguished scientists who made their work accessible to a young audience through the essays that form *The User's Guide to the Universe*. They are Bernard Carr, Seth Shostak, Brandon Carter, Martin Rees, and Geoff Marcy. Their expert knowledge and enthusiasm for this project made it a joy to work on.

Stuart Rankin at the University of Cambridge, for writing so brilliantly about how light and sound travel.

Our friends at NASA and all the people in the different departments who took the time and trouble to talk to us about what NASA does and how it works. In particular, we would like to thank Michael Griffin, Michael O'Brien, Michael Curie, and Bob Jacobs.

Kimberly Lievense and Marc Rayman at the Jet Propulsion Laboratory in California, for their help with the wonders of robotic spaceflight.

Kip Thorne and Leonard Mlodinow at Caltech, for their advice and friendship.

Richard Garriott and Peter Diamandis at Space Adventures, for their energy and enthusiasm, and Richard for including us—and the first George book—in his real-life space adventure! Thanks to him, *George's Secret Key to the Universe* has now visited the International Space Station.

Markus Poessel, for his attention to detail and helpful comment.

George Becker and Daniel Stark at the Institute of Astronomy, Cambridge, for their invaluable comments.

Sam Blackburn and Tom Kendall, for patiently answering endless quirky science, engineering, and computing questions.

Tif Loehnis and all at Janklow and Nesbit, UK, for their kindness and hard work on the George series. And Eric Simonoff in the New York office, for sending George to the United States once more.

At Random House, our wonderful editor Sue Cook, for her tremendous work, which brought the *Cosmic Treasure Hunt* together and made it into such a beautiful book. Lauren Buckland, for her great work on the text and the images; Sophie Nelson, for the careful copyedit; and James Fraser, for his wonderful front cover. Also Maeve Banham and her team in the Rights department, for helping to ensure that the George books truly do reach an international audience. And a special thank you to Annie Eaton, for her dedication and warmth toward the George series.

Keso Kendall, for her help with how a teenage supercomputer should speak.

All the "team"—at home and at the university—for their patience and generosity toward another George book.

Finally, but most importantly, we would like to thank our young readers—Melissa Ball, Poppy and Oscar Wallington, Anthony Redford, and Joanna Fox, for their thoughtful feedback and their very helpful comments on the *Cosmic Treasure Hunt*. And we would like to thank all the kids who asked the questions, who wrote, e-mailed, or came to lectures and were brave enough to stand up and ask something at the end. We hope this book gives you a few answers. And we hope you never stop asking "Why?"

Lucy and Stephen Hawking

Here's a sneak peak at a forthcoming book!

George and the Big Bang

By Lucy and Stephen Hawking

Illustrated by Garry Parsons

Enjoy this excerpt from the third book about George, Annie, and the super-computer Cosmos, which will be coming in the fall. The final book will be heavily illustrated and will feature essays by prestigious scientists throughout.

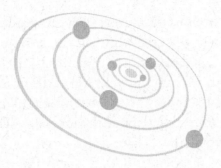

Who were *who*?" said a voice as Eric himself pushed open the door to his study, a steaming mug of tea in one hand and a pile of scientific papers jammed under his tweed-jacketed arm. "Hello, Annie and George!" he said. "Enjoying your last day of school vacation?"

The two friends stared blankly back at him.

"Oh dear! I'll take that as 'no,' shall I?" said Eric. "Is something wrong?" He smiled at them both. Eric couldn't stop smiling these days. If George had to describe Annie's father at the moment, he would have used the words "incredibly happy." Or "incredibly busy." In fact, the busier Eric was, the happier he seemed. Since he had moved back from the United States, where he had been working on a space mission to try and find traces of life on Mars, the scientist always seemed to be in a rush and always seemed to be enjoying himself. He was happy at home with his family, he loved his new job as Professor of Mathematics at Foxbridge University, and he was super-excited about the big experiment he was running at the Large Hadron Collider in Switzerland.

The project at the LHC was the continuation of work

started by scientists hundreds of years earlier. The aim was to discover what the world was made of, and how the tiny fundamental pieces fit together to form the contents of the Universe. To do this, Eric and the other scientists were trying to find a theory that would allow them to understand everything about the Universe. They gave it the simple name the "Theory of Everything." It was the greatest goal in science. If they could find it, scientists would be able to understand not only the beginning of the Universe, but possibly even how—and why—the Universe we live in came about.

THE THEORY OF EVERYTHING

Throughout history, people have looked around and tried to understand the amazing things they saw, asking: What are these things? Why do they move and change like that? Were they always there? What do they tell us about why we're here? Only in the last few centuries have we started to find scientific answers.

Classical Theory

In 1687 Isaac Newton published his *Laws of Motion*, describing how forces change the way objects move, and the *Law of Universal Gravitation*, which says that every two objects in the Universe attract each other with a force—*gravity*—which is why we are stuck to the Earth's surface, why the Earth orbits the Sun, and how planets and stars were created.

On the scale of planets, stars, and galaxies, gravity is the architect who controls the grand structure of the Universe. Newton's laws are still good enough for placing satellites in orbit and sending spacecraft to other planets. But more modern classical theories, namely Einstein's theories of relativity, are needed when objects are very fast, or very massive.

NEWTON'S LAWS
The Laws of Motion

1. Every particle remains at rest, or in motion along a straight line with constant velocity, unless acted on by an external force.

2. The rate of change of momentum of a particle is equal in magnitude to the external force, and in the same direction as the force.

3. If a particle exerts a force on a second particle, then the second particle exerts an equal but opposite force on the first particle.

THE THEORY OF EVERYTHING

The Law of Universal Gravitation

Every particle in the Universe attracts every other particle with a force, pointing along the line between the particles, which is directly proportional to the product of their masses and inversely proportional to the square of the distance between them.

Quantum Theory

Classical Theory is fine for big things, like galaxies, cars, or even bacteria. But it can't explain how atoms work—in fact, it says atoms can't exist! In the early twentieth century, physicists realized they needed to develop a completely new theory to account for the properties of very small things like atoms or electrons: quantum theory. The version that sums up our current knowledge of fundamental particles and forces is known as the *Standard Model*. It has quarks and leptons (the component particles of matter), force particles (the gluon, photon, W and Z), and the Higgs (which is needed to explain part of the masses of the other particles, but has not yet been seen).

Many scientists think this is too complicated, and would like a simpler model. Also, where is the dark matter astronomers have discovered? And what about gravity? The force particle for gravity is called the *graviton*, but adding it to the Standard Model is difficult because gravity is very different—it changes the shape of spacetime.

THE THEORY OF EVERYTHING

The Challenge—the Theory of Everything . . .

A theory explaining *all* the forces and *all* the particles—
a *Theory of Everything*—might look very different to
anything we have seen before, because it would need
to explain spacetime as well as gravity. But if it exists,
it should explain the physical workings of the whole
Universe, including the heart of black holes, the Big
Bang, and the far future of the cosmos.

Finding it would be a spectacular achievement.

With this astonishing prospect in sight, thanks to the new results from the LHC, it wasn't surprising that Eric was in a good mood. Such a good mood, in fact, that he didn't even object to the kids using Cosmos when they weren't supposed to.

"I see you've been using my computer!" Eric raised an eyebrow, but he didn't look angry. "I hope you haven't got strawberry jam between the keys again," he said mildly, leaning over to look at Cosmos.

"Where's the best place in the Universe for a pig to live?" Eric read off the screen. "Ah!" His face cleared. "Now I understand." He ruffled Annie's hair. "Your mom said you were both worried about Freddy."

"We were looking for somewhere else for him to go," said Annie.

"And what did you find?" asked her father, taking off his tweed jacket and pulling up a rickety old swivel chair so he could sit between Annie and George, who were still gazing wide-eyed at Cosmos's screen.

"Um . . . well, Cosmos looked around the solar system but we didn't find anywhere," said George.

"I bet you didn't," murmured Eric. "Can't quite imagine Freddy on Pluto."

"So we thought about taking him to a planet that would be suitable for human life, but we haven't found one yet," continued George.

"Then we looked in Foxbridge instead—to find somewhere close to home to keep Freddy for a few days," Annie burst out. "But we found a group of horrible people in a basement, saying that your experiment at the Large Hadron Collider would exterminate the Universe!"

Suddenly Eric looked furious. "Cosmos!" he barked. "What have you been doing?"

"I was only trying to help," said Cosmos sheepishly.

"Gallumphing galaxies!" Eric didn't look quite so happy now. "What were you thinking of, allowing the kids to eavesdrop on those idiots?"

"They said that you're going to destroy the False Vacuum. . . ." said George slowly. "And that this will make the Universe dissolve. Is this true?"

"No! Of course not! It's a crazy theory," said Eric irately. "Don't pay them any attention! They're just trying to frighten people because they don't like the work we're doing at the great experiment in Switzerland."

"But they were at your college!" squeaked Annie.

"College schmollege," said Eric, dismissively. "They could be anywhere, it doesn't make them any more credible."

"So you *do* know who they are?"

"Not entirely," admitted Eric. "They've concealed their identities because it's a secret organization—all we know is that they call themselves 'Theory of Everything Resists Addition of Gravity.'"

"'Theory of Everything Resists Addition of Gravity,'" repeated Annie. "That's T-O-E-R-A-G. That makes TOERAG! Is that really their name?"

Eric laughed. "It's certainly the perfect one for them! They are absolutely a bunch of total toe rags."

"What do they want?"

"Last year," said Eric, "TOERAG, as I'm now going to call them, wanted us to abandon the Collider. They said we would create a black hole if we started the experiment. Well, we ignored them and turned it on. As we're all still here today, you can tell the world wasn't actually swallowed up by a black hole. After that we thought they'd give up. But now they've seized on this 'vacuum' nonsense to prevent us from starting our next experiment, which uses more energy than the ones we've conducted in the past."

"But why?" said George. "Why would they keep on dreaming up mad theories?"

"Because they don't want us to succeed," Eric explained. "Our goal is to understand the Universe at the deepest level. So we need to know not just how the Universe behaves but *why*. Why is there something rather than nothing? Why do we exist? Why this set of particular laws and not some others? This is the ultimate question of life, the Universe, and everything. And some people simply don't want us to find that out."

"So this 'bubble of destruction' stuff, it really *is* all nonsense?" George double-checked, just to be sure.

"Complete cosmic cobblers!" exclaimed Eric. "But"—a frown crept over his brow—"despite that, more and more people seem to believe what TOERAG is saying. So we changed the plans for our new experiment, just in case TOERAG decided to surprise us with something nasty."

"So when does it start?" asked George.

"We've already started it!" said Eric. "The accelerator is up, the detectors are online, and we even achieved our design luminosity a few weeks ago." The scientist shook his head sadly. "We're keeping it as quiet as we can to stop TOERAG from interfering. Those losers . . . Now, back to the real stuff—where are we going to put Freddy? Cosmos?"

As though trying to make up for his earlier mistake, Cosmos quickly brought up a new image on his screen. It was a beautiful picture, which showed the sun hanging low over a peaceful wooded valley, with gently swaying trees, wild flowers, and colorful butterflies dancing across the hedges.

"This would be a good place for your pig," quavered Cosmos.

"What about it?" said Eric briskly to George and Annie. "Does that look all right? Would you be happy about Freddy living here?"

"It looks lovely . . ." George managed to squeeze in. *Where is it?* he wanted to ask, but Eric, who was obviously in a great hurry, had already moved on to the next task.

"Great!" said the scientist, tapping a few commands onto the keyboard. "Now, kids, this is a bit complicated but I think I can make a double portal."

Before the two friends could say anything, Cosmos had opened up a portal to Freddy's farm, and Eric had hopped through into the pigpen. The giant pig looked so shocked to see Eric appear out of nowhere that he didn't resist when he was gently pushed through another doorway that Cosmos had created. He happily trotted away into the wooded valley that was still displayed on the screen.

George and Annie watched eagerly as Freddy disappeared through one doorway from the farm, only to reappear in the valley, scampering through the thick grass, his snout twitching excitedly in the fresh country air, eyes sparkling once more.

Eric backed out of the portal doorway and closed it down. "We'll go back in to check up on Freddy very soon," he said. George noticed a faint dusting of straw on his corduroy trousers. "I'd better do something about the farm too—stop them from panicking that a pig has escaped and is on the loose."

"What will you say to them?" asked Annie.

"I don't know!" admitted Eric. "But I've managed to explain how a Universe could arise out of nothing, so I expect I can explain away a disappearing pig."

"Pig relocation mission completed. Pig safe and happy in new home. Food, water, and shelter all provided. Threat status to pig—zero," Cosmos flashed up on his screen.

"And now," said Eric in the voice that the children knew meant the subject was firmly closed, "it is time for me to do some work. I need to prepare for the talk I'm giving at the university the day after tomorrow.

And you two should be getting ready for school in the morning."

The two friends slouched reluctantly out of Eric's study. This meant the summer break was over. Annie had one evening to do all the preparation homework she had stored up all summer long. George realized it was time to go home to his real family. He hoped the babies wouldn't cry constantly the night before he had to go to his new school for the first time.

Annie sighed. "Bye, George."

"Bye, Annie," said George sadly. The next morning they were both starting at different schools: Annie was attending a private school, and George wasn't.

"Why do we have to go to middle school?" Annie burst out as they hovered by the back door, neither of them wanting to take the next step. "Why can't we go to a School for Space Exploration? We'd be totally top of the class! No one else has seen the rings of Saturn from close up or nearly fallen into a lake of methane on Titan."

"Or seen a sunrise with two suns in the sky," said George, thinking of the hot planet in a binary solar system that they'd once visited by mistake.

"It isn't fair," said Annie, "to make us pretend to be ordinary kids when we're not!"

"Annie!" Eric's voice floated along from his study. "I can hear you! People who don't do their homework don't get to travel into space at all! That's the rule, as well you know."

Annie made a face. "May the Force be with you," she whispered to George.

"And with you," said George, before turning and heading home.

The Search is just the beginning. . . .

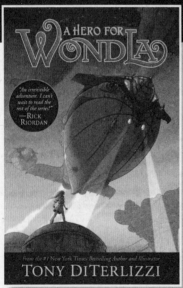

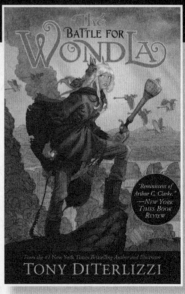

Also by
Lucy & Stephen Hawking

GEORGE'S SECRET KEY TO THE UNIVERSE

GEORGE'S COSMIC TREASURE HUNT

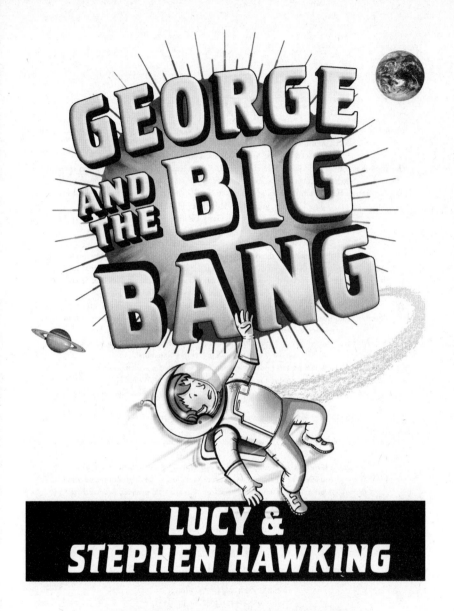

GEORGE AND THE BIG BANG

LUCY & STEPHEN HAWKING

ILLUSTRATED BY GARRY PARSONS

Simon & Schuster Books for Young Readers
New York   London   Toronto   Sydney   New Delhi

For Willa, Lola and George,
Rose, George, William and Charlotte

THE LATEST SCIENTIFIC THEORIES!

Within the story are a number of terrific essays on scientific topics that give readers real insight into some of the latest theories. These have been written by the following eminent scientists:

SPECIFIC FACTUAL SECTIONS

There is lots of science within this book, but there are also a number of separate sections where facts and information are provided on specific subjects. Some readers may wish to refer to these pages in particular.

Chapter One

W*here's the best place in the Universe for a pig to live?* Annie was typing onto the keyboard of Cosmos, the supercomputer. "Cosmos will know!" she declared. "He must be able to find Freddy somewhere better than that shabby old farm."

The farm where Freddy, the pig, now lived was actually perfectly nice—at least, all the other animals seemed happy there. Only Freddy, George's precious pig, was miserable.

"I feel awful," said George sadly as Cosmos, the world's greatest supercomputer, ran through his millions and billions of files to try to answer Annie's question about pigs. "Freddy was so angry he wouldn't even look at me."

"He looked at *me*!" said Annie hotly, glaring at the screen. "I defi-nitely saw him send me a message with his piggy eyes.

It was: *HELP! GET ME OUT OF HERE!*"

The day trip to visit Freddy at the farm just outside Foxbridge, the university town where George and Annie lived, had not been a success. When Annie's mom, Susan, arrived to pick them up at the end of the afternoon, she was surprised to see George red-faced and furious and Annie on the verge of tears.

"George! Annie!" said Susan. "What is the matter with the two of you?"

"It's Freddy!" burst out Annie, leaping into the backseat of the car. "He hates it at the farm."

Freddy was George's pet pig. He had been a Christmas present from George's gran when he was a piglet. George's parents were eco-activists, which also meant they weren't very interested in presents. They didn't like the way all the discarded, broken, and unwanted toys left over from Christmas built up into huge mounds of old plastic and metal, floating across the seas, choking whales and strangling seagulls, or making mountains of ugly junk on the land.

George's gran knew that if she gave George an ordinary present, his parents would give it right back, and everyone would get upset. So if he was to keep his Christmas present, she realized she would have to think of something special—something that *helped* the planet rather than destroyed it.

That's why, one cold Christmas Eve, George found a cardboard box on the doorstep. Inside it was a little pink piglet and a note from Gran saying: *Can you give this young pig a nice home?* George had been thrilled. He had a Christmas present his parents had to let him keep; and, even better, he had his very own pig.

The problem with little pink piglets, however, is that they get bigger. Bigger and bigger, until they are enormous—too large for the backyard of an ordinary row house with a narrow strip of land and scattered vegetables growing between the two fences separating it from the neighboring yards. But George's parents had kind hearts really, so Freddy, as George named the pig, had continued living in his pigsty in the backyard until he reached a gigantic size—he was now more like a baby elephant than a pig. George didn't care how big Freddy got—he was very fond of his pig and spent long hours in the yard, chatting to him or just sitting in his huge shadow, reading books about the wonders of the cosmos.

But George's dad, Terence, had never really liked

Freddy. Freddy was too big, too piggy, too pink, and he enjoyed dancing on Terence's carefully arranged vegetable plot, trampling his spinach and broccoli and munching thoughtlessly on his carrot tops. Last summer, before the twins were born, the whole family had been going away. Terence had been super-quick to find Freddy a place at a nearby children's petting farm, promising George that when they all got back, the pig would be able to come home.

Only this never happened. George and his parents returned from their adventures, and George's next-door neighbors—the scientist Eric, his wife, Susan, and their daughter, Annie—came back from living in America. Then George's mother had twin baby girls, Juno and Hera, who cried and gurgled and smiled. And then cried some more. And every time one of them stopped crying, there would be a beautiful half-second of silence. Then the other baby would start up, wailing until George thought his brain would explode and start leaking out of his ears. His mom and dad always looked stressed and tired, and George felt bad about asking them for anything at all. So once Annie came back from America, he started slipping through the hole in the back fence more and more often, until he was practically living with his friend, her crazy family, and the world's greatest supercomputer in the house next door.

But it was worse for Freddy, because he never made it home at all.

Once the baby girls were born, George's dad said they had enough on their hands without a great big pig taking up most of the backyard. "Anyway," he told George rather pompously when he protested, "Freddy is a creature of planet Earth. He doesn't belong to you—he belongs to nature."

But Freddy couldn't even stay in his small, friendly petting farm, which had to close at the beginning of this summer vacation. Freddy—along with the other animals there—had been moved to a bigger place where there were unusual breeds of farm animal, and lots of visitors, especially during summer vacation. It was a bit like him and Annie moving up to middle school, George thought to himself—going somewhere much bigger. It was a bit scary.

"Nature, huh!" he snorted to himself as he remembered his dad's comments now. Cosmos the computer was still chewing over the complicated question of the best location in the Universe for a homeless pig. "I don't think Freddy knows he's a creature of planet Earth—he just wants to be with us," said George.

"He looked so sad!" said Annie. "I'm sure he was crying."

On their trip to the farm earlier that day, George and Annie had come across Freddy lying flat on his stomach on the floor of his pig pen, legs splayed out on either side, his eyes dull and his cheeks sunken. The other pigs were trotting around, looking cheerful and

5

healthy. The pen was spacious and airy, the farm clean, and the people that worked there friendly. But even so, Freddy seemed lost in a piggy hell of his own. George felt incredibly guilty. Summer vacation had passed and he hadn't done anything about getting Freddy home again. It was Annie who had suggested making the trip to the farm today, badgering her mom into driving them there and picking them up again afterward.

George and Annie had asked the workers what was wrong with Freddy. They'd looked worried too. The vet had examined him: Freddy wasn't sick, she'd said; he just seemed very unhappy, as though he was pining away. After all, he had grown up in George's quiet backyard, and had then moved to a small farm with just a few children coming to pet him. In the new place he was surrounded by noisy, unfamiliar animals and had lots of visitors every day: It was probably a big shock. Freddy had never lived with his fellow pigs before. He was totally unused to other animals: In fact, he considered himself more as a person than a pig. He didn't understand what he was doing on a farm where visitors hung over the edge of the pig pen to stare at him.

"Can't we take him home?" George had asked.

The helpers looked a little perplexed. There were lots of rules and regulations about moving animals around, and anyway, they felt that Freddy was simply too big now to live in an urban backyard. "He'll feel better soon!" they reassured George. "Just you wait and see— next time you come to visit, it'll be quite different."

"But he's been here for weeks already," protested George.

The helpers either didn't hear or chose to ignore him.

Annie, however, had other ideas. As soon as they got back to her house, she started making plans. "We can't bring Freddy back to your place," she said, switching on Cosmos, "because your dad will just take him straight back to the farm. And he can't live here with us."

Unfortunately George knew this was true. He looked around Eric's study: Cosmos was perched on the desk, on top of piles and piles of scientific papers, surrounded by wobbling towers of books, cups of half-drunk tea, and scraps of paper with important equations scrawled on them. Annie's dad used the supercomputer to work on his theories about the origins of the Universe. Finding a home for a pig was, it seemed, almost as difficult.

When Annie and her family had first moved into this house, George's pig had made a dramatic entrance, charging through Eric's study, sending books flying into the air. Eric had been quite pleased, because in all the chaos Freddy had actually helped him to find a book he'd been searching for. But these days, George and Annie both knew that Eric wouldn't welcome a spare pig. He had too much work to do to look after a pig.

"We need to find somewhere nice for Freddy," said Annie firmly.

Ping! Cosmos's screen came to life again and started flashing with different colored lights—a sure sign that the great computer was pleased with himself. "I have prepared for you a summary of the conditions within our local cosmic area and their suitability for porcine life," he said. "Please click on each box to see a readout of your pig's existence on each planet within our Solar System. I have taken the liberty of providing"—the computer chortled to himself—"an illustration for each planet with my own comments."

"Wowzers!" said Annie. "Cosmos, you are the *best*."

On Cosmos's screen were eight little boxes, each marked with the name of a planet in the Solar System. She checked the one labeled MERCURY . . .

Mercury
Scorched pig

Jupiter
Sinking pig

Venus
Smelly pig

Saturn
Orbital pig

Earth
Happy pig

Uranus
Upside-down pig

Mars
Bouncy pig

Neptune
Windy pig

OUR SOLAR SYSTEM

The Solar System is the name we give to the family of planets that orbit our star, the Sun.

How Our Solar System Was Created

Our Solar System was formed around 4.6 billion years ago

 Step One:
A cloud of gas and dust begins to collapse—possibly triggered by shock waves from a nearby supernova.

 Step Two:
A ball of dust formed, spinning round and flattening into a disk as it attracted more dust, gradually growing larger and spinning faster.

 Step Three:
The central region of this collapsed cloud got hotter and hotter until it started to burn, turning it into a star.

 Step Four:
As the star burned, the dust in the disk around it slowly stuck together to form clusters, which became rocks, which eventually formed planets, all still orbiting the star—our Sun—at the center. These planets ended up forming two main groups: close to the Sun, where it is hot, the rocky planets; farther out, beyond Mars, the gas planets, which consist of a thick atmosphere of gas surrounding a liquid inner region with, very probably, a solid core.

Stars with a mass like our Sun take around ten million years to form.

Step Five:

The planets cleaned up their orbits by gobbling up any chunks of material they came across.

Because Jupiter is the largest, it may have done most of the cleaning up itself.

Step Six:

Hundreds of millions of years later, the planets settled into stable orbits—the same orbits that they follow today. The bits of stuff left over ended up either in the asteroid belt between Mars and Jupiter, or much farther out beyond Pluto in the Kuiper belt.

Are There Other Solar Systems Like Ours?

For several hundred years astronomers suspected that other stars in the Universe might have planets in orbit around them. However, the first exoplanet was not confirmed until 1992, orbiting the corpse of a massive star. The first planet around a real, brightly shining star was discovered in 1995. Since then, more than four hundred exoplanets have been discovered—some around stars very similar to our Sun!

An exoplanet is a planet in orbit around a star other than the Earth's Sun.

This is just the beginning. Even if only 10% of the stars in our Galaxy had planets in orbit around them, that would still mean more than *two hundred billion solar systems* within the Milky Way alone.

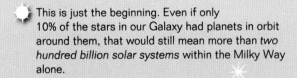

Some of these may be similar to our Solar System. Others might look very different. Planets in a binary solar system, for example, might see two suns rise and set in the sky. Knowing the distance from their star to the planets—and the size and age of the star—helps us to calculate how likely it is that we might find life on those planets.

Most of the exoplanets we know about in other solar systems are huge—as big as Jupiter or larger—mainly because those are easier to detect than smaller planets. But astronomers are beginning to discover smaller, rocky planets orbiting at the right distance from their star that might be more like planet Earth.

In early 2011, NASA confirmed their Kepler mission had spotted an Earth-like planet around a star five hundred light-years away! At only 1.4 times the size of our home planet, this new planet, Kepler 10-b, may be the most similar to Earth we have found so far.

Chapter Two

"But I don't think Freddy could actually live on any of those planets," objected George after they had looked through Cosmos's tour of the Solar System for pigs. "He'd boil on Mercury, get blown away on Neptune, or sink through layers of poisonous gas on Saturn. He'd probably wish he was back on the farm."

"Except for on Earth . . . ," murmured Annie. "That's the only planet in our Solar System that's suitable for life." Her nose was scrunched up, meaning she was thinking hard. "It's just like for humans," she said suddenly. "You know how my dad was talking about finding a new home for human beings, in case our planet becomes uninhabitable?"

"You mean, if we get struck by a huge comet or global warming takes over?" said George. "We won't be able to live on this planet if there are volcanic eruptions or it becomes a huge, dry desert." George knew all about the frightening things that might happen to planet Earth if humans didn't start taking better care of it from his eco-activist parents.

ASTEROID ATTACK!

 An asteroid is a rocky fragment left over from the formation of the Solar System about 4.6 billion years ago. Scientists estimate there are probably millions of asteroids in our Solar System.

Asteroids typically range in size from as little as a few yards to hundreds of miles across.

 Once in a while an asteroid will get nudged out of its orbit—for example by the gravity of nearby planets—possibly sending it on a collision course with the Earth.

 Around once a year, a rock the size of a family car crashes into the Earth's atmosphere but burns up before it reaches the surface.

Once every few thousand years, a chunk of rock about the size of a football field hits the Earth, and every few million years, Earth suffers an impact from a space object—an asteroid or a comet—large enough to threaten civilization.

 If an asteroid or a comet—a rocky ice ball that slingshots around the Sun—were to hit the surface of the Earth, it is possible that it could crash through the surface, releasing a flood of volcanic eruptions. Nothing would survive the impact.

A **meteoroid** is a chunk of rock that flies through our Solar System; a **meteorite** is what you call that piece of rock if it lands on the Earth.

Sixty-five million years ago, an asteroid smashed into the Earth. This could be what wiped out the dinosaurs—the impact sent up a cloud of fine dust, which blocked out the sunlight, dooming the dinosaurs' and many other species to extinction.

GAMMA RAY BURST . . . GAME OVER!

We also face the exotic threat of extinction by gamma rays from space.

When very massive stars reach the ends of their lives and explode, they not only send hot dust and gas across the cosmos in an expanding cloud. They also shoot out deadly twin beams of gamma rays, like lighthouse beams. If the Earth were directly in the path of such a beam, and if the gamma-ray burst happened close enough to us, the beam could rip our atmosphere apart, causing clouds of brown nitrogen to fill the skies.

Such explosions are rare. One would need to happen within a few thousand light-years to do real damage, and the beam would need to hit us very precisely. Thus, astronomers who have studied the problem in detail are not that worried!

SELF-DESTRUCT!

☆ We've already done a lot of damage to our planet—without any help from asteroids or gamma rays.

The Earth is home to more than seven billion people.

☆ The Earth is suffering from overpopulation.

☆ All those extra people mean we will need to grow more food, putting a greater strain on the Earth's natural resources and sending even more gases into the Earth's atmosphere. There's been a lot of argument about climate change. But scientists are clear that the planet is getting warmer and that human activity is the reason for this change. They expect this change to continue, meaning that the world will get hotter and some areas will experience heavy rainfall while others suffer from drought. Sea levels are expected to rise, which could make life very difficult for people who live on coastlines.

☆ There are more and more humans on Earth but fewer and fewer other species. Extinction of other animals is a growing problem, and we are seeing whole groups of species disappear from the face of the Earth. It seems a real pity that we are destroying our beautiful and unique planet just as we are learning how it really works.

Globally, nearly a quarter of all mammal species and a third of amphibians are threatened with extinction.

"Exactly! My dad says humans need to look for a new home," said Annie, "just like Freddy does. Pigs need about the same conditions as people, so if we can find a place in the Universe that's suitable for human life, then Freddy would be fine there as well."

"So all Cosmos has to do is find a new home for humanity and we've found somewhere to keep my pig?"

"Precisely!" said Annie happily. "And we can visit him in space from time to time, so he doesn't get lonely and sad again." They both fell silent. They knew that their master plan was rather less than perfect.

"How long is it going take us to find somewhere for Freddy in space?" asked George eventually. "Your dad has been searching and searching for a new place for human beings to start a colony, and he still isn't sure he's found the right place."

"Um, yeah," admitted Annie. "We might—just *might*—want to think about finding Freddy somewhere a bit closer to home, just for now."

"Somewhere on planet Earth would be good," agreed George. "But how are we going to get him to his new home—in space or on Earth? How are we going to carry a great big pig around?"

"Now that is the great geniosity of my brilliant plan!" cried Annie, perking up. "We're going to use Cosmos. If Cosmos can send us on great big journeys across the Universe, then he can take a pig just a short hop across planet Earth. Cosmos, am I right?" she demanded.

"Annie, you are," confirmed Cosmos. "I am so clever and intelligent that I can do any or all of the things you have mentioned."

"But is he *supposed* to?" asked George. "I mean, isn't your dad going to be angry if he finds we've used his supercomputer to transport a pig?"

"Unless you order me to do so," said Cosmos slyly, "I would have no reason to inform Eric that we have taken a porcine adventure together."

"See?" said Annie. "If we ask Cosmos to take Freddy to somewhere he'll be safe, then Cosmos will do it."

"Hmm," said George, still sounding doubtful. He'd been on journeys before where Cosmos had been allowed to pick the destination, and he wasn't sure that the supercomputer always got it right. George didn't want to push his pig through the portal—the amazing doorway into space that Cosmos could open up—and find he'd been sent to a sausage factory. Or the top of the Empire State Building. Or a remote tropical island that would be too hot for Freddy— not to mention too lonely.

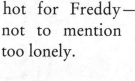

"Cosmos," he said politely, "could you show us the places you'd take Freddy before you actually send him there? Oh, and for the moment, until we find some-where permanent, they all have to be close enough for us to bike to, because I don't think we should keep using you—we might get caught."

"Processing your request," replied Cosmos. When Annie's family had come back from America, Cosmos had suffered a mega breakdown. Eric had managed to fix him, but he had returned with a much more user-friendly attitude. Now, his circuits whirred for a few seconds, and then an image appeared, floating in the air in the center of Eric's study, connected to Cosmos by two thin beams of light.

"It's a map!" said George. "It looks like . . . Hold on! It's Foxbridge!"

"Indeed," said Cosmos. "It is a three-D image. Anything Google can do, I can do better." He harrumphed. "The presumptuous upstarts."

"Oh my, it's beautiful!" sighed Annie. Every feature of the ancient and distinguished university town of Foxbridge was drawn in loving detail on Cosmos's map—each tower, rampart, spire, and quadrangle represented in perfect miniature.

In a corner of one of the courtyards, a little red light was flashing.

"That's my dad's college!" said Annie in surprise. "Where that light is flashing. Why are you showing us Dad's college?"

"My files tell me that pigs need a quiet, dark space with fresh air and some sunlight," said Cosmos. "The place marked is an empty wine cellar at the base of an old tower. It has a ventilation system, so the air is clean, and a small skylight. It hasn't been used for many years, so your pig should be safe and comfortable there for a few days, provided you take the precaution of bringing some straw with him from the farm."

"Are you sure?" said George. "Won't he feel a little cooped up?"

"For a short while your pig will enjoy perfect peace and quiet," replied Cosmos. "It will be a little break for him until you decide where you would like him to be permanently housed."

"We have to get him out of that farm!" exclaimed Annie. "And quickly! He's having a terrible time and we must, must, *must* save him!"

"Can we see the cellar?" asked George.

"Certainly," said Cosmos. "I will open a small window into the cellar so that you can verify the information I have given you."

The map melted into thin air and was replaced by a rectangle of light as Cosmos created his portal: Annie and George had gone through it many times to journey into space. On those occasions, Cosmos had made a door. But if he just wanted to show them something, he drew a small window for them to look through.

"This is so exciting!" exclaimed Annie while they waited. "Why did we never think of using Cosmos to travel around the Earth before?"

The rectangle went dark. George and Annie peered at it more closely.

"Cosmos, we can't see anything!" said George. "I thought you said there would be some daylight. We don't want Freddy to think he's gone to prison!"

Cosmos sounded confused. "I have checked the coordinates, and this is the right location. Perhaps the window has been covered."

"Jeepers!" whispered Annie. "The darkness—it's moving!" Through the window, the blackness seemed to be swaying from side to side.

"Listen!" she hissed. "I can hear voices."

"Not possible," replied Cosmos. "My data tells me that the cellar is no longer in use."

"Then what are all those people doing there?" said Annie in a hollow voice. "Look!"

Staring through the window, George realized she was right. What they were seeing was not a dark room where no light penetrated. It was a throng of tightly packed people, all wearing black clothes. He could just make out shoulders and backs—the crowd seemed to be facing away from them.

"Can they see us?" whispered Annie.

"If they turn around, they will see the portal window," said Cosmos, who had conducted a brief scan of the room. "Although it is entirely inconsistent with logic, probability, and reason, the cellar appears to be filled with human beings."

"Alive ones?" said Annie in a terrified voice. "Or dead ones?"

"Breathing and functional ones," said Cosmos.

"What are they doing?"

"They are—"

"Turning around," interrupted George in horror. "Cosmos, close the portal!"

Cosmos snapped the window shut so fast that no one in the cellar noticed the tiny flash of light. Even if they had, none of them would have guessed that their secret meeting had just been witnessed by two very puzzled kids and an agitated super-computer in an ordinary suburban house somewhere on the edge of Foxbridge.

However, a voice from inside the cellar drifted into the room where Annie and George sat, motionless and shocked.

"All hail the False Vacuum!" it said. "Bringer of life, energy, and light." In Cosmos's hurry to shut down the portal before anyone saw it—and them—he had closed the visual monitor but not the audio port, so they could hear but not see the events in the cellar.

A deathly hush followed. Annie and George hardly dared to breathe. Then, as though they were listening to a particularly horrible radio show, the voice continued.

"These are dangerous times!" it hissed. "We may be living through the last days before the Universe itself is ripped to shreds by a bubble of cosmic destruction. Criminal scientists at the Large Hadron Collider will soon begin their new, high-energy experiment. We failed to stop them from using the Collider last time. But now, the situation is far more serious. The moment these crazy fools switch on their machine, a cosmic catastrophe will be unleashed that will exterminate the entire Universe! Their plans to take the work at the Large Hadron Collider to the next level could reduce us all to nothing."

Annie and George heard the densely packed crowd in the room hiss and boo at these words.

"Quiet!" said the voice. "Please—our distinguished scientific expert will explain."

A new voice spoke. This time it was an older, soft-spoken one. "These dangerous lunatics are led by a Foxbridge scientist called Eric Bellis."

Annie squeaked and clapped her hand over her mouth. Eric Bellis was her dad!

"Bellis is masterminding the high-energy collision experiment using the ATLAS detector at the Large Hadron Collider—the LHC. It is about to enter its most dangerous phase. If Bellis achieves the collision energy he intends, then I calculate that there is a significant probability of causing the Universe to spontaneously decay by creating a piece of the True Vacuum.

"If the tiniest bubble of the True Vacuum is created in a particle collision at the LHC, the bubble will expand—

at the speed of light—replacing the False Vacuum and obliterating all matter! All atoms on Earth will dissolve in less than a twentieth of a second. Within eight hours, the Solar System will be gone. Of course, it does not end there . . ."

But the voices from the cellar were fading now as Cosmos struggled to hold the connection.

"The bubble will continue to expand forever," the voice went on in a menacing whisper. "Bellis will have accomplished the unthinkable—the destruction of the entire Universe!" With the last "sssssss" of "Universe" left hanging in the air, the voice was silent once more.

For a moment George, Cosmos, and Annie froze. Cosmos snapped out of it first.

DANGEROUS ENVIRONMENT FOR PIG RELOCATION! flashed up across his screen in big red letters several times.

"We're not sending Freddy there!" agreed Annie, who looked rather dazed. "We're not having our pig spend time with those creepy people! 'Specially not if they're going to be rude about my dad!"

George gulped. What had those black-clad people been talking about? "Cosmos, Annie," he said urgently, "who *were* they?"

Chapter Three

"Who were who?" said a voice as Eric himself pushed open the door to his study, a steaming mug of tea in one hand and a pile of scientific papers jammed under his tweed-jacketed arm. "Hello, Annie and George!" he said. "Enjoying the last day of summer vacation?"

The two friends stared blankly back at him.

"Oh dear! Should I take that as a 'no'?" said Eric. "Is something wrong?" He smiled at them both. Eric couldn't stop smiling these days. If George had to describe Annie's father at the moment, he would have used the words "incredibly happy." Or "incredibly busy." In fact, the busier Eric was, the happier he seemed. Since he had moved back from America, where he had been working on a space mission to try to find traces of life on Mars, the scientist always seemed to be in a rush and always seemed to be enjoying himself. He was happy at home with his family, he loved his new job as professor of mathematics at Foxbridge University, and he was super-excited about the big experiment he was running at the Large Hadron Collider in Switzerland.

The project at the LHC was the continuation of work started by scientists hundreds of years earlier. The aim was to discover what the world was made of, and how the tiny fundamental pieces had fitted together to form the contents of the Universe. To do this, Eric and the other scientists were trying to find a theory that would allow them to understand everything about the Universe. They gave it the simple name the "Theory of Everything": It was the greatest goal in science. If they could only find it, scientists would be able to understand not only the beginning of the Universe but possibly even how—and why—the Universe we live in came about.

THE THEORY OF EVERYTHING

Throughout history, people have looked around and tried to understand the amazing things they saw, asking: What are these objects? Why do they move and change like that? Were they always there? What do they tell us about why we're here? Only in the last few centuries have we started to find scientific answers.

Classical Theory

In 1687 Isaac Newton published his *Laws of Motion*, describing how forces change the way objects move, and the *Law of Universal Gravitation*, which says that every two objects in the Universe attract each other with a force—*gravity*—which is why we are stuck to the Earth's surface, why the Earth orbits the Sun, and how planets and stars were created. On the scale of planets, stars, and galaxies, gravity is the architect who controls the grand structure of the Universe. Newton's Laws are still good enough for placing satellites in orbit and sending spacecraft to other planets. But more modern classical theories, namely Einstein's theories of relativity, are needed when objects are very fast, or very massive.

THE THEORY OF EVERYTHING

NEWTON'S LAWS

The Laws of Motion

1. Every particle remains at rest, or in motion along a straight line with constant velocity, unless acted on by an external force.
2. The rate of change of momentum of a particle is equal in magnitude to the external force, and in the same direction as the force.
3. If a particle exerts a force on a second particle, then the second particle exerts an equal but opposite force on the first particle.

The Law of Universal Gravitation

- Every particle in the Universe attracts every other particle with a force, pointing along the line between the particles, which is directly proportional to the product of their masses and inversely proportional to the square of the distance between them.

Quantum Theory

Classical Theory is fine for big things, like galaxies, cars, or even bacteria. But it can't explain how atoms work—in fact, it says atoms can't exist! In the early twentieth century, physicists realized they needed to develop a completely new theory to account for the properties of very small things like atoms or electrons: quantum theory. The version that sums up our current knowledge of fundamental particles and forces is known as the *Standard Model*. It has quarks and leptons (the component particles of matter), force particles (the gluon, photon, W and Z), and the Higgs (which is needed to explain part of the masses of the other particles, but has not yet been seen). Many scientists think this is too complicated, and would like a simpler model. Also, where is the dark matter astronomers have discovered? And what about gravity? The force particle for gravity is called the *graviton*, but adding it to the Standard Model is difficult because gravity is very different—it changes the shape of space-time.

The Challenge—the Theory of Everything . . .

A theory explaining *all* the forces and *all* the particles—a *Theory of Everything*—might look very different from anything we have seen before, because it would need to explain space-time as well as gravity. But if it exists, it should explain the physical workings of the whole Universe, including the heart of black holes, the Big Bang, and the far future of the cosmos. Finding it would be a spectacular achievement.

With this astonishing prospect in sight, thanks to the new results from the LHC, it wasn't surprising that Eric was in a good mood. Such a good mood, in fact, that he didn't even object to the kids using Cosmos when they weren't supposed to.

"I see you've been on my computer!" He raised an eyebrow, but he didn't look angry. "I hope you didn't get strawberry jam between the keys again," he said mildly, leaning over to look at Cosmos.

"*Where's the best place in the Universe for a pig to live?*" Eric read off the screen. "Ah!" His face cleared. "Now I understand." He ruffled Annie's hair. "Your mom said you were both worried about Freddy."

"We were looking for somewhere else for him to go," said Annie.

"And what did you find?" asked her father, pulling up a rickety old swivel chair so he could sit between Annie and George, who were still gazing wide-eyed at Cosmos's screen.

"Erm . . . well, Cosmos looked around the Solar System but we didn't find anywhere," said George.

"I bet you didn't," murmured Eric. "Can't quite imagine Freddy on Pluto."

"So we thought about taking him to a planet that would be suitable for human life, but we haven't found one yet," continued George.

"Then we looked in Foxbridge instead—to find somewhere close to home to keep Freddy for a few days," Annie burst out. "But we found a group of horrible people in a basement, saying that your experiment at the Large Hadron Collider would exterminate the Universe!"

Suddenly Eric looked furious. "Cosmos!" he barked. "What have you been doing?"

"I was only trying to help," said Cosmos sheepishly.

"Gallumphing galaxies!" Eric didn't look quite so happy now. "What were you thinking of, allowing the kids to eavesdrop on those idiots?"

"They said that you're going to destroy the False Vacuum . . . ," said George slowly. "And that this will make the Universe dissolve. Is this true?"

"No! Of course not! It's a crazy theory," said Eric angrily. "Don't pay them any attention! They're just trying to frighten people because they don't like the work we're doing at the great experiment in Switzerland."

"But they were at your college!" squeaked Annie.

"College schmollege," said Eric dismissively. "They could be anywhere—it doesn't make them any more credible."

"So you *do* know who they are?"

"Not entirely," admitted Eric. "They've concealed

LUCY & STEPHEN HAWKING

their identities because it's a secret organization—all we know is that they call themselves 'Theory of Everything Resists Addition of Gravity.'"

"Theory of Everything Resists Addition of Gravity . . . ," repeated Annie. "That's T-O-E-R-A-G. That makes TOERAG! Is that really their name?"

Eric laughed. "It's certainly the perfect one for them! They are absolutely a bunch of total toerags."

"What do they want?"

"Last year," said Eric, "TOERAG, as I'm now going to call them, wanted us to abandon the Collider. They said we would create a black hole if we started the experiment. Well, we ignored them and turned it on. Since we're all still here today, you can tell the world wasn't actually swallowed up by a black hole. After that we thought they'd give up. But now they've seized on this 'vacuum' nonsense to prevent us from starting our next experiment, which uses more energy than the ones we've conducted in the past."

"But why?" said George. "Why would they keep on dreaming up crazy theories?"

"Because they don't want us to succeed," Eric explained. "Our goal is to understand the Universe at the deepest level. So we need to know not just *how* the Universe behaves, but *why*. Why is there something rather than nothing? Why do we exist? Why this set of particular laws and not some others? This is the ultimate question of life, the Universe, and everything.

And some people simply don't want us to find that out."

"So this 'bubble of destruction' stuff—it really *is* all nonsense?" George double-checked, just to be sure.

"Complete cosmic cobblers!" exclaimed Eric. "But"—a frown crept over his brow—"despite that, more and more people seem to believe what TOERAG is saying. So we changed the plans for our new experiment, just in case TOERAG decided to surprise us with something nasty."

"So when does it start?" asked George.

"We already started it!" said Eric. "The accelerator is up, the detectors are online, and we even achieved our design luminosity a few weeks ago." The scientist shook his head sadly. "We're keeping it as quiet as we can to stop TOERAG from interfering. Those losers . . . Now, back to the real stuff—where are we going to put Freddy? Cosmos?"

As though trying to make up for his earlier mistake, Cosmos quickly brought up a new image on his screen. It was a beautiful s c e n e , which showed the sun hanging

low over a peaceful wooded valley, with gently swaying trees, wild flowers, and colorful butterflies dancing across the hedges.

"This would be a good place for your pig," suggested Cosmos.

"What about it?" Eric said briskly to George and Annie. "Does that look all right? Would you be happy about Freddy living here?"

"It looks lovely—" George managed to squeeze in. *Where is it?* he wanted to ask, but Eric, who was obviously in a great hurry, had already moved on to the next task.

"Great!" said the scientist, tapping a few commands onto the keyboard. "Now, kids, this is a bit complicated but I think I can make a double portal."

Before the two friends could say anything, Cosmos had opened up a portal to Freddy's farm and Eric had hopped through into the pig pen. The giant pig looked so shocked to see Eric appear out of nowhere that he didn't resist when he was gently pushed through another doorway that Cosmos had created. He trotted away happily into the wooded valley that was still displayed on the screen.

George and Annie watched in amazement as Freddy disappeared through one doorway from the farm, only to reappear in the valley, scampering through the thick grass, his snout twitching excitedly in the fresh country air, eyes sparkling once more.

Eric backed out of the portal doorway and closed it down. "We'll go back in to check up on Freddy very soon," he said. George noticed a faint dusting of straw on his corduroy pants. "I'd better do something about the farm too—stop them from panicking that a pig has escaped and is on the loose."

"What will you say to them?" asked Annie.

"I don't know!" admitted Eric. "But I've managed to explain how a Universe could arise out of nothing, so I expect I can explain away a disappearing pig."

"Pig relocation mission completed. Pig safe and happy in new home. Food, water, and shelter all provided. Threat status to pig—zero," Cosmos flashed up on his screen.

"And now," said Eric in the voice that the children knew meant the subject was firmly closed, "it is time for me to do some work—I need to prepare for the talk I'm giving at the university. And you two should be getting ready for school in the morning."

The two friends slouched reluctantly out of Eric's study. This meant that summer vacation was over. Annie had one evening to do all the preparation homework she had stored up throughout summer vacation. George realized that it was time to go home to his real family. He hoped the babies wouldn't cry constantly the night before he had to go to his new school for the first time.

Annie sighed. "Bye, George."

"Bye, Annie," said George sadly. The next morning they were both starting at different schools: Annie was attending a private school, while George was going to the local school.

"Why do we have to go to middle school?" Annie burst out as they hovered by the back door, neither of them wanting to take the next step. "Why can't we go to a School for Space Exploration? We'd totally be top of the class! No one else has seen the rings of Saturn from close up or nearly fallen into a lake of methane on Titan."

"Or seen a sunrise with two suns in the sky," said

George, thinking of the hot planet in a binary solar system that they'd once visited by mistake.

"It isn't fair!" said Annie. "To make us pretend to be ordinary kids when we're not!"

"Annie!" Eric's voice floated out from his study. "I can hear you! People who don't do their homework don't get to travel into space at all! That's the rule, as well you know."

Annie made a face. "May the Force be with you," she whispered to George.

"And with you," said George, before turning and heading home.

Chapter Four

George's first day at his new school passed in a blur of long corridors and confusing schedules. Again and again he found himself in classrooms for the wrong subjects with older or younger kids.

It was noisy, perplexing, and a bit scary at this enormous school. George wondered if this was how Freddy had felt when he'd moved from the quiet, safe world of George's backyard, first to the small, bustling petting farm and then to the huge, scary new farm. No wonder Freddy hadn't looked happy. On the first day at middle school, even those kids who had been super-confident at George's old school looked lost and worried as they wandered around the huge maze of a building, trying to find the right classrooms. It didn't matter if you hadn't been friends at elementary school—it was such a relief to see a familiar face, rather than all these terrifying grown-up kids—that even sworn enemies suddenly became best friends.

George had only just worked out where he was supposed to be when it was time to go home. He headed out of the gates. Long ago, at his old school, he used to hide in the coatroom every afternoon until everyone else had left, to make sure he wasn't pounced on during his walk home.

But that was before he had learned how to travel across the Universe and unravel great cosmic mysteries. Ever since he'd become friends with Annie and learned about the wonders that surround our planet, George had stopped feeling scared. After all, he'd faced down a mad scientist in a distant solar system; after that, there hadn't been much to be afraid of.

But it wasn't just the journeys that had changed George's life; the knowledge he had gained from those trips had made him feel intrepid. He had used his brain to solve great challenges, and he now knew that he could cope with anything.

As he walked home, George thought about Eric and the adventure with Freddy the evening before. Perhaps, he thought, he could pop over and see Eric to ask if they could check up on his pig. George kicked himself for not asking where Freddy actually was. That valley had looked lovely, but George didn't even know if his pig was still on planet Earth or whether clever Cosmos had transferred him to some other far-off, miraculous place that could support life as we know it. George was sure that Eric knew where Freddy was, but he'd feel happier if he also knew himself.

At home, he dumped his school bag in the hall, then

raced right through his house, only stopping to say a quick hello to his mother and baby sisters and scoop up a pea and cabbage muffin, which he crammed into his mouth in one bite. (George's mom only cooked with the vegetables from their garden; sometimes she had strange ideas about which recipes to use for her home-grown produce . . .) He ran straight out of the back door and into the yard where Freddy had once lived. Jumping through the hole in the fence that led to Annie's backyard, George tore up the path to their back door. He banged on it, but there was no reply. He hammered on it again.

The door opened a few inches. It was Annie, back from school, wearing her new green school uniform.

"Oh, George!" she said. She didn't look entirely pleased to see him.

"Hi, Annie," said George cheerfully. "How's your school? Mine was weird, but I think it might be okay."

"Um, it was all right," she replied, rather quietly. "Did you, er, want something?"

George was surprised. He came over all the time and she'd never before asked him why.

"Er, yeah!" he said, a bit startled. "I was going to ask your dad if he knows where Freddy is. So I can go and visit him."

"Dad's not here," said Annie apologetically. "I'll tell him you asked. I expect he'll e-mail you later."

Then she actually started to close the door in his face. George couldn't believe his eyes. What was going on? Then it all became clear.

"Who is it?" came an older boy's voice from behind Annie.

"Oh, it's, um . . . it's someone who lives next door," said Annie, looking to and fro as though trapped between the two of them. "He wants to see my dad."

She opened the door a tiny little bit wider, and George could now see the other boy. He was taller than both George and Annie, with black spiky hair and skin the color of caramel. Like Annie, he wore a green school uniform.

"Hi!" He nodded to George over Annie's head. "I'm sorry Eric's not here. You'd better go. We'll tell him you came over."

George's jaw dropped in disbelief.

"I'm Vincent, by the way," said the boy casually.

"Vincent also started at my school today," said Annie, not quite meeting George's eye.

"Seriously?" said George in surprise. "You're in sixth grade?"

"No!" Vincent looked annoyed. "Eighth grade. I know Annie from outside school."

"You do?" said George.

"Vincent's dad is a film director," said Annie shyly, but in a way that George just knew meant she was super-impressed by Vincent. "He knows my dad — he made Dad's new TV series."

"A film director," said George, feeling defeated. "Nice. My dad's an organic gardener," he said defiantly to Vincent.

"C'mon, Annie," said Vincent. "We should get rolling."

"Mom's taking us to the skate park," Annie told George. "Vincent is a champion skateboarder."

"You roll, then," he said, trying to sound normal. "You just roll along." He turned around and walked back along the backyard path until he reached the hole in the fence. Annie and Vincent were still standing in the doorway, watching him.

George tried to hop casually through the hole in the fence, as he had done so many times in the past. But it didn't quite work and he crashed into the wooden planks instead, falling to the ground with a thump. George couldn't help looking around. Annie and Vincent were still there, which was super-annoying and unfair. When

he'd been at the door, they hadn't wanted to open it. Now they wouldn't go away.

With as much dignity as he could manage, he picked himself up and calmly stepped through the gap, trying to behave as if nothing had happened. But inside, he felt wounded and left out. It was only day one of the school year, and already Annie had a new friend to do cool stuff with.

Where did that leave George?

Now he had no pig, and no Annie either. He suddenly felt empty and alone. He trailed into the house, looking miserable.

A little later that afternoon, when George had done his chores and finished his homework, he decided to go back next door, just in case Eric had come home before Annie and the champion skateboarder Vincent returned.

George found the back door ajar. He pushed it open and sidled in. The house was quiet, dark, and unusually cold, as though, inside, winter had started, while outside it was still only the beginning of autumn. There didn't seem to be anyone home. But if the back door was unlocked, George thought, somebody *must* be home. He listened carefully for signs of life: nothing.

In the gloom, he suddenly noticed a pale blue light coming from under the door of Eric's study. He tapped on it lightly.

"Eric!" he called. "Eric?" He put his ear to the door. There was no sound other than the occasional mechanical beep, which signaled that, inside the study, Cosmos was operational.

George hesitated. Should he open the door? He didn't want to disturb Eric if he was working on an important theory, but it might be his only chance to catch him on his own. Using his fingertips, he carefully pushed open the study door.

Unless you counted Cosmos the supercomputer as a person, there was no one inside Eric's study. Cosmos sat in his usual place on the desk, twinkling away like a Christmas tree, with all his lights on full alert.

From his screen shone the twin beams of light that Cosmos used to draw the space portal—the doorway that had taken George and Annie on so many cosmic journeys. In the middle of the study hung the doorway to space, suspended by the two rays of light and propped open by one of Eric's suede loafers.

Through the crack George could see a desolate

cratered surface under a deep-black sky. He leaned forward to push the door open a little farther so that he could see better, but he was dazzled by brilliant sunlight and had to shield his eyes with his arm.

He stepped back from the portal doorway and looked around Eric's study. Suddenly he spotted his old space suit, left crumpled on an armchair in the corner. Quickly he pulled it on, checked the levels in his air tank, buckled himself in as Eric had shown him, and prepared to step closer to the entrance to space.

With his hands safely encased in space gloves, George pushed at the portal doorway and had a close-up view of the surface of the Moon, the closest celestial body to the Earth. A grayish expanse of dusty ground stretched far into the distance; it was bathed in harsh sunlight that cast strong shadows across the crevasses.

Between the portal and the mountains, George could make out a tiny figure, bouncing enthusiastically toward a crater in the distance. Even though it was wearing an all-in-one white space suit with a fitted space helmet, George could still tell from the uneven, joyous way it was leaping about that it must be Eric. On Earth, Eric tended to shamble along in a distracted haze, but in space he behaved as if he had been set free from earthly cares to enjoy and revel in the wonders of the Universe.

Taking a bold step forward, George crossed the threshold and set first one and then the other boot on the Moon.

As he left planet Earth behind him, he floated up off the ground, the surface of the Moon scrunching under his feet as he landed again. In the Moon's low gravity, he could bounce several feet into the air just by gently pushing off with his space boots.

THE MOON

Q: *When did our Moon form?*

A: It's estimated that the Moon formed over four billion years ago.

Q: *How did it form?*

A: Scientists think that a planet-sized object struck the Earth, causing a dusty hot cloud of rocky fragments to be catapulted into Earth's orbit. As this cloud cooled down, its component bits and pieces stuck together, eventually forming the Moon.

Q: *How big is it?*

A: The Moon is much smaller than the Earth—you could fit around forty-nine Moons into the Earth. It also has less gravity. If you weigh one hundred pounds here on Earth, you would weigh less than seventeen pounds on the Moon!

Q: *Does it have an atmosphere?*

A: No. This explains why the sky is always dark on the Moon, meaning that if you stay in the shade, the stars are visible all the time.

Q: *What explanations did people have for the Moon before scientists discovered how it was formed?*

A: A long time ago, people on Earth believed that the Moon was a mirror, or perhaps a bowl of fire in the night sky. For centuries, humans thought the Moon had magical powers to influence life on Earth. In one way, they were right—the Moon *does* affect the Earth, but not by magic. The Moon's gravity exerts a pull on the oceans, which creates the tides.

Q: Could life exist on the Moon?

A: The Moon cannot support life—
unless it's wearing a space suit. But
as a consolation prize, evidence is
mounting that the Moon contains
much more water—the prime
ingredient for life as we know it—
than scientists thought just a few
years ago. It's frozen, though, and
any Earth emigrants to the Moon will
need to put substantial effort into
transforming it into its
life-friendly liquid form.

*Q: Has our Moon ever been visited by other
civilizations?*

A: The nearest celestial object to us has been
visited twelve times by astronauts from
Earth. Between 1969 and 1972, twelve
NASA astronauts walked on the surface
of the Moon. Could the Moon have been
visited before human civilization even began on
Earth by extraterrestrials who left deposits behind
them? Could the aliens have come as close as "next
door" to us? It's a (very, very) long shot, but some
scientists on Earth are looking again at Moon rock to
see whether it holds any clues.

"Hello, Earthlings!" shouted George, taking a few bounds forward. He knew no one on Earth could hear him, but he just had to say something to mark his first steps on the Moon. Set against the darkness of the sky, his home planet looked like a blue-green jewel, flecked with white clouds. Although both Annie and George had been on exciting cosmic adventures before, this was the first time George had seen his home planet from so close.

From Mars, the Earth had been just a tiny bright fleck in the sky.

From Titan, George and Annie hadn't been able to see the Earth at all through the thick, gaseous clouds on that strange frozen moon of Saturn.

And by the time they'd reached the Cancri 55 solar system, Earth had been hidden from their eyes altogether. Even using a telescope from that distance, they would have only known that the Earth was there from the very slight variable shift in the color of the light coming from our Sun, the star at the center of our Solar System.

On the Moon, however, he was near enough to see the detail of his home planet but far enough away to marvel at its beauty.

After admiring the view, he bounced off in Eric's direction, covering the distance between them very quickly. By the time he reached the scientist, Eric had disappeared into the shallow crater and was looking at a dusty machine, stuck in the bottom of it.

"Eric!" shouted George into his voice transmitter. "Eric! It's me, George!"

"Great gravitational waves!" exclaimed Eric in shock, looking up from the broken-down lunar vehicle. "You gave me quite a scare! I wasn't expecting to meet anyone else up here." He hadn't heard the great shout of joy when George first stood on the Moon as George's voice transmitter had been out of range.

"I came into the study and the door was open," explained George. "What are you doing here?"

"I only meant to go to the Moon for a minute," said Eric rather guiltily. "I wanted to get a little bit of Moon rock to take a closer look at it. I've got this theory about alien civilizations that I want to work on. I figure that if we were visited by aliens sometime in the past—say a hundred million years ago—they would have left traces somewhere. I don't believe anyone has investigated Moon rock to see whether it shows traces of alien visitation. I want to look at Moon rock again with fresh eyes, to see whether there is any signature of life in it. No one has examined Moon rock this way before so I thought I'd get some and try myself. Look what I came across when I was collecting samples! It's a lunar rover!"

"Does it still work?" asked George, quickly scrambling down to where Eric stood. It looked as though a dune buggy had crashed and been abandoned on the Moon. Eric climbed into the driver's seat while George surveyed the rover thoughtfully. "Can you make it go?"

"I expect the batteries are dead by now," said Eric, brushing some dust off the rover with the arm of his space suit.

"There's no steering wheel," noticed George. "How do we drive it?"

"Good question!" Eric wiped his sleeves on his legs, leaving long gray trails of moondust on his white space suit. "There must be some way to switch it on . . ." He fiddled around with a T-shaped joystick between the front seats. But nothing happened. The joystick seemed to be part of a console. Wiping away the lunar dust around it with the thumb of his space glove, Eric uncovered a series of switches with the labels POWER, DRIVE POWER, and DRIVE ENABLE. "Aha!" said Eric happily. "Houston, we have the answer!"

George leaped into the rover alongside Eric. "What happens if you flip those switches?" he asked excitedly. "Can we find out?" He hoped Eric wouldn't turn all grown-up on him and say they shouldn't mess around with someone else's moon buggy. But Eric didn't let him down.

"Yes, we certainly can!" replied Eric. He flipped the switches one at a time and then pushed the joystick, making the rover shoot forward very suddenly. The unexpected movement catapulted them both up into the air and out of the vehicle.

"It works!" Eric cried, climbing back in. "George, could you give the rover a push from behind while

I drive it out of the crater. With the Moon's lack of gravity, it'll be easy."

"Why do *I* have to push?" grumbled George. "Why don't I get to drive it?" But he took up a position behind the moon buggy and braced himself. Eric pushed the joystick forward once more. As he did so, the rover churned its wheels into the ground, showering George with fountains of dust and Moon rock.

"Push harder!" shouted Eric. At that moment George gave an almighty heave, and the lunar rover struggled out of the crater and onto the flat plain above.

"There!" said Eric, brushing his gloved hands together happily and hopping out of the driver's seat. "That's better!" He patted the lunar rover in admiration. "What a piece of machinery! It can't have been used for forty years and it still works! Now that's what I call a car."

"Who does it belong to?" asked George, who was now almost entirely covered in moon rock and dust.

"Left by the Apollo Moon landers, I would think," said Eric. "Look, over there! That must be the descent stage of the Lunar Module." Eric pointed to a four-legged object, squatting in the distance. "This is a piece of space history."

There was a brief silence as they both paused in wonder at what they had found. Then, suddenly, Eric seemed to realize that he was in fact standing on the Moon in the company of his next-door neighbor, a schoolboy called George.

"George, what are you *doing* following me out to the Moon?" he asked.

"I came to ask you about Freddy," explained George. "You didn't tell me where his new home is—I don't even know which planet he's on!"

"Oh, quivering quasars!" exclaimed Eric, hitting himself on the space helmet with his space glove. "Neither do I! We'll have to ask Cosmos. Don't worry—

we know that Freddy is perfectly safe and well—we just need to find out *where*! Was there anything else I forgot?"

Eric was famous for forgetting things, as he freely admitted. He never forgot important matters like his theories about the Universe, but he often forgot day-to-day tasks like putting on his socks or eating his lunch.

"Well, it's not so much that you forgot," explained George. "More that I didn't get to ask you."

"Ask what?" said Eric.

"Your work . . . Looking into the origins of the Universe—is that a dangerous thing to do?"

"No, George," said Eric firmly. "It is *not* dangerous. In fact, I think it would be dangerous if we *didn't* think about the origins of the Universe—if we dealt in speculation rather than in facts about where we come from and what we're doing here. That's dangerous.

"What we're trying to do is understand how this magnificent Universe"—Eric swept his arm around to point at the craggy mountain ranges, the huge dark expanse of black sky, with the distant bauble of planet Earth hanging above the moonscape—"came into being. We want to know how and why these billions of stars, the infinite and beautiful galaxies, planets, black holes, and the incredible diversity of life on planet Earth came about—how did it all begin? We're trying to go back to the Big Bang to find out. That is what the science

of cosmology, studying the origins of the universe, is all about. The Large Hadron Collider will let us re-create the first few moments of time so we can understand better the way the Universe formed.

"What we're doing isn't dangerous and neither is the LHC. The only real danger comes from people who want to stop us: Why don't they want the secrets of the early Universe to be revealed? Why do they want people to be scared and afraid of science and what it could do for us? That, George, is the great mystery to me." Eric sounded mildly frustrated.

"But do you think those people will try to harm you and the other scientists?" asked George.

"No, I don't think so," said Eric. "They'll just sneak around being a nuisance—they're not even brave enough to show their faces, so I don't think we have much to fear from them. Forget them, George. They are just a bunch of losers."

George felt much better now—both about Freddy *and* the origins of the Universe. Suddenly nothing seemed so bad after all. He and Eric turned and bounced back toward the portal, which was still glimmering in the distance. Usually they closed the portal down when they were on a space adventure, but because Eric had only meant to be gone for a couple of minutes, he'd left it propped open with an old shoe.

Before they reached the doorway Eric got his space camera out of his pocket. "We should take our photo! Say, 'Cheese! The Moon is made of!'" he said, holding the camera out and snapping a picture of them as

George made the thumbs-up sign with both hands.

"Will anyone notice that we moved the rover?" asked George as Eric put the camera away.

"Only if they look very carefully," said Eric. "This part of the Moon isn't under constant surveillance. That's why I chose it as a safe place to land."

"Anyway, they should be pleased," George pointed out. "We got their rover out of a hole in the ground and made it work again."

"Hold on a minute," said Eric as he looked up into the sky. "That light over there—*that's* not a comet." A pinprick of light was moving through the dark sky toward them.

"What is it?"

"I don't know . . . But whatever it is, it's man-made—so it's time to go. I've got the rock I need—let's go!"

Together, Eric and George leaped through Cosmos's space portal, back to the place where all their space adventures had begun.

THE CREATION
OF THE UNIVERSE

There are many different stories about how the world started off. For example, according to the Boshongo people of central Africa, in the beginning there was only darkness, water, and the great god Bumba. One day Bumba, in pain from a stomachache, vomited up the Sun. The Sun dried up some of the water, leaving land. Still in pain, Bumba vomited up the Moon, the stars, and then some animals—the leopard, the crocodile, the turtle, and, finally, man.

Other peoples have other stories. They were early attempts to answer the Big Questions:

- Why are we here?
- Where did we come from?

THE LATEST SCIENTIFIC THEORIES

The first scientific evidence to answer these questions was discovered about eighty years ago. It was found that other galaxies are moving away from us. The Universe is expanding; galaxies are getting farther apart. This means that galaxies were closer together in the past. Nearly fourteen billion years ago, the Universe would have been in a very hot and dense state called the Big Bang.

The Universe started off in the Big Bang, expanding faster and faster. This is called *inflation* because it is like the way in which prices in the stores can go up and up. Inflation in the early Universe was much more rapid than inflation in prices: We think inflation is high if prices double in a year, but the Universe doubled in size many times in a tiny fraction of a second.

Inflation made the Universe very large and very smooth and flat. But it wasn't completely smooth: There were tiny variations in the Universe from place to place. These variations caused tiny differences in the temperature of the early Universe, which we can see in the cosmic microwave background. The variations mean that some regions will be expanding slightly less fast. The slower regions will eventually stop expanding and collapse again to form galaxies and stars. We owe our existence to these variations. If the early Universe had been completely smooth, there would be no galaxies or stars and so life couldn't have developed.

Stephen

Chapter Five

They tumbled back into the scientist's messy study. In their hurry to avoid being spotted by the mystery satellite, they fell over in a dirty jumble of space suits that were once—but no longer—white.

"The portal is closed," Cosmos informed them. "You have been brought back to your terrestrial home, the beautiful planet Earth."

"Cosmos, you are the most amazing and intelligent computer ever created," said George, who knew how much the supercomputer enjoyed a compliment.

"While I suspect you are flattering me," replied Cosmos, his screen turning rose-pink, as it always did when he blushed, "nevertheless I find your statements to be consistent with reality."

As soon as he had gotten to his feet, George started to wriggle out of his space suit. It now lay on the floor, looking like an empty caterpillar cocoon after the butterfly has broken free. Eric was carefully wrapping up his pieces of precious Moon rock, still wearing his space suit, when they heard footsteps outside the door.

"Quick!" hissed Eric. "Hide your space suit."

George bundled it into the big cupboard in the corner of the study. The air was full of floating fragments of dust, brought back from the Moon.

"Hello!" called Eric in a rather high voice. "Susan, is that you?" After the last adventure, when they had very nearly not made it back from a distant solar system forty-one light-years across the Galaxy, Susan, Annie's mom, had banned the kids from accompanying Eric into space.

"Hello, yes, it's us," said Susan. She didn't come into the study but walked past into the kitchen instead. The sound of thumping feet announced that Annie was back too.

"It was very cool!" she cried, flinging back the study door. "Dad, can I have a skateboard for my birth—?" She stopped in surprise. "Why have you got a space suit on?" she asked. "Why is George here?"

"Shush!" said her dad quickly.

"No! You *haven't* . . . You *have*! Have you been into space without me?" She glared at George.

"You went to the skate park," he said sweetly. "It was . . . very cool. Much cooler than *the Moon*, I should think."

Annie looked like she might erupt. Eric just looked baffled, as though the kids were speaking Vulcan and he had forgotten to plug in his translator.

"I've got to go," said George. "Dinnertime! Bye, Annie. Bye, Eric. Bye, Susan!"

As he dashed out of the back door, Susan called after him, "Don't forget, George! You're coming to the lecture with us tomorrow evening! We've got your ticket . . ."

* * *

The next day, as arranged, George went over to Annie's house before Eric's lecture at the university. Annie was not pleased to see him.

"How was the Moon?" she asked angrily as they strapped on their bike helmets. "Actually, no, don't tell me—I bet that it was totally stupid."

"But you went to the skate park," protested George. "With Vincent. You didn't ask *me* to come!"

"You never said!" Annie muttered, hopping onto her bicycle. "You never said you liked skateboarding! But you *knew* I wanted to go to the Moon. More than anything! It's the place I most want to go to in the whole Universe. And you went without me. You're not my friend."

Even though George knew there was something very unfair about the way Annie was behaving, he was stumped for a reply. Why was she angry with him for doing something with Eric when she was busy anyway, doing something fun with Vincent son-of-the-film-director? But George couldn't ask her that. Instead he just circled mutinously on his bike in

front of their houses until Susan came out, carrying a large cardboard box that she balanced awkwardly on her handlebars.

"C'mon, you two," she said cheerfully, deciding to ignore the fact that Annie and George looked really fed up with each other.

Together, the three of them rode toward the center of town. For several centuries the Math Department had been located in a grand building on a narrow street in the heart of old Foxbridge. But as they turned off the bike path to ride down the street, they found it was so full of people that they had no choice but to get off their bikes and push.

"Who are all these people?" asked Annie as they tried to shove their way through the crowd.

"Let's leave our bikes here," said Susan, pointing to a bike rack. "I don't think we can get any closer to the department with them." They locked up their bikes, then sidled through the crowd of people toward the entrance: A flight of steps led up to a pair of glass double doors with columns on either side. In front of the doors stood a university official, looking anxiously out over the heaving throng below.

"They're all here for your dad's talk!" said George to Annie as he squeezed his way toward the steps after Susan. "Look! They're trying to get into the building!" The crowd surged around them, all pushing forward toward the old stone building

with the inscription AD EUNDEM AUDACTER above the portico.

"What for?" muttered Annie, struggling to keep up with George. "Why would so many people want to come and hear my dad talk about math?"

They ducked and wove their way up the steps to where the official stood guard. Immediately he held out his arm to stop them from going in.

"No entrance to the professor's talk!" he snapped.

"Excuse me," said Susan politely, "but I am Professor Bellis's wife, and this is his daughter, Annie, and her friend George. We've come to help set up the hall for Eric's talk."

"Oh, I am sorry, Mrs. Professor!" said the official apologetically. "We don't usually do security for the Math Department—it's not like this place to cause much of a stir!" He took a handkerchief out and mopped his brow. "But it seems your husband has become pretty famous."

As Susan and the two children turned to look at the waiting people, they heard a sudden commotion from the back of the crowd.

"Stop the criminal scientist!" came the chant. A small line of people dressed in black, wearing masks, were waving banners. "Don't let the advance of science destroy our Universe!"

The official looked horrified and spoke quickly into his two-way radio. "Math Department—send back-up.

Get inside, Mrs. Bellis," he said, opening the door and ushering Susan and the kids through. "We'll deal with the likes of them," he muttered grimly. "We don't tolerate this kind of behavior in Foxbridge. It just isn't done around here."

Chapter Six

Once they were inside, Susan quickly dragged the gaping kids away from the doors and through the entrance hall. They made their way into the big auditorium. "Ignore what's going on outside. Put one of these on every seat," Susan said calmly, giving them each a small cardboard box containing dozens of pairs of dark glasses.

Everything was nearly ready for Eric to take to the stage and give his very first public lecture as the new professor of mathematics at the ancient and very brilliant University of Foxbridge.

Annie and George moved between the rows, carefully putting one pair of glasses on each chair. Annie had for once been really scared by the protestors outside, and she was still trembling slightly.

"Mom, what's going on?" she asked. "Are those the people from TOERAG—that organization Dad was telling us about?"

"I don't exactly know," her mom replied gently. "But they do seem to be objecting to your father's experiments to explore the origins of the Universe. They believe that they are just too dangerous and should be stopped before they can go any further."

"But that's crazy!" said George. "We know that Eric's experiments are safe! And they might show us how the Universe really began. They're, like, the final piece of a jigsaw puzzle that scientists have been working on almost forever! We can't just throw the last piece away before we've seen the whole picture."

By now, they'd worked their way along all the rows from the big double doors at the back of the hall right to the front, where Eric would be speaking. The doors suddenly flew open, and a tall boy zoomed down toward them. He leaped off his skateboard and landed next to George, the wheels still spinning as he caught it in his hands.

"Ta-dah!" he announced.

"Vincent!" squeaked Annie in delight. "I didn't know you were coming. At least I've got *one* friend here!" she added pointedly in George's direction.

"I thought the doors were locked," George muttered grumpily, wishing they still were.

"They just opened them, and"—Vincent pointed

to his skateboard—"I rode straight to the front of the line."

"Have all the people in black gone?" asked Annie. Fans were now streaming into the lecture hall, taking their seats, examining the dark glasses left on the chairs and wondering why they might need them.

"Yup, they've legged it," said Vincent. "Weirdos. What was all that about? 'Criminal scientist'—the morons!" Annie was smiling at Vincent in a way that made George want to pull her hair quite sharply, just to wipe that look off her face.

"One of them tried to talk to me," Vincent added, flipping his board up and down with his left foot.

"What did he say?" asked George.

"I couldn't really make it out," admitted Vincent. "He had a mask on, so I suppose it was like trying to speak through a woolly sock. But it did sound as if he was trying to say a word."

"What word?" asked George curiously.

Vincent eyed him cautiously. "To be honest, buddy," he said, "it sounded like he was saying your name. It sounded like he said 'George.'"

"Why would one of the protesters be saying 'George'?" asked Annie in confusion.

"Maybe he wasn't saying George," said Vincent very reasonably. "Maybe it just sounded like that. Or perhaps that word means something else in I'm-a-crazy-person-who-dresses-up-in-black-for-no-good-reason language. My dad always has trouble at his film premieres," he bragged. "You're really no one at all if you don't have a few loony fans. It's just, like, one of the things that goes with being famous."

"Oh, yeah," said Annie admiringly. "Film premieres. That must be so, like, amazing!"

"Yeah," echoed George vaguely. "Amazing!" He wasn't even being sarcastic. He was too preoccupied with wondering why someone at the protest would be saying his name. There must be a connection, he thought, between the strange people in the abandoned college cellar underneath a tower in Foxbridge and the demonstration outside. Who else would call Eric an evil, criminal scientist other than a faceless group of dark bodies who believed his work had the power to rip the Universe into shreds in a matter of minutes? But how could any of that group know George's name? How could—?

At that moment the lights in the hall flashed on and off a couple of times, and a disembodied voice—which George and Annie recognized as Cosmos—told everyone to take their seats.

"Ladies, gentlemen, kids, and cosmic travelers," the voice went on. "Today we are going on a journey unlike any you will ever experience. Prepare, ladies, gentlemen, and young travelers! Prepare to meet your Universe!"

With that, the whole hall went dark.

Chapter Seven

George, Annie, and Vincent quickly sat down in their seats. They were on the end of the front row, with just one empty chair next to George. The whole of the rest of the hall was packed with people—there wasn't another free spot in the house. In the darkness, they heard the audience shuffle and then fall silent.

"Cosmic travelers," said Cosmos, his voice booming magnificently across the packed hall. "We have many billions of years to cover. You must be ready! Ready to go back to the beginning, ready to understand how it all began.

"Please, put on your dark glasses," he continued. "We will be showing you brilliance and brightness, and we don't want to damage your eyes." Above the heads of the audience, a tiny little pinprick of extremely bright white light had appeared, suspended in the middle of the total darkness. All at once George noticed that the seat next to him was no longer empty. A man had snuck in and sat down. George turned to look at him just as Cosmos projected a huge flash of light that illuminated

the whole hall. It lasted just long enough for George to see the man sitting next to him and to notice that he was wearing a very unusual pair of glasses in which the glass, instead of being clear or black, was bright yellow.

Only once in his life had George seen such glasses before. When he, Annie, and Cosmos had rescued Eric from the inside of a black hole, the scientist had come out wearing a pair of identical yellow glasses. They hadn't belonged to him, and the mystery of what those odd-looking glasses might have been doing in the middle of a super-massive black hole had never been solved.

"Where did you get those glass—?" George started to ask, but his voice was drowned out by Cosmos.

"Our story begins thirteen point seven billion years ago." As Cosmos spoke, the tiny speck of light hovered above their heads, with the hall in darkness once more. "At that time, everything we can now see in the Universe— and everything we can't see because it is invisible—began as a tiny speck, much smaller than a proton.

"The available space itself was also tiny, so everything had to be crammed together. If we peer back in time as far as we can, conditions were so extreme that physics can no longer describe exactly what was happening at this moment. But it looks as if space as we know it started at zero size thirteen point seven billion years ago, and then expanded."

The dot of light grew very suddenly, like a balloon being inflated. The balloon was slightly transparent, and it was possible to see bright swirling patterns moving all over its surface; otherwise it seemed to have nothing inside.

"This hot soup of stuff," continued Cosmos, "will become our Universe. Note that the Universe is only the surface of the sphere—this is a two-dimensional model of three-dimensional space. As the sphere grows, so the surface expands and the contents spread out.

"Time also began along with space. This is the traditional picture of the Big Bang in which everything, including space and time, comes into being very suddenly at the beginning of history."

Above their heads, the balloon exploded outward, and the audience seemed to be absorbed into its hot, swirling surface. The writhing colors twisted, then dimmed and broke up like a cloud, leaving total darkness in the hall. There were "Oohs" and "Aahs" of wonder.

After a moment, dim, moving patches of light began to appear on the dark ceiling; the patches then took on the shapes of galaxies, spreading out and away from each other until they had all vanished and darkness had returned once again.

"Was it really like this?" questioned Cosmos. "Some scientists wonder whether the Big Bang really *was* the beginning of history. We don't know for sure, but let's pick up the story at a moment just a minuscule fraction of a second after the Big Bang, when the whole observable Universe was scrunched into a tiny amount of space, smaller than a proton."

"Imagine . . . ," said another voice, and a spotlight showed Eric, standing on the stage with a big smile on his face. The audience burst into applause. "Imagine that you are sitting inside the Universe at this very early time . . ."

THE BIG BANG—A Science Lecture

Imagine that you are sitting inside the Universe at this very early time (obviously, you couldn't sit *outside* it). You would have to be very tough because the temperatures and pressures inside this Big Bang soup are so tremendously high. Back then, all the matter that we see around us today was squeezed into a region much smaller than an atom.

This would be a tiny fraction of a second after the Big Bang, but everything looks much the same in all directions. There is no fireball racing outward; instead, there is a hot sea of material, filling all of space. What is this material? We aren't certain— it may be particles of a type we don't see today; it may even be little loops of "string"; but it will definitely be "exotic" stuff that we couldn't expect to see now, even in our largest particle accelerators.

This tiny ocean of very hot exotic matter is expanding as the space it fills grows bigger—matter in all directions is streaming away from you, and the ocean is becoming less dense. The farther away the matter is, the more space is expanding between you and it, so the faster the matter moves away. The farthest material in the ocean is actually moving away from you faster than the speed of light.

A lot of complicated changes now happen very fast—all in the first second after the Big Bang. The expansion of the tiny Universe allows the hot exotic fluid in the little ocean to cool. This causes sudden changes, like when water changes as it cools to form ice.

When the early Universe is still much smaller than an atom, one of these changes in the fluid causes a stupendous increase in the speed of expansion, called *inflation*. The size of the Universe doubles, then doubles again, and again, and so on until it has doubled in size around ninety times, increasing from subatomic to human scale.

Like pulling a bedspread straight, this enormous stretching flattens out any big bumps in the material so that the Universe we eventually see will be very smooth and almost the same in all directions.

On the other hand, microscopic ripples in the fluid are also stretched and made much bigger, and these will trigger the formation of stars and galaxies later.

Inflation ends abruptly and releases a large amount of energy, which creates a wash of new particles. The exotic matter has disappeared and been replaced by more familiar particles—quarks (the building blocks of protons and neutrons, although it is still too hot for these to form), antiquarks, gluons (which fly between both quarks and antiquarks), photons (the particles light is made of), electrons, and other particles well known to physicists. There may also be particles of dark matter, but although it seems these have to appear, we don't yet understand what they are.

Where did the exotic matter go? Some of it was hurled away from us during inflation, to regions of the Universe we may never see; some of it decayed into less exotic particles as the temperature fell. The material all around is now much less hot and dense than it was, though still much hotter and denser than anywhere today (including inside stars). The Universe is now filled with a hot, luminous fog (or plasma) made mainly from quarks, antiquarks, and gluons.

Expansion continues (at a much slower rate than during inflation), and eventually the temperature falls enough for the quarks and antiquarks to bind together in groups of two or three, forming protons, neutrons and other particles of a type known as hadrons; and also antiprotons, antineutrons, and other antihadrons. Still little can be seen through the luminous foggy plasma as the Universe reaches one second old.

Now, over the next few seconds, there are fireworks as most of the matter and antimatter produced so far annihilate each other, producing floods of new photons. The fog is now mainly protons, neutrons, electrons, dark matter, and (most of all) photons, but the charged protons and electrons stop the photons traveling very far, so visibility in this expanding and cooling fog is still very poor.

When the Universe is a few minutes old, the surviving protons and the neutrons combine to form atomic nuclei, mainly of hydrogen and helium. These are still charged, so the fog remains impossible to see through. At this point the foggy material is not unlike what you would find inside a star today, but of course it fills the whole Universe.

After the frantic action of the first few minutes of life, the Universe then stays much the same for the next few hundred thousand years, continuing to expand and cool down, the hot fog becoming steadily thinner, dimmer, and redder as the wavelengths of light are stretched by the expansion of space. Then, after 380,000 years, when the part of the Universe that we will eventually see from Earth has grown to be millions of light-years across, the fog finally clears—electrons are captured by the hydrogen and helium nuclei to form whole atoms. Because the electric charges of the electrons and nuclei cancel each other out, the complete atoms are not charged, so the photons can now travel uninterrupted—the Universe has become transparent.

After this long wait in the fog, what do you see? Only a fading red glow in all directions, which becomes redder and dimmer as the expansion of space continues to stretch the wavelengths of the photons. Finally the light ceases to be visible at all and there is only darkness everywhere—we have entered the Cosmic Dark Ages.

The photons from that last glow have been traveling through the Universe ever since, steadily becoming even redder—today they can be detected as the cosmic microwave background (CMB) radiation and are still arriving on Earth from every direction in the sky.

The Universe's Dark Ages last for a few hundred million years, during which time there is literally nothing to see. The Universe is still filled with matter, but almost all of it is dark matter, and the rest hydrogen and helium gas, and none of this produces any new light. In the darkness, however, there are quiet changes.

The microscopic ripples, which were magnified by inflation, mean that some regions contain slightly more mass than average. This increases the pull of gravity toward those regions, bringing even more mass in, and the dark matter, hydrogen and helium gas already there are pulled closer together. Slowly, over millions of years, dense patches of dark matter and gas gather as a result of this increased gravity, growing gradually by pulling in more matter, and more rapidly by colliding and merging with other patches. As the gas falls into these patches, the atoms speed up and become hotter. Every now and then, the gas becomes hot enough to stop collapsing, unless it can cool down by emitting photons, or is compressed by collision with another cloud of matter.

If the gas cloud collapses far enough, it breaks into spherical blobs so dense that the heat inside can no longer get out—finally, a point is reached when hydrogen nuclei in the cores of the blobs are so hot and squashed together that they start to merge (fuse) into nuclei of helium and release nuclear energy. You are sitting inside one of these collapsing patches of dark matter and gas (because this is where the Earth's galaxy will be one day), and you may be surprised when the darkness around you is broken by the first of these nearby blobs bursting into bright light—these are the first stars to be born, and the Dark Ages are over.

The first stars burn their hydrogen quickly, and in their final stages fuse together whatever nuclei they can find to create heavier atoms than helium: carbon, nitrogen, oxygen, and the other heavier types of atom that are all around us (and *in* us) today. These atoms are scattered like ashes back into the nearby gas clouds in great explosions and get swept up in the creation of the next generation of stars. The process continues—new stars form from the accumulating gas and ash, die, and create more ash. As younger stars are created, the familiar spiral shape of our Galaxy—the Milky Way—takes form. The same thing is happening in similar patches of dark matter and gas peppered across the visible Universe.

Nine billion years have passed since the Big Bang, and now a young star surrounded by planets, built from hydrogen and helium gas and the ash from dead stars, takes shape and ignites.

In another four and a half billion years the third planet out from this star will be the only place in the known Universe where human beings can comfortably exist. They—you—will see stars, clouds of gas and dust, galaxies, and cosmic microwave background radiation everywhere in the sky—but not the dark matter, which is most of what lies there. Neither will you be able to see anything of those parts that are so distant that even the CMB photons from there have yet to arrive, and indeed there may be parts of the Universe from which light will never reach our planet at all.

This is our beautiful Earth . . .

Chapter Eight

As Eric finished his talk and the lights went up, the whole audience jumped to their feet, bursting into loud applause, which rang and rang around the lecture hall.

Modestly Eric took a few bows and then stumbled off the stage, where he was immediately mobbed by eager fans, flash bulbs popping, and television cameras shadowing his every move. The crush around him was so dense that Annie and George had no hope of getting anywhere near him. The pressure of the crowd drove them slowly backward, away from where Eric was standing.

Annie's cheeks were pink with excitement. "Amazing!" she kept saying to no one in particular. "That was amazing!" she babbled on to Vincent, who seemed dazed, as though he had looked into the heart of a burning star and now couldn't return to reality on planet Earth.

George suddenly heard a polite but pointed cough near him, and turned to see the man who had taken the seat beside him standing there. George realized that

he was very old, with white hair and a soft drooping mustache. He wore a suit of pressed tweed with a vest, and a watch chain looped across the front of it. The old man gripped George's arm.

"You were sitting next to Eric's daughter," he whispered urgently. "Do you know Eric?"

"Yes . . ." George tried to back away. The old man's whiskers were almost tickling his face.

"What is your name?" asked the old man.

"George," said George, still trying to move backward.

"You must get him," replied the mustachioed man

91

urgently. "I must speak to him. It is very important."

The old man was now wearing an ordinary pair of clear glasses, making George wonder if he had imagined the yellow ones earlier.

"But who are you?" he asked.

The old man frowned. "You mean you don't know?"

George thought very hard. Had he met this man before? Somehow he didn't think so. But there was something familiar about him—something about the way he spoke—that was trying to ring bells in George's mind.

"You recognize me, don't you?" persisted the old man. "Go on, tell me my name."

George racked his brains but he just couldn't think who this might be. Embarrassed, he shook his head.

"Really?" The man's face fell. He was obviously disappointed. "I was very well known in my day," he said sadly. "Every school child knew of my theories. You mean, you have never heard of Zuzubin?"

George grimaced. He felt awful. "No, I'm sorry, Professor Zuzubin . . ." He couldn't finish.

"I am sad," said the old professor sorrowfully, "to hear this. I was Eric's tutor, you know!"

"Yes!" cried George in relief that he had something positive to say. "That's where I've seen you before—in the photo of Eric at the university! You're his great teacher!"

Professor Zuzubin didn't look any happier. "Eric's

great teacher . . . ," he murmured. "Yah, that is how I
would be remembered. That is what they would think
of me if . . ." He seemed to check himself. "Never
mind," he said decisively. "Bring me Eric. I will be
waiting in his office. Now hurry, George!"

George had to fight his way through to Eric, who
was busy answering questions from the fans grouped
around him in starstruck clusters. "Stop pushing!" they
hissed to George as he tried to barge through. He saw
that Eric had unplugged Cosmos, folded him up, and
tucked him under his arm.

Finally George got close enough to whisper into his
ear. "Eric," he said, "Professor Zuzubin is here and he
wants to speak to you. He's says it's very important."

"Zuzubin is here?" said Eric, turning to George in
surprise. "Here? In this lecture hall? Are you sure? *The*
Zuzubin?"

"Zuzubin," George confirmed as people wanting to
talk to Eric shoved and pushed him. "He's waiting for
you in your office. He says it's urgent."

"Then I must go!" said Eric. He clapped his hands
together loudly. The hall fell silent. "Thank you all for
listening!" he told his fans. "Please come back next
month, when we will be discussing baby black holes
and the end of the Universe. Good evening, ladies,
gentlemen, and children!"

Eric left the lecture hall to another huge burst of
applause, with George following behind him, a frown

on his face. There was something about Professor Zuzubin—whether it was the yellow glasses or the strange way he had said Eric's name—that made George feel uneasy about him. Whatever was about to happen to Eric, George needed to know . . .

"What," said Professor Zuzubin, slamming a photograph down on Eric's desk, which made all the half-drunk cups of tea, unopened envelopes, scientific papers, and piles of books perched on it jiggle nervously, "is the meaning of this?"

"Professor Zuzubin," said Eric, turning red and fidgeting. "I . . . I . . ."

George gazed at him in amazement. He had never seen Annie's father being told off before.

Professor Zuzubin just stood there, watching his former pupil. "Eric Bellis, I know this has something to do with you. Kindly explain yourself."

George sneaked a look at the photo. It showed a grayish cratered surface. But in the middle of the fuzzy photo seemed to stand two indistinct figures in space suits.

"Oh dear," murmured Eric.

"Oh dear indeed," said Professor Zuzubin.

"This is all *my* fault," said Eric immediately. "You can't blame George."

"*George!*" Professor Zuzubin exploded. "Now you're taking children out into space? What is next? Taking a trip to the Moon with a whole school party? What were you thinking?"

"No, it was just me," said George bravely. "I followed Eric out to the Moon because I wanted to ask him a question. He didn't invite me to go there; I went out all by myself." As soon as the words were out of his mouth, George realized that his explanation actually made everything sound much worse.

"So you left the space portal unsecured during a cosmic journey . . . ," said Zuzubin slowly, "which allowed a *child* to use the portal unsupervised in order to join you in space? Do you know how serious this is?"

"I'm so sorry," said Eric, looking very ashamed. "I had no idea there would be a satellite in that location."

"You were very careless. This photo," retorted Zuzubin, "was sent to me by Dr. Ling at the Chinese branch of the Order of Science. He would like to know how a Chinese satellite managed to take a timed and dated photo of two astronauts on the Moon when no manned spacecraft have visited it since 1972."

"It's not that bad," said George hopefully, "is it? If they can't see the portal, then Cosmos is still a secret and they might think the photo is just a mistake."

"A *mistake*?" yelled Zuzubin. "You used the super-computer to take a little day trip to the Moon and got caught, and you think this counts as a *mistake*?"

"Don't shout at George," said Eric, rallying a little. He took a swig from one of his cold cups of tea, which seemed to fortify him. "I admit—we went to the Moon using Cosmos so I could investigate a theory I'm working on. I needed some Moon rock as a sample. But that's it! End of story."

"No!" said Zuzubin, turning red. "Not end of story! For now this photograph is still highly confidential—Dr. Ling has managed to see to that—but if it gets out, then we are all in very deep trouble. You knew that Cosmos could only be an effective tool for scientific discovery if we kept his existence a complete secret. You knew what might happen if he became public knowledge. You are the guardian of the world's greatest supercomputer. And yet you . . . you . . ."

He looked so angry, George thought his head might explode like an erupting volcano.

"This has come at the worst possible time for the Order of Science to Benefit Humanity," he continued, more calmly now.

The Order of Science to Benefit Humanity was a special and very distinguished group of scientists who had come together to make sure that science was used for good and not evil. Eric was a member—and so, in fact, were George and Annie. George had become the youngest member ever to join during his adventures with Eric and the black hole.

"You must have seen the protest today outside your lecture," Zuzubin ranted on. "You must realize that T.O.E. Resists Addition of Gravity is gathering strength right now."

George noticed that he made a great effort to call the protest group something other than TOERAG, which George thought was rather odd. After all, the name seemed to suit them extremely well, so why didn't the mysterious cosmologist want to use it?

"They are getting braver," Zuzubin went on. "They have never appeared in public before today. But they know people worldwide are turning away from science, and so they are gaining in confidence. In this atmosphere, if the public finds out through your foolish actions that we kept a supercomputer secret, they will start to ask what else we keep from them—perhaps the Collider really *is* dangerous, they will say. Perhaps none of us should be allowed to continue our work? Our lives in science could be over. Science itself could be over."

George thought Eric was about to burst into tears. He had never seen him so upset.

"What can I do?" said the scientist, wringing his hands. "How can I make this better?"

"We have called an emergency all-members meeting," said Zuzubin, checking the round silver watch looped across his vest, "of the Order of Science to Benefit Humanity. You must leave immediately and take Cosmos with you. They will review all the activities that Cosmos has undertaken while he has been in your care to see whether your use of the supercomputer has been justified."

George and Eric both gulped. The thought of the Order of Science looking through Cosmos's log and finding that he had recently been used to transport a pig was not a comfortable one.

"You will explain to the Order what you have done," said Zuzubin.

"That could be very awkward . . . ," murmured Eric, still thinking about Freddy.

"And they will decide whether you will remain as Cosmos's guardian and custodian. I have arranged your transport."

Eric turned pale. "You mean, they want to take Cosmos away from me?"

"They can't do that!" cried George. "That's wrong!"

"We shall see," said Zuzubin. "Eric, you must leave now. You will be collected from your house."

"Where am I going?" asked Eric.

"To the great experiment."

"I'm coming with you," said George. "I'm a member of the Order of Science. I should be there."

"Certainly not," thundered Zuzubin. "You will stay here. This is not a matter for children."

"Zuzubin is right," said Eric gently. "This doesn't concern you, George."

"But where are you going?" he asked. "Where is the meeting? When will you come home?"

Eric gulped. "The Large Hadron Collider," he said quietly. "I'm going back to the beginning of time."

With that, the three of them filed silently out of Eric's office and headed for the double doors at the entrance. Eric and George went out onto the street, but as George looked back through the glass, he saw that Zuzubin was not following them. Instead, the old professor disappeared down the stairs by the front door. That's curious, he thought. Where was Zuzubin going?

"Eric," said George as the scientist unlocked his bike, "what's underneath the Math Department?"

"*Underneath?*" said Eric. He looked completely dazed. "I haven't been down there since I was a student."

"What's down there?" persisted George.

"A load of old junk, I should think. Old computers, mostly. I don't know . . ." Eric shook his head. "I'm sorry, George. I've got a lot on my mind right now. Find your bike and we'll ride home."

Chapter Nine

Back at Eric's house, Annie was whooping with glee at how well his lecture had gone.

"Vincent said you were awesome," she said happily. "He said you totally rocked!"

But the happy atmosphere didn't last long. One look at Eric and George told Susan that something very unexpected must have happened. She took Eric into the study and closed the door. It didn't make any difference—through the thin walls the two children could still hear every word Annie's parents said.

"What do you mean?" they heard Susan ask Eric once he'd broken the news. "How can you be leaving for Switzerland tonight? It's the beginning of term. What about your students? What about *us*? You promised you would help with our anniversary party! It's been planned for ages—don't let me down, Eric. Not again."

"What's going on?" whispered Annie to George. They were hovering in the kitchen.

"A satellite took a photo of us on the Moon," George told her. "It was sent to some ancient professor by the

Chinese branch of the Order of Science. And now your dad is in trouble. He's got to go to a meeting at the Large Hadron Collider right away: He has to explain what happened to see whether they will let him keep Cosmos."

Annie turned green. "We might *lose* Cosmos?" she hissed.

"Susan," said Eric in the next room, "I'm really sorry."

"You *promised* me," said Susan. "You promised me you wouldn't mess our lives up anymore!"

Annie and George didn't want to listen but they couldn't help hearing. Every word was horribly clear.

"If I don't go now, I will *definitely* lose Cosmos," said Eric.

"Cosmos!" retorted Susan angrily. "I'm so sick of that computer! It's been nothing but trouble."

"That's not true," protested Eric feebly.

Annie ran out of the kitchen and burst into the study. "Stop!" she announced dramatically. "I can't stand it! Don't argue anymore!! Stop it! Just stop it!"

George stood frozen in the kitchen. For the first time since he'd known the family next door, he would have given anything to be back in his own house with his own parents. Even though his baby sisters made lots of

noise and his mom cooked weird food, he just wanted to get out of Annie, Susan, and Eric's lives and back into his own.

"Annie, please," said Susan. "This is between your father and me."

"*Are* they going to take Cosmos away?" Annie asked her dad, who seemed to have drifted off into a universe of his own.

"What?" said Eric, sounding startled.

"You weren't even listening, were you?" sighed Susan. Suddenly she sounded totally defeated. "I was talking to you and you were thinking about science."

"I . . . I . . ." Eric couldn't deny it.

"Maybe it would be better if you *did* lose Cosmos," said Susan rashly. "I hope they take that dratted computer away from you, then we can get back to being a normal family."

"Mom!" Annie cried out in horror. "You don't mean that."

"Oh yes I do," said Susan. "If the Order of Science doesn't destroy that blasted machine, I'll do it myself."

After that, it got very awkward and frosty in the house. Eric stomped upstairs to pack, followed by Annie, full of suggestions of what to say to the Order of Science. "Annie! I will handle this by myself!" George heard her father say in an unusually loud voice. "Stay out of it! This is none of your business!"

As George stood there, still stuck in the same spot in the kitchen, he heard Annie run down the stairs and into Eric's study, slamming the door behind her. The sound of noisy sobs rang through the house.

"Annie . . ." Susan tapped gently on the study door.

"Go away!" shouted Annie. "I hate you! I hate you all!"

Susan came into the kitchen, her face pale and drawn. "I'm so sorry, George," she said in a tired voice.

"That's okay," said George. But it wasn't. He'd never heard grown-ups arguing like that and it made him feel sick.

"You should go home now," said Susan kindly.

Eric appeared in the doorway. "Here, take this . . . ," he said, handing George the hamster, Pooky, in its cage.

"Oh—and this. It's a souvenir," he added sadly. "In case they come and confiscate all my space stuff while I'm away. I thought you'd want to keep it." It looked like a large off-white duvet had been stuffed into a knapsack. But George knew exactly what it was: Eric was giving him his space suit.

"Are you sure?" he said, shouldering the knapsack and taking the cage in both hands. The hamster, Pooky, was no ordinary pet. He was in fact the only nano supercomputer in existence. Designed by Dr. Reeper, Eric's former colleague, Pooky was almost as powerful as the great Cosmos himself.

At least, in *theory* Pooky was that powerful—the only problem was, Eric had no idea how to operate him. The nano computer was disguised as a very life-like small furry animal, but it had no control panel and didn't respond to any commands or instructions. Without his creator, Dr. Reeper, supercomputer Pooky was entirely useless. Eric had hoped to link him up with Cosmos, but this plan had failed. Instead, Pooky had been living quietly in a spacious hamster cage where he cleaned his whiskers, slept, and ran on his wheel—not much to challenge the world's second most intelligent computer . . . But until Dr. Reeper returned from his extended vacation at a distant physics institute, there was nothing Eric could do with Pooky. Except keep him safe—and secret.

Apart from Reeper, only George, Eric, and Annie knew about Pooky. Which, George suddenly realized, meant the Order of Science to Benefit Humanity could have no idea that a second supercomputer existed. They only knew about Cosmos.

"Bye, George," said Eric. "Good luck."

"What about Annie?" asked George. The sobbing had now stopped.

"I'll ask her to text you," said Susan. "When we have things figured out."

George slipped out of Annie's kitchen door and back across the yard, hopping through the hole in the fence.

In the darkness, his house glowed with a welcoming, familiar light. The solar-powered electricity generator his eco-friendly dad had rigged up didn't provide a strong current, and the battery it fed was often rather flat in the evenings.

George opened the back door and went into the kitchen, where his mother, Daisy, was processing vegetable purée for the babies. The smell of home overwhelmed him. His mother turned and smiled.

"Have you come home? To stay, I mean?" she asked, seeing her eldest child hovering in the doorway, clutching a large hamster cage and a knapsack. A lump came into George's throat. He nodded.

"I'm so glad," Daisy said gently. "I know it's been difficult for you here with the girls . . ." The twins were snoozing in two rush baskets on either side of the stove, their long, dark eyelashes sweeping down over petal-perfect cheeks. "It will get better," she went on, hugging George, "when they're a little older. And not quite so noisy."

One of the twins—George still wasn't quite sure which—laughed in her sleep, a pretty tinkling sound, like stardust falling to Earth.

"You'll be amazed when they're older—you won't be able to imagine what life was like without them."

George's dad, Terence, was standing in the doorway, watching. George realized that his parents had never said anything about the huge amount of time he spent at the house next door, and suddenly he loved them even more for not mentioning it.

"It's good that you're back, George," his dad said gruffly. "We missed you. Here, let me help." He took the hamster cage and peered in at the world's second most powerful computer who, like the babies, was now asleep. "Who's this . . . ?"

"That's Pooky," said George. "Can he stay in my room?"

His parents smiled. "Of course," Daisy said. "What a dear little thing! A little smaller than that funny old pig."

"I'll take him upstairs," said Terence.

With that, George climbed the stairs to his own room and went to sleep in his own bed, the curtains left open a crack just in case he should wake up in the night and look out to see a shooting star.

Chapter Ten

In the quiet, dark street below, a long shiny black car pulled up in front of Eric's house. The driver got out and rang the doorbell. A white-faced Eric was waiting behind the front door, clutching a very small suitcase, with Cosmos in a laptop bag. He turned on the threshold to say good-bye. Susan and Annie hugged him tightly.

"I have to go," he said. His eyes burned like two dying stars in his pale face.

"Good luck," said Susan quietly. "Eric, please be careful! Please! Watch out for yourself. There are bad people out there, and they don't like you."

"Hush, hush, I'll be fine!" said Eric, trying to sound cheerful. Now that he was actually leaving, Susan and Annie couldn't be angry with him anymore. "In a few days I'll be back and we'll all be laughing about this! It's just a silly misunderstanding—once I've had a chance to explain, everyone will be fine. I'll be home before you know I've gone! Maybe even in time for the party!"

"Bye, Dad!" said Annie, her bottom lip wobbling.

"C'mon, Professor." The driver was getting impatient. "Get in the car, sir. We're on a schedule."

Eric turned away and climbed into the sleek vehicle, the driver carefully shutting the door on him. The windows were made of dark glass, so Annie and Susan didn't see the tear running down his cheek as he sat, alone with his computer, on the soft leather seat.

The car rolled away down the street, the powerful engine purring. They drove in silence to a nearby airfield—it was a private strip where only a few planes landed and took off each day. A few words from the driver to the guard at the gate, and the car was through, heading right onto the airfield.

A jet was waiting in the brilliant light of a full Moon, the small staircase folded down so that Eric could get right out of the car and into the plane. He climbed aboard, and found that he was the only passenger.

After only a few minutes the pilot's voice came over the loudspeaker. "Good evening, Professor Bellis. It is our great honor to be flying you this evening. We will

be landing at an airfield near the Large Hadron Collider in about an hour and a half. Could we ask you to fasten your seat belt for the journey?"

With that, the little plane accelerated down the runway and smoothly lifted its nose until they were flying through the night sky toward what could be the end of Eric's career.

Even though George had fallen into a deep sleep the moment his head touched the pillow, it didn't last long. After what felt like just a few seconds, he found himself sitting bolt upright in bed, cold sweat trickling down his back. His sleep had been full of confused dreams in which people in black were chasing Freddy through thick orange grass on a faraway planet where the sun was green. "Stop the criminal pig!" they shouted in his nightmare. George tried to call out, to tell them to leave Freddy alone, but he could only manage a terri-fied croak.

Waking in his bedroom, George was struck by a horrible thought. If Eric came back without Cosmos, he would never find out where Freddy had gone! Eric hadn't told him where the pig's new home was because he had still needed to look it up on Cosmos. If Cosmos was lost to them, then so was Freddy! What if the computer had sent him right out to the farthest reaches of the Universe? That would mean he'd be moving farther and farther away from him . . . George might never see him again, and it would be his own fault for not taking better care of his pig in the first place.

THE EXPANSION OF THE UNIVERSE

The
astronomer Edwin
Hubble used the one-hundred-inch
telescope on Mount Wilson, California, to
study the night sky. He found that some of the
nebulae—fuzzy, luminous specks in the night sky—are
in fact galaxies, like our Milky Way (although the galaxies
could be of widely varying sizes), each containing billions
and billions of stars. And he discovered a remarkable
fact: Other galaxies appear to be moving away from us, and
the farther they are from us, the faster their apparent speed.
Suddenly, humanity's Universe became much, much larger.

The Universe is expanding: Distances between galaxies are
increasing with time. The Universe can be thought of as
the surface of a balloon on which one has painted blobs
to represent galaxies. If one blows up the balloon,
the blobs or galaxies move away from each
other; the farther apart they are, the
faster the distance between
them increases.

THE REDSHIFT

Very hot objects in space,
like stars, produce visible light,
but as the Universe is constantly expanding,
these distant stars and their home galaxies are
moving away from Earth. This stretches their light as
it travels through space toward us—the farther it travels,
the more stretched it becomes. The stretching makes visible
light look redder—which is known as the cosmological redshift.

George lay there in bed, feeling miserable and sorry for himself—and for Freddy. It occurred to him that a midnight muffin and a glass of milk might provide some consolation. So he slipped out of bed and tiptoed very lightly downstairs in his pajamas, knowing his parents would not be happy if he woke up the babies when they were sleeping.

But halfway down the stairs he heard a noise; it came from the dark, and supposedly empty, ground floor.

George froze, too scared to go any farther down but not wanting to go back upstairs either in case he drew attention to himself. He listened really carefully, straining his ears for any faint sound.

Just as he was starting to think that he must have imagined the noise, he heard it again. It was quiet but distinct—footsteps, as stealthy and careful as his own. Outside, the Moon was full and shining so brightly that it seemed almost like day in the silvery light that flooded in through the downstairs windows. From where he stood, 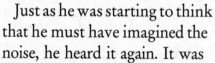 pinned by fear against the staircase wall, George saw a long shadow pass the foot of the stairs and continue into the kitchen. He heard the back door open and

close as the catlike footsteps padded away.

As noiselessly as he
could, George snuck
back up the stairs to
look out of the window
into the garden. By the
light of his old friend the
Moon, George saw the

long shadow creep down to the end of the yard, where
it seemed to float over the back fence and disappear.
George's blood was pumping so hard in his ears that he
felt dizzy. He ran into his parents' bedroom and shook
his dad awake.

"*Rumppffff!*" his dad snorted, turning over.

"*Dad!*" hissed George urgently. "Dad! Wake up!"

"Grugfmp!" Terence was talking in his sleep. "Ban
the bomb! Save the whale! Meat is murder!"

George shook him again.

"Ban the whale! Murder the bomb! Save the meat!"
Terence carried on sleep-talking while, beside him,
Daisy was snoring softly, her head underneath the
pillow.

Finally he woke up. "George! . . . Is it the babies?"
Terence groaned. "Do they need feeding—again?"

"Dad, I saw someone!" George told him. "There was
someone in the house! I saw them climb over the fence
at the end of the yard."

Terence grunted unhappily but got heavily to his feet. "Good luck finding anything to steal in this place," he muttered to himself. "Good luck finding anything at all." But he went downstairs to check, coming back with a serious but very sleepy face.

"The back door was open," he said to George. "I've locked it now. It was probably just a cat, you know. Go back to sleep now, before the babies—"

At that moment they both heard a wail from one of the cribs. "Oh no," groaned Terence. "There goes one . . ." Another baby wail joined in. "And there goes the other. Back to bed, Georgie. See you in the morning."

The next day at school, George's head was pounding. He slumped over his desk, hardly able to keep his eyes open. His dad had decided not to report anything to the police—nothing had been stolen, and anyway, Terence was sure that it was some kind of animal, probably a cat, that had nosed its way into the kitchen in search of food.

George didn't agree: The footsteps he had heard were too heavy to belong to a cat, unless it was the size of a leopard. It was much more likely that it had been a person. But he didn't argue with his dad. He gave a huge yawn. It was exhausting, trying to work all this out.

"Are we keeping you up?" said George's new history teacher pleasantly.

"No, sir," said George.

"Then kindly get out your textbook and turn to page thirty-four."

George fumbled in his bag and found the book. He opened it at the page he had marked to read for homework the evening before but, in all the excitement of Eric's talk, completely forgotten about.

Someone else, however, had got there before him. Tucked into that very page was a note, folded in half and with his name written on it in a familiar old-fashioned, curly script. Heart sinking, George unfolded the piece of paper, and read:

George,
Evil is at work in the Universe. Our friend Eric is in danger. We must speak. Do not try to contact me by any means. I will come to you.
Courteously yours,
Dr. R.

George felt a chill creep down his spine. His bag had been downstairs the night before. He'd left it on the table in the living room. That meant the shadow he had seen and the footsteps he had heard must have belonged to none other than Dr. Reeper, Eric's old enemy.

Why visit me? thought George in horror. *Why not visit Eric?*

As soon as he'd asked himself the question, he knew the answer. Eric wasn't there—by last night he'd already gone, taking Cosmos with him. And Pooky, the nano supercomputer that strange Dr. Reeper might have expected to find at Eric's, had been upstairs in George's house, where Reeper hadn't dared venture. If he had intended to visit Eric, he would have already been too late to find him. So he came looking for George instead. If Reeper was creeping around in the dead of night, then he must have something very important to tell him. George knew he needed to find Reeper and ask him what was going on. But could he trust him?

Annie, George knew, would say "No way!" Reeper had got them into deep cosmic trouble twice before. But he had turned out okay in the end: He'd saved all their lives when they had got stuck on a distant moon with no way back. And once they'd returned to planet Earth, Reeper had sworn to put his dark past behind him. He wanted to be friends with Eric, he'd said. He wanted to work as a real scientist again, and not live in the shadows any longer.

Judging by the note that George had found in his textbook, it looked as though Reeper had information that would help Eric. George had a thousand questions running through his head, the first of which was: How on earth would he ever find Reeper?

"If I was a crazy ex-scientist, where would I be?" he thought to himself. At least, he *meant* to think it to himself, but it soon became apparent that he'd said it out loud.

"I don't know where a crazy ex-scientist might be," replied his teacher mildly. "But if I was George Greenby, I would be on page thirty-four right now, and about to give my teacher the answer to the question written on the board."

The rest of the class tittered. "Sorry, sir," said George,

Our beautiful Earth, with our one Moon.

NASA/courtesy of nasaimages.org.

Above:
A setting last quarter crescent
Moon and the thin line of the
Earth's atmosphere; photo taken
from the International Space Station.

NASA/courtesy of nasaimages.org.

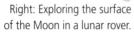
Right: Exploring the surface
of the Moon in a lunar rover.

ESA/NASA/SOHO

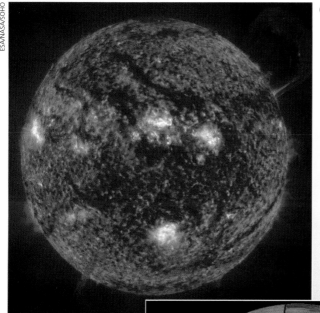

Our Sun.

NASA/courtesy of nasaimages.org.

Twin probes beam
back views of our Sun—
both front and back!
This amazing composite
image was created in
February 2011.

LOOKING AT OUR EARTH FROM SPACE

NASA/courtesy of nasaimages.org.

The Semien mountains of Ethiopia, Africa.

NASA/courtesy of nasaimages.org.

The Great Sand Dunes National Park and Preserve in Colorado.

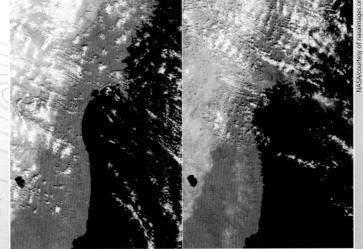

NASA/courtesy of nasaimages.org.

The horrifying results of the tsunami and earthquake in March 2011 in Japan.

Hubble's deepest views of the cosmos suggest that the first stars after the Big Bang lit up the heavens like a fireworks display.

A young glittering collection of stars—NGC3603 in the constellation Carina, twenty thousand light-years away.

The faint red blob—an infrared image—shows one of the very earliest galaxies ever seen in our Universe.

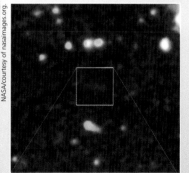

A tiny building block of today's giant galaxies, this compact galaxy existed only 480 million years after the Big Bang.

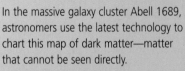

In the massive galaxy cluster Abell 1689, astronomers use the latest technology to chart this map of dark matter—matter that cannot be seen directly.

and for the next thirty minutes he tried to make his brain return to 1066 and all that, instead of focusing on the evil at work in the Universe.

But he found it almost impossible. One thought kept flashing through his mind, as clearly as if Cosmos had shouted it in huge red capital letters:

ERIC IS IN DANGER.

Chapter Eleven

After school, George rode around Foxbridge on his bicycle before going home. It was very unlikely that he would just run into Reeper on the street, but he didn't know what else to do. And then he remembered Cosmos's map of Foxbridge. The basement! If he could find the basement where the secret meeting had been held, he might be able to discover more information about TOERAG. He just *knew* that Reeper's message had something to do with those people in black.

Had Reeper been at the demonstration?

Was Reeper the figure in black who had tried to talk to Vincent?

George pedaled very fast. He knew Foxbridge really well, and Cosmos's map had shown him exactly where the secret basement was.

When George got there, he realized that this was, of course, Eric's college—the one where he and Reeper had been students of the great Zuzubin. Reeper, Zuzubin, and Eric were all members of the same college community.

Zuzubin, thought George. *Zuzubin*. Why did he seem to be everywhere and nowhere all at the same time?

The huge gates of Eric's college were closed and bolted, but a little door cut into the wood of the main entrance was left open for students to come in and out. George hopped through, only to find a fierce-looking porter, the guardian of the college, waiting for him.

"I have something for Professor Bellis," George lied, not knowing what else to say.

"Leave it at the desk," growled the porter, who had just finished straightening every single blade of grass in the bright green lawn behind him. He'd dusted down the marigold petals in the herbaceous borders, swept all

the paving stones, and polished the brass door knockers, so the last thing he wanted was a scruffy schoolboy messing up his perfect courtyard. "College is closed."

The porter stood there, glaring at George over his handlebar mustache, giving George no choice but to back out and go home. After he'd had a snack George went next door to see Annie, but he found only Susan, Annie's mom, who appeared frazzled for a change. Normally it was George's mom who looked like she'd got out of the wrong side of bed. This time, Susan had the messy hair, mismatched clothes, and worried eyes.

"Annie's not here," she told George. "She's gone to a karate lesson with Vincent. Apparently he's a black belt."

Of course he is, thought George. He would be.

"I would ask you in," continued Susan, looking stressed, "but I've been trying to get everything ready for this big party we're having on Sunday and Annie and I need to go to my sister's tonight so I'm very busy. And look! This window is broken—we don't know how. There's glass every-where."

George's heart sank. "Did that happen last

night?" he asked. He didn't want to tell Susan that his house had received a midnight visit too. She looked anxious enough as it was.

"It looks like it," she replied. George thought she was going to cry. "We didn't hear anything—and nothing's been taken. It's very strange."

"Is Eric back soon?" he asked to try to cheer her up.

"I've hardly heard from him. But he says the big meeting is tomorrow night," said Susan. "And he hopes they'll figure everything out so that he can fly back the morning after. I must leave now, George. I can't stay any longer."

With that, she shut the back door, and George heard the sound of the key turning in the lock, followed by the sharp noise of bolts being shot across. He sighed. There was nothing more for him to do here so he went home.

As he came into the kitchen, his father had just switched on the radio for the news.

"*Could the Universe be swallowed by a bubble of destruction, leaked from the Large Hadron Collider?*" said the newsreader in a cheerful voice. "*That's the big question on everyone's lips this evening.*"

"George!" said Terence. "Do you know anything about this?"

"Shush!" said George. "Please, Dad, I need to listen!"

The news report continued:

"*A dramatic statement released today by anti-science*

group *The Theory of Everything Resists Addition of Gravity* claims that the new experiment at the Large Hadron Collider could be extremely dangerous! In an open letter to the Universe, Theory of Everything scientists state that the experiment is reckless and unsafe, as it may produce a tiny amount of something called the True Vacuum.

"According to Theory of Everything sources, our existence in the Universe depends on the False Vacuum, which could be destroyed as a result of the high-energy experiments scheduled to begin shortly at the Collider. Within eight hours, Theory of Everything estimates, the bubble of destruction could have ripped our whole Solar System apart! Professor Eric Bellis, leader of the Collider Experimental Group, was this evening unavailable for comment. However, in the last few minutes a statement has been issued on behalf of the those working with him: 'The Collider is perfectly safe and no one should be afraid of the advances of science.'

"And now, in other news—"

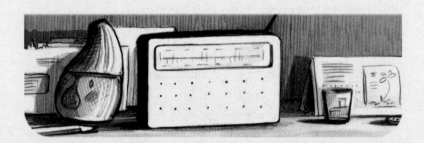

What is a vacuum, and what does it have to do with vacuum cleaners?

A vacuum means a space so empty it doesn't even have air in it. So if we pumped all the air out of a room, for example, we would create a vacuum.

A vacuum cleaner uses an air pump to create a puny sort of "would-be" vacuum that helps it to sweep up all the particles of dust when you're cleaning your house. But you couldn't use a vacuum cleaner to make the sort of vacuum that we're talking about here. You'd need something with a much more powerful pump for our experiment.

VACUA IS THE PLURAL OF VACUUM

The vacuum in the beam pipes of the Large Hadron Collider is as empty of gas molecules as some regions of outer space!

VACUA

Removing all the air particles from a room is not an easy job. Even a room completely empty of *atoms* still contains *radiation*:

- Infra-red photons emitted by the warm walls of the room

- radio photons from TV transmitters

- microwave photons left over from the Big Bang

- other particles whizzing through from space (e.g. neutrinos produced by the Sun)

- It also would still contain dark matter!

What if we could remove the radiation by cooling down the warm walls? Then the room would be emptier than the space between galaxies! But it would still contain something called *quantum fields*. These are what are behind photons, neutrinos, electrons, and the other particles. Physicists call the lowest energy state of the quantum fields the *vacuum state*, and it is this state—the state without any observable particles—that would now fill our imaginary room.

If we could look closely enough, we would also be able to see tiny ripples in space-time and gravity called *gravitational waves*.

So, although we may think that the room has been completely emptied when we pumped the air molecules out, close up, this vacuum actually buzzes with activity!

Put energy into a vacuum state (physicists would say *excite* it), and particles (and antiparticles) appear. It is thought that the vacuum is the state of *lowest energy*. There may be many other vacuum states with equally low energy—when excited they would create familiar-looking particles. In the early Universe, when the temperature was much higher, space may have existed for a little while in a *false vacuum* state with higher energy, whose particles would seem exotic today. As the temperature fell, this false vacuum would have decayed into our current lower-energy vacuum. A *true vacuum* is one which really does have the lowest possible energy.

There is no reason to think that any experiment on Earth could kick us into a different vacuum!

Terence switched off the radio. "Is this true?" he said somberly to George. "Are we really at risk from Eric's experiments?"

"No!" exclaimed George. "Of course not! Eric wants to help human beings, not destroy them!"

"Then why are they saying those things about him on the radio?"

"I don't know," said George. "Someone wants to stop him from making discoveries, so they've invented this bogus theory about the True Vacuum. I have to find out why! I need to help Eric."

"You need to do your homework," said his dad seriously. "And stay away from Eric and his family for now. I don't want you getting mixed up in this—do you understand me, George? If there is a reasonable explanation, we'll wait to hear it from Eric himself. Until then, you keep out of the way. Do you promise me?"

"I promise," said George. But even though he hated to deceive his father, he had his fingers crossed behind his back.

The next morning was Saturday, and George was lying sprawled on top of his bed, fully dressed and wondering what to do next, when his phone rang. Now that he had started at middle school, his parents had finally let him have a cell phone.

"Annie!" He had never been more pleased to hear from her. He'd sent hundreds of texts the evening before, and called her, but she hadn't replied.

"Did you hear what they said about my dad on the news?" she asked him.

"Erm . . . yes," said George cautiously. It must be horrible, he thought, to have a famous dad. "Has he called you?"

"Nope," sniffed Annie. "He hasn't texted or e-mailed or anything. Just nothing. But all the over the Internet, people are saying he's a dangerous lunatic and must be stopped from doing any more experiments because he's about to destroy the whole Universe. All I know is that Mom says he's got this big meeting with the Order of Science tonight at seven thirty and she hopes he's coming home after that."

"I had a weird note," confessed George. "From Reeper."

"From *Doctor Reeper*?" screeched Annie. "What does it say?"

"It says that your dad is in danger and that evil is at work in the Universe."

"What use is that?" she exclaimed. "We *know* that already! Why can't he say something helpful for a change? Did you speak to him?"

"Nuh-uh," said George. "He didn't, like, give a number to call. Just a note, Reeper-style, written on parchment in loopy old writing. Like he'd dipped a feather pen in blood or something."

"How very Reeper-the-Creeper," said Annie in a hollow voice.

"I tried to get Pooky working," George continued.

"And did you?"

"Nuh-uh," said George again, looking over at Pooky's cage. The hamster supercomputer was snuffling around in some hay, his little eyes blue and blank and empty of any meaning whatsoever. For once he wasn't running crazily in his hamster wheel, spinning round and round and round for hours on end. "I even got in touch with Emmett last night, and tried connecting remotely, but he said he couldn't figure it out either." Emmett was Annie and George's computer genius friend in America.

"Rats!" said Annie sadly. "Or rather—hamsters! If the master geek can't do it, then we've got no chance."

"Emmett did say one thing about Pooky, though," George told her. "He said that he thinks all this running in the wheel is Pooky's way of keeping his CPU cool while he's computing something. Something about coolant pumping around his brain when he's active."

"So Pooky is active, but we can't get him to work!" Annie sighed. "That's so frustrating! Why won't Pooky help us?"

George didn't get to answer, because at that moment a piercing high-pitched noise burst out of the hamster's cage.

"Was that the babies?" asked Annie, who'd heard it on the other end of the phone.

"Not the babies . . . ," said George slowly. "I think that noise came from Pooky."

Pooky was standing on his hind legs with his nose pointing directly up at the ceiling. His paws scrabbled wildly in the air and he screeched again, a bloodcurdling sound that seemed too loud to come from such a small animal. Suddenly Pooky's head swung around and he turned to glare at George with his little hamster eyes, which had turned from sky blue to flashing yellow.

"What's going on?" said Annie sharply.

"Pooky's having some kind of fit!"

But then Pooky opened his mouth. "George," he said, in a voice that sounded like a rusty nail scraping across a blackboard. "George."

"*Who said that?*" Annie screamed into the phone.

"Pooky . . . ," whispered George, whose hair was prickling on the back of his neck. "Pooky just spoke!" Pooky, as far as he knew, had never before uttered a single word. Unlike Cosmos, he was a silent super-computer. Until a few moments ago.

But the voice Pooky used hadn't been the voice of a hamster, or even a computer: It was the voice of a human being, and one whom they both knew quite well.

"Reeper!" said Annie. "Pooky spoke to you in the voice of Doctor Reeper!"

"George," said Pooky again, this time more clearly, "you must help me."

"What do I do?" said George to Annie, panicking.

"Find out what he wants," she urged. "But don't be fooled! Remember what he did to us before!"

"How can I help you?" asked George, horribly aware that he was now having a conversation with an electronic hamster.

"You must come and meet me," said Pooky, his eyes flashing. "You must travel into space to find me. We need to talk."

"Reeper, is that you?"

"Who else could it be?" said the hamster in Dr. Reeper's voice.

"The last time we met," said George bravely, "you wanted to abandon us to run out of oxygen on a moon forty-one light-years away from Earth. And the time before, you tried to throw Eric into a black hole."

"I've changed," said Pooky simply. "I want to help you."

"Why should I believe you?"

"You don't have to, but if you don't come and find out what I have to say, Eric will never come home . . ."

The thought of Freddy, abandoned and alone in a strange place forever, flashed through George's mind as well.

"Why can't you tell me now?" he said, seizing the little hamster with both hands. "What's happening to Eric?"

"Eric is in grave danger . . . Only you can save him, George. Only you. Meet me. Pooky will bring you to me. I don't have much time. You must leave immediately. Good-bye, George. See you in space!"

"Reeper!" George shouted at the hamster. "Reeper! Come back!" But Pooky's eyes had turned blue again, and George realized that the connection had been lost.

"What did he say?" Annie yelled into the phone.

At that moment the hamster gave a shudder, and a tiny pellet dropped out of his furry backside.

"He said"—the phone was shaking in George's hand—"that I must come and meet him in space!"

"But where?" cried Annie. "Where in space are you supposed to meet him?"

"He didn't say. He didn't tell me where to come or how to get there."

"Try Pooky again!" ordered Annie.

George picked up the little hamster and gently pressed all over his tiny furry body to see whether there was some hidden switch they hadn't yet found. But the hamster just gazed back at him with the same empty expression as before.

"I'm on my way over," said Annie.

"No, don't come!" said George. "There isn't time." He picked up the tiny pellet that Pooky had deposited on the floor of his cage. It was a screwed-up ball of paper. George unraveled the pellet, which turned out to be a long thin ribbon of paper with a line of numbers on it, ending in a capital H. "There seems to be another message ... Perhaps it's the destination . . . ," he said slowly, remembering a letter that Dr. Reeper had once sent to Eric, giving him the coordinates of a distant planet he wanted Eric to visit. The string of numbers reminded him of the way Reeper had written the location of that planet—the snag being that it had turned out not to exist, and Reeper had actually sent Eric right into the path of a super-massive black hole. "Maybe this is where I'm supposed to meet Reeper ..."

"But how will you get there?" asked Annie. "And how do we know it will be safe? Maybe you're going to fall into a black hole!"

"I can't talk now," said George, who had the phone jammed between his shoulder and his ear as he jumped off the bed and wrenched open his cupboard to find the space suit that Eric had given him as a souvenir of their cosmic journeys.

Pooky was stirring again, his blue eyes slowly

changing color—the signal, George now knew, that he was about to spring into action.

"I'm coming over," said Annie firmly. "I'll be there really fast—I've got my bike with me. Don't go anywhere before I get there."

"Sorry, Annie," said George. "I don't have time to wait."

Pooky had sat bolt upright and his eyes were now flashing red; they shot out two little beams of light that stopped halfway across the room and started spinning, forming a brilliant circle that whizzed round and round like Pooky's hamster wheel.

"George!" said Annie into the phone. "Don't hang up!" At that moment he was struggling into his space suit. "Don't go into space alone!"

"I don't have a choice!" George shouted before he put on his space helmet so he could still speak with his normal voice rather than through the voice transmitter. "If I don't go now, we won't know what Reeper has to tell us! Annie, I have to go . . ."

He put the cell phone down on his bed. In front of him, Pooky's circle of light had grown. Beyond it he saw a silver tunnel, which led off into the distance with no sign of what lay on the other side. George put on his space helmet and took a deep breath from his air tank. Through the transmitter, he could hear Reeper's voice again.

"George," he rasped. "George—enter the tunnel of light."

"Where are you?" asked George, trying to sound brave. He didn't feel brave. He had never been so scared in all his life. His blood felt like it had frozen in his veins, but his heart was pounding so loudly that he thought his ears might explode.

"I am at the other end, waiting for you," said Reeper. "Follow the tunnel, George. Come to me."

When George had stepped through Cosmos's portal on his previous journeys around the Universe, he had usually been able to see where he was going on the other side. But this time there was only the shimmering silver tunnel, which curved away without showing where it was taking him.

What would he find at the other end? A parallel Universe? Another place in time? Did the tunnel bend away because it followed the curvature of space-time, leading to some mysterious destination far away from the Earth's gravitational field? What lay in wait for him at the other end? There was only one way to find out.

"If you want to save Eric," whispered Reeper, "you must go on this journey. Just take the step, George. The tunnel will bring you to me."

"*George!*" Annie screamed from the phone on the bed. George could still pick up noises around him, thanks to the external microphone in his helmet. "I can hear Reeper as well! Don't go!"

George hesitated. Then he heard another voice speaking on the phone. It was Vincent.

"George, buddy," he said. "Don't go by yourself! It isn't safe. Annie's told me about the portal and Doctor Reeper. You mustn't do this."

What? thought George, feeling miffed. What was Vincent doing with Annie at her aunt's house? All the time he'd been talking to Annie, Vincent had been listening in? Vincent knew about the portal and Cosmos and Dr. Reeper? Vincent knew all the secrets that he and Annie had faithfully sworn never to tell anyone? And now Vincent, karate champion and ace skateboarder as well as Annie's new BFF, was telling *him* what to do?

So Vincent thought he couldn't handle it, did he? Vincent thought he wasn't brave enough to save Eric, George's mentor and teacher and Annie's dad? "I'll show you, Vincent," he muttered to himself. "And I'll save you, Eric, even if no one else will.

"Good-bye, Earth people," he

went on haughtily. "I am going into space. I may be gone for a while."

He stepped forward toward Pooky's wheel of light, which quickly sucked him into the tunnel as though he had dived down a waterslide at the park. George whooshed headfirst through the silver tunnel, his arms stretched out in front of him, turning this way and that as he was whisked out of his bedroom to an unknown location.

George didn't have time to think—he was traveling at immense speed through a blur of shining light on his way to meet his former deadly enemy, Dr. Reeper, somewhere out there in the great cosmic expanse that makes up our Universe.

From a place already light-years behind him, he thought he heard Annie scream, the sound echoing around his space helmet: "*Noooooo!*"

But it was too late. George was gone.

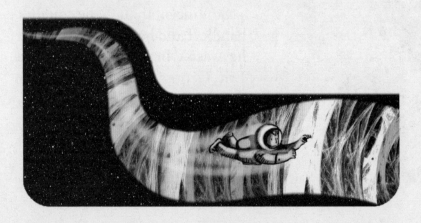

Four-Dimensional Space-Time

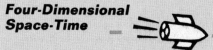

When we want to go somewhere on Earth, usually we only think in two dimensions—how far north or south, and how far east or west. That is how maps work. We use two-dimensional directions all the time. For example, to drive anywhere you only need to go forward (or reverse), or turn left (or right). This is because the surface of the Earth is a two-dimensional space.

The pilot of an airplane, on the other hand, isn't stuck to the Earth's surface! The airplane can also go up and down—so as well as its position over the Earth's surface, it can also change its altitude. When the pilot is flying the plane, "north," "east," or "up" will depend on the airplane's position. "Up," for example, means away from the center of the Earth, so over Australia this would be very different from over Great Britain!

The same is true for the commander of a spaceship far away from the Earth. The commander can choose three reference directions any way he or she wishes—but there must always be three, because the space in which we, the Earth, our Sun, the stars, and all the galaxies exist is three-dimensional.

SPACE, TIME, AND RELATIVITY

Of course, if we have something we need to get to, like a party or a sports event, it isn't enough to know *where* it will be held! We also need to know *when*. Any event in the history of the Universe therefore needs four distances, or coordinates: three of space and one of time. So to describe the Universe and what happens within it completely, we are dealing with a four-dimensional space-time.

Relativity

Einstein's Special Theory of Relativity says that the laws of nature, and in particular the speed of light, will be the same, no matter how fast one is moving. It's easy to see that two people who are moving relative to each other will not agree on the distance between two events: For example, two events that take place at the same spot in a jet aircraft will appear to an observer on the ground to be separated by the distance the jet has traveled between the events. So if these two people try to measure the speed of a pulse of light traveling from the tail of the aircraft to its nose, they will not agree on the distance the light has traveled from its emission to its reception at the nose. But because speed is distance traveled divided by the travel time, they will also not agree on the time interval between emission and reception—if they agree on the speed of light, as Einstein's theory says they do!

This shows that time cannot be absolute, as Newton thought: That is, one cannot assign a time to each event to which everyone will agree. Instead, each person will have their own measure of time, and the times measured by two people that are moving relative to each other will not agree.

This has been tested by flying a very accurate atomic clock around the world. When it returned, it had measured slightly less time than a similar clock that had remained at the same place on the Earth. This means you could extend your life by constantly flying around the world! However, this effect is very small (about 0.000002 second per circuit) and would be more than canceled by eating all those airline meals!

Chapter Twelve

George shot out of the other end of the tunnel, skidding facedown along a stretch of bare rock. His vision was still blurry from the bright, swirling lights of the silvery tunnel. For a second he saw stars before his eyes; then he lifted his head and saw thousands more of them, burning brightly in the black sky around him.

As he peered up, he saw something else. A large black boot appeared in front him, and then another. George rolled over and looked up at a figure in a black space suit looming over him, its face hidden by the darkened glass of the space helmet. It didn't make any difference. George didn't need to see his features to know that this was Dr. Reeper: the thwarted scientist and madman was on the loose in the Universe once more.

Behind Reeper's head there was an immense expanse of sky, so dark that his shape seemed to blend into it. Beside him, George could see nothing but bare gray rock pitted with great craters. He struggled to sit up, his muscles jellified by the journey.

"You can stand," said Reeper drily. "I picked an

asteroid with enough mass that you wouldn't float off."

When George had landed on a comet, on his first space journey with Annie, they'd had to tether themselves to the potato-shaped ball of rock and ice because its gravitational force was not strong enough to keep them on the surface. While the comet had been mostly dust, ice, and frozen gas, this asteroid was bigger, and made from much denser material: The gravity here seemed to be holding George firmly in place.

"Where are we?" he wondered, staggering a little as he got to his feet.

"Don't see anything you recognize?" asked Reeper. "No lovely blue-green planet hanging in the distance, just waiting for you to save it?"

George could see nothing but stars. The mouth of the tunnel had disappeared entirely, leaving him no escape from Reeper and this strange, rocky place.

"Of course you don't," continued Reeper. "You wouldn't recognize much of your own Galaxy if I'd taken you out into the Milky Way. But you are no longer in your home Galaxy. You've journeyed farther than ever before."

"Are we in another Universe?" asked George. "Was that a wormhole?"

"No," said Reeper. "That's my updated version of the portal. A doorway seems terribly old school, don't you think? Eric always was such a traditionalist. You wouldn't think it, would you? His theories tore up everything we thought we knew about the Universe, and yet when it comes to designing a portal, he models it on his own front door.

"This, George, is Andromeda."

The Andromeda Galaxy (also known as M31) is the *nearest large galaxy* to our own Milky Way, and together they are the largest objects in our Local Group of galaxies. The Local Group is a group of at least forty nearby galaxies that are strongly influenced by each other's gravity.

 At 2.5 million light-years away, Andromeda is not actually the closest galaxy to us (that title probably goes to the *Canis Major* dwarf galaxy), but is the closest with a comparable size and mass.

 Current estimates suggest that the Milky Way has more *mass* (including dark matter), but Andromeda has more *stars*.

 Andromeda has a *spiral* shape, like the Milky Way.

 Like the Milky Way, Andromeda has a *super-massive black hole at its center*.

 Also like the Milky Way, Andromeda has several (at least fourteen) satellite dwarf galaxies in orbit around it.

ANDROMEDA

Unlike most galaxies, light received from Andromeda is blue-shifted. This is because the expansion of the Universe— which makes galaxies move away from each other—is being overcome by gravity between the two galaxies, and Andromeda is falling toward the Milky Way at around 300 kilometers per second (186 miles per second). The two galaxies may collide in around 4.5 billion years, and eventually merge— or they may just miss. Collisions between galaxies are thought not to be unusual— the small Canis Major dwarf galaxy appears to be merging with the Milky Way right now!

"Another galaxy . . . ?" said George in awe.

"Our neighbor," confirmed Reeper, sweeping an arm around him. "This is, if you like, the galaxy equivalent of the house next door. Given the size of the Universe, it might as well be. Notice anything?"

"The stars look the same . . . ," said George slowly. "This asteroid looks like an asteroid. I suppose we must be orbiting a star, so we're in another solar system. It's not so very different from being in the Milky Way."

"Yes, indeed," agreed Reeper. "Remarkable, isn't it? Close up, no two pieces of rock are exactly the same. No two planets, no two stars, no two galaxies. Some regions of space contain just clouds of gas and dark matter, but in other places you find stars, asteroids, and planets. So much variety! Yet here we are, two and half million light-years away from Earth, and things don't look that different. This asteroid could be in our own Solar System; those stars could be in our own Milky Way. The variations here are the same as in our own Galaxy. What do you think that means, George? Answer me that and I'll tell you why we are here."

"It means," said George, thinking about Eric's lecture, "that everything everywhere was formed in the same way, from the same material and by the same rules, but the tiny fluctuations at the beginning of time caused everything to turn out a little bit different from everything else."

UNIFORMITY IN SPACE

In order to apply General Relativity to the Universe as a whole, we usually make some assumptions:

> every location in space should behave in the same way (*homogeneity*)

> and every direction in space should look the same (*isotropy*).

This leads to a picture of the Universe that is

> uniform in space

> starts with a Big Bang

> and then expands equally everywhere.

This picture is strongly supported by astronomical observations—what we can see in space through telescopes on the ground and in space.

Yet the Universe can't be *exactly* uniform in space, because this would mean that structures like galaxies, stars, solar systems, planets, and people couldn't exist. A pattern of tiny *ripples* over the uniformity is needed to explain how the first patches of gas and dark matter could begin to collapse, so that the laws of physics could go on to create stars and planets.

Because the gas and dark matter start out nearly uniform, and because we believe the same laws of physics apply everywhere, we expect that all galaxies form in a similar way. So distant galaxies should have similar types of stars, planets, asteroids, and comets to those that we can see in our own Milky Way.

Where the initial tiny ripples came from is not yet completely understood. The best theory at the moment is that they came from microscopic quantum jitters that were magnified by a very rapid early expansion phase—called *inflation*—that took place during a very tiny fraction of the first second after the Big Bang.

"Well done! I am glad to know that one of my ex-pupils at least can show that he has benefited from his education."

"Why have you brought me here?" asked George bravely. "What is it this time?"

"I don't think I like your tone." Reeper now sounded more like he had when he'd been a teacher at George's old school.

"I don't think I like being catapulted into space by a talking hamster," George shot back at him.

"Of course," said Reeper hastily. "I can see that was a bit of a surprise. But I had no other way of contacting you."

"Oh, really?" said George. "Didn't you break into my house at night and leave a note in my schoolbook?"

"Yes, yes, I did," said Reeper. He seemed unusually nervous, unlike the Reeper of old, who was always totally confident of his evil powers. "I was trying to attract your attention. I couldn't find Eric next door so I came and left a note for you instead."

"Why didn't you just come and talk to me, if it was so important?"

"Because I can't," said Reeper in frustration. "I can't go anywhere or do anything—I'm trapped. Since I slipped away to your houses the other night, they've put me under even closer surveillance. They don't know I visited you, but they know I went somewhere and it has made them suspicious. That's why I had to meet you in space. It's the only safe place for us to talk. I couldn't possibly have contacted you—and certainly not Eric—by earthly means. I would have blown our only chance of stopping them."

"Who is it who's watching you?" asked George.

"Them," said Reeper. "TOERAG. They are everywhere." He looked around as he spoke, as though they might be floating past the asteroid in this unknown part of the Andromeda galaxy. "They are the unseen, the dark force. They are all around us."

"I think that's dark matter you're thinking of," said George. "The invisible material that makes up twenty-three percent of the known Universe."

"George," said Reeper earnestly, "you are so right. They are humanity's dark matter. You can't see them, but you know they are there by the effect they have on the Universe around them."

For once, he seemed to be speaking from the heart—if indeed he actually had one.

"Were they the people in black at Eric's lecture?" demanded George.

"That was a few of them. There are many more—they are a vast network. I was there too at the demonstration—I couldn't get near you so I tried to alert you via that boy but it didn't work."

"I knew it!" said George. "I knew it was you! But I couldn't work out why. I don't understand why TOERAG is doing this. Why would it be so bad if

Eric discovered the Theory of Everything? Why would it be so dangerous to understand the origins of the Universe?"

"For you and me it would be a great step forward. For TOERAG it would be a terrible, wounding blow."

"Because of the True Vacuum," asked George, "and what it might do?"

"The leaders don't really believe that the Universe will be ripped apart in a growing bubble of destruction, leaked from the Large Hadron Collider," Reeper told him. "That's just a terrible apocalyptic prospect they use to frighten people into joining their organization so that their network keeps on growing. What they're really scared of is something very different."

"Such as?"

The asteroid sped onward on its orbit, circling a very bright young star that was a few billion years younger than our Sun. As George watched, two hundred-yard-

long chunks of rock smashed into each other with the energy of a nuclear explosion. A cloud of pulverized dust expanded outward. This young solar system was a very violent place, with many such chunks hurtling around the central star. Eventually planets would form and vacuum up all the debris left lying around after these collisions, but for now, it was a chaotic, dangerous place to be. Although, thought George, from what Reeper had to say, it sounded like almost anywhere in the Universe was a better bet than planet Earth right now.

"The leaders of TOERAG are convinced that Eric's experiments will eventually have other results," said Reeper. "Once we have the Theory of Everything, they believe that scientists will be able to use this knowledge in a number of ways. For example, they think it will become possible to create a new source of clean, cheap renewable energy."

"But who doesn't want that?" cried George.

"I have hacked into their secret membership files," Reeper explained, "so I am one of the very few people who can actually identify the leaders of TOERAG. It's made up first of big companies—who would prefer us to keep on using coal, oil, gas, or nuclear energy rather than look for sources of renewable energy. They think that experiments at the LHC might one day give us the clue as to how to produce clean, cheap energy and they don't want that."

"Urgh!" said George. "You mean the people who mess up the seas and poison the atmosphere with green-house gases?" He thought of his eco-activist parents and how they tried their hardest to protect the planet. They were just normal, ordinary, kind people who wanted to make a difference to the future of the life on Earth. What chance did they have against such powerful opponents?

"Not just them," warned Reeper. "There's also a group within TOERAG who think that once we find one unified theory for the four forces, it will result in the elimination of war. They think that we will come to understand that we are all the same, all part of the same human race. This could raise our awareness of the problems on planet Earth, end competition for resources, and make the rich countries want to help the poor nations."

"Don't they want peace?" George was bewildered.

"No," said Reeper shortly. "They make a lot of

money selling weapons so that people can kill each other. They'd really prefer it if we kept waging war."

"Anyone else?" said George.

"Well, there are a few astrologers who think their predictions will become worthless once Eric and the other scientists can explain everything. So they won't be able to make money by telling your fortune on the Internet. There's a television evangelist who fears that no one will want to be saved by him if Eric is successful. Another group has joined out of fear—fear of science and what it will do in the future. There are even some scientists."

"Scientists?" said George in shock. "Why would they join TOERAG?"

"Well, there's me, for a start," said Reeper. "I didn't really join—I infiltrated TOERAG in order to spy on them. I heard about this secret, anti-science organization, and so to find out more, I became one of their number—my codename is *Isaac*, after one of the greatest scientists of all, Isaac Newton. In order to gain acceptance, I lied and told them that Eric and I were still sworn enemies. No one yet knows that he and I made peace with each other, so they believed me and let me in."

"Does Eric know you are part of TOERAG?" asked George.

"No," admitted Reeper. "I wish he did. I wanted to talk to him about their plans, but I realized it would put him in even more danger if I contacted him directly."

"Who are the other scientists?"

"That's more difficult," said Reeper. "We're never allowed to meet each other. We have separate jobs to do and our paths never cross."

"What was your job?"

"My job"—there was a trace of pride in Reeper's voice—"was to create a bomb, a really powerful and intelligent one. They wanted me to make a bomb that would be impossible to defuse. The thing about most bombs is that you can cut the wires to stop  them detonating. TOERAG wanted a bomb that even if you snipped the wires or knew the code, you still couldn't prevent the explosion. They said," Reeper added hastily, "it was just a prototype, for experimental purposes only."

"You didn't really do it, did you?" asked George. "I mean, you didn't actually make a bomb that works and give it to a dangerous underground anti-science group?"

"Of course I did!" said Reeper, sounding startled. "How could I make something that didn't work?"

"Duh, quite easily!" said George. "Then it wouldn't be able to blow anything up. Problem solved!"

"But I'm a scientist!" bleated Reeper. "I can't make something that doesn't work! I have to get it right—otherwise I'm not a scientist! And that would be . . ." He trailed off.

"You'd better tell me about this bomb," George said, trying to be patient.

"Right, well," said Reeper, sounding more enthusiastic. "It's really brilliant! And it can blow up anything—I mean, just anything!"

"Yup, I got that," said George. "You keep on telling me."

"Sorry, sorry!" said Reeper. "Okay, I designed a bomb with eight switches. You input a code on a numerical pad to make the switches go live. Then, when you push all eight of the switches, it creates a superposition of eight states. Once all eight switches are thrown, the countdown automatically begins."

"So what is the really super-clever part?" asked George.

"Because it's a quantum mechanical bomb"—Reeper sounded like he was boasting, just a little—"it has created a quantum superposition of the different alternatives inside the detonator. This means that anyone who tries to defuse the bomb by cutting one of the cables or flipping one of the switches would just blow themselves and everyone else up. That's the point—they wanted a bomb that couldn't be shut down, in case there were traitors inside TOERAG."

"I don't get it," said George.

"The bomb has been armed in such a way that no one switch can turn it off; it is in a quantum superposition of eight different possible switches. The detonator does not 'decide' which switch is actually being used until someone presses one to try to stop the bomb going off, and the circuit checks whether it is correct. At that point the wave function collapses randomly to one of the eight possible alternatives. Even if you pressed all eight at once, the bomb will very probably detonate immediately. What I mean is—it will explode, no matter what you do to it."

"Why did you do this?" asked George grimly.

"Because I wanted someone to know how clever I am," said Reeper sulkily. "I didn't realize they actually intended to use the wretched thing. They said it was just an experiment."

"And where is this impossible-to-defuse quantum mechanical bomb?"

"Well, I don't know!" said Reeper, sounding panicky. "That's the problem—it's gone!"

"Gone where?"

"They've taken it away. And from what I've learned by hacking into their computers, it looks like they mean to use it, after all. Where's Eric?"

"He's at the Large Hadron Collider . . . ," said George slowly as the true horror of the situation became clear to him. "At a meeting of the Order of Science to Benefit

Humanity. Every single full-member of the Order will be there. They've been asked to come together."

"That's it!" cried Reeper. "That's where they are going to use the bomb! They're going to use it to destroy the Collider, and not just Eric, but all the leading physicists in the world!"

"But . . . but . . . but how could they know that the Order of Science is having a meeting?" gasped George.

"I have long suspected that the Order contains a mole," said Reeper, speaking quickly now. "One of the scientists in TOERAG must also be a member of the Order of Science. He or she must have betrayed the Order to TOERAG."

"And that person definitely isn't you?" asked George fiercely.

"I'm not even a member of the Order," said Reeper sadly. "So it couldn't be me. My membership was revoked many years ago and I was not allowed to rejoin. It is someone else, someone really dangerous."

"Why are you trying to help Eric now?" wondered George.

"George," said Reeper, "I know you don't have a high opinion of me. But believe me, what I love above all else is science. I can't just stand by and, after all these centuries of work, see it extinguished by idiots who are acting out of greed or prejudice. I joined TOERAG to try to stop them. That's why I'm here."

George's head was spinning. Could Reeper really

PARTICLE COLLISIONS

If there were no forces, particles colliding inside machines like the LHC would come out the same as they went in. Forces allow fundamental particles to influence each other in collisions (even to change into different particles!) by emitting and absorbing special force-carrying particles called *gauge bosons*.

Physicists can represent a collision by using **Feynman diagrams**. Such diagrams show the ways in which it is possible for particles to scatter off each other. One Feynman diagram is one part of describing such a collision and the diagrams need to be summed up for a complete description of a single collision.

Here is the simplest kind, in which two electrons approach, exchange a single photon, and then continue on their way. Time goes from left to right, the wiggly line is a photon, and the solid lines show the electrons (marked as e). This diagram includes all the cases where the photon travels up to down or down to up (which is why the wiggly line is drawn vertically):

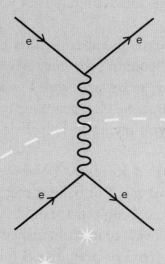

More complicated processes have more than one virtual particle in more complex Feynman diagrams. For example, here is one with two virtual photons and two virtual electrons:

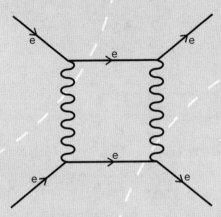

An infinite number of many diagrams are needed to fully describe each kind of particle reaction, though thankfully scientists can often obtain very good approximations by only using the simplest ones. Here's one that could represent what might happen at the Large Hadron Collider when protons collide! The letters u, d, and b are quarks; while g shows gluons:

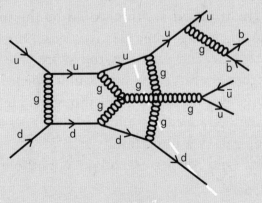

be telling the truth? If so, this would be the first time he wasn't concealing some deadly trick, intended to exterminate Eric and even up the score. He looked over at Reeper . . . but something had happened to him while George was absorbed in his thoughts. He seemed to be fading, disappearing into the blackness of the Andromeda galaxy around him.

"George," said Reeper urgently. "We have less time than I thought."

"What's happening to you?"

"I'm not real." Reeper was talking very fast now. George could no longer see his outline—only small triangles of reflected starlight on his shiny helmet and boots. "I am a computer-generated avatar of myself. It was the only way I could meet you. When I couldn't find Pooky or Eric or Cosmos, I broke into your house and secretly left a re-router downstairs. Through that re-router, I used Pooky to send myself here and open the portal remotely to transport you."

"Why don't you avatar *yourself* to the Collider and tell them?" cried George. "Why *me*?"

"I cannot get to the Collider!" said Reeper, his voice distorting. "I will not be able to escape them again."

"What about the quantum mechanical bomb?" cried George.

"There's a way! I'm not a complete fool! I made an observation! Pooky sent you a code . . ."

"What! How do I use Pooky's code? How do I defuse the bomb?"

But the only reply George got was a faint whisper through his voice transmitter: "George . . ."

And with that, the Universe around him fell silent. In front of him, where Reeper had stood, the silvery tunnel had opened up once more, pulling him forward into its river of light.

He twisted and turned at unimaginable speed across

the Universe, flying quintillions of miles from Andromeda back to our own Galaxy, the Milky Way, which is made up of matter and dark matter—that mysterious dark substance that surrounds us but which we can't see, feel, or hear. As he traveled, a thought flew into his brain—*I have been to the dark side*, he said to himself. *I have been to the dark.*

THE DARK SIDE
OF THE UNIVERSE

One of the simplest questions we can ask is: What is the world made of?

Long ago, the Greek Democritus postulated that everything is made of indivisible building blocks he called *atoms*. And he was right—and over the past two thousand years we have filled in the details.

All the stuff in our everyday world is made of combinations of the ninety-two different types of atoms: the elements of the periodic table—hydrogen, helium, lithium, beryllium, boron, carbon, nitrogen, oxygen, and all the way up to uranium, number ninety-two. Plants, animals, rocks, minerals, the air we breathe, and everything on Earth is made of these ninety-two building blocks. We also know that our Sun, the other planets in our Solar System, and other stars far away are made of the same ninety-two chemical elements. We understand atoms very well, and are masters at rearranging them into all kinds of different things, including my favorite, French fries! The science of chemistry is all about building different things with atoms, a kind of "Lego with atoms."

Today, we know there is a whole lot more out there than just our Solar System—a mindbogglingly large Universe, with billions of galaxies, each made of billions of stars and planets. So what is the Universe made of? Surprise—while our Solar System and other stars and planets are made of atoms, most of the stuff in the Universe is *not*; it is made of very strange stuff—dark matter and dark energy—that we do not understand as well as atoms.

First the numbers: In the Universe as a whole, atoms account for 4.5%, dark matter for 22.5%, while dark energy comes in at 73%. An aside: Only about one in ten of those atoms is in the form of stars, planets, or living things, with the rest existing in a gaseous form too hot to have made stars and planets.

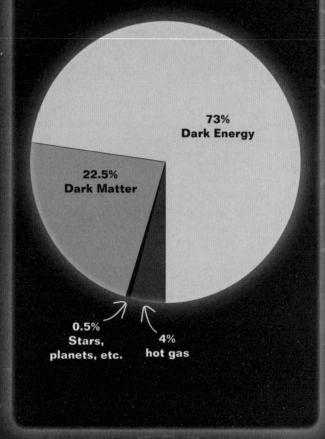

73%
Dark Energy

22.5%
Dark Matter

0.5%
Stars,
planets, etc.

4%
hot gas

Let's begin with dark matter. How do we know it is there? What is it? And how come we don't find it on Earth or even in our Sun?

We know it is there because the force of its gravity holds together our Galaxy, the Andromeda galaxy, and all the other big structures in the Universe. The visible part of the Andromeda galaxy (and all other galaxies) sits in the middle of an enormous (ten times larger) sphere of dark matter (astronomers call it the dark halo). Without the gravity of the dark matter, most of the stars, solar systems, and everything else in galaxies would go flying off into space, which would be a very bad thing.

At the moment we don't know exactly what the dark matter is made of (not unlike Democritus, who had an idea—atoms—but didn't have the details). But here is what we *do* know.

Dark matter particles are not made of the same parts that atoms are (protons, neutrons, and electrons); it is a new form of matter! Don't be too surprised—it took nearly two hundred years to identify all the different kinds of atoms, and over the course of time, many new forms of atomic matter were discovered.

Because dark matter is not made of the same pieces as atoms, it is pretty much oblivious to atoms (and vice versa). Moreover, dark matter particles are oblivious to other dark matter particles. A physicist would say that dark matter particles interact with atoms and with themselves very weakly, if at all. Because of this fact, when our Galaxy and other galaxies formed, the dark matter remained in the very large and diffuse dark matter halo, while the atoms collided with one another and sank to the center of the dark halo, eventually forming stars and planets made almost completely of atoms.

The "shyness" of dark matter particles, then, is why stars, planets, and we are made of atoms and not of dark matter.

Nonetheless, dark matter particles are buzzing around our neighborhood—at any given time there is about one dark matter particle in a good-sized tea cup. And this is key to testing this bold idea. Dark matter particles are shy, but can occasionally leave a telltale signature in a very, very sensitive particle detector. For this reason, physicists have built large detectors and placed them underground (to shield them from the cosmic rays that bombard the surface of the Earth) to see if dark matter particles really do comprise our halo.

Even more exciting is creating new dark matter particles at a particle accelerator by turning energy into mass, according to Einstein's famous formula, $E = mc^2$.

The Large Hadron Collider in Geneva, Switzerland, the most powerful particle accelerator ever built, is trying to create and detect dark matter particles.

And satellites in the sky are looking for pieces of atoms that are created when dark matter particles in the halo occasionally collide and produce ordinary matter (the reverse of what particle accelerators are trying to do).

If one or more of these methods are successful—and I hope that at least one will be—we will be able to confirm that something other than atoms makes up the bulk of the matter in the Universe. Wow!

And now we are ready to talk about the biggest mystery in all science: *dark energy*. This is such a big puzzle that I am confident it will be around for one of you to solve. Solving it might even topple Einstein's theory of gravity, General Relativity!

We all know that the Universe is expanding, having grown in size for the past 13.7 billion years after the Big Bang. Since Edwin Hubble discovered the expansion more than eighty years ago, astronomers have been trying to measure the slowing of the expansion due to gravity. Gravity is the force that holds us to the Earth, keeps all the planets orbiting the Sun, and is generally nature's cosmic glue. Gravity is an attractive force—it pulls things together, slows down balls and rockets that are launched from Earth—and so the expansion of Universe should be slowing down due to all the stuff attracting all the other stuff.

In 1998 astronomers discovered that this simple but very logical idea couldn't be more *wrong*; they discovered that the expansion of the Universe is not slowing down, but instead it is *speeding up*. (They did this by using the time-machine aspect of telescopes: Because light takes time to travel from across the Universe to us, when we look at distant objects we see them as they were long ago. Using powerful telescopes—including the Hubble Space Telescope—they were able to determine that the Universe was expanding more slowly long ago.)

How can this be? According to Einstein's theory, some stuff—stuff even weirder than dark matter—has repulsive gravity. *Repulsive gravity* means gravity that pushes things apart rather than pulling them together, which is very strange indeed!) It goes by the name of *dark energy* and could be something as simple as the energy of quantum nothingness or as weird as the influence of additional space-time dimensions! Or there may be no dark energy at all, and we need to replace Einstein's Theory of General Relativity with something better.

Part of what makes dark energy such an important puzzle is the fact that it holds the fate of the Universe in its hands. Right now, dark energy is stepping on the gas pedal and the Universe is speeding up, suggesting that it will expand forever, with the sky returning to darkness in about one hundred billion years.

Since we don't understand dark energy, we can't rule out the possibility that it will put its foot on the brake at some time in the future, perhaps even causing the Universe to recollapse.

These are all challenges for the scientists of the future—you, maybe?—to explore and understand.

Michael

Chapter Thirteen

Eric was standing in the main control room at the LHC, in front of the CCTV screens that showed ATLAS, 100 meters (328 feet) below in its cave, one of the gargantuan detectors at the Large Hadron Collider. ATLAS was the largest of its kind ever built, a colossal piece of engineering that dwarfed the tiny human beings who had created its mighty bulk. But entry to the mile-long tunnels housing the accelerator, and the huge man-made caves housing ATLAS and the other detectors, was now forbidden, and all the doors were sealed. No one was allowed into that part of the underground complex while the LHC was running.

According to the official schedule, the start of the great experiment—complete with politicians pressing a red button—was still weeks away. This was meant to be the dress rehearsal, a time when the scientists could work out whether they had thought of everything and could sort out their last technical problems before the experiment began for real. However, everything had gone so well that the trial run was now indistinguishable from the real thing. The proton beams were already circling in opposite directions through the tunnels more than eleven thousand times per second, creating six hundred million collisions per second, and ATLAS was reading the collision data.

The Large Hadron Collider (LHC)

CERN

CERN—properly known as the European Organization for Nuclear Research—is an international particle physics laboratory on the border of France and Switzerland.

In 1990 a CERN scientist, Tim Berners-Lee, invented the World Wide Web as a way of allowing particle physicists to share information easily—now the Web is an everyday tool for many people!

Founded in 1954, CERN has been operating colliders for more than fifty years now as part of its research into fundamental particles.

In 1983, the Super Proton Synchrotron (SPS) collided protons and antiprotons (the antimatter version of the proton) together and discovered the W and Z particles, which carry the weak nuclear force. The SPS is built inside a circular tunnel 7 kilometers (4.3 miles) in circumference, and today feeds protons to the LHC.

In 1988, after three years of digging, a new 27-kilometer (17-mile)-circumference circular tunnel 100 meters (328 feet) underground was completed to house the Large Electron-Positron collider (LEP). The LEP collided electrons with positrons (the antimatter version of the electron).

In 1998, work began on digging the detector caverns for the LHC. The LEP was turned off in November 2000 to make way for this new collider in the same tunnel.

The LHC was fully turned on for the first time in September 2008.

The Large Hadron Collider (LHC)

THE LHC

This is world's largest particle accelerator.

Two beam pipes run along the 27-kilometer (17-mile) circular tunnel of the LHC, each carrying a beam of protons, traveling in opposite directions. It's like a huge electromagnetic racetrack!

Inside the pipes, almost all the air has been pumped out to create a vacuum like there is in outer space, so that the protons can travel without hitting air molecules.

The core of the LHC is the most lifeless place on Earth!

Because the tunnel is curved, more than 1200 powerful magnets around the tunnel bend the protons' course so that they don't hit the walls of the pipe. The magnets are superconducting, which means they can generate very large fields with very little loss of energy. This requires them to be cooled with liquid helium down to -456 degrees Farenheit (-271 degrees Celsius)—colder than outer space!

All in all, there are around 9,300 magnets at the LHC.

At full power, each proton will perform 11,245 laps of the ring per second, traveling at more than 99.99% of the speed of light. There will be up to six hundred million head-on collisions between protons per second.

As well as protons, the LHC is also designed to collide lead ions (nuclei of lead atoms).

THE GRID

With about one megabyte of data per collision, the LHC detectors produce too much data for even the most modern storage equipment. Computer algorithms select only the most interesting collision events—the rest, more than 99% of the data, are discarded.

Even so, the data from collisions at the LHC in one year is expected to be fifteen million gigabytes (which would fill seventeen thousand PCs with a two-hundred-gigabyte hard drive each). This creates a massive storage and processing problem, especially since the physicists who need the data are based all over the world.

The storage and processing is shared by sending the data rapidly over the Internet to computers in other countries. These computers, together with the computers at CERN, form the worldwide *LHC Computing Grid*.

The Large Hadron Collider (LHC)

The Detectors

The LHC has four main detectors situated in underground caverns at different points around the circumference of the tunnel. Special magnets are used to make the two beams collide at each of the four points along the ring where the detector caverns are situated.

ATLAS is the biggest particle detector ever built. It is 46 meters (151 feet) long, 25 meters (82 feet) high, 25 meters (82 feet) wide, and weighs 7,000 metric tons (15,432,359 pounds). It will identify the particles produced in high-energy collisions by tracing their flight through the detector and recording their energy.

CMS (Compact Muon Solenoid) uses a different design to study similar processes to ATLAS (having two different designs of detector helps to confirm any discoveries). It is 21 meters (69 feet) long, 15 meters (49 feet) wide, and 15 meters (49 feet) high, but weighs more than ATLAS at 14,000 metric tons (30,864,716 pounds).

ALICE (A Large Ion Collider Experiment) is designed specifically to search for quark-gluon plasma produced by colliding lead ions. This plasma is believed to have existed very soon after the Big Bang. ALICE is 26 meters (85 feet) long, 16 meters (52 feet) wide, 16 meters (52 feet) high, and weighs about 10,000 metric tons (22,046,226 pounds).

LHCb (Large Hadron Collider-beauty)—the "beauty" in the name of this experiment refers to the beauty, or *b* quark, which it is designed to study. The aim is to clarify the difference between matter and antimatter. It is 21 meters (69 feet) long, 10 meters (33 feet) high, 13 meters (43 feet) wide, and weighs 5,600 metric tons (12,345,886 pounds).

50m —

40m —

30m —

20m —

10m —

0m —

ATLAS
46 meters (Length)
25 meters (Width)
25 meters (Height)

CMS
21 meters (Length)
15 meters (Width)
15 meters (Height)

ALICE
26 meters (Length)
16 meters (Width)
16 meters (Height)

LHCb
21 meters (Length)
13 meters (Width)
10 meters (Height)

	Length	Width	Height
ATLAS 7,000 metric tons	46 meters	25 meters	25 meters
CMS 14,000 metric tons	21 meters	15 meters	15 meters
ALICE 10,000 metric tons	26 meters	16 meters	16 meters
LHCb 5,600 metric tons	21 meters	13 meters	10 meters

The Large Hadron Collider (LHC)

New Discoveries?

The Standard Model of particle physics describes the fundamental forces, the particles that transmit those forces, and three generations of matter particles.

But . . .

Only 4.6% of the Universe is made from the type of matter we know. What is the rest made of (the dark matter and dark energy)?

Why do elementary particles have masses? The Higgs boson—a particle predicted by the Standard Model but never observed—could explain this. Hopefully the LHC will see the Higgs for the first time.

Why does the Universe contain so much more matter than antimatter?

For a brief time, just after the Big Bang, quarks and gluons were so hot that they couldn't yet combine to form protons and neutrons—the Universe was filled with a strange state of matter called quark-gluon plasma. The LHC will re-create this plasma, and the ALICE experiment is set to detect and study it. In this way, scientists hope to learn more about the strong nuclear force and the development of the Universe.

New theories are trying to bring gravity (and space and time) into the same quantum theory that already describes the other forces and subatomic particles. Some of these ideas suggest there may be more than the familiar four dimensions of space-time. Collisions at the LHC could allow us to see these "extra dimensions," if they exist!

Even though the smooth running of the great experiment should have been a source of great happiness for Eric, instead it was a lonely and strange time. His colleagues and friends were sympathetic but distant. Until the Order resolved the dark cloud hanging over his name, Eric was a controversial figure whom people tended politely to avoid.

Even worse than the isolation from his peers, Eric realized he was on the cusp of becoming alienated from his work. The round of experiments being prepared were the most powerful of all, and might unlock the answers to the great questions of physics. But, Eric suddenly realized, if the meeting went against him and he was thrown out of the Order of Science, he would have to leave immediately; he might not be here to witness the most important moment in science since the Big Bang. No matter what the results of the experiment, Eric realized he might be banned from reading the data. Until he was reinstated as a trusted and responsible colleague, he remained a solitary and suspect individual, on the fringes of the scientific world. Was this, he wondered, what he himself had done to Dr. Reeper all those years ago? Was this how Reeper had felt when he found himself reviled and rejected by all his peers? Eric sank in gloom as he considered his future, spent far away from the work he loved above all else.

His pager beeped.

Meeting confirmed tonight at 19.30 hrs. Underground

trigger room, read the flashing letters. Eric gulped. At last, his fate would be decided.

Eric had been waiting for some time now. It had taken all the members of the Order of Science longer to get here than they had at first calculated. Eric didn't even have Cosmos for company. The supercomputer had been confiscated the minute he had stepped onto the tarmac in Switzerland from his small jet. Dr. Ling, the Chinese scientist who had spotted Eric and George on the Moon, had been waiting for him at the airfield.

"I'm so sorry, Eric," Dr. Ling had said, looking very embarrassed, unable to meet Eric's eye as the rain poured down from the night sky, "but you must hand Cosmos over immediately."

"What will happen to him?" asked Eric.

"He will be interviewed by The Grid," said Dr. Ling. "The Grid will review all Cosmos's activities since he was put in your care."

An image of Freddy flashed into Eric's mind. He wondered what The Grid, the vast and sprawling computer network that analyzed data from the Large Hadron Collider, would make of Cosmos and Eric transporting a pig from a farmyard to a peaceful rural setting. And of Eric and George's recent trip to the Moon—not to mention his various journeys around the Universe with not one but two kids in tow.

The Grid was one of the mightiest computers in the world, but he wasn't like Cosmos. Cosmos had a special power that The Grid completely lacked: He had empathy, and this allowed him to be creative, making him the world's most intelligent computer. Despite his name, The Grid was unable to bypass his own rigid rules or make intuitive connections between different pieces of information. In a straight contest, Eric knew clever little Cosmos would win every time against the enormous bully. But even so, Eric was sad to see his little silver friend taken away for such a challenging experience.

As he waited in the main control room Eric looked at the clock. Not long to go now until the meeting to decide his fate. He was still baffled by the speed at which his life had unraveled. Was it really so drastic, that photo taken on the Moon? Did it really merit this extraordinary meeting of the Order? Weren't they making a very big mountain out of what was, after all, just a lunar molehill?

A scientist walked past him, nose in the air, attempting to evade Eric's gaze.

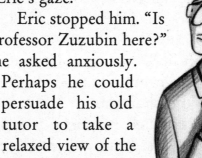

Eric stopped him. "Is Professor Zuzubin here?" he asked anxiously. Perhaps he could persuade his old tutor to take a relaxed view of the incident. Maybe Zuzubin would ask the Order to go easy on Eric, provided he promised never to do anything like this again . . . ?

"Zuzubin?" said the scientist. "He's gone."

"Gone?" said Eric in surprise. "But I thought he called this meeting! Why wouldn't he stay when the result must be so important to him?" The other scientist didn't hang around to answer him, so Eric was left alone with his thoughts once more.

Something was very wrong here. The meeting had been arranged too quickly and on too flimsy an excuse. Zuzubin, who'd seemed to be in charge, had suddenly vanished, and Cosmos was now handcuffed to The Grid, being examined circuit by circuit. This, Eric suddenly realized, was not the way things should be. Something was very wrong indeed. But what could he do?

He looked at his cell phone. The screen was blank. Even here in the main control room, the Grid exerted a powerful blocking signal, meaning you could only use the internal paging system or the LHC phone network. Anyway, he realized with a shock, he didn't have anyone to call. The only person who would unquestioningly believe him was George, and this really wasn't the moment to bring a kid into this difficult and uncomfortable situation.

Sighing, Eric felt he might as well switch off his phone before the battery died. He mooched around the control room for a few more minutes but suddenly felt he couldn't stand it any longer. There was only one thing for it. Faced with the hostility and suspicion of his peers, bored of his isolation and lack of activity, and frustrated at the manner in which his opinion was being disregarded, Eric decided he would go for a long, soothing walk.

Chapter Fourteen

George shot out of the silver tunnel and landed on his belly, skidding across his bedroom floor. He lay there, panting, until he realized that, as on the asteroid, he was not alone. This time, two pairs of feet in sneakers were waiting for him. He rolled over onto his back. Through the window of his space helmet, two blurred faces peered down at him, distorted by the curved glass. One was fringed with blonde hair and had round, worried blue eyes. The other, topped by a plume of black spikes, looked totally astonished.

"George"—the smaller figure shook him—"you're back! You shouldn't have gone by yourself!"

Who were these people? George struggled to place them. It was as if they'd met once, in a strange dream, and he could no longer remember why or how he knew them. Lights danced in front of his eyes as he battled with the shifting, multi-colored cloud inside his head to form thoughts that meant something. But they just seemed to evaporate into the mist in his brain before he could seize on any of them to make sense of what was happening to him.

The taller figure grabbed George's hands in their space gloves and pulled him to his feet. But George couldn't stand up. It was as though his bones had melted and his muscles turned to mush.

"Oh, man!" the larger figure said, catching George as he crumpled to the floor. George's vision went in and out of focus, the swirling silver light of the tunnel still turning before his eyes. "Where did you come from? *What* was *that*?"

Looking around blearily, George could just about see that the portal had closed again and Pooky was still and quiet. Only these two facts seemed to signify anything to his confused mind. This strange person had him in his arms now, half-carrying him to the bed, where he laid George down, still wearing his space suit and perched uncomfortably on top of his oxygen tank. A pair of hands undid the clasp on his space helmet and took it off, then mopped George's soaking face with a corner of the duvet cover.

"Water!" shouted the smaller figure. "Get him some water!"

The other person dashed out of the room, coming back with a mug in his hands. "Here, drink this." He dribbled a few drops into George's mouth.

The small person was tugging off George's space boots. "George! It's me—Annie. Vincent, help me!" she ordered. "We need to get him out of this space suit."

They each took a boot, unclipped the fasteners, and pulled, both flying backward with a thump as they suddenly released George's feet from the heavy boots. But this didn't stop them for a second—they just got up and rushed back over to George, who was looking worse by the minute. His face was white as a sheet, except for his cheeks, which were mottled with bright pink patches, and his eyes rolled around

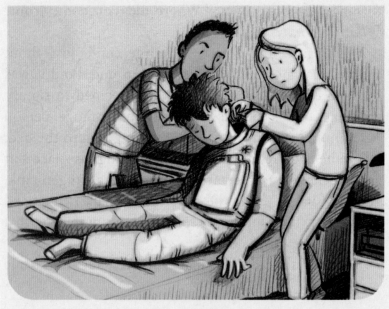

in their sockets as he tried and failed to focus them.

"What's happened to him?" cried Vincent as Annie sat George upright and unsnapped the oxygen tank from his back.

"Unzip him," she commanded.

Vincent unzipped the suit and dragged George's arms out of it. "Stand up," he said, lifting George up so that he could pull off the space suit, revealing George's shirt and jeans underneath.

George just flopped into Vincent's arms, as though he had no bones in his body. Vincent laid him carefully back down on the bed, using a T-shirt he found on the floor to wipe George's face, which was again covered in beads of sweat.

"The suit!" shouted Annie. "Give me the suit!" Vincent threw the heavy suit over to her and she started rifling through the pockets. "Where is it?" she muttered.

"He doesn't look so good," warned Vincent. "Shall I call a doctor?"

Annie looked up from the suit. "And say what?" she asked desperately. "*Our friend got back from space and he's not feeling well*? How can we explain that he traveled through an unauthorized portal that clearly wasn't safe?" Her voice was rising hysterically. Some green drool was now snaking out of George's mouth and dribbling down his chin.

"Help me!" said Annie. "Help me find the emergency space drops—they're in one of these pockets."

Vincent slid off the bed and grabbed the other half of the suit, which he patted all over, trying to feel for something in its depths. "Is this it?" He'd located a small plastic bottle in an arm pocket. SPACE RESCUE REMEDY it said in cheery red letters on the bottle. Vincent read out the words on the label. "*Do you need a space rescue? Have you had a bad space experience? Nausea? Loss of vision? Muscles turned to glue? Hair loss?*" He looked anxiously at George, who still seemed to have a full head of hair.

"Give!" shouted Annie.

"Have you taken this before?" said Vincent suspiciously, holding onto the bottle.

"Never needed to," she admitted. "But Dad always told us to take it if we were travel-sick after a space journey."

"Where does it come from?" said Vincent.

"We get it from Space Adventures R Us. They send it with each space suit my dad buys," said Annie. "But I never imagined we'd actually use it."

Vincent tossed it over to her and noticed that George was now twitching violently. Annie gently squirted a few drops from the nozzle of the small bottle into George's mouth. Some of the amber liquid oozed out between his numb lips, which were now turning blue.

"Please, planets and stars," muttered Annie, "make

this work for George!" She carefully squirted a few more drops into his mouth.

"Did you check the dose?" Vincent asked her.

"It's okay," she said. "The bottle only contains one dose, so you can't take too much; that's what Dad said."

As she spoke, George's lips started turning pink again, and his face was changing from mottled white and pink to its usual healthy color. His breathing slowed from rapid gasps to a gentle whoosh, and his eyelids fluttered as the Space Rescue Remedy ran though his system, putting right the things the cosmic journey had messed up.

"Oh, George!" said Annie—and burst into tears. Vincent came over to give her a hug—just as George's eyes opened again.

"What the . . . ?" mumbled George.

Annie and Vincent sprang apart and rushed over to either side of the bed.

"George! You're alive!" Annie kissed him sloppily on the cheek.

George's head was pounding. "Annie . . . ?" he mumbled. "Is that you?"

"It's me!" she said joyfully. "And Vincent," she added. "We saved you! You came through some weird-looking tunnel in your space suit and started having a fit."

"I had a fit?" repeated George, who was feeling stronger by the second. He sat up and looked around his bedroom.

"You were dribbling," said Vincent helpfully. "And your eyes had gone crazy."

George lay back down on the bed and let his eyelids close. This was all super-weird. He tried to remember what had happened, but the only image he could focus on was Annie hugging Vincent when he'd come out of his brightly colored delirium.

"George," she said urgently. "Where were you? What were you doing, out in space without us?"

"*Us?*"

"Me and Vincent," said Annie, a touch impatiently now that she could see George was going to be fine. "We would have come with you, if you'd just waited. We got here as quickly as we could, once you stopped talking on the phone."

"How did you get in the house?" George's brain had not yet recovered enough to take him back to space—it could only deal with the details of what was going on immediately around him.

A wail from downstairs answered the question. "Your mom and the twins," said Annie. "Daisy let us in."

"Does she know? About the space portal?" said George, sitting up again in panic.

"No, she's too busy with the babies—they make so much noise, I don't think she heard anything," said Annie.

"Here, drink this." Vincent handed George a mug of water.

George took a huge gulp and then nearly spat it out. "What is that?" he said in disgust.

"Sorry," said Vincent. "It's the toothbrush mug. It was the first thing that came to hand."

"C'mon," urged Annie. "C'mon, George, *think*! Where have you been? Why did you go?"

George's mind snapped into focus. It all came whooshing back to him, brilliantly clear and very, very urgent.

"Oh, holy supersymmetric strings . . . ," he said slowly, using Emmett the computer geek's favorite phrase. He looked at Annie and Vincent, deciding on what to say. "Vincent, can I trust you?"

"I think you have to," said Annie, putting her arm around George, "given what he's just seen. And he helped save your life. Just tell us, George—what happened to you out there?"

He thought for a second. There was more at stake here than just his feelings. He might not be super-fond of Vincent, but the karate kid was here now, and obviously he knew everything.

George took a deep breath. "I've seen Reeper," he told them.

"So he was there," said Annie, "waiting for you."

"That's the creepy guy, right?" said Vincent, reaching over and taking a swig out of George's toothbrush mug.

"Um—yeah," said George. "He took me out to an asteroid in Andromeda."

"Andromeda!" squeaked Annie. "Wow! I've never been that far." She almost sounded jealous.

"I wouldn't recommend it." George grimaced. "I don't think Pooky's portal would pass any safety checks."

"You looked rough, man," said Vincent admiringly.  "You must be made of strong stuff."

"Er, thanks," said George.

At that moment his mom knocked on the door and poked her head in. "I brought you some broccoli and spinach muffins!" She passed a plate into the room.

"Thanks, Mrs. G," said Annie, swiftly taking the plate and

blocking the doorway until Daisy had disappeared downstairs, summoned by another angry wail from one of the twins. "They look delicious!" Annie called after her.

Vincent, who was always hungry, fell on the plate of muffins with a little cry of joy. As he tasted them, his expression changed from delight to surprise.

"Oh my God!" he exclaimed through a mouthful of crumbs.

Annie kicked him sharply before he could make any rude comments about Daisy's cooking. It was all right for her and George to laugh about it, but suddenly she realized that it wasn't okay for Vincent to make fun of George's mom.

"I just meant this tastes like serious energy food," Vincent assured her. "Like we eat before a karate championship. That's all. No wonder George is a man of steel, if this is what he lives on."

"What time is it?" asked George.

Vincent checked his watch. "Five-o-six," he replied.

"Five! We haven't got long! Hold on—what time is it in Switzerland?"

"Six-o-six," said Vincent.

"Right, we have to work fast," said George, speaking as quickly as he could. "Annie, you told me that the meeting of the Order is at seven thirty tonight. Reeper said that TOERAG has a bomb—a quantum mechanical bomb—and I bet they've primed it to go off when the meeting starts so that the Collider—and everyone near it—will be blown to kingdom come, and science will be set back by centuries."

"A quantum mechanical bomb?" said Annie, looking almost as sick as George had been a few minutes earlier. "What's *that*?"

"Well, I know what it *is*," confessed George, "but I'm not sure how to turn it off. We'd better take this with us." He picked up Pooky's string of numbers. "I'm not sure, but it might be the code to defuse the bomb. Or one of them, anyway."

"What makes you think Reeper is telling the truth?" demanded Annie.

"We can't know for sure, but I think he's on our side this time. And Eric's side. Reeper wants to stop the Collider and everyone around it from being blown up by those weirdos we saw in the cellar when we were looking for somewhere to put Freddy."

"How can you trust this Reeper guy?" threw in Vincent. "Hasn't he always double-crossed you in the past?"

Annie had pulled her cell phone out of her pocket. She tried calling her dad, but she couldn't get through. She couldn't even leave a message.

"I don't know if we can," said George. "We're taking a chance on him. But if we don't do something, it's likely that the Collider will explode during the meeting of the Order of Science this evening."

"How can we get there in time?" cried Annie. "We'd need to travel through a portal to do that, and we haven't got Cosmos!"

"There is another portal," said George, finally working it out in his head and discovering the missing link he had been searching for since his visit to the Math Department, "and I know where it is!"

"Where?" said Annie in confusion. "I thought Cosmos was the only supercomputer in the world—apart from Pooky, who isn't safe."

"You're right," agreed George. "We can't use Pooky again—we don't know how, and his portal is no good anyway. But we do know how to use *new* Cosmos, which means we might be able to operate *old* Cosmos."

"*Old* Cosmos . . . ?"

"Do you remember your dad's lecture?" George's brain was now working at the speed of light. "That crummy professor, Zuzubin, was there. He's the one who told Eric he had to go to Switzerland, and he's the one who called the emergency meeting of the Order of Science to Benefit Humanity."

"So what?" said Annie. "What are you saying?"

"When we left the Math Department, Zuzubin didn't

follow us," George continued. "He went down the stairs, instead of coming out."

"And . . . ?"

"Your dad once told us that when he was a student at Foxbridge, old Cosmos—the first supercomputer—lived in the basement of the Math Department. And after your dad's lecture, I saw Zuzubin go down the stairs to the basement when we were going out of the front door. *And* I saw him wearing a pair of yellow glasses, just like the ones Eric found when he fell into the black hole. Which means that someone has been traveling around the Universe, dropping stuff."

"And to do that, they must have a supercomputer," said Annie, catching on. "So you think that old Cosmos is in the basement of the Math Department and Zuzubin has been using him . . . ?"

"But Annie's dad was a student, like, zillions of years ago," Vincent pointed out. "Surely that computer's been shut down by now."

"That's what we're supposed to think," said George. "We're supposed to think that old Cosmos doesn't work. But if he does, and he can send Zuzubin to look at black holes, he could also send us to the Collider in time to defuse the quantum mechanical bomb."

"But why would Zuzubin keep a secret like that?" asked Annie.

"I don't know . . ." George's voice was full of foreboding. "But I think we're about to find out. We need

© CERN

Looking back to the beginning of time with the LHC (Large Hadron Collider)—an international project based in Europe.

NASA, ESA, S. Beckwith (STScI), and the Hubble Heritage Team (STScI/AURA)

NASA, ESA, M. Regan and B. Whitmore (STScI), and R. Chandar (University of Toledo)

Two dramatically different views of the Whirlpool Galaxy.

NASA, ESA, A. Feild (STScI), and P. van Dokkum (Yale University)

The comparative sizes of our Milky Way galaxy (left) and an ultracompact galaxy in the early Universe (right). Both have the same number of stars!

The formative years of spiral galaxies—shown here by four barred spiral galaxies at varied distances from the Earth.

NASA, ESA, and Z. Levay (STScI)

6.4 billion light-years

NASA, ESA, and Z. Levay (STScI)

5.3 billion light-years

NASA, ESA, and Z. Levay (STScI)

3.8 billion light-years

NASA, ESA, and Z. Levay (STScI)

2.1 billion light-years

Cosmic ice sculptures in the Carina Nebula . . .

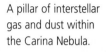

A pillar of interstellar gas and dust within the Carina Nebula.

NASA, ESA, and M. Livio and the Hubble 20th Anniversary Team (STScI)

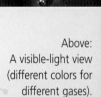

Above:
A visible-light view (different colors for different gases).

Right:
An infra-red view (colors assigned to different wavelengths).

to get to the Math Department. As fast as we can. Zuzubin will be at the Large Hadron Collider for the meeting, so we should be able to try old Cosmos."

He and Annie thumped down the stairs two at a time, sped out of the door, and got their bikes, with Vincent following closely behind. "What I don't get . . . ," Annie's friend said as he hopped onto his skateboard. "Why math? What has math got to do with anything? It's just a bunch of numbers on a blackboard that all add up to another number. What's that got to do with the Universe anyway? What use is math to anyone?"

HOW MATHEMATICS IS SURPRISINGLY USEFUL IN UNDERSTANDING THE UNIVERSE

It is obvious that some things in our everyday world are simple and others complex. We know our Sun will come up day after day exactly on time, but the weather changes in annoying and haphazard ways—unless like me you live in Arizona, where it is almost always warm and sunny. So you can set your alarm clock the night before and be sure you will wake up at the right time of day, but if you choose your clothes ahead of time you might get it badly wrong.

Those things that are simple, regular, and dependable can be described by *numbers*, like the number of hours in a day, or the number of days in a year. We can also use numbers to describe complicated things like the weather—such as the highest temperature each day—but in that case it's often hard to spot any patterns in the numbers.

Our ancestors noticed many patterns in nature: not just day and night, but the seasons, the movements of the Moon, stars, and planets in the sky, and the rise and fall of the tides. Sometimes they used numbers to describe the patterns; sometimes they used songs or poetry instead. Many ancient peoples went to a lot of effort with numbers and patterns to describe the movement of heavenly bodies. They liked to predict eclipses—scary but exciting events where the Moon blots out the light of the Sun and you can see the stars in the daytime. Knowing when an eclipse would happen required lots of boring calculations, and they didn't always get it right. But when they did, people were impressed.

Long ago, nobody knew why numbers and simple patterns occur so often in nature. But about four hundred years ago, some people began to study the patterns more carefully. Especially in Europe, there were beautiful and quite skillfully made instruments to help observe and measure things accurately. People had clocks and sundials and all sorts of metal gadgets for distances and angles and times. Eventually they had small telescopes, too. These curious people called themselves "natural philosophers"—and were what we would now call scientists.

One thing natural philosophers puzzled over was *motion*. At first, there seemed to be two sorts: stars and planets moving in the sky, and objects moving around on Earth. Everybody knows that when you throw a ball it travels in a curved path, and it doesn't take too many tries to see that the curve is always the same if the ball is thrown at the same speed and angle.

Of course, our ancestors were well aware that moving objects followed simple predictable paths. They knew it because their lives depended on it. Hunters needed to be sure that when a stone left a sling or an arrow left a bow, it would behave the same way today as it did yesterday. In Australia, the ancient people known as Aboriginals were so ingenious they could make a flat stick called a boomerang, and when it was thrown it would follow a special path that would cause it to curve back toward the thrower.

THE LATEST SCIENTIFIC THEORIES

By the sixteenth century, mathematics had gone some way beyond simple arithmetic, to include algebra and other fancy methods, and the natural philosophers were able to write down equations to describe many of the patterns found in nature. In particular, they could write equations to describe curves like the paths of arrows and balls. For example, a simple equation describes a circle, a slightly different one a squashed circle called an ellipse, and yet another describes the curve of a rope hanging between two poles. Using this more advanced mathematics, a huge variety of patterns and shapes could be described not just in words, but in symbols and equations, written on paper and printed for other scientists and mathematicians to study.

Useful though all this was, it was still just a description of patterns in nature, not an explanation. The big breakthrough began with the work of Galileo Galilei in Italy in the early seventeenth century. Everybody knows that when an object is dropped from a height, it rushes toward the ground faster and faster. Galileo wanted to make this precise: How much faster does it go after one second, two seconds, three seconds . . . ? Was there a pattern? He found the answer by experimenting—he tried dropping things and timing them. He rolled balls down slopes so everything happened more slowly and easily. Then he sat down with all the measurements and did some arithmetic and algebra, until he found a single formula that correctly describes the way that all falling bodies *accelerate*; that is, go faster and faster as they fall.

Galileo's formula is pretty simple: If the object is

dropped from rest its speed increases in proportion to the time it has been falling. This means that when the object has been falling for two seconds it's going exactly twice as fast as it was at one second. And there's more. If the object is thrown from a height at an angle instead of just dropped, it will still fall in the same way but it will also move horizontally, and Galileo's formula says that the shape of the path the object follows is a *parabola*—one of the curves mathematicians already knew about from studying geometry.

The decisive step came when Isaac Newton in England worked out how objects like balls change their motion (that is, accelerate or decelerate) when they are pushed or pulled by forces. He wrote down a very simple equation to describe it.

In the case of Galileo's falling objects, the force concerned is, of course, *gravity*. We feel the force of gravity all the time. Newton suggested that the Earth pulls everything downward, toward its center, with a force proportional to the amount of matter the object contains (known as its mass). Newton's equation connecting force and acceleration then explained Galileo's formula for falling bodies.

But this was just the start. Newton also suggested that not just the Earth, but every object in the Universe—including the Sun, Moon, planets, stars, and even people—pull on every other object with a force of gravity that gets weaker with distance in a precise way, called an *inverse square*. That's a fancy way of saying that at *twice* the distance from the center of the Earth (or the Sun, or the Moon) the force is one-*quarter* as strong; at *three* times the distance it is one-*ninth*, and so on.

Using this formula plus his equation for how force and acceleration are related, Newton was able to do some cool mathematics (some of which he invented) to work out how planets and comets move around the Sun, pulled by the Sun's gravity. He also calculated how the Moon goes around the Earth. And the numbers all came out right! More than that, the *shapes* of the orbits were also correctly described by his calculations. For example, astronomers had measured that the orbits of the planets are ellipses, and the great Newton showed they *should* be—from his calculations! No wonder everybody thought he was a hero and a genius. The government was so pleased they put him in charge of printing all England's money.

The really important thing about Newton's work on motion and gravitation is deeper, however. He proposed that his formula for gravity and his equation for force and acceleration were *laws of nature*. That is, they should be the same everywhere in the Universe and at all times, and can never change—rather like God, whom Newton believed in. Before Newton, some people thought the motions of objects on Earth, like balls and boats and birds, had nothing to do with the motions of bodies in the sky, like the Moon and planets. Now we knew they all obeyed the same laws. While other scientists had *described* motion, Newton *explained* it in terms of mathematical laws.

In practical terms, this was a huge leap forward, because now anyone could sit in a chair and work out how such-and-such an object would move, without ever seeing it, or even leaving the room. For example, you can calculate where a cannonball will land if it is fired at a certain speed and angle. You can work out how fast it would need to go to fly off the Earth and never come back. Using Newton's simple equations, engineers can figure out exactly how to point a rocket to send a spacecraft to the Moon or Mars—before they even have the money to build the rocket.

All this made physics—the study of the basic laws of the Universe—a *predictive* science. Physicists could play with their equations and predict things that nobody knew before, like the existence of unknown planets. Uranus and Neptune were found after astronomers used Newton's laws to work out where in the sky they should be, and we now use those laws to predict the existence of planets going around other stars.

Very soon physicists began applying the same ideas to other forces, like electricity and magnetism, and sure enough, they were found to obey simple mathematical laws, too. Then atoms and their nuclei were studied, and they also can be explained in detail with mathematical formulas. So there are now quite a number of equations in physics textbooks.

Some physicists wonder whether it will go on like this forever, or whether all the laws and equations can be merged in some way, into some super-duper law that contains all the others. Quite a lot of smart people have peered at the equations to look for links, and a few have been found that turned out to be right.

A famous example was when James Clerk Maxwell, a Scottish physicist in the nineteenth century, found that the laws of electricity and magnetism could be joined, and when he had done that he solved the equations and discovered that the combined *electromagnetic* force could generate waves of electromagnetism. When he worked out the speed of the waves from his equations, he found it was the same as the speed of light. Bingo! Light must be an electromagnetic wave, he said.

The quest for a super-duper law combining *all* the forces goes on. It needs a really bright youngster to pull everything together.

When I was a schoolboy, I liked a pretty girl called Lindsay. One day I was doing a homework problem in physics. I had to calculate (that is, predict) what angle to throw a ball for it to go the maximum distance up a hill of a certain slope. Lindsay (who was studying liberal arts) sat opposite me in the school library, which was nice, although it made me a little nervous. She asked what I was doing, and when I described the problem she remarked in wonderment, "But how can you find out what a ball will do by writing things on a piece of paper?" At the time I thought this was a silly question. After all, this was my homework! But Lindsay had actually touched on a very deep issue. Why can we use simple mathematical laws to describe, and even predict, things that go on in the world around us? Where do the laws come from? That is, why does nature have laws at all? And even if for some reason there have to be laws of nature, why are they so simple (like the inverse square law of gravity)? We can imagine a universe with mathematical laws that are so subtle and complicated that even the brainiest human mathematician would be baffled.

Nobody knows why the Universe can be explained with simple mathematics, or why human brains are good enough to work it all out. Maybe we just got lucky? Some people think there is a Mathematician God who made the Universe that way. Scientists are not very interested in gods, though. Could it be that life will arise only if the Universe has simple mathematical laws, so nature *has* to be mathematical or we wouldn't be here arguing about it? Perhaps there are many universes, each with laws different from our own, and maybe some with no laws to speak of at all. These other universes may be devoid of scientists and mathematicians. Or maybe not.

To be honest, it's all a mystery, and most scientists think it's not part of their job to worry about it. They just take the mathematical laws of nature as a fact, and get on with their calculations.

I'm not one of them. I lie awake at night turning it all over in my mind. I'd like an answer. But whether or not there is a reason for the mathematical simplicity of the Universe, it's clear that physics and mathematics are deeply interwoven, and that we will always need people who can do experiments and people who can do mathematics. And they had better keep talking to each other!

Paul

Chapter Fifteen

Geoorge and Annie pedaled furiously past Foxbridge's curiously shaped citadels of learning, Vincent curving gracefully beside them on his skateboard. The town was full of old and beautiful buildings, where for centuries scholars had dreamed up great theories, explaining the Universe and all its wonders to a world that only sometimes wanted to know.

Some of the colleges looked like fortresses—for good reason. Throughout the ages they had at times been forced to lock their gates to keep out angry mobs, furious at some of the new ideas their scholars had propounded. Gravity, for example. The orbit of the Earth around the Sun, rather than the other way around. Evolution. The Big Bang. The double helix of DNA, and the possibilities of life in other universes. The walls of these colleges were thick, with tiny windows to protect those within from a real and often unfriendly world outside.

The three children scooted into the court-yard of the Math Department,

throwing the bikes against the black railings and running up the steps to the front entrance. Today the glass doors just swung in the breeze, and no one stopped them as they dashed into the hallway. They were greeted only by the familiar smell of chalk dust and old socks, and by the distant clank of the tea tray being unloaded.

"Don't take the elevator!" hissed Annie as Vincent started to press the button. "It's too noisy! Let's go down the stairs."

Vincent parked his precious skateboard under the notice board in the hallway—he noticed ads for enticing events such as DOUBLY PERIODIC MONOPOLES: A 3D INTEGRABLE SYSTEM or THE EARLY UNIVERSE: TRANSITIONAL PHASES!—and the three of them tiptoed down the steps to the basement, George first, Annie next, and Vincent following behind.

When they reached the bottom of the stairs, they found that the dim lights in the basement were already on. They could just about see across the big room: It turned out to be full of junk—old office equipment, discarded computers, broken chairs, splintered desks, and reams and reams of computer paper. They picked their way cautiously through the terrible mess, guided by the sound of a computer whirring away somewhere behind the wall of debris. It soon became clear that they were not alone in the basement. Above the sound of the computer they heard a very clear and very human voice.

"No!" A howl of frustration. "Why, you stupid computer, won't you let me do what I want to do?"

Moving carefully forward—Annie and George in front, with Vincent, who was taller, poised behind them—they could see through the mess to where an old man in a tweed suit was attempting to operate an enormous computer. It stretched across one whole wall of the basement, such an antique that it was made up of compartments, what looked like cupboard doors, and great stacks of machinery, all piled on top of each other. In the middle was a monitor screen, on which the old man seemed to be watching a film. Only the top half of the set showed a picture—the bottom half had text scrolling across it in bright green letters on a black background.

"It's Professor Zuzubin," George whispered into Annie's ear. "He's here! He should be at the Collider— he said it was a meeting for all the Order of Science to Benefit Humanity and that means him as well."

"What's he doing?" asked Annie, speaking into George's ear in turn. They watched, agog, as Zuzubin ran the footage again in reverse, and the words scrolled backward off the bottom half of the screen. He pressed PLAY and the film started once more. As they watched the images, they could see a man who looked like a much younger version of Zuzubin himself, standing at the front of a packed auditorium in front of an old-fashioned overhead projector.

"It's the lecture hall where your dad gave his talk!" said George to Annie. "It's Zuzubin, and he's giving a lecture at Foxbridge!"

"He once had Dad's job," she murmured. "He was a math professor here."

"Maybe he wants his old job back," muttered George grimly; he didn't like the look of what he was seeing. "Look—in the audience! It's your dad!"

In the film, a young man with a thick shock of black hair, wonky glasses, and a big smile had just stood up.

"It *is* my dad!" said Annie, tears coming to her eyes. "Oh my God! I can't believe he was ever that young! What's he doing?"

Old Cosmos answered that question for them. "Professor Zuzubin," he said in a mechanical voice, speaking the words the young Eric was mouthing on the screen. "I have shown that your theory contains a flaw!" In typical Eric style, he looked as though

Zuzubin should be pleased by his remarks.

In the film, Zuzubin kept smiling, although his grin was becoming fixed onto his face as though stuck on with superglue.

Eric continued in the voice of old Cosmos: "I have shown that the model of the Universe that you propose violates the weak energy condition."

On the screen, Zuzubin's nostrils flared and he looked angry.

A singularity is a place where the mathematics used by physicists goes horribly wrong! For example, as you approach the center of a black hole—one type of singularity—space-time curvature grows to infinity and the normal rules of mathematics fail at the exact center (they say to divide by zero, which everyone knows isn't allowed!).

Sometimes a physics calculation makes an assumption that turns out to be wrong at a particular point, and a singularity is found. Once this is understood, the calculation can be adapted so that the error is fixed, the math works properly, and the singularity disappears. Good result!

The more interesting singularities are harder to get rid of and suggest that a new theory is needed. For example, black hole and Big Bang singularities occur in the math of General Relativity. Perhaps a theory with very different math is needed to understand what is really going on, and to get sensible results at such places in the Universe.

This is a busy area of research for scientists who hope that a Theory of Everything will get rid of these singularities.

The Big Bang

the space-time curvature becomes
infinite

the density of matter becomes
infinite

the temperature becomes
infinite

the space containing all we see around us
in the Universe reaches
zero size

and all paths going back in time come . . .
to an end.

This singularity is also known as an *initial singularity*
because it sits at the beginning of time.

"Bellis," recited old Cosmos, the words scrolling along on the text screen. "Your theories concerning this 'Big Bang' are interesting, but impossible to prove."

"I believe not!" said the young Eric. "The recently discovered microwave background radiation provides direct evidence in favor of the Big Bang model. Furthermore, I am firmly of the opinion that one day we will be able to build a great experiment that will show that the mathematical theories I have developed here at Foxbridge with my colleagues"—he gestured modestly to the people sitting around him—"are consistent with reality."

The real-life Zuzubin pressed PAUSE, and the picture froze. He frantically hammered the command buttons on Cosmos's keyboard. A little paintbrush appeared on the screen. Zuzubin swirled it around using a computer mouse he had attached to old Cosmos. The little paintbrush swept ineffectively over the picture, but nothing changed.

"Pah!" exclaimed Zuzubin. "Why won't this work!" he muttered to himself. "In that case, I shall try something else . . ."

He deleted all the text visible on the screen. Typing rapidly, he inserted the words: *Not so. The properties of the zuzon particle are the key to understanding the relationship between the four forces and the creation of matter. I predict that any experiment at the energy scale you propose will end in a dramatic and life-threatening explosion, which will prove that my theories about the*

*nature of fundamental particles and the dynamics of the
Universe are correct.*

But as soon as Zuzubin typed in the new text, the
cursor moved back and erased it again, replacing it with
the original speech.

"It's not a movie," murmured George. "It's the *past*!
He's using Cosmos to view himself in the past, giving
a lecture at Foxbridge! And he's trying to change it—it
looks like he's made Cosmos some kind of Photoshop
program to change what he said and did back then."

"Why?" asked Annie.

"He's trying to make it look like he predicted what's
about to happen," said George. "He's using Cosmos to
go back and change the past to make *his* theories look
right—and your dad's wrong. And he's trying to show
that he predicted that the Collider would explode."

Zuzubin had been too focused on what he was doing
to notice any noise the kids might have made. But even
he couldn't ignore the sound of George's cell phone
bursting into song as the theme song from *Star Wars*
rang through the basement.

George acted quickly. He dropped the phone on the
floor, kicking it back toward Vincent, who knelt down
to scoop it up, pressing END CALL and changing the
ringtone to SILENT.

But it was too late. Zuzubin was on to them. Turning
around, he glared—and then smiled as he saw two pairs
of eyes staring back at him from the carefully arranged

mountain of junk that he'd been using to hide the original supercomputer from the rest of the world.

"Ah, George!" he said, baring his teeth in a grin. "And look—my friend, little Annie. Come forward, my dear children. Come, come! Annie, I held you on my knee as a baby—you have nothing to fear from me!"

George and Annie had no choice. As they stepped forward, Vincent stayed down among the old furniture. Realizing that Zuzubin might not have spotted him, he figured that if he could hide in the basement, he might be able to  help Annie and George if they got into trouble. Vincent hadn't understood much of what the old scientist had said, but it was clear to him that anyone who was trying to change the past to make himself right and someone else wrong was not a person to be trusted.

"Annie," cooed Zuzubin. "So grown-up! So tall! So clever! How nice it is to see you again. But why so worried, children? Why so anxious? What can Professor Zuzubin do for you? Tell me, my dears. You can trust me!"

George pinched Annie to stop her speaking, but it

was no good. Annie was desperate enough to believe anyone who told her they could help.

"Professor Zuzubin...," she said in a quavering voice. The old man reached behind and surreptitiously turned off old Cosmos's monitor, so that the film of the past was no longer playing.

"We need to get to the Large Hadron Collider," Annie continued. "Something terrible is going to happen there! We must save my dad! We want you to send us to the LHC using old Cosmos, so that we get there in time to stop the bomb from going off."

"Your father is in trouble?" Zuzubin pretended to be concerned. "A bomb? The LHC? No, I don't believe it! Not Eric, surely . . ." He trailed off, viewing George with a suspicious eye.

"Don't say any more . . ." George was only whispering to Annie, but Zuzubin heard him.

"Whyever not?" he said. "Eric was my favorite pupil, my best ever success story. If he needs my help, then it would be my honor and privilege to provide it." He bowed low to show that this was indeed so.

Annie turned to George. "We don't have any other options," she said wildly. "There's no one else we can ask!"

"So you want to go to the Collider!" said Zuzubin smoothly. "Sure, that is no problem. You can be there in under a second." He entered a few commands on the keyboard, his hand hovering on a doorway into the great computer.

"When I open this door," Zuzubin purred, "Cosmos will take you directly to the place you need to be—directly to the right destination for you. You, Annie, can be the hero today. You, Annie, will solve all the problems and make everything good once more."

Annie's eyes sparkled. For once, *she* would be the hero. For once, *she* would be the person who made a difference, the one who saved the day. Not her dad, not her mom, not George. *Her.*

"I'll do it!" she said decisively. "Take me to the Collider!"

"Oh, but you can't travel alone," tutted Zuzubin, shaking his head. "Your little friend will have to travel with you. It must be you *and* George, or I cannot open Cosmos to transport you."

"Annie . . ." George tugged frantically at her T-shirt. "No! That doesn't make sense!"

"I don't care!" declared Annie. "Professor Zuzubin, open Cosmos and send us"—she turned and glared at George—"to the Collider."

"What about space suits?" said George desperately. "We haven't got them."

"You're not going into space," said Zuzubin in the same oily tone, "so why would you need them? This is just a short hop from one country to another. You step through the portal here"—his hand was on the doorknob—"and you will emerge almost instantly at your destination. I promise you this. I swear on my oath as a member of the Order of Science to Benefit Humanity that this is true."

"See?" said Annie. "He swore on the Oath—the one you took, the one I took—the one Dad and all his scientist friends took! He wouldn't lie, not about the Oath!"

"I most certainly would not," said Zuzubin gravely. "Now, Annie, listen carefully. You are the hero . . . you are going to travel through the portal . . . you are going to save the day." His voice had an oddly hypnotic quality. Annie blinked rapidly and her head seemed to sway around on her neck.

George looked at his watch. It was already six p.m. in Foxbridge, which meant it was seven p.m. in Switzerland—only thirty minutes until the quantum bomb went off, taking the great experiment, Eric, and all the world's top scientists with it. Zuzubin, sensing that George was weakening, winked at Annie and pulled the doorway open. Beyond it, they could see nothing—only darkness.

"Step through," said Zuzubin insistently. "Step through, dear children! Zuzubin will make sure you are safe and sound . . . safe and sound . . . nice dear little children.”

As though in a trance, Annie stepped forward, sleep-walking into the dark doorway, through which she disappeared in a matter of seconds.

George couldn't let her go alone. He had no idea where she would end up: Even if some miracle *did* transport her to the Collider, she wouldn't be able to defuse the quantum mechanical bomb because she didn't have the code. He ran after her.

How different, he thought, the original Cosmos—the world's first ever supercomputer—was to new Cosmos, the sleek, personable, chatty little computer they had grown to know and love. Old Cosmos was like trying to steer a huge cruise liner when you were used to a sleek little speedboat.

Bracing himself, George stepped forward and passed once more through a portal to an unknown world of discovery and adventure, the darkness swallowing him whole.

Chapter Sixteen

From his vantage point among the junk, Vincent noted everything that happened. He watched Zuzubin's sinister face, and although he couldn't make out each word the old man said, he could see Annie looking conflicted and confused, and George turning red with anger. Vincent saw George protest but knew there was little the other boy could do.

Once Zuzubin opened the portal door, which Annie believed would lead them straight to the Collider and her father, Vincent—like George—knew their fate was sealed. He prepared himself to leap out of his hiding place. As always, before Vincent used his karate skills, he recited the karate mantra to himself:

"*I come to you with only karate, empty hands. I have no weapons, but should I be forced to defend myself, my principles or my honor; should it be a matter of life or death, of right or wrong; then here are my weapons, karate, my empty hands.*"

But when Vincent looked up, Annie and George had disappeared, and only the old man Zuzubin was there in front of the great silent computer, laughing and laughing until the tears ran down his wrinkled cheeks and he had to bring out a perfectly pressed white handkerchief to wipe them away. When he finally stopped laughing, he switched the monitor back on, but this time he changed the channel.

Vincent peered through the debris to see what the old man was doing now—on the screen he could just make out the image of a room with two smallish figures moving around inside it. He edged closer, as quietly as he could, just as Zuzubin picked up an old-fashioned microphone and started speaking into it.

"George and Annie . . . ," he said.

On the other side of old Cosmos's doorway, George and Annie had stepped through and found themselves in complete darkness. Behind them, the portal door clicked shut. They had absolutely no idea where they were—until a light flipped on, illuminating their new surroundings. For a second, they just stood open-mouthed in surprise. They had never before stepped through a computer doorway and found themselves anywhere like this before. They were quite used to emerging from Cosmos's portal into different gravitational conditions, where they flew upward into the atmosphere of a strange planet, or got dragged down onto the surface. On their previous journeys, they'd stepped through Cosmos's portal to encounter lakes of dark methane, volcanoes that erupted in plumes of slow-moving, sticky lava, or planet-swallowing sandstorms. They'd seen a sunset with two suns in the sky as well as witnessing the fast-forwarded fate of an exploding black hole. But they'd never been anywhere like this before.

In some ways, it was just a room, so it was hard to say why it felt so creepy. It was square, the ceilings were of normal height, it had a comfy-looking sofa, a television set and a couple of cosy armchairs, a patterned rug on the floor, and bookshelves that held hundreds of hardcover books, their spines neatly arranged in alphabetical order.

On one of the armchairs, a cat stretched and purred. The curtains were closed, but Annie ran straight over to them and pulled them back. The two friends saw a view of a snow-capped mountain range, with dark fir trees on the lower slopes and a blue sky above the peaks, darker clouds gathering beyond the more

distant mountains. "Where are we?" Annie asked.

"I don't know," said George slowly, looking around. "But this is definitely not the Large Hadron Collider." They could both feel that something about this room was terribly, horribly wrong.

"Are those the Alps outside the window?" wondered Annie hopefully. "Should we open the door? Perhaps the Collider is nearby." The door they had come through had closed behind them. They both looked at it.

"Won't that just take us back to Foxbridge?" said George. "Don't we need another door to exit from wherever this is?"

At that moment the antique television set spontaneously crackled into life. Black and white flashes shot across the screen, showing only a small part of the fuzzy picture behind them. But the voice that addressed

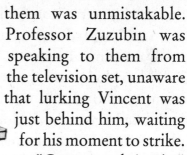

them was unmistakable. Professor Zuzubin was speaking to them from the television set, unaware that lurking Vincent was just behind him, waiting for his moment to strike.

"George and Annie," said the professor, his image settling onto the screen.

"It's *Zuzubin*!" screamed Annie. They could see

him clearly now, the collection of junk in the background as he loomed closer. Everything fell into place for George—the voices they had heard in the cellar, the yellow glasses Zuzubin had been wearing, the phrases he had heard on the radio news broadcast, the secret use of old Cosmos in the basement.

"It was *you* all along!" said George, speaking into the television set. "You've been traveling around the Universe, leaving things inside black holes! *You* invented the True Vacuum theory in order to scare ordinary people into joining TOERAG! *You* were the insider who betrayed the Order of Science. You set up the meeting tonight so that all the top physicists would be in one place—then you could blow them all up and be the only one left! You want to change what happened in the past to make it look like you were right all along—that your theories, which everyone has forgotten about, showed that the Large Hadron Collider would explode!"

"And," said Zuzubin nastily, "I have succeeded—in all my aims. In just a short while the Collider will indeed explode, and the world will realize that I am a scientist who should not have been forgotten! It will look like I was right all along and there will be no other physicists to contradict me. I have won!"

"No, you've cheated!" shouted George at the TV. "That's not winning—that's being the biggest loser of all."

Annie interrupted him. "Where *are* we?" she cried,

pressing her face against the screen. "You promised us we would arrive safely at the LHC! You swore on the Oath."

"Oh no, my dear," cackled Zuzubin. "If you listened more carefully and did not give in to your immature habit of making rash assumptions, you would have heard me correctly. I said you would arrive safely at your destination. Which you have. I never told you where that destination would be."

Annie ran over to the door and paused just in front of it.

"Wait!" said George. "Annie, don't open the door. We don't know what we'll find."

"Exactly," said Zuzubin. "You, my dear little friends, are in the Inverse Schrödinger Trap. It was so easy! You just walked straight in."

"What does that mean?" asked Annie in bewilderment.

"It means"—George gave a heavy sigh—"that we will only know where we are when we open the door. We could be anywhere at all, but we won't find out for sure while the door is still closed."

"Too good, too good," mused Zuzubin. "While the door remains closed, you are in an infinite number of locations. Shall I show you some of the possibilities?" The scene through the window changed to a vista of something glowing white-hot, with a yellowish tinge. Annie and George both recoiled from the glare coming through the window.

"Perhaps," said Zuzubin, "you are in the middle of planet Earth, held in the crystalline center of the inner core. In that case, you would be right in the heart of a one-and-a-half-thousand-mile ball of solid iron, which is about as hot as the surface of the Sun. The pressure is three point five million times the pressure on the surface of the planet. Open the door—please! Be my guest! I will be most intrigued to know what happens—will you fry or will you be crushed? Which will be first?"

George's jaw had dropped. He stared in horror at the window.

"Nothing to say for once?" said Zuzubin. "Then I will continue our lesson in geology. Around this iron ball lies an outer core of liquid iron—which, by the way, is exceedingly toasty as well—and around that, another mantle of rock through which volcanic lava sometimes escapes. Even if you did get that far, your blood would bubble in your veins, as it is unbelievably hot down there. But that isn't the end of it. From there, you'd have to dig through twenty-five miles of the rocky crust to get to the surface. Of course, after just a few miles, you might find that you'd broken through to the bottom of the ocean! Oh, children!" He clasped his hands together.

"Let's look at what that would be like for you!"

Annie sat down very suddenly on top of the cat, which yowled indignantly and wriggled out from under her to take up a position on the sofa, from where it shot her murderous looks as it washed its paws.

The picture through the window changed again. This time they were underwater in a deep trench, so far down that the sunlight never penetrated. In the light from the room behind them they could see squiggly reef formations and a plume of black smoke coming out of a hole in the ocean floor.

"Let's say you find yourself at the bottom of the Pacific, in a hot spring," gloated Zuzubin, "where strange prehistoric life-forms exist, hidden from human eyes, able to survive on the minerals expelled through the vents from the core of the Earth itself."

A massive worm, longer than either of the kids, swam straight at the window, bashing into it. Its long pallid body squelched along the glass as it retreated in surprise.

"Oh dear, he didn't see us!" exclaimed Professor Zuzubin. "Well, that is because he has no eyes. He's a giant tubeworm—what a lovely creature. You'd like to take a little swim with him, wouldn't you? He's quite friendly," said Zuzubin vaguely. "Which doesn't really

matter. After all, you'll boil alive in the heat from the hydrothermal vent. If you don't drown first, that is."

George sat down next to Annie and put his arm around her. She was shaking. "Don't look anymore," he said. "He's trying to frighten us. Don't let him." But George himself couldn't tear his eyes away from the hideous picture outside the window.

"I see I still don't please you!" said Zuzubin sorrowfully. Once more, the view from the window shifted. This time, all they could see was mile upon mile of ice floes, stretching away from the window for eternity. "Perhaps you don't like to be warm! Let's try a different view. Maybe you are at the South Pole, in the middle of the Antarctic winter." Strong winds buffeted

the window. A group of penguins could be seen, their heads bowed against the fierce gusts of freezing air.

"You see, little children," Zuzubin continued, enjoying his captive audience, "on the other side of that doorway are all the infinite possibilities. Perhaps you have been shrunk down to quantum size so you can find out what it would be like to be a quark!"

"That can't happen," said George. "It isn't possible."

"Oh, really?" said Zuzubin. "You couldn't become confined forever with the three quarks and the myriad quark-antiquark pairs and gluons swarming around inside a proton? The probability of ever escaping would be very small. No one has ever seen a quark outside a hadron, George, and no one will ever see you—"

"No," insisted George. "That's totally bogus and wrong."

"I leave it to you to find out," said Zuzubin smoothly. "Experiments are a fundamental part of science, and I look forward to watching the results of your attempt to prove me incorrect."

"*Shut up!*" shouted Annie. "We have to get out of here!"

"Please," said Zuzubin. "Don't stay a minute longer than you wish. All you have to do is open the door."

"But we can't!" said Annie, sinking onto the sofa. "Can we? If we open the door, we'll probably die . . ."

"Only probably," said Zuzubin comfortingly.

UNCERTAINTY AND SCHRÖDINGER'S CAT

The *quantum* world is the world of atoms and subatomic particles; the *classical* world is the world of people and planets. They seem to be very different places:

C	Q
Classical: We can know both *where* something is and *how fast* it's moving.	**Quantum:** We *can't* know both exactly, and perhaps we know neither—this is *Heisenberg's Uncertainty Principle.*
Classical: A ball traveling from *A* to *B* takes a definite path. If there is a wall in the way with two holes, then the ball either goes through one hole or the other.	**Quantum:** A particle takes *all* paths from *A* to *B*, including paths through different holes— the paths add up to produce a *wavefunction* rippling out from *A*.
Classical: We know the ball is going to *B*, and not to somewhere else.	**Quantum:** The particle can reach anywhere the wavefunction can reach. We only discover where it is when we make an observation.
Classical: Gentle observations don't affect the motion of the ball.	**Quantum:** Observations completely change the wavefunction—e.g., if we observe our particle at *C*, the wavefunction *collapses* to be completely at *C* (then ripples out again).

A Cat in a Box!

But cats (classical!) are made of atoms (quantum!).
Erwin Schrödinger imagined what this might mean
for a cat—though don't do this to your pet cat
(Schrödinger didn't actually do it either)!
He imagined shutting a cat inside a (completely
light- and soundproof) box with some poison,
a radiation detector, and a small amount of
radioactive material. When the detector bleeps
(because an atom produces radiation), then the
poison is automatically released. After a while
in the box, is the cat still alive? The atoms in the
box (including the cat's) take all possible paths:
In some, radiation is produced and the poison
released; but not in others. Only when we make an
observation by opening the box do we discover if
the cat has survived. Before that, the cat is neither
definitely dead nor definitely alive—in a way, it's a
combination of both!

"That means we are trapped . . . ," said George slowly. "In this room . . . forever."

"I have provided plenty of reading material," said Zuzubin. "You'll find all the major texts on the bookshelves, and there is some nourishment in the fridge."

Annie leaped up and went over to the fridge, as though it might show her a way out of this trap. But all it contained was a box of breakfast cereal and five large chocolate bars, with a bottle of milk marked CAT.

"Shredded Wheat and chocolate?" protested Annie.

"A perfectly adequate diet, I have always found," said Zuzubin coldly. "I would have asked you for your culinary preferences, but there really wasn't time. You were in such a terrible hurry."

"This is *your* room, isn't it?" said George, the truth dawning on him. "You live here when you go into hiding—when you disappear, you come here."

"It's peaceful," admitted Zuzubin. "It gives me time to think."

"So there *is* a way out," said George, pointing at Zuzubin through the TV screen. "*You* return to

Foxbridge, so we must be able to. You don't come in here and just take a chance on where you'll end up when you open the door. I bet you've used this room to get to the LHC and to all the other places as well. It's how you travel around."

"Well, yes, of course!" said Zuzubin. "Using the TV remote control, I can make an observation that causes the portal to pick a definite location. So when I open the door, it has taken me to my chosen destination."

"The remote control!" shouted George. "Annie, we must find the remote control for the TV set!"

"Look as hard as you like," sneered Zuzubin. He dangled an object in front of the screen. George slumped in defeat as he realized Zuzubin had the remote in his hand.

"Are you just going to leave us here while my father gets blown up?" said Annie very quietly. It seemed like all hope had gone.

"I am," confirmed Zuzubin. "Would you like to watch? I can play it for you on the television set, if you would like. I am eager to make my guests happy."

"Nooooo!" cried Annie, so loudly and painfully that, back in Foxbridge, Vincent heard her and knew it was time to act.

Chapter Seventeen

Vincent had been hovering behind the old professor, hoping that he would somehow give him a clue how to get Annie and George out of the trap. He knew he could easily overpower the old man, but what good would *that* do? If Zuzubin wouldn't tell him how to extract George and Annie from the bizarre room that he could see on the screen, they could be in even more trouble than before.

Vincent glanced down at George's cell phone, which he'd picked up off the floor, and saw that the screen bore the message: MISSED CALL—HOME. It was at that moment that he heard Annie's cry of pain, and realized he could stand by no longer.

Readying himself, he leaped out from behind the pile of old furniture with a great battle cry. He flew through the air and landed immediately behind Zuzubin, felling him with one swift and totally accurate karate chop. Zuzubin had half turned in surprise, but he toppled like an ancient tree, his eyes rolling back in his head as he crumpled to the floor and lay there, unconscious.

On the screen, Vincent saw Annie and George's astonished faces peering back at him.

"Vincent!" Annie covered the TV screen with kisses.

George dragged her back. "Vincent!" he said. "That was amazing!"

"Vincent, you're the best!" said Annie.

George elbowed her out of the way again. "But, Vince, how are we going to get out?"

"Call my dad!" shouted Annie. "Tell him about the bomb at the LHC!"

Using George's cell phone, Vincent scrolled through and found Eric. He pressed the green phone icon and waited. But all he got was an electronic voice, telling him that the phone was switched off and he would have to try again later.

"The remote control!" shouted George. "Vince, get the remote control from Zuzubin!"

Vincent looked down at the prone figure of Zuzubin, splayed on the floor in his tweed suit, his mustache drooping to one side. He leaned down and pried a remote control out of Zuzubin's fingers, holding it up to the TV screen so George and Annie could see it.

"Is this the one?" said Vincent.

"Yeah!" said George. "That's it! Now can you get us out?"

"Like, er, how?" asked Vincent quietly. "How does this thing work?"

"Oh no," said George. "I didn't think of that. I don't know."

"What if you look at it more closely?" Vincent held the control right next to the screen.

"It's no good," said George in frustration. "The picture isn't clear enough. And Vince," added George, "you've got to be quick. There isn't much time!"

"Call the LHC!" said Annie. "Tell them there's a bomb!"

"Forget it—they wouldn't believe him," said George. "There's only one way—that's to get there and defuse the bomb ourselves."

On the other side, Vincent was staring at the remote control. "When I press 'menu' on my TV remote at home," he said slowly, "it makes the television change between functions. Which is sort of what we need the Inverse Schrödinger Trap to do—we need it to change from a trap to a portal. Shall I try it?" he asked nervously.

"You have to!" said George. "It's our only hope!"

Vincent took a deep breath and pressed the menu button. Nothing happened. He pressed it again and a list came up on Cosmos's screen. The same list of options appeared on the television screen, inside the Schrödinger Trap. He read out loud the first option on the list: "Foxbridge." And then he read out to his friends, waiting inside the Inverse Schrödinger Trap, the second option: "Large Hadron Collider."

"Those must be the locations Zuzubin has visited! If we choose the Collider, perhaps it will take us to the place where he left the bomb! If there are arrow buttons on the remote," said George, speaking very fast, "use them to select LHC."

"I don't know!" fretted Vincent. When it came to dangerous sports like skateboarding and karate, he knew no fear. But faced with sending his friends into certain danger, he felt terrified. "I can't!" he said. "I can't send you to the LHC! We know there's a bomb!"

"Vincent, do it!" said Annie, shoving George out of the way again. "You have to get us to the LHC! If you don't, my dad will never come home—that's what Reeper said! The quicker you do it, the more time we have when we arrive to find the bomb and defuse it. Press the button, Vince! And we'll open the door. Send us there!"

Vincent gave a heart-wrenching sigh and pushed the select button, the cursor hovering over the highlighted "LHC" letters on the screen.

As he did so, George reached forward and pulled open the door . . .

The last Vincent saw of his friends on the television monitor were their backs, disappearing through the portal doorway. Had he managed to work Cosmos correctly? Would they arrive safely at the LHC? Was the LHC, with the bomb primed to go off, a place where he should have sent them? Should he have made them come back to Foxbridge? And what if he'd pressed the wrong button and opened something exotic like a wormhole for them to pass through? What if he'd accidentally sent them back in time? What then?

Vincent gently sank to the floor and waited, his head in his hands, while Zuzubin, the progenitor of all this evil, snored on the floor beside him.

WORMHOLES
AND TIME TRAVEL

Imagine that you are an ant, and you live on the surface of an apple. The apple hangs from the ceiling by a thread so thin that you can't climb up it, so the apple's surface is your entire Universe. You can't go anywhere else. Now imagine that a worm has eaten a hole through the apple, so you can walk from one side of the apple to the other by either of two routes: around the apple's surface (your Universe), or by a short cut, through the wormhole.

Could our Universe be like this apple? Could there be wormholes that link one place in our Universe to another? If so, what would such a wormhole look like to us?

The wormhole would have two mouths, one at each end. One mouth might be at Buckingham Palace in London, and the other on a beach in California. The mouths might be spherical. Looking into the London mouth (a little like looking into a crystal ball), you could see the California beach, with lapping waves and swaying palm trees. Looking into the California mouth, your friend might see you in London, with the palace and its guards behind you. Unlike a crystal ball, the mouths are not solid. You could step right into the big spherical mouth in London, and then after a brief float through a weird sort of tunnel, you would arrive on the beach in California, and could spend the day surfing with your friend. Wouldn't it be wonderful to have such a wormhole?

The apple's interior has three dimensions (east–west, north–south, and up–down), while its surface has only two. The apple's wormhole connects points on the two-dimensional surface by penetrating through the three-dimensional interior. Similarly, your wormhole connects London and California in our three-dimensional Universe by penetrating through a four-dimensional (or maybe even more-dimensional) *hyperspace* that is not part of our Universe.

Our Universe is governed by *laws of physics*. These laws dictate what can happen in our Universe and what cannot. Do these laws permit wormholes to exist? Amazingly, the answer is yes!

Unfortunately (according to those laws) most wormholes will implode—their tunnel walls will collapse—so quickly that nobody and nothing can travel through and survive. To prevent this implosion we must insert into the wormhole a weird form of matter: Matter that has *negative energy*, which produces a sort of anti-gravity force that holds the wormhole open.

Can matter with negative energy exist? Amazingly, again, the answer is yes! And such matter is made daily in physics laboratories, but only in tiny amounts or only for a short moment of time. It is made by borrowing some energy from a region of space that has none, that is by borrowing energy from *the vacuum*. What is borrowed, however, must be returned very quickly when the lender is the vacuum, unless the amount borrowed is very tiny. How do we know? We learn this by scrutinizing the laws of physics closely, using mathematics.

Suppose you are a superb engineer, and you want to hold a wormhole open. Is it possible to assemble enough negative energy inside a wormhole and hold it there long enough to permit your friends to travel through? My best guess is "no," but nobody on Earth knows for sure—yet. We haven't been smart enough to figure it out.

If the laws *do* permit wormholes to be held open, might such wormholes occur naturally in our Universe? Very probably not. They would almost certainly have to be made and held open artificially, by engineers.

How far are human engineers today from being able to make wormholes and hold them open? Very, very far. Wormhole technology, if it is possible at all, may be as difficult for us as spaceflight was for cavemen. But for a very advanced civilization that has mastered wormhole technology, wormholes would be wonderful: the ideal means for interstellar travel!

Imagine you are an engineer in such a civilization. Put one wormhole mouth (one of the crystal-ball-like spheres) into a spaceship and carry it out into the Universe at very high speed and then back to your home planet. The laws of physics tell us that this trip could take a few days as seen and felt and measured in the spaceship, but several years as seen, felt, and measured on the planet. The result is weird: If you now walk into the space-travel mouth, through the tunnel-like wormhole, and out the stay-at-home mouth, you will go back in time by several years. The wormhole has become a machine for traveling backward in time!

With such a machine, you could try to change history: You could go back in time, meet your younger self on a certain day, and tell yourself to stay at home because when you left for work that day, you got hit by a truck.

Stephen Hawking has conjectured that the laws of physics prevent anyone from ever making a time machine, and thereby prevent history from ever being changed. Because the word *chronology*

means "the arrangement of events or dates in the order of their occurrence," this is called the *Chronology Protection Conjecture*. We don't know for sure whether Stephen is right, but we do know two ways in which the laws of physics *might* prevent time machines from being made and thereby protect chronology.

First, the laws might always prevent even the most advanced of engineers from collecting enough negative energy to hold a wormhole open and let us travel through it. Remarkably, Stephen has proved (using the laws of physics) that every time machine requires negative energy, so this would prevent *any* time machine from being made, and not just time machines that use wormholes.

The second way to prevent time machines is this: My physicist colleagues and I have shown that time machines *might* always destroy themselves, perhaps by a gigantic explosion, at the moment when anyone tries to turn them on. The laws of physics give strong hints that this may be so; but we don't yet understand the laws and their predictions well enough to be sure.

So the final verdict is unclear. We do not know for sure whether the laws of physics allow very advanced civilizations to construct wormholes for interstellar travel, or machines for traveling back in time. To find out for certain requires a deeper understanding of the laws than Stephen or I or other scientists have yet achieved.

That is a challenge for you—the next generation of scientists.

Kip

Chapter Eighteen

A t TOERAG's secret headquarters, the leaders of the movement also sat glued to a TV screen that gave them a secret insider view of the trigger room at the Large Hadron Collider.

"You will enjoy this," one of the leaders told Reeper, who was pretending he wanted to watch. He dared not show his true feelings in case TOERAG realized he had given away their plans. "Finally you will see Eric Bellis, your old enemy, finished off forever! And best of all, when the Collider is destroyed, the public will think that it exploded because the experiment was too dangerous and that he has lied all along about the risks that it posed."

"Ha ha." Reeper forced a hollow laugh. "How . . . extremely riveting . . ." He'd hoped that his escape into space to meet George on the fast-orbiting asteroid would somehow have foiled this appalling plot.

The clock ticked onward. The meeting at the Collider was scheduled to start at seven thirty. It was already seven fifteen. The trigger room was filling up with scientists. The trigger room in the electronics cavity was a very secret and secure place to hold a meeting. Although it was underground, like the accelerator tunnels and the detector cavities, this part was not sealed off because a very thick wall protected the scientists in the trigger room from the workings of the experiment.

It was also safe and private. Or so the Order of Science to Benefit Humanity believed. Not knowing that someone had deliberately planted a hidden camera, they thought there was no way they could be seen or overheard in this location. As it was, their every word and action was seen elsewhere, by the very same people the Order had such good reason to avoid.

In the middle of the room sat little Cosmos, slightly

the worse for wear after his lengthy interviews with The Grid, his screen smudged and wonky, and several wires sticking out at the back. A scientist walked into the room and inspected him, wincing as he noticed the damage done to the silver laptop.

"Is that Bellis?" said the television evangelist, peering at the screen.

"No," said Reeper. "Bellis is not in the room yet." How he wished he knew for sure that Eric was elsewhere in the Collider, receiving information from George about the quantum mechanical bomb!

"He must get there by seven forty," said another of TOERAG's leaders angrily. "He must be at the nucleus of the explosion."

The minutes ticked by and Reeper held his breath. But just as the clock reached seven thirty, the door to the trigger room flew open and Eric sauntered in, back from his refreshing stroll and determined to meet his fate in fighting form . . .

On the other side of the two-yard-thick wall, George and Annie dashed through the doorway from the Inverse Schrödinger Trap, tripping each other up as they flew through, landing in a tangled heap on a metal floor.

"Get off me!" cried Annie from underneath George. He tumbled to one side and tried to stand up, but his legs felt wobbly. He lay on the floor for a moment, looking at the enormous metal disk that loomed up in front of them.

It was shaped like a very simple drawing of the Sun, round and shiny, with sunbeams radiating out from the central disk. Around the edge of the circle was a ring of blue metal plates, and farther out, huge gray tubular arms stretched forward, as though extending a mighty embrace. The machine towered over them like a cathedral—lofty, silent, and impressive in its sheer bulk. It was the kind of place that made you want to whisper.

George rose unsteadily to his feet. He and Annie seemed to have landed on some kind of platform. She hadn't gotten up yet, but lay scrunched up in a ball on the floor. "Are you okay?" George asked her.

She turned her face up toward him, her eyes still closed. They flickered open for a second, and George saw a flash of brilliant blue; then she squeezed them shut again. "Yeah, I'm fine," she said. "It's like when you've been asleep and someone switches the light on. Just give me a second."

George looked around. "Hello?" he called softly. The noise was lost in the vast empty space, as though the machine had gobbled it up. He could hear a mix of strange repetitive whistling sounds: *PEEooooo—PEEoooooo—PEEooooo*. But there didn't seem to be anyone else around.

What George didn't notice were the tiny motion detectors that had immediately picked up on the unauthorized human arrivals, setting off the alarm system as security cameras transmitted images of him and Annie to security monitors throughout the complex. Down among the intricate machinery, which was carefully blanketed by those thick walls, George and Annie couldn't hear the Klaxons that announced the interlock system had been triggered, initiating a *beam dump.* This meant the proton beams were kicked out of the accelerator's beam pipes and ended up slamming into seven-meter-long graphite cylinders, each contained in a steel cylinder. They had no clue that their presence had been detected and had set off a dramatic and noisy reaction.

Annie staggered to her feet, blinking rapidly. "Are

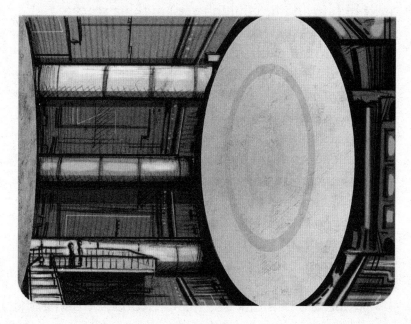

we on a spaceship?" she whispered, looking around. "Is this the engine room of a spacecraft?"

"Don't think so." George shook his head. "It's got normal gravity. And we can breathe without an oxygen tank. I think we're on Earth. This must be the Large Hadron Collider—which means old Cosmos took us to the right place."

"Phew, that's lucky," said Annie, sidling closer to him, as she always did when she was nervous. "But where do we go now? How do we find Dad? And what about—?"

George was just about to reply when, very suddenly, Annie screamed.

"What?" he said, in panic. Annie was standing right next to him and he couldn't see anything scary.

"There's—something—furry—on my leg!" she gasped, frozen with fear. George looked down. The black and white cat from Zuzubin's fiendish trap was winding itself around her ankles.

George gathered the cat up in his arms. "It's okay," he said soothingly to both Annie and the cat. "It's just Zuzubin's kitty. It must have come through the wormhole with us." He scratched the cat, which purred and snuggled closer to him.

"Are you sure it's safe?" said Annie doubtfully, recovering from her fright. "You don't think Zuzubin turned himself into a cat and came with us, to do more evil stuff?"

"Nope, don't think so," said George, stroking the

soft black and white fur. "The cat's friendly now—I think it wanted to get out of that room as much as we did. Look . . ." Under the cat's chin hung an engraved medal. "What does it say?"

Annie twisted the disk around so that she could read it. "*Reward!*" she read. "*Found dead or alive!*" She turned it over. "*Schrödy*—that must be his name. Hold on, it says something else." In smaller letters underneath was written: *I am the cat that walks alone.*

Suddenly the cat hissed and dug his claws into George, who promptly dropped him.

"*Ye-ouch!*" he cried.

"See?" said Annie darkly. "You can't trust anything that came from that horrible room!"

The cat landed on all fours, standing up on his paws like a ballerina *en pointe.* He hissed several times and scratched the metal floor. The fur on his back stood up

LUCY & STEPHEN HAWKING

and he arched his body, as though confronting an invisible foe. He looked up at George, whiskers quivering, then looked away again.

"What is it, Schrödy?" asked George, squatting down next to him.

"Another trick, I suppose," warned Annie.

Schrödy padded forward a few paces, turned, and came back. He circled George a few times, moved away, and came back once more, all the while casting meaningful glances in George's direction.

"He wants us to follow him," said George slowly.

"You want us to follow a *cat*?" Annie frowned in disbelief.

"I was sent into space by a talking hamster," George pointed out. "And trapped in a weird room by a loony scientist who wants to blow up the LHC. So why not follow a cat? He is Zuzubin's cat, after all."

"I thought he was Schrödinger's cat," threw in Annie.

"Whatever! He's a physics cat—maybe he knows something. Maybe he saw Zuzubin through the window in the Schrödinger Trap, hiding the bomb in the LHC. And"—George looked around the huge almost silent expanse of machinery—"we don't have any other clues to follow right now, or any idea how to find your dad— or the bomb for that matter."

Annie had her phone in her hand but it had no signal.

"If this *is* the Large Hadron Collider," George continued, "which it kinda *has* to be, that means we're underground. That thing"—he pointed at the machine—"is probably some kind of detector, wrapped around the tube where the protons collide."

"Which means we're under the Earth . . . ," said Annie slowly. "Like being in the subway."

"Yup," said George. "We've come out of one trap straight into another. Only this one is a whole lot more dangerous than the last. But we must have arrived here for a reason—Cosmos has brought us to a place at the LHC where Zuzubin has been before. Which must mean the bomb is around here somewhere."

Schrödy hissed again and pawed impatiently at the floor. In the spooky quiet by the great detector, both children imagined they could hear the bomb, ticking down the last few minutes until it exploded, destroying humanity's greatest ever experiment—and a large number of human lives with it.

"So we follow the cat!" Annie broke the silence. "C'mon, Schrödy, show us the way."

Schrödy licked his whiskers and gave them a smug little smile before high-stepping it toward the edge of the platform. A series of blue staircases led downward. At the top of the steps, the cat paused and looked expectantly up at George.

"He wants you to carry him," Annie translated.

"No claws, Schrödy!" George scooped the cat up into his arms and clattered down the stairs. Annie thumped after him, making a ringing noise as she struck

each metal tread on the way down. When they reached the bottom, Schrödy promptly wriggled out of George's arms and landed gracefully on the floor. The kids followed as he stalked along below the curved side of the enormous ATLAS detector.

"George," said Annie, tugging at his sleeve as they tiptoed after the handsome black and white cat. "What if Schrödy isn't showing us the bomb? What then?"

George felt sick to his stomach. "I don't know," he admitted, trying to sound brave. "We'll try and find your dad, and he'll be able to stop it. He *will*, Annie!"

But they both knew they were now deep underground, surrounded by concrete, rock, and layers of metal machinery. If the bomb went off before they could defuse it, there was no way they could escape the blast.

They followed the cat, who led them right to the back of the huge underground chamber. The vast underbelly of ATLAS loomed over them, curving upward, composed of millions of component parts. The kids gazed upward at the largest experiment humanity had ever created.

"If the bomb's in there, we'll never find it," whispered Annie.

George felt despair settle over him . . . but Schrödy had other ideas. Hissing, he flexed his claws once more and dug them into Annie's leg. Even though she was wearing jeans, she still felt it.

"*Oww!* Horrible cat!" she cried.

The cat was unperturbed. He looked up at them both expectantly, waved his long tail, and headed over to a soda machine in the corner. The kids hadn't even noticed it—it was such a familiar object surrounded by so much that was extraordinary that it had melted into the background to become almost invisible.

"Schrödy!" said Annie indignantly. "We're not getting you a drink right now! We have other things to worry about!"

But George was scrutinizing the soda machine. "Annie," he said softly. "Do you notice anything odd about this soda machine?"

She looked at it more closely. The top half was divided into compartments, each with a picture of the drink it would dispense and a button to press to order it. Underneath the different soda options, a handwritten sign was stuck to the front of the machine. It read:

"I've never heard of any of these drinks before," Annie said, turning back to George. "They're not real sodas! I mean, Quark-O-taster! Gloopy Gluon! Nutty Neutrino! What are those? And the lights are on, even though it says 'out of order.'"

George did a quick count. "Eight," he said grimly. "There are eight drink options here. And Reeper said there were eight switches on the bomb."

Annie gasped. "The bomb is inside the soda machine,

isn't it?" she said. "We have to select the right drink to defuse the bomb."

George got out the scrap of paper with the long numerical code that Pooky had kindly excreted for him. "That's it!" he said. "This is the code that makes the switches go live so you can arm—or disarm—the bomb. But the quantum superposition means that all eight switches have been used to arm it, but only one is the important one. But we don't know which one it will be."

"So if we press the wrong button, it will explode?" said Annie.

"Yes," said George. "And there should be no way at all of knowing what the right soda is until we try one, and then it will probably turn out to be the wrong one. But Reeper said he'd done something to the bomb so that you could turn it off after all. He said he'd already made an observation . . ."

"If he made an observation," said Annie, quickly working it out, "that means he must have already looked to see which soda the bomb was going to use so that the quantum superposition thing wouldn't happen. Reeper must have known what switch to use to disarm it. Pooky sent you the code to make the switches go live . . ."

"And we just have to choose the right soda," said George. "That's all."

"That's all . . . ," echoed Annie, staring at the sodas in the machine. She took a step forward.

"Don't touch the machine," George warned her. "We don't know if it's been booby-trapped."

"I won't touch it. But we have to choose . . . Look!"

Underneath the slot where you inserted your money was the display that counted up the coins you'd paid for the drink of your choice. The display showed two numbers, which were rapidly counting down—eighty was now replaced by seventy-nine. "I bet that's the number of seconds left until the explosion," said Annie. "So we have to choose something—and fast—or the bomb will go off anyway. What would happen if we pressed all eight switches at once? Would that work?"

"Well, no," said George. "Because it's a soda machine—that's why it's so clever! Think about it—

with a normal soda machine, you can only press one button at a time and get one drink. It will only let you make one choice. So we can't press more than one button now either."

"But which button do we press?" asked Annie.

George gulped and read along the top row of drinks. "*Fizzy-Wi Zzzz*," he read. "*Quark-O-Taster! Gloopy Gluon. Phrozen Photon. Nutty Neutrino. Electron Energy Drink. Hi-Hi-Hi-GG-Up! Lemon-flavored Iced Tau.*" The figures on the time display were now at sixty, showing that the seconds were dwindling fast. George looked down at Schrödy. "Any ideas?" he asked. The cat seemed to shake his head sadly, as if to say he'd done all he could. He curled up on George's feet and started washing his whiskers. "Annie?" said George hopefully.

"One of them," said Annie, "must be the odd one out . . . One of them must be the setting that Reeper used to make the quantum observation so that the bomb was made to choose one of the eight codes. But which one?"

"W and Z bosons . . . ," George repeated to himself. "Quark . . . Gluon, Photon, Neutrino. Electron, Higgs, and Tau. Which one are you?" Suddenly his brain lit up like the lights on the soda machine. "Eureka!" he cried. "I've got it! It's the Higgs! That's the odd one out."

"Are you sure?" said Annie. The time display now showed they were only thirty seconds away from the explosion.

"Higgs," said George quickly. "It's the only particle that doesn't spin on its axis. The Gluon and Photon have one unit of spin and Neutrino, Electro, and Tau have half a unit."

"Press it!" urged Annie. "Press it, George, *now*! Before it's too late!"

As George leaned forward, the time display showed fifteen seconds left. His hand hovered.

What if he was wrong?

What if he pressed the wrong button and was responsible for blowing up the Large Hadron Collider—and everyone and everything inside it?

A memory nagged at the back of his mind. Eric had once talked about how all observations in quantum theory were fundamentally unpredictable ("indeterminate" had been the word he'd used). Physicists could only calculate the *probability* of a particular result, and only in special situations was the probability a certainty. How, then, had Reeper been able to force the bomb to choose "Hi-Hi-Hi-GG-Up"? He looked down at Pooky's piece of paper—and realized that the last character on the line of symbols was not a number at all, but a capital *H*.

The display was still ticking down—9—8—7—6—5—when George, finally sure that he had worked it out, struck the button to choose the Higgs drink.

Immediately the lights stopped flashing on the <u>front</u> of the machine. Only the Hi-Hi-Hi-GG-Up button continued flashing. The time display froze at four seconds. ENTER CODE scrolled across a window by the drinks button.

George quickly punched in the number part of Pooky's code, upon which the whole machine briefly lit up and trembled. The time display disappeared and the word DISARMED appeared in its place.

As the kids watched in amazement, they heard a clunking noise, and the machine dispensed a can of soda into the transparent tray at the bottom and promptly switched itself off.

"Well!" said George. "That's not at all what I expected!"

Schrödy purred happily, and Annie sank to the floor in relief. Suddenly they heard something else— this time the sound of a heavy door being flung back and footsteps approaching. The footsteps got closer, and a disheveled-looking Eric came round the edge of the great machine and ground to a halt when he saw the kids.

"Annie! George!" cried Eric. "What the blazing stars is going on?" Behind him appeared a phalanx of bemused-looking scientists who had hot-footed it to the ATLAS cavern.

When the alarms had gone off, the scientists had quickly realized that somehow there were two small people in the ATLAS Detector Cavern! Pushing his way through the crowd gathered around the computer screen, which showed the image of the intruders, Eric had realized to his horror that the duo bore a striking resemblance to his daughter Annie and her best friend, George. With the other scientists, he had watched in shock as the two figures had set off down the staircase in front of ATLAS and fallen out of view of the cameras. At that moment, Eric snapped into action and ran from the trigger room, determinedly striking out in the direction of the ATLAS detector.

"Dad!" said Annie, falling on him and hugging him. "You're safe! The LHC isn't going to blow up! Science isn't over!"

"What are you talking about?" exclaimed Eric.

"Professor Bellis," said one of the other scientists. "Can you explain why two children, apparently related to you, have managed to appear in the sealed underground section of the Large Hadron Collider, thus triggering the interlock system and forcing a beam dump?"

"Ah, Doctor Ling," said Eric, nodding at the scientist who had just spoken.

"Could you kindly explain what is going on?" Under Dr. Ling's arm was Cosmos, the little silver laptop. Even in his hurry to follow Eric as he had shot out of the trigger room, headed for the ATLAS detector cavern, Dr. Ling had clearly not wanted to leave Cosmos unguarded.

"Er, well, no!" said Eric, and the scientists began to frown. But George quickly stepped forward.

"Um…hello, everyone," he said. "Sorry about this. There was this quantum mechanical bomb inside the soda machine."

"The soda machine?" said Dr. Ling. "But that's been out

271

of order for ages! No one ever uses it . . . ah," he said. "So that it made it a really clever place to hide a bomb."

"If the bomb had gone off," continued George, "the whole Collider would have been destroyed. We—that is, me and Annie, because I would never have worked it out all by myself—knew there were eight switches that arm or disarm the bomb. There are eight different soda options in the machine, which means each one represents one of the switches on the bomb. We had the code here"—he waved the scrap of paper with Pooky's code on it—"and we knew that the designer of the bomb had, in secret, already made an observation. So we just had to work out which option it was—and that was all about picking the right soda. We thought it must be the 'Higgs,' because all the others are the names of particles that spin on their axis and the Higgs doesn't; but actually"—he looked over at Annie—"it was the right choice because the code here ends in *H*. We picked Higgs, entered the code, and the bomb has now been disarmed."

"Ah . . . the first time the Higgs has definitely been observed at the Large Hadron Collider," said one scientist. "And it was via a soda machine!"

The other scientists whispered among themselves. "A quantum mechanical bomb?" they muttered. "Who could think up such a fiendish device?"

"But how could this awful thing have happened?" said Dr. Ling, sounding anxious. "Who could have wanted to cause such devastation and destruction?"

George and Annie looked at each other. Annie stood up and started to explain this time.

"This organization—TOERAG . . ." The scientists groaned, but Annie carried on: "TOERAG wanted to blow up the Collider while you were all here so that it would appear that the high-energy experiment had gone wrong. They thought that it would kill two birds with one stone—all the world's top physicists would be gone *and* people would think that these kind of experiments were too dangerous and they would never be tried again."

"I don't understand," said Dr. Ling. "How did they manage this? We have maximum security at the Collider. How could they have gotten in?"

"They had an insider," George explained.

"It was Zuzubin, wasn't it?" broke in Eric sorrowfully. "He betrayed us, didn't he? George, do you know why?"

Eric looked so sad that George didn't want to mention Zuzubin's treachery anymore. But he had to answer the question.

"Er, well, Annie and I—we think that Zuzubin wanted to use old Cosmos as a time machine and go back to the past. He wanted to make it look like his theories—the ones that everyone has forgotten about— were right after all. And that you were wrong. He was also trying to show that he predicted the Large Hadron

Collider would explode so that his theories would appear to be correct."

Eric took off his glasses and polished them on his shirttails. "Oh dear," he said. "Poor old Zuzubin."

"What do you mean, *poor old Zuzubin*?" said George hotly. "He tried to blow us all up! You can't feel sorry for him."

"He must have gone crazy," said Eric, shaking his head. "The Zuzubin I knew would never have done anything like this. He would have known that science is an ongoing story. It isn't about who's right or wrong, it's about progression. It's about doing the best work you can and then letting the scientists who come after you build on what you created. It may be that your theories are disproved—that's the risk you take. To try anything new means taking risks and if you don't do that, then you will never achieve anything meaningful. And of course we get it wrong sometimes. That's the point. You have to try and fail and start again, and keep going—not just in science; in life as well."

"Indeed," added Dr. Ling. "The greatest challenges come not when our predictions turn out to be accurate, but when they're not and instead, we discover new information that means we have to change everything we thought we knew."

Just then, Dr. Ling's pager bleeped furiously, as did the pagers of all the other scientists present, making a chirping noise—it sounded as if a flock of starlings had flown into the room. Everyone seized their pager and read the short message. A huge shout went up.

"What is it?" George asked Eric. "What's going on?"

He hugged both children again. "It's ATLAS!" he said. "He's got a result for us! Just when we least expected it! He's got some new information about the early Universe. Now, if I can put that information into Cosmos . . ." He trailed off.

All the scientists fell silent as they remembered that the difficult question of Eric's guardianship of Cosmos had not yet been resolved.

Dr. Ling stood there, looking thoughtful. "Professor Bellis," he said very courteously, "I believe there is a matter that we must deal with before we can investigate this new and exciting piece of information from ATLAS. Before I ask the Order of Science to vote on whether you should remain as the sole custodian of Cosmos, I would like to know—how is it that these two children know so much? How have two mere kids managed to use their unexpected knowledge of quantum theory to prevent an enormous and catastrophic event today at the Large Hadron Collider—an event that would have put back the progress of humanity by centuries?"

Eric didn't get a chance to speak as George interrupted.

"I can tell you that," he answered. "We know stuff because Eric is always explaining things to us. But he doesn't just *tell* us—he gets us to go on journeys with him so that we have to work stuff out for ourselves. He helps us by giving us knowledge, but he also gets us to use our brains to make that knowledge mean something."

"And he uses Cosmos to do this?" queried Dr. Ling.

"Cosmos helps him to make it fun and exciting for us," said George. "That way, we learn things, and then, when we face new challenges, we know how to apply what we learned to different situations and come up with answers. But also"—George shot a worried look at Eric but decided to continue—"we wouldn't have been able to do this—to save all these lives and the Large Hadron Collider—if it hadn't been for Doctor Reeper. He put himself in danger to join TOERAG— who knows what they might have done to him if they had found out he betrayed them? And he sent his avatar into space to tell me about the bomb. Without him, we could never have stopped them. Will you think again about letting him rejoin the Order of Science? He really deserves to be welcomed back."

"Hm," said Dr. Ling. "Very interesting. I will put these matters to a vote. All those in favor of Eric Bellis remaining as the operator of Cosmos, please raise your hands."

A forest of hands went up.

"All those not in favor?"

Not a single arm was raised.

"All those who would like to readmit Graham Reeper to the Order of Science?"

Even with Eric's hand raised, they were still two votes short of a yes.

"George and Annie," said Eric pleasantly, "I believe you are both members of the Order. Would you like to vote?"

They both smiled and raised their hands.

"In that case," said Dr. Ling, handing Cosmos over to Eric, "I would like to return Cosmos to your guardianship once more. And we will find Doctor Reeper and re-award him his fellowship. For saving science from destruction . . ."

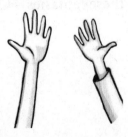

"Thank you," said Eric, clutching Cosmos gratefully. "Thank you,

Doctor Ling. Thank you, colleagues from the Order of Science. But most of all, thank *you*, Annie and George."

"Just one thing," said Dr. Ling as the group started to disperse toward the elevator. "Professor Bellis— no more pigs. Please. Not with the supercomputer, anyway."

"Of course," said Eric hastily. "I'll use my car next time I need to move a pig . . . When I've found him again," he added to himself under his breath. This would be the first item on his to-do list, after he'd examined the results of the experiments into the beginning of the Universe.

"Incidentally," said Dr. Ling as they joined the back of the line for the elevator, "did I see a *cat* in here? I can't believe it—how could a cat get down here?"

"Oh yes, that was Schrödy. He was—" Annie started to say, but then fell silent. Looking around, she saw no sign of the black and white cat. "Perhaps he's gone into another dimension," she speculated in surprise. "After all, he has ten to choose from, if M-Theory is correct."

"Schrödy?" Dr. Ling enquired.

"An imaginary friend," said George firmly. "Of Annie's. She's still very young, sir, and she still has these fantasies— Ouch! Ouch! Annie, get off me . . ."

M–THEORY—ELEVEN DIMENSIONS!

How can we combine Einstein's classical Theory of General Relativity, which describes gravity and the shape of the whole Universe, with the quantum theory explaining tiny fundamental particles and all the other forces?

The most successful attempts all involve *extra space dimensions* and *supersymmetry*.

The extra dimensions are rolled up very tightly so that large objects don't notice them!

Supersymmetry would mean more fundamental particles: e.g., photinos to go with photons, and squarks to go with quarks! (The LHC may see these, and perhaps even detect extra dimensions.)

The theory of *superstrings* (supersymmetric strings) replaces particles (dots) with tiny "strings" (lines). By vibrating in different ways—like different notes on a guitar string—strings behave like different types of particle. Although this sounds strange, strings *can* explain gravity!

Superstrings must exist in ten dimensions—so six extra space dimensions must be hidden away. We don't understand yet exactly how this happens.

In 1995 Ed Witten suggested that the varied types of superstring theories are all different approximations to a *single* theory in *eleven* dimensions, which he called *M-Theory*.

Scientists disagree on what the *M* means: Is it magic, mystery, master, mother, or perhaps membrane? Future generations of physicists will discover the truth!

Scientists have studied M-Theory very hard since then, but still don't know exactly what it is, or if it really is a Theory of Everything.

Chapter Nineteen

Back at ground level, in the control room at CERN, the scientists gathered gleefully around the banks of computer monitors to review the surprising new data uncovered by ATLAS and the high-energy collisions that were taking place in the tunnels below. Dr. Ling and Eric were very busy, inputting these results into Cosmos.

"This is very exciting," Eric said to George and Annie. "This new information from ATLAS will allow us to run a simulation of the Universe backward on Cosmos. We can start at today and work all the way back for thirteen point seven billion years. It's going to be quite a show!"

"Um, Dad . . . ," said Annie. "Before you do that, could you give Mom a call? She was really worried about you. She'll want to know that you're okay."

"Oh, of course!" said Eric, picking up one of the phones on the desk and dialing. "Hello, Susan!" he said into the handset. "Yes, yes, I'm fine . . . What? Annie? Lost? No, she's here with me . . . How did she get to Switzerland? Ah, well, that's a long story . . . No, no, George is here too . . . Yes, we will be back in time for the party . . . No, I haven't forgotten that I promised to pick up the cake . . ."

As Eric struggled to explain how the two kids had shown up safe and sound at the Large Hadron Collider, George tapped Dr. Ling on the shoulder.

"Doctor Ling," he said. "What about TOERAG? What will happen to them now?"

The scientist looked very serious. "I have put out an international alert," he told George. "I hope that they will be found and arrested. They endangered lives with their actions, and if it hadn't been for you and Annie, today would have been a tragedy."

"Will you find them?"

"Wherever they are on this planet, we will track them down."

"TOERAG wasn't trying to protect people at all, was it?" asked George. "They just frightened people into joining them."

"Yes, George," said Dr. Ling. "They pretended they wanted to watch over humanity, but that wasn't true. They used a good motive to hide a bad one—which is a truly evil thing to do."

"My parents don't like science much," confessed George. "They think it damages the planet. They're trying to live a green life."

"Then they are people to whom we, as scientists, should listen. We shouldn't ignore their point of view. The planet belongs to all of us, and we need to be able to work together to make a difference."

George felt quietly proud of his mom and dad.

Meanwhile Annie had grabbed one of the other LHC phones and was talking to Vincent, back in Foxbridge.

"You did *what*?" She burst out laughing. Covering the phone with one hand, she turned to George. "Vincent put Zuzubin into the Inverse Schrödinger Trap! Zuzubin was just coming to when Vincent opened the doorway and pushed him through it!"

George took the phone from Annie. "Wow! That was a cool move," he said admiringly to Vincent. George had to admit he was grateful to Vincent, and that perhaps, just perhaps, he and Vincent might become friends in the future.

On the other end of the line Vincent was laughing. "It was nothing!" he said modestly. "Nothing like what you did, anyway. I just thought it was the safest place to keep him, until Eric gets back. I can see him on the monitor—he's furious! But I've locked the door so he can't open it again."

"Can he escape?" asked George.

"Nope," said Eric, who'd overheard the conversation. "Zuzubin is pretty much stuck there. Until we get back to Foxbridge tomorrow—by airplane, just like normal people. Don't you worry, kids, I'll deal with Zuzubin when we get back. And yes, George, I'll track down Freddy and we'll find him a permanent home too."

Annie took the phone from George. "Bye, Vince!" she said happily. "See you tomorrow! We have to go now—my dad is about to run the Universe backward on Cosmos! We're about to go back to the beginning of everything and see what it was like at the Big Bang!"

Eric sat in front of the supercomputer, pecking away at the keys, Dr. Ling peering intently over his shoulder. Annie and George pushed through the small crowd of scientists who were gathering silently around them so that they could see the screen—columns of numbers were quickly scrolling across it, while in the corner a graph with a little red line was inching across and down, heading toward the bottom of the screen. "That's the diameter of the Universe," Eric said, pointing. "It's shrinking to zero as Cosmos approaches the Big Bang."

As George watched, the line suddenly headed

steeply downward, plunging almost vertically toward the bottom of the graph. "That's inflation," murmured Dr. Ling. "A period of exponential expansion. We are already well into the first second of the Universe's life."

Only the steady noise of computers and air conditioning broke the silence for the next few minutes. George couldn't take his eyes off the little line. It was almost at the bottom of the screen—then seemed to pull up a tiny bit. It was still falling, but not quite so steeply.

George stared—and it did it again. Someone behind

him took a deep breath. George glanced at Eric—and saw that he was beaming in delight, his eyes flicking back and forth over the unceasing columns of numbers.

"Not what we expected!" Eric whispered to himself. "Not what we expected at all!"

"What isn't?" asked Annie.

Her father turned to face her, smiling in delight. "What we've hoped for from the start, Annie. New physics! You see, it seems there isn't one at the Big Bang after all!" He turned back to Cosmos, and started typing rapidly.

Annie turned to George. "There isn't what?" she asked.

George was still watching the graph. The little line was still going down, but had leveled off so much now that it was hugging the bottom of the screen, almost horizontal. "I think I know . . . ," he replied.

Eric sat back with an air of triumph. "You'll see!" he cried, then leaned forward and pressed F4. With that, a small beam of light shot out from Cosmos's screen and sketched the shape of a window, hanging in the air above the heads of the assembled scientists, Dr. Ling and Eric and Annie and George. At first the window looked dark, with a round blurred object hanging in the center of it. But very quickly the blue and green sphere came into sharp focus, and they were looking at planet Earth, turning on its axis as it traveled along its orbit around its parent star, the Sun. Cosmos brought the window closer to the Earth, so that it could be clearly seen, with its familiar patterns of continents and oceans, with the deserts and great forests that cover the surface of this most beautiful and habitable of planets. But even as they watched, the surface of the Earth seemed to be changing shape . . .

TIME: **NOW** **13.7 billion years since the Big Bang**

TIME: 200,000 years ago

MODERN HUMANS APPEAR.

TIME: 65 million years ago

THE AGE OF THE DINOSAURS COMES TO AN END.

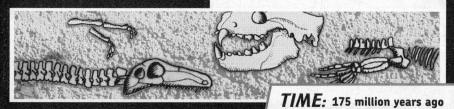

TIME: 175 million years ago

PANGAE—ALL THE EARTH'S CONTINENTS UNITED IN ONE BIG LAND MASS—BREAKS APART.

TIME: about 200 million years ago

DINOSAURS BEGIN TO ROAM OUR PLANET.

TIME: roughly 2 billion (that's 2,000,000,000) years ago

OXYGEN FROM PHOTOSYNTHESIS BEGINS TO COLLECT IN THE EARTH'S ATMOSPHERE.

1 billion = 1,000 million, or 1,000,000,000

TIME: about 3.5 billion years ago

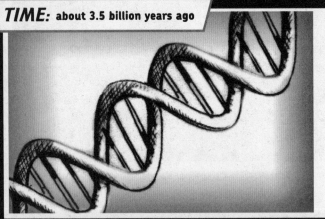

LIFE ON EARTH BEGINS . . .

THE EARLY EARTH IS A DANGEROUS PLACE . . .

. . . AS IS THE EARLY SOLAR SYSTEM AS THE PLANETS FORM.

OUR SUN IS BORN.

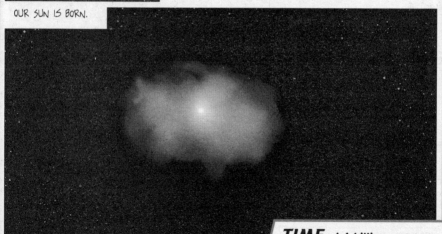

TIME: 4.6 billion years ago

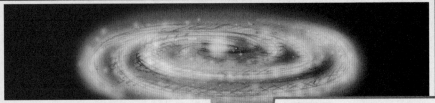

A BEAUTIFUL SPIRAL GALAXY—THE MILKY WAY.

THE FIRST STARS EXPLODE AND BLAST A MIX OF DIFFERENT ATOMS INTO SPACE, WHICH WILL END UP IN THE NEXT GENERATION OF STARS ALL ACROSS THE UNIVERSE.

PATCHES OF GAS COLLAPSE INTO BLOBS THAT HEAT UP SO MUCH THEY RELEASE NUCLEAR ENERGY—TO BECOME THE FIRST STARS.

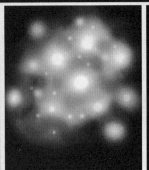

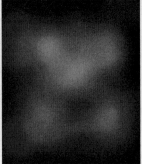

DENSE PATCHES OF DARK MATTER AND GAS ARE ATTRACTED TOGETHER BY GRAVITY.

THE COSMIC DARK AGES LAST A FEW HUNDRED MILLION YEARS.

THE FOG LIFTS AS THE FIRST WHOLE ATOMS APPEAR—THE COSMIC MICROWAVE BACKGROUND RADIATION IS NOW FREE TO TRAVEL ACROSS THE UNIVERSE.

HOT FOG FILLS THE UNIVERSE AS THE FIRST NUCLEI FORM.

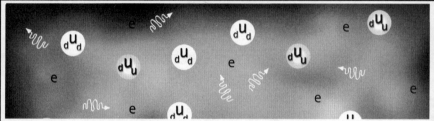

THE QUARK-GLUON PLASMA HAS COOLED, ALLOWING PROTONS AND NEUTRONS TO FORM. MATTER AND ANTIMATTER ANNIHILATE, RELEASING PHOTONS (PARTICLES OF LIGHT), WHICH CAN'T TRAVEL FAR THROUGH THE FOGLIKE PLASMA.

ALL PARTICLES HAVE ACQUIRED MASS WITH HELP FROM THE HIGGS FIELD.

THE UNIVERSE HAS JUST STOPPED INFLATING AND RELEASED A LARGE AMOUNT OF ENERGY. THE UNIVERSE IS FILLED WITH A QUARK-GLUON PLASMA.

TIME: The Inflationary Epoch. Almost at the Big Bang . . .

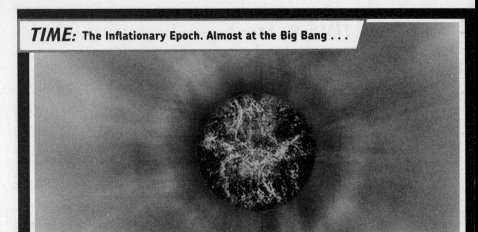

THE UNIVERSE IS SHRINKING VERY FAST AS WE APPROACH THE BIG BANG!

TIME: The Planck Epoch—New Physics!

THE REALM OF EXOTIC MATTER AND M-THEORY. STILL SHRINKING BUT NOT QUITE SO FAST . . .

THIS IS WHEN SPACE AND TIME—AS WE UNDERSTAND IT—SHOULD BEGIN. BUT THE UNIVERSE IS STILL HERE, INCREDIBLY SMALL AND STILL SHRINKING. PERHAPS IT WILL NEVER REACH A SINGULARITY AFTER ALL. . . .

Acknowledgments

A book like *George and the Big Bang* doesn't just appear out of nowhere. Many people are involved in making it happen. Working on the whole George series—and in particular, this third volume—has been a pleasure and a privilege. We would like to thank the team at Simon & Schuster for their dedication to publishing the George trilogy in the United States. We would especially like to say a huge thank-you to David Gale, who championed George from the very first and has seen the series through to this final adventure. We'd also like to thank very warmly Navah Wolfe, Dorothy Gribbin, Krista Vossen, Michelle Kratz, and Paul Crichton for their kindness, commitment, and professional expertise.

Gary Parsons has brought George and his friends and foes to life—this time, taking on the challenge of illustrating the Universe backward. And our distinguished researcher Stuart Rankin did a terrific and inventive job. Stuart's contribution incudes the genius of the IST, the essay on the Big Bang, and the deceptively simple explanations of quantum theory and other bizarre and fabulous phenomena. Very dedicated thanks go to Markus Poessel at the Max Planck Institute for his excellent input into the final version of the text.

Once more a roll call of very eminent scientists came forward to explain their work to a young audience. Our thanks go to Paul Davies, Michael S. Turner, Lawrence Krauss, and Kip S. Thorne for their brilliant contributions. We'd also like to thank Roger Weiss at NASA for his photographic insights into the wonders of the Universe and all our friends at NASA for the use of the cosmic images.

And, most of all, we would like to thank our young readers for wanting another George book! Good luck on all your cosmic journeys!

Lucy Hawking